KERRIGAN IN COPENHAGEN

KERRIGAN IN COPENHAGEN

A Love Story

THOMAS E. KENNEDY

BLOOMSBURY

NEW YORK · LONDON · NEW DELHI · SYDNEY

Published by Bloomsbury USA, New York
Bloomsbury is a trademark of Bloomsbury Publishing Plc

This is a work of fiction. Names, characters, places and incidents either are the product of the author's imagination or are used fictitiously and any resemblance between the characters and actual persons living or dead, businesses, companies, events or locales is entirely coincidental.

The quotes and references from Jens August Schade are from *Schades Digte* (*Schades Poetry*), Copenhagen: Gyldendal Publishers, 1999, and are used with kind permission of Gyldendal and the copyright holders.

Translations of Jens August Schade, Henrik Ibsen, Johannes Ewald, Johan Herman Wessel, and Ole Pedersen Kollerød are by Thomas E. Kennedy.

The lines of verse quoted on page 7 are by A. E. Housman.

Some of this material was previously published in a different form in *New Letters*, *Epoch*, *The Southern Review*, *ServingHouseJournal*, *Kerrigan's Copenhagen*, and *Best American Magazine Writing* 2008.

All papers used by Bloomsbury USA are natural, recyclable products made from wood grown in well-managed forests. The manufacturing processes conform to the environmental regulations of the country of origin.

LIBRARY OF CONGRESS CATALOGING-IN-PUBLICATION DATA HAS BEEN APPLIED FOR.

First U.S. edition published by Bloomsbury USA in 2013
This paperback edition published in 2014

Paperback ISBN: 978-1-62040-640-3

1 3 5 7 9 10 8 6 4 2

Typeset by Westchester Book Group
Printed and bound in the U.S.A. by Thomson-Shore, Inc., Dexter, Michigan

For Copenhagen,
city of the ever-changing light,
with love

With deep and sincere thanks to
Anton Mueller & Helen Garnons-Williams &
all their associates at Bloomsbury
Nat Sobel & Judith Weber & all their associates at Sobel Weber
Roger & Brenda Derham & Valerie Shortland
Duff Brenna, Walter Cummins, Greg Herriges, Mike Lee,
Robert Stewart & Gladys Swan

With special thanks to
Junot Díaz, Alain de Botton & Andre Dubus III for their
invaluable encouragement

Always for Daniel, Isabel, Søren & Leo

CONTENTS

Zero: A Love Affair

Kerrigan, Kerrigan,
Whither rovest thou?
—GILGAMESH

Terrence Einhorn Kerrigan is in love.

When his wife and child were taken from him, he told himself he would never love a woman again, and he never has, not in the way that requires a surrender of the sovereign spirit. But a man must love nonetheless, and thus a love affair begins this story—a love affair with a city.

Here he has made his home, returning after the death of his parents to the city of his mother, a city whose moods are unpredictable, unfathomable, unimpeachable as a woman's, often still and dark, perfidious as its April weather—now light and sweet as the touch of a summer girl who fancies you, now cold as snow, false as ice, merciless as the howling beating wind that swoops around his building, now quietly enigmatic as the stirring of the great chestnut trees that line the banks of the lake beneath his windows.

The city is Copenhagen, the city of the Danish smile and blue eye, the Danish national character that one of its great unknown sons, Tom Kristensen, described in his great unknown 1930 novel *Hærværk*, made into the great unknown 1977 film *Havoc*, as "false blue eyes and blond treachery."

Here he will clothe himself in its thousand years of history, let its wounds be his wounds, let its poets' songs fill his soul, let its food fill his belly, its drink temper his reason, its jazz sing in the ears of his mind, its light and art and nature and seasons wrap themselves about him and keep him safe from chaos.

It is the city of a hundred vices and fifteen hundred serving houses, bars, cafés—more of them than one will ever come to know in a lifetime without a very major effort. Kerrigan has decided to make that effort. He came to Copenhagen to find serenity, to find a life, and was surprised to find love, and then astonished to lose it, and he searched for it, searched his heart for it, but like Gilgamesh he kept finding instead a Divine Alewife who filled his glass and chanted:

> Kerrigan Kerrigan
> Whither rovest thou?
> What you seek, you shall not find.
> Rather, let full be your belly.
> Make merry day and night
> And forget the darkness.
> Of each day make you a feast of light.
> Let your raiment be sparkling and fresh.
> Wash your head and bathe in water.
> Scrape smooth the stubble from your jowls.
> And reach for the hand of the little one
> Who reaches for yours.
> Lay with the woman who delights in you,
> For this is the greatest a man can achieve.

Kerrigan agrees, even if there is no little one anymore. Gone the woman who delights in him. Gone the child. And that is how all stories end. With the naked, withered Christmas tree tilted against the trash barrel.

Yet he knows no better city in which to follow the Alewife's bidding, as far as he is able.

He does not know precisely how many serving houses there are in Copenhagen. He has not yet decided how many of them he will visit over what time scale or how many of them he will include in his book. He has no idea what might happen in each of the places he visits, what adventures he might encounter, what dark nights of the soul he might descend to, what radiant bodies he might win with a flattering tongue.

And not to know, he decides, is good.

One: Kerrigan's Associate

Whiskey, it keepeth the reason from stifling.
—RAPHAEL HOLINSHED, 1577

Kerrigan's path to meet his Research Associate and her jade-green eyes leads him diagonally across the Botanical Gardens to Nørreport. He hoofs over to Fiolstræde; then, at the intersection of Skindergade, it occurs to him that he still has some time and that there are three choices open to him. There are always three choices.

He has a good hour before he will meet his Associate and considers whether to turn left to the **Booktrader**, right to **Charlie Scott's Pub**, or continue directly forward through Jorck's Passage to **Farrelly's Irish Rover**.

If he goes left to the Booktrader, at Skindergade 23, he will enjoy the company of his good friend, the antiquarian bookseller Lars Rasmussen, in addition to the possible company of an artist and a bookbinder, Natacha and Iben, two lovely young women who are often there, and diverse others: artists, singers, musicians, poets, professors, writers, a criminologist friend named Dave from New York who includes Kerrigan on his field trips to Danish prisons, an ornithologist in the employ of Kastrup airport to discourage the birds from being sucked into jet motors, and a found-art practitioner who collects what she calls *kussesten*—stones found along the beach and in the forest that resemble *kusse*, Danish for *cunt*—thus, cunt-stones. (Danes rarely call a spade a shovel.) At the Booktrader, Kerrigan would stand leaning on the remainder table of books for a buck and a half (ten crowns) beneath the elaborate plaster sculpture on the ceiling titled *The Book Lovers* by Kasper Holten—a wreath of nine naked figures coiling out of a book, each performing some variety of erotic act on the next and the whole wreath of them spiraling toward a distant heart. But he will also be tempted to drink the wine poured liberally by Lars into glasses that hold more than they would appear to, and on top of what he has had already he will get drunk and show up late and sloppy to meet his Associate, and he does not wish to see his bad behavior reflected in her jade-green eyes.

If he goes right, to Charlie Scott's at Skindergade 53, he will have the opportunity to enjoy Jazz Under the Stairs, featuring the astonishingly energetic Australian clarinetist and singer Chris Tanner, and possibly bump into guitarist and composer Billy Cross, who is the nephew of Lionel Trilling and does the best arrangement of "Blue Suede Shoes" that Kerrigan has ever heard and who inter alia has been lead guitar for Bob Dylan and occasionally comes into Charlie Scott's, although there, Kerrigan no doubt will drink many pints of inexpensive pilsner and will also be drunk and late for his Associate.

On the third hand, he is more hungry than he is thirsty. He has been roaming this midmorning and early afternoon around the north side, sampling pints here and there, and wandered past the building at Skt. Hans Gade 18 where Knut Hamsun in 1890 wrote the novel *Hunger* about a consciousness starving to express itself. Kerrigan is literally feeling peckish, and he knows that if he walks straight ahead through Jorck's Passage, a half turn to the right will put him at Vimmelskaftet 46, on the Walking Street, outside Farrelly's Irish Rover, where at all hours he can get a full or, alternatively, diminutive Irish breakfast served by his favorite Irish-American waitress, Cathy.

His choice has been chosen.

It's a bit nippy for the outdoor tables so he steps inside the great dark cave of the bar, and Cathy greets him instantly with her Chicago accent, "Gad, Kerrigan, where you been hidin'? Want Irish breakfast? Big or little?"

"Little, please."

"You always let me down!"

Round and blue-eyed with some manner of sweet street-smart curl to her lips, she approaches his table with cutlery wrapped in a skimpy green paper napkin and a tumbler of ice and amber fluid.

"What's this?" Kerrigan asks with alarm, and sips.

"It's Paddy's," she whispers, "and keep your voice down, cancha? You wanna get me in trouble?"

"A goddamn full glass of Irish whiskey? I can't drink all this on top of what I already had!"

"Aw, you fuckin' drama queen!"

"I have a meeting with my research associate!"

"And you don't wanna fuck *that* up!"

"I can't drink this."

"You always disappoint me, Kerrigan! Get it down your neck now. It's good for you."

Despite himself he sips the Paddy's, knowing he must come up for a spell of air soon, and suddenly knows that that air must be the air of Dubh Lin—fort of the Dane, Garrison of the Saxons—on the banks of the River Liffey. Why, he wonders, does he feel he must go to Dublin? The compulsion seems to take force from a constellation of coincidences: the fact that the lake outside the window of his east side apartment here is called Sortedams Sø, which means Black Dam Lake, and Dubh Lin means Dark Pool, and his own name, Kerrigan, is originally Ciarogan, a double diminutive of *ciar*—dark, black—and incredibly his mother's maiden name was Mørk, Danish for dark. He discovered these facts one by one with an increasing sense of amazement. Moreover, Dublin was also founded by the Danes twelve hundred years ago, and his branch of the Kerrigans originated, according to his father, on the curving street that is said to be the bank of the Dark Pool into which the Vikings sailed.

He intuits a connection between the Dark Pool and the Black Lake, between the Vikings there and the Irish here, between his Irish father and his Danish mother and the origin of his name, that he might find a life in wrapping the cloak of these international, cross-cultural, historical facts around him, the life and love that had been stolen from him by Licia.

This is at least part of it. This is definitely part of it, part of what he must fill his mind with. Sometimes, lying in his solitary bed some nights, some mornings, he feels disconnected from all of time, existing purely in the present, as though he has had no past, as though he only just arrives each moment in the present and all of the past is mere illusion, the future melting back into the present, the present disappearing in the unfathomable bottomless past . . .

Maybe, he thinks, *I have been drinking too much.*

The time is not right, he knows, to go to Dublin. First he must meet his newly employed Associate and must begin his project with her.

He manages to get out of the Irish Rover after only one whiskey by leaving money on the table, ducking out while Cathy's in the back. He leaves a generous tip to discourage her from future compulsions to serve him gratis whiskey. He dodges around to Skindergade again, heading for Frederiksberg, where he is to meet his Associate, at Wine Room 90.

And now it is there again—the illusion. Suddenly the day is gone, and he and his Associate sit close in the little taxi, knees touching occasionally— by accident? Kerrigan wonders. Late-afternoon pastel facades of west Copenhagen reel past the window on either side. Secretly he hopes their project will never conclude.

Quite another matter is his Associate herself, a handsome woman of seven and fifty years who in her youth was a beauty. *Why is a young girl so pretty and why does it last so short a time?* Søren Kierkegaard asked in *Either/Or.* Or was it in *Seducer's Diary?* Same thing. On the other hand, his Associate is not bad at all. Not bad at all, Kerrigan speculates. Anyway he himself is only a year younger.

His project, what he has contracted for, what he is being paid to do, is to select a sampling of one hundred of the best, the most historic, the most congenial of Copenhagen's 1,525 serving houses and write them up for one of a one-hundred-volume travel guide: *The Great Bars of the Western World.* Kerrigan thinks of himself as a failed poet, which is a less complicated concept than a failed human being, and he has accepted this commission under false pretenses. He does not wish the book to be written. He wants only to research it. Forever. For whatever of forever remains him.

* * *

They have just come from **Wine Room** 90 in the Frederiksberg section, an elegant old establishment that, however, drove him to distraction because of management's insistence that beer be tapped in accordance with some scientific principles that involve frequent work with a spatula in foam and require twenty minutes to draw a single pint. Which meant for him more thirst than the quaffing of it. If it takes twenty minutes to tap a pint and ten minutes to drink it, a serious time deficit is involved. The minutes haunt him with their mocking brevity. All glasses are essentially empty, defining an empty space. Every clock wears the face of a pompously indifferent sadist, measuring life's depletion with a series of equally measured hand strokes.

Kerrigan is the writer, his Associate the researcher; he the form, she the content—or, in another more hopeful context, she will be the form and he the content. As a body fills a grave, he thinks, remembering a line from Malamud's *Fidelman*. Kerrigan is a man of quotes. They substitute nicely for thought. And he is well versed in dates, which seem to place him in history, in relation to persons and events. It is nice to be placed and to have a substitute for thought. He is aware of this as well as of the double bind of his ironic nature. No matter. *Enivrez-vous. Could man be drunk forever, on liquor, love or fights, / Lief would I rise of morning, and lief lie down of night / But men at times are sober, they think by fits and starts, / and if they think they fasten their hands upon their hearts.*

He feels himself perched on the edge of the turning millennium, knows what this past millennium contained, or at least to some personal extent the last fifty-six years of it, yet speculating on the contents of the next seems to him like practicing science fiction.

"Why must it take so long to fill my glass?" he demanded of her, nursing the little bit of beer remaining of his first pint.

"You have an interesting accent," she said. "Where did you learn your Danish?"

"In bed," snapped Kerrigan.

"Did you have many instructors?" she asked with a teasing curl to her lip.

He chuckled, sipped a drop of the remaining beer. "You didn't answer *my* question," he said. "Why does it take so long?"

On the table before her was a slender Moleskine notebook filled with the minute spidery scrawl of her penmanship, a seemingly endless cornucopia of facts. She ran her slender, chiseled finger down the handwritten contents page, thumped with a red pointed fingernail the line she was seeking, and flipped halfway through the book. "I have that right here," she said with a smile. "They tap it very slowly so the acid foams off, giving it a soft and stomach-friendly taste . . ."

"Stomach friendly?" he said with a smirk. Her smile was both warm and sphinxlike, slightly naughty, for she could see, he saw, that when he looked into her luminous, in this light, forest-green eyes, the pupils ringed with a thin circle of distinct yellow, he was harboring naughty thoughts about her. This was not the first time she had assisted him with research. Last time they worked together they were close to getting involved and almost did, but not quite. He was about to be a husband then, soon to be a father. Free now, he would not mind taking up where they left off then, though he deeply and sincerely does not want to get involved.

But at the rate the silver-bearded, white-aproned bartender tapped beer, Kerrigan could not get out of Wine Room 90 on Old King's Road fast enough.

Now, in the taxicab, she leans toward him, unbuttoned forest-green woolen coat hanging open, leaving him to wonder if it is her wish for him to see there what he sees in her décolletage—what the Danes call "the cavalier passage" and in English has the harsh and uncharming title of "cleavage." Always a mystery. Devilish strategy. How lovely, he thinks, is the process of the grain in the blood, and says, "I see a sweet country. I could rest my weapon there. That's a quote from *The Tain*."

"*The Tain*," she says, and shifts to English. "Is that not Irish high poetry? Let me respond from Odin's *Sayings of the High One*: "Remember always to praise the voman's radiant body, for he who flatters, gets." The undertone is ironic, though irony in Danish, Kerrigan knows, is often a mask of affection.

Now, however, she asks the taxi to stop outside the **Railway Café** on Reventlow's Street. The sign outside the bar says *Øl* in red neon and *Bier* in flat blue. A sidewalk placard gives the English translation, BEER. A life-size cardboard cutout of a golden Tuborg girl in an aquamarine frame stands alongside the door, holding a tray with a bottle of gold Tuborg.

"This von is a must," his Associate says.

He loves the way she says "one." "Why?"

"Because I haf to pee."

Kerrigan pays the driver, gets a receipt, and follows her, his leather satchel crooked beneath his arm. In the satchel he carries his fat, over-size, annotated, dog-eared paperback copy of *Finnegans Wake* around with him. Not that he expects ever to finish reading it, but its presence alleviates any danger of his having to worry about being alone with his mind.

Inside the bar there is no tap, so he orders two bottles of green Tuborg while his Associate finds the loo. He sits at the bar and surveys the art on the walls: paintings of locomotives, street scenes of old Copenhagen, a faithful dog, a plashy seascape, photos of steam engines, and a long glass case of HO gauge model trains. This is, after all, across the street from the central station.

"Nice-looking pictures," he says to the nice-looking, plump, blonde, fortyish barmaid. *A man can never know too many barmaids*, he thinks.

"Yeah," she says. "Some of them."

"When was this establishment established?"

With one eye closed she puffs her cigarette, and it wobbles between her lips as she speaks. "Long time. Three generations in any case."

Kerrigan notices there is a functioning transom over the entry door, tilted open. "Don't see many of them around anymore."

"You're right enough there," the barmaid says without looking at him and trims her cigarette on the edge of a heaped-full black plastic ashtray.

Half a dozen men sit at a long table gambling for drinks with a leather cup of dice—raffling, they call it. As Kerrigan sips his green, an old guy comes out of the gents' while a short, broad, crew-cutted woman barges through the front door and stands in the middle of the floor. From a large carpetty purse she pulls out a pistol and points it at the old guy, orders, "Hands up or trousers down!"

Kerrigan gasps, ducks. The woman shouts, "You're all wet!" and squeezes the trigger. A limp jet of water squirts into the man's face. Then, giggling hysterically, she puts the water pistol away again.

"Daft goose," the old man mutters and hobbles away, mopping his face with a gray handkerchief, while the woman shouts, "Good day!" and looks at the barmaid. "My God, you do look sexy today, sweetheart!"

"I usually do," says the barmaid quietly, and the crew-cutted woman moves to the bar. "Damn, give me a beer, my wife's been breaking my balls!" Then she turns to the older man beside her, says, "Tivoli is open." Danish for "your fly is unzipped." The old man says, "Out doing research again, ey?" She reaches and rearranges the material around his flies, saying, "If you had that cut a little different, it might look like you really had something there, old fellow."

"Sweetheart!" the man grumbles in his gravelly voice, "my nuts have been hanging there just like that since before you were born!"

They both laugh, and she turns to Kerrigan and says, "I got to catch a train back to Sorø so my wife can start breaking my balls again. So if you were thinking of buying me a bitter, you'll have to be fast. I don't have much time."

Kerrigan lifts his beer. "Did you say Sorø! That's a charming place. The old Sorø Academy. The Eton of Denmark. The great Ludvig Holberg is buried there in the chapel. I was there once."

"*Once?*" she says. "Try and *live* there." She makes mouths of both hands and has them gossip rapidly at each other. "Bla bla bla bla bla . . ."

His Associate emerges from the loo and takes a place at the bar on the other side of Kerrigan.

"Sorry, honey," says the crew-cutted woman. "I saw him first."

"You're velcome to him," she says.

"Well, wait, hel-lo!" says the woman, looking more closely at the Associate. "Where have *you* been all my life, sweetheart?"

"Growing up," says the Associate, and the woman barks a single note of laughter, says, "Don't go away now, I just have to water my herring."

"So what do you have in your Moleskine book about this joint?" Kerrigan asks. His Associate digs it out of her bag, and Kerrigan notices several starfish stickers on the black cover. Endearing, he thinks, as she pages through. "Nothing," she says finally. "Only that the street was named for Christian Ditlev Frederik Reventlow, 1748–1827, early in this century. He led the way to the end of adscription, which freed the serfs."

The crew-cutted woman swaggers back toward the bar. Sotto voce, Kerrigan suggests, "Shall we drink up?" He orders a bitter for the crew-cutted woman to keep her occupied at the bar when they leave.

They cross the street and move on, look back at a place called **The Stick (Pinden)**, and Kerrigan notices that it has a typical feature of many Copenhagen serving houses. From across the street it looks positively uninviting, particularly with the graffiti on its side door. Approached from the same side of the street, however, it is a little more welcoming, with a cutout of a kindly-looking waiter bearing a tray of beer steins by the door. And inside, when they go to hang their coats, the large wardrobe window, painted with a seated black cat, is even better.

At the bar, they order: a green for him, a bottle of sweet red Tuborg for her. She reads her notes to him. "This place opened in 1907 and was acquired a dozen years later by Betty Nansen. You know, the actress— the theater in Frederiksberg near where we were at Wine Room 90, the Betty Nansen Theater. Its name, The Stick, came from a game of chance played with matchsticks." She leans closer and lowers her voice. "Only women are allowed to serve in this bar. '*Kun en pige*,'" she says. "*Only a Girl.*"

"What's that?"

"A book. By Lise Nørgaard. The woman who wrote *Matador*, the television play that ran in about fifty parts telling the whole story of Danish social changes from about 1920 to maybe the late '60s? *Only a Girl* is Nørgaard's memoir of her life in the 1920s and '30s. Her father opposed her doing anything but girlish stuff."

"Isn't that like against the law or something?" Kerrigan asks her. "Only to hire women for the bar?"

She comments with an inhalation that is not the usual inhalated Scandinavian affirmative but a subtly bitter expression of irony. He puzzles over it for a moment, then remembers another story she told him last time they were together. Originally it had been her wish in life to be a journalist, but she was "blocked from it."

"How blocked?" he asked.

"Well," she said mildly. "Let's say it was because I have a cunt."

She was a good student, judged "*egnet*"—suitable—to proceed from primary school to secondary school in the academic line. There are three categories: suitable, unsuitable, possibly suitable. When a Danish child is thirteen or fourteen, one of these is stamped upon him or her. (His ex-wife Licia revealed to Kerrigan, if she was telling the truth, that she was judged "unsuitable." But he could never be sure whether she was telling the truth. About anything.) The novelist Peter Høeg, best known for his *Smilla's Sense of Snow* (1992), also wrote a novel entitled *De Måske Egnede*—literally *The Possibly Suitable*, although it was published under the translated title *Borderliners*, which does not quite convey the harshness of it. Høeg himself had been judged "possibly suitable" when he was a boy.

But Kerrigan's Associate was suitable and went on to gymnasium— the Danish secondary school for those judged suitable to go on to university, which she was. Her father, himself a lawyer at a publishing house, pulled strings to get her a job as a secretary in the editorial offices of Copenhagen's oldest daily newspaper, *Berlingsketidende*— *Berling's Times*. He said getting into the offices was a foot in the door, better than university. She worked there for a year waiting for the head of personnel to do what her father had promised he would, begin to try her out on small journalistic assignments, obituaries, social notices. Finally, when nothing happened, she approached him about it, and he expressed surprise. He told her there was never any connection between the administrative and editorial or journalistic functions at the paper, that it had never been his idea that she should do anything more than secretarial work. "*Du* er *kun en pige*," he said with a smile. "You *are* just a girl."

"He really said that to you?" Kerrigan asked.

"It was a conservative paper. It was 1959. And he was a conservative guy."

Kerrigan's Associate confronted her father about it, and he denied ever having promised anything of the sort. She should be happy to work for that fine newspaper. It was a good, solid job. She didn't have to keep those terrible hours journalists did. It was a good job for a young woman who was not yet married, and she wouldn't turn hard the way journalists do.

Kerrigan gazes at her.

"I was stupid," she tells him now. "By then I was used to the money. I didn't know how to fight. Maybe I was afraid to. I met a handsome young lawyer from the newspaper's legal department. He was seven years older than me and I was . . ."

"You were a knockout. I've seen pictures of you. Remember? You're still a knockout."

Whether she remembers or not she does not say; instead she says, "I had a cunt instead of a prick. So here I am now, nearly forty years, two husbands, three daughters, and five grandsons later. I see some of them. Once a year. I work as a freelance research secretary. On the weekends I go barefoot around my east side flat in leotards and play at being an artist. I know it's no excuse," she says. "But you know what really galls me? Many years later, my father gave me a copy of that book for Christmas. *Only a Girl*. He got Lise Nørgaard to sign it for me. He knew her. I just don't understand what he was thinking. Maybe he wasn't thinking at all. Maybe he just took it for granted. Because I have a cunt."

"I certainly hope you don't hate your cunt."

"I really like my cunt," she says. "But it has been something of a handicap at times."

"'The Speed of Darkness,'" Kerrigan says.

Her eyes hang a question toward him, and he recites a poem by Muriel Rukeyser, as best he can remember it, about the chain of consequence that the person who hates the cunt hates the child.

The tilt of her head and her mouth expresses skepticism.

"American poet," he says. "She died almost twenty years ago." He pauses for a moment, thinking back to other events, Licia, his babies, but jettisons the memory and continues, "She was writing about the poet not yet born who will be the voice of our time."

When she says nothing, he asks politely, "You say you have daughters?"

"Three. And five grandchildren. Two of the girls live in the U.S., the third in Canada. Once a year one or the other visits me. Or I visit them."

He sees a shadow in her gaze. "It really is incredible to think that in my lifetime, only like thirty, forty years ago, women were mocked, cheated of their rights, even had to use titles that revealed whether or not they were married, for Christ's sake!" And thinks of Licia—the new woman. He slides down from the barstool. "Shall we move on?"

"Don't forget your little briefcase now."

The thick novel bulges in the satchel. She asks what he is reading, and he finds himself telling her a little about Joyce and Dublin as they step out into Reventlowsgade.

"Lot of connections between Dublin and Scandinavia," he says. "Dublin was settled by Vikings, especially the Danes. Joyce believed he had Danish blood in him."

"How is the book?" she asks.

"A rough trudge. But it has its merry moments."

Across Reventlowsgade, his Associate points at the back of the Astoria Hotel. She has her Moleskine open in her hands. "When that was built in 1935, they nicknamed it *Penalhuset*—the Penal House. For obvious reasons."

"Good illustration for Kafka's 'Penal Colony,'" says Kerrigan. "Moody art. You paint, yourself? I hope I can get to see your paintings?"

"A little," she says.

Passing the Central Station, he glances down from the sidewalk bridge to the tracks below. He thinks of the poet Dan Turèll, the long poem he wrote in his thirties, the scene set in this station, imagining his last walk through the city; Turèll could not have known, in his thirties, the poem was predicting his early death at forty-six of throat cancer.

They cross Vesterbrogade—West Bridge Street—past **Fridhedsstøtten**, the Liberty Pillar, erected between 1792 and 1797. "It is to commemorate the liberation of the serfs," she says, "with the repeal in 1788 of adscription; before this, the peasants were the property of the person who owned the land they worked. The pillar is mentioned many times in Tom Kristensen's 1930 novel *Havoc*. You know, Ole 'Jazz' Jastrau in *Havoc* lived just around the corner from the Railway Café where we just were," she says. "He walks past this monument numerous times in the novel—I think that is saying he belongs in a way to the newspaper he works for."

They are passing Tivoli on the other side of the street. "Look at the trees!" she exclaims. They pause to gaze across Vesterbrogade at the front of the Tivoli Park. "The park is more than a hundred and fifty years old now," she tells him, "and the trees are just that shade of green only once a year."

She leads the way to Axeltorv—Axel Square—bounded by the broad front of the Scala Building, the Circus Building across the other end, and the many colors of the Palace Theater, which looks like a birthday cake.

She says, "Those rainbow pastels in the Palace Theater were done by Paul Gernes, the painter who overturned the idea that hospital rooms have to be sterile white. Which is especially nice for sick kids, to be surrounded by a rainbow of colors. Do you have children, yourself?" she asks, and he feels his face harden.

"Let's not go there," he mutters, caught unawares by the question at a moment when he felt he was expanding, being filled with a sense of place. To know facts is to have a handle.

She says, "I just thought . . . you'd make a good father. You're gentle. And enthusiastic."

They stand over the sheer vast pool of the shimmering fountain, so full it seems convex, always about to spill over, but it never does. He is battling memories: how his two-year-old daughter would sit on his lap and point at things for him to name—lamp, table, chair, carpet, repeating the words after him, the delicate features of her fresh-minted face, same blue eyes as her mother's. He thinks again of Licia, thinks, *Cunt!* and feels the anger as further loss. Gabrielle would be five now, the little one three. He didn't even know her name. If there really was a little one. If it was his. If it was just another lie.

He remembers the Rukeyser poem he quoted for his Associate in the bar, and suddenly in his mind he's jotting the line of a poem—*the cunt giveth and the cunt taketh away*—and in his mind he slashes out the line and reminds himself that he is not a poet.

When he says nothing more, the Associate turns a page in her Moleskine. "This square was built in 1863 when the old Central Station was opened," and he welcomes the lilting, soothing feminine music of her voice. "The square is named for Bishop Absalon, who founded Copenhagen in 1167, although evidence now proves the city is actually older than that, from the last half of the year 1000. You can see Absalon's statue on a rearing horse wielding an ax down on **Højbro Plads**, just off the **Strøget**, the Walking Street."

"A bishop wielding an ax? Interesting. He should ride his horse over to the Town Hall Square and do battle with the evil Burger King."

She chuckles, goes on: "The Danish literary critic Georg Brandes spoke at the unveiling of the statue in 1902 and pointed out that the ax was not only a weapon of battle but also a tool of civilization—to chop trees and firewood. Absalon, by the way, is the Hebrew version of the Danish name Axel."

"Here's **Axelborg Bodega**," she says, and leads him in. Glad to be delivered of bottled beer, he orders a pint and sits unspeaking, from time to time lifting his glass to his mouth. He does not toast and she respects his silence, which does not fail to escape his attention—he feels her watching him and wishes she would stop, but at the same time thinks of her question about children and hopes she does not pursue the subject. To make sure she doesn't, he changes it.

"I hope I can see your pictures sometime," he says.

"Let's see," she says. "If you're ever hungry and low on funds, they serve an excellent *skipperlabsskovs* here—lobscouse, sailor's stew, a huge portion of potatoes and boiled beef in a pale gravy made with beer—it's served with dark rye bread and pickled beets."

The place is nearly empty, and Kerrigan slowly relaxes, absently watching a man who sits alone at an adjoining table. The man is about his own age, drinking a bottle of Tuborg *Påske Bryg*, Easter Brew, strong beer, 7 to 8 percent, brewed around the Easter season for a few weeks every year. It has been brewed for over a century. The day it hits the streets—known since 1952 as P-Day (Easter Beer Day)—the young people in Copenhagen go on a rampage with it.

The man glances at them a couple of times—wistfully, Kerrigan thinks.

"What does your little book have about Danish beer?" he asks, and her delicate fingers rattle pages.

"It's been brewed in Denmark since around 4000 B.C.—six thousand years ago. They've found a preserved body of a Bronze Age girl—the Egtved Girl—in Jutland at a grave site with a pail of beer between her legs. She was in her mid-twenties, and the beer was made from malt wheat, cranberries, pollen, and instead of hops, bog myrtle for a bitter spice, also known as 'sweet gale.'"

"Sweet gale. I like that. Beer was known as 'mead,' right?"

"Wrong. Mead is fermented honey. A kind of wine. Beer is made from grain water, yeast, and seasoning. Hops didn't reach Denmark until about the year 1000. Until then they used sweet gale to give it the bitter taste. The Vikings used to drink to Freja, their goddess of fertility." She turns a page.

"But it wasn't until the nineteenth century that the Danish beer really began to excel. Thanks to the German yeast culture provided by Emil Christian Hansen to I. C. Jacobsen—the brewer of Carlsberg. The alcohol content of the various Danish beers—and there are more than 150 types brewed by fifteen breweries—ranges from under 1 percent to nearly 10 percent. Pilsner is 4.6, gold beer 5.8, Easter and Christmas beer are up to 7.9, Giraf is about 7.3 and Elephant is about the same, Jacob's Cognac Beer is 8.5 percent, and superpremiums up to 9.7. There is another that is 10 or 11 percent, Special Brew. The stronger beer is better with richer, heavier, or spicier food. And the Easter or Christmas beers are best after dinner—nice instead of sweet dessert wine."

"How about snaps?"

"Much younger than beer. Only about six hundred years old. Actually, it was originally known as *brændevin*, brandywine, and the best of it was called *aquavit*, 'water of life' in Latin, which is also the origin of whiskey—from the Irish *uisce beathadh* or the Scot Gællic *uisge beatha*, also literally 'water of life.'"

She turns another page. "At the end of the 1700s, the word *snaps* was adopted to replace brandywine. It means 'dram' or 'mouthful' but also is from *snappe*—to snap or take quickly—which is when you bite the snaps down in one shot. It was around that time the snaps glass was introduced, too. Otherwise they used to drink from the bottle. Or from a pocket flask. Which in Danish is called a *lommelærk*, a pocket lark, because it 'chirps' when you drink from it. Snaps was *very* central to Danish life up until 1917. It was also used for toothache, sluggishness, bad stomach, arthritis, all sorts of pain, and as a sleeping medicine for children, and for washing windows. It was 47.5 percent alcohol then, much stronger than now—it's usually 40 percent now, although some Christmas snaps is stronger. Then in 1917, the tax was raised so the price of a bottle of snaps quintupled, which achieved the goal of reducing consumption. The German and English word is *schnapps*, but that seems too long to me, don't you think? *Snaps* is quicker and better."

"Let's have one," says Kerrigan, and signals the waiter by tipping an imaginary snaps glass to his lips. The waiter comes with a bottle of Jubilaeum and two glasses.

"Doubles, please," says Kerrigan.

"Adult size," says the barman, and fills the glasses to the lip so that the liquor is almost convex atop the glasses.

"Know what that is called?" she asks, pointing to the top of the pour. "A meniscus."

They raise the glasses by the stems carefully, nod, snap them dry. "To the meniscus," he says. "Sounds a bit naughty. Is there also something called a womeniscus?"

She smiles. "That's called a pussy."

The man with the *Påske Bryg* looks over again, still wistful, and his wistfulness makes Kerrigan feel fortunate by comparison.

They cross **H. C. Andersens Boulevard** to the **Town Hall Square**, pausing to glance at the statue of Hans Christian Andersen seated in bronze, gazing up toward **Tivoli Gardens**. She is into her Moleskine again.

"This was done by Henry Luckow-Nielsen in the fifties." They stand gazing at Hans Christian in his bronze chair.

"There's also another, much older one in **Kongens Have**, the King's Garden," she tells him. "The Erotic Museum on **Købmagergade** used to have a big poster of that Andersen sculpture with a naked woman seated on his knee. How Andersen would have blushed. That sculpture was made during his lifetime. There was a competition for his seventieth birthday, and the first couple of entries Andersen looked at showed him reading to children—which had been stipulated in the competition guidelines. He didn't like it. 'Madonna with child,' he hissed. He picked the winner—his solitary self, telling a story to an imaginary audience he didn't have to share his pedestal with. He was a vain man in his old age. All his life, actually. Poor H. C.," she says, pronouncing the *h* as "ho" in the Danish fashion. "Poor Ho. C. Such success and so unhappy. All the women he adored, to no avail, poor man. He was always being spurned. But he always 'got his money back,' as he referred to writing about his sorrows—whether it was a toothache or a heartache. He puts one of his spurners, Louise Collin, in his tale 'The Swineherd' as the haughty princess, and in 'The Little Mermaid' as the prince. Hans Christian himself was the mermaid, by the way."

Kerrigan, lighting a small cigar, snorts and sits on a bench just back from the statue. She joins him at the opposite end of the bench. He glances at her face, her lips, charmed by her knowledge, her enthusiasm, her wit and irony. He wants to kiss her mouth, considers taking a bold course and doing just that, but he doesn't dare run the risk of scaring her off. He is also titillated by the thought of her visiting the Erotic Museum, and saying *pussy*.

But his attraction makes him remember how hard he fell for Licia. He remembers Licia rolling in the Ionian surf in a bikini the blue of her eyes on the north shore of Cephalonia. How she smiled and stared deep into his eyes. *Her love made me into the me I always wanted to be, had been waiting all my life to be: a man loved by a woman like Licia. A man who made a beautiful baby girl with a woman like Licia. She was the woman I hungered for all my life*. Then he remembers the neighbor woman on the one side visiting him once, after Licia was gone, inferring, quite unmistakably, that Licia had spent a lot of time with the neighbor man on the other side.

But in some way he is comforted by the information on Andersen—*great men have been unhappy, too*, he thinks. *You are not the only man who has been thrown away*.

He says, "Hard to picture that lovely little bronze lady on her rock in the water off Langelinje as a transvestite. Andersen in scaly drag."

"Not everyone shares your view of her as lovely." She digs a packet of Prince from her bag, lights one, chin tipped up as smoke issues from her lovely pursed lips.

"Yeah," he says, "I hear someone cut her head off."

"Twice. The statue was sculpted by Edvard Eriksen and had sat there peacefully since 1913, donated by Carl Jacobsen, the founder of Carlsberg Breweries. He donated many sculptures to Copenhagen. One night in 1964, someone climbed out to her rock with a metal saw and cut her head off. Many believe it was done by the artist Jørgen Nash, referred to as the 'Mermaid Killer.' The mermaid's head was recast and replaced, but someone did it again about twenty-five years later. The theory is that the first time, Nash did it because as an artist he was furious that such a sentimental statue based on such a sentimental tale should come to be a symbol of Copenhagen. The second time, however, it was said to be a journalist trying to make news and a name for himself."

"I don't recall the story being as bad as that."

"Are you a sentimentalist? Some love it. But the way it ends! Her soaring to the heavens and all those rosy clouds!"

He reaches over to touch the bronze book on Andersen's bronze knee. "So who else did the old boy have the hots for?"

"Sophie Ørsted—the daughter of H. C. Ørsted . . ." She consults her book. "1777 to 1851. He discovered electromagnetism in 1820—you know they still call the unit of magnetic strength for him—an oersted."

"Isn't there also a park named for him here in Copenhagen? Ørsted Park?"

"Yes," she says. "And there is a fine sculpture garden there. They have also named an avenue, an institute, and an electrical plant for Ørsted. Anyway, Sophie's father was one of Andersen's friends—one of the first to recognize that Andersen's true greatness was not in his plays or novels or travel books, but in his tales. Most of the critics of the time thought the tales trivial and offensive. They were nonacademic, even antiacademic, because they were written in colloquial language. Andersen became an international success in 1835 with his novel *The Improvisatore*, the same year that he published his first book of *Fairy Tales, Told for Children*. Ørsted had better sense than the critics of the time. He told Andersen that the novel may have made him famous, but the tales would make him immortal. Andersen always believed he would be famous. He came to Copenhagen at the age of fourteen as a pauper and threw himself at the mercy of society. 'First you go through a cruel time and then you become famous,' he explained, and, by the time he was thirty, he had proven that was true. But his love life was always a cruel time. As you can read in his journals. It is said that for every day that he sets an X he practiced onanism."

"Honeymoon of the hand, ey? Did he set a double X when he used the stranger?"

"Stranger?"

"His left."

She sniggers and glances at him with light in her eyes.

"Moving right along," he says. "What cafés did he frequent in Copenhagen?"

"The only café I know of that Andersen frequented was the Caffé Greco in the Via Condotti in Rome, which was the haunt of everyone in Rome," she continues. "Casanova, Canova, Goethe, Gogol, Byron, Liszt, the Danish sculptor Bertel Thorvaldsen. Andersen used to go to Greco in 1833 when he was in Rome for the first time. He was twenty-eight. Just before he got famous."

"Let's see," Kerrigan says. "In 1833, Kierkegaard would have been twenty, right?"

"Yes. And writing in his journals about the sins of passion and the heart being nearer salvation than the sins of reason!"

"Sounds a bit like Andersen."

"To Kierkegaard," she says, "Andersen was a 'sniveler,' the word he used in a review of Andersen's third novel. Kierkegaard was one of his sternest critics."

"How did Andersen take to criticism?"

"Generally he would weep," she says, laughing, and he cannot resist joining her, and somehow their laughter at Andersen's misery and weak nature a century and a half ago makes him feel stronger in the realization that despite being a great artist, Andersen was pretty much a jerk and a baby.

"I read somewhere," she continues, "that when he visited Charles Dickens in England, Dickens found Andersen lying facedown on the lawn of Gad's Hill, Dickens's home, weeping. Another bad review. Andersen also stood on the bank of **Peblinge Lake**—just a few blocks from here—and wept."

Kerrigan snickers, and she joins him.

"But he always got his revenge," she says, "always got his 'money back.' He didn't take his final revenge on Kierkegaard until twenty-five years after the philosopher's attack on him—and six years after Kierkegaard's death—when he wrote the tale 'The Snail and the Rose Bush,' in 1861. Kierkegaard is the snail, spitting at the world and retiring into his shell, while the rose—"

"Andersen?"

"Naturally . . . keeps on blooming because it can do nothing else."

They fall silent in the cool spring evening air. Then she says, "Kierkegaard wasn't really *discovered* until twenty years after his death, when Georg Brandes lectured on his work in Germany, and the French made him 'the father of existentialism.' Brandes didn't like 'The Little Mermaid' either. Or 'The Ugly Duckling,' because the swan that emerges is a domesticated one, not a wild swan. In the folktales and ballads in Denmark, some wildness is shown in nature and in our soul and fate. Many of the old Danish folk ballads were about the elfin women who lure men so they become elfin-struck, elfin-wild, making them dance in the woods and lie with them."

"Like Keats's 'La Belle Dame Sans Merci.'" An image of dancing in the woods with Licia flashes through his mind.

"Yes. And there were also elfin women who stood glittering at the edge of the road through the woods waving to lonely travelers to come and dance with them, but if a traveler left the road to go to her, he was led in deeper and deeper as the elfin woman backed away. Finally, when he reached her, she would turn and he would discover she had no back, and he would disappear into the back that was not there, never to be seen again."

Kerrigan shifts on the bench, wondering that she is able to sit so still and straight with her cigarette while producing such a wealth of facts. He studies the face of the bronze Andersen sculpture seated so high above him. The thick lips curving out over protruding false teeth, the Hebraic nose, the narrow eyes. "He must have been a pain in the arse."

"He traveled with a length of rope in his luggage in case the hotel caught fire, so he could lower himself from the window. He was even said to leave a note by his bedside every night: 'I only seem dead.' In case he should slip into a coma while sleeping."

Kerrigan asks, "I wonder if he ever read Poe?" at the same time appreciating the conjuncture of the possibility, even probability, feeling enriched in spirit by the moment. "Did he have any friends at all?"

"Well, he had many fans and royal champions. He knew Mendelssohn, Heinrich Heine, the Grimm brothers, Liszt, Victor Hugo, Alexandre Dumas. Charles Dickens presented him with a twelve-volume illustrated edition of his works, every volume of which was inscribed with the words, 'To Hans Christian Andersen from his friend and admirer Charles Dickens.' In fact, one of Andersen's tales, 'The Dung Beetle,' was written on a public challenge by Dickens to write a story about such a creature. Andersen dedicated the first English edition of his tales to Dickens. He was also Dickens's houseguest in 1857, but he overstayed his welcome by about three weeks—ignoring the visdom of the old Danish proverb that a fish and a guest begin to stink after three days. After that, Dickens stopped answering his letters. Andersen wrote sadly about the end of the friendship in his journals: *All over, and that is the way of every story.* Which are the closing words of his own tale 'The Fir Tree.'"

When Kerrigan hears that line—*All over, and that is the way of every story*—he feels penetrated by it, wounded. He finds himself watching not the statue of Andersen but the face of his Associate, her eyes like green lamps flickering to green shadow. The sureness with which she speaks, the volume of information, faltering only occasionally to consult her Moleskine.

He drops his cigar and steps on it, looks at her again. "You are a very learned person," he says softly.

She gazes at him with a mild blankness. "I am an autodidact," she says. "A good research secretary. I don't *know* anything. I just repeat facts."

"I think you know a lot more than you know. But you did say you go barefoot on the weekends. I find that a rather charming picture." *I would love to see your naked little trotters.* "Do you paint your toenails?"

"Would you not like to know." She stubs out her cigarette against the iron foundation of the bench and tosses it into the gutter. "Shall we push onward to the Palace?"

The **Palace Hotel** is just across the Town Hall Square. Kerrigan is startled once again to see, among this elegant architecture, the Burger King and 7-Eleven shops on either prime corner of the square leading into the Walking Street, and the Kentucky Fried Chicken joint a few doors away.

"This whole place," she says as they cross the Town Hall Square, "used to be crisscrossed with trolley tracks. Tom Kristensen describes it in *Havoc* as a kind of desert that he crosses each evening from his job there in the newspaper, over to the west side, where we've just come from." She points diagonally across the square to the windows of the newspaper *Politiken.*

"*Hærværk,*" says Kerrigan. "*Havoc.* I know the Danish title literally means 'vandalism,' but 'havoc' is the right translation, I think. It's very contemporary. About a man—a person—destroying his best possibilities for position. And destroying his position to win back the greater part of his nature." Then he wonders how that applies to him. Licia destroyed his best possibilities. He examines that thought for self-pity but can find only a statement of fact.

They are standing under the tall pedestal, atop which is the statue of the Lyre Blowers, and she checks her book. "Incidentally," she says, "it is said that the horns of the lyre blowers in this sculpture sound only if a virgin over the age of fifteen walks past and that, in fact, they've never been heard."

Kerrigan smiles but is thinking about Jazz Jastrau in *Havoc* raising his Lindblom cocktail—one part gin, four parts absinthe—and whispering, *Now we begin, quietly, slowly to go to the dogs.* "It was a religious book, really," he says. "Spiritual. A man revolting against the lies of a 'profession,' of 'employment.' At one point in the book, he says he can never forget Jesus among the whores, and the more he squanders and drinks, the closer Jesus comes to him, rising amidst the havoc of his heart."

"So simple?" she says, glancing at him, and he averts his eyes.

They cross past the looming dark structure of St. Nicholas Church, no longer a church at all but a restaurant, among other things, with a green metal pissoir on the street outside it. Behind the church (Skt. Nikolaj Kirke), his Associate takes him around one side to show him a bust, half hidden in a nook of red bricks. "That's Tausser, the artist. His real name was Svende Aage Tauscher. Lived from 1911 to '82. He was a vagabond, a bum really, a drunk, homeless. Still, he painted something like nine thousand pictures in his life, most of them sold to buy drink. When his gallery owner scolded him for selling the pictures so cheap, Tausser said he needed the money because it made him feel so sad when he didn't have enough when it came his turn to buy a round."

Kerrigan studies the bust—a bearded, rumpled, sagging face beneath a rumpled fedora, but with character in the sags, the wrinkles. He thinks how often he passed this church, never noticing Tausser. And he wonders how the man continued to work, to be productive, despite his homelessness, his alcoholism.

In the **Café Nick** down the street, Kerrigan asks, "What did Hans Christian Andersen drink?"

"He liked porter."

"Let's drink a porter then," says Kerrigan as they sit beneath a large 1920s painting of a woman in a lilac shirt smoking a cigarette, no doubt a racy matter at the time, and the waiter brings them bottles of Carlsberg black stuff.

They toast the dead tale-teller with a *skål*, then they drink to a sketched portrait of Tausser on the wall here, too—one that was done by the same man who did his bust, Troels Lybecker. There is another sketched Tausser portrait on the wall, from 1976 by Rune Dyremark. "They say the church was full when Tausser was buried," Kerrigan's Associate says.

"Pretty good for a homeless guy. How wonderful if there are really ghosts," says Kerrigan. "If Andersen's spirit were here right now, witnessing our toast. And Tausser."

"They say when you speak of a dead person, he comes back to life for the time you speak."

Then they sit in silence among the paintings and dim light of the Nick. Kerrigan is a little tight and wonders if she is really as sober as she seems. He glances at her Moleskine book on the table, wondering how such a slender pad can contain so much information; she dutifully opens it, though he thinks he sees some hesitation pull at the corner of her comely mouth.

"There used to be an expression, 'Nicolai Bohemians.' It applied to the customers of all the small bars and cafés that were around this square, around the church, Sankt Nikolaj. You know who Saint Nikolaj was?"

He shakes his head.

"Santa Claus! Father Christmas. This café opened in 1904. It was the main café frequented by artists, but they called the whole area the Minefield because there were so many bars here, tempting people."

Kerrigan considers the nearly century-old café, the seven centuries of church here, the great fire of 1795, places himself in the midst of it. Then he remembers the name of a poet who used to drink here. "I know something about this place," he says. "A poem. Want to hear?"

"If I say yes, I can preserve the illusion of free will."

He smiles, says, "Smart-ass," drinks some porter. "Now you'll have to beg me."

Her green eyes look up beseechingly at him. "Please?" she says softly, and his blood jumps. He clears his throat, but then he says, "Actually I'm not allowed to. I could get sued for reciting it in public. And the night has a thousand ears. But if you go buy a copy of *Schades Digte*— *Schade's Poems* from Gyldendal, published earlier this year, you'll find it in toto under the title 'The Dancing Painter.'" He leans close to her, says, "If you put your ear to my lips, I'll whisper a few lines."

Her eyes lighten as he whispers, and her excited reaction excites him.

"I don't know his poetry," she says.

"Ah-ha! So your little junior woodchuck's Moleskine manual doesn't contain *every*thing after all! Poul Borum called Schade the greatest Danish poet of the twenties and the liveliest force in modern Danish literature. Born in 1903, the year before this café opened. He died in '78. He was considered a pornographer for years because he wrote about all the things dearest to our hearts—sex and love and drink. Borum compares him to D. H. Lawrence, E. E. Cummings, and Henry Miller. His first book of poetry, *The Living Violin*, came out in 1926 and was subtitled *spiritual and sensual songs*, and that's his force; he joins body and soul. Borum calls him a happy Baudelaire. But the last book, *I'm Mad About You*, is about eros as obsession, as psychosis."

"And Borum is dead now, too," she says.

"They all go into the dark," says Kerrigan. "You know he once invited me to collaborate with him on a translation. I declined."

"*Why?*"

"Because I was stupid. I was afraid. I guess I was afraid I couldn't measure up, that Borum, that Denmark maybe, would swallow me alive. Now I know myself a little better. I *know* I can't measure up, so there's nothing to be afraid of. You just have to know that a good translator— as a friend of mine who is a good translator told me, Stacey Knecht—has to put himself second. For many years that was too difficult for me."

"Have you translated Danish writers?"

"A few, a bit of Pia Tafdrup. Currently mostly Henrik Nordbrandt and Dan Turèll."

Her green eyes, he notes, lighten when they widen. "Dan Turèll? Uncle Danny!"

"Yes, a painter who'd known Turèll—Barry Lereng Wilmont—saw my translations of Nordbrandt and suggested I translate Turèll. I thought he'd been translated years ago, but no. Barry had promised Dan before he died that he would have him sent across the ocean in translation. Barry introduced me to Dan's widow, Chili, and she gave permission."

Her gaze rests on his face, as if taking him in again, reassessing him, and a flicker of unexpected hope lights in him. But hope for what? No.

He takes out his Petit Sumatra cigarillos, sees her still watching him, extends the box, and to his surprise she takes one. He strikes a stick match, holds it across the table, and she lightly guides his hand with her fingertips. The touch runs across the surface of his flesh, and he thinks of Schade in the Copenhagen bars and serving houses, surrounded by the women he loved so—his muses, he called them—drunk on red wine and desire, writing his poetry even under the table. He feels the water in his eyes, thinking of the man, thinking he might have met him once before he died in 1978, had he only stirred himself to action, but in the seventies Kerrigan was trying to reenter society after having squandered the sixties hitchhiking around the United States. His parents died and he cashed in their assets and invested the money in Denmark, where his mother was born, and found work here as a suit, a humanistic, nonprofit suit, while he completed his university work with no time to look and see the world around him. He never met Dan Turèll either, although he had had opportunities. He thinks of all the things he could experience still if only he could stir himself to do so, to overcome his ego, to overcome his fear of what the "false blue eyes and blonde treachery" reduced him to.

"There's another one by Schade set here," he says. "I think it's called 'In the Café,' about a song on the jukebox and kissing a girl with ugly teeth and a Finnish girl who shows him her breasts—or is that another one?"

She flicks a crumb of tobacco off her pink tongue, asks, "What is your education?"

"My education? I have a doctorate. A Ph.D."

"Oh! Can I touch you?"

He thinks of the Norwegian-Danish Aksel Sandemose's novel about the so-called *Jantelov*. "The Law of Jante," he says. "First commandment, *Thou shalt not think thou art something*. It's just a piece of paper," he says, "right?"

"Meaning," she says, "*wrong*, right? That it is something *more* than just a piece of paper, *right*?"

He shrugs, smiles, caught out in his sentimental hypocrisy and seduction and pride. He doesn't mind. He glimpses a mildness lurking beneath her caution and mockery.

"You know James Joyce—the Irish novelist?"

She nods. "A little."

"Well, he wrote what is considered by many people to be the greatest novel of the twentieth century with one of the most admired and often quoted women lead characters of, well, maybe of all literature, at least since Chaucer's Wife of Bath—actually, you remind me of both those characters; you even have a bit of a gap tooth like the Wife of Bath. Very sexy! The Joyce character is Molly Bloom, and you know what she says in the book about university knowledge? She says, 'I wouldn't give a snap of my two fingers for all their learning. Why don't they go and create something . . .'"

His Associate smiles so warmly it gladdens his own heart, and he puts his hand on hers on the table. She looks at his hand, but she does not stop smiling or withdraw from his touch. He squeezes her fingers and takes his own hand away, suddenly shy. In the silence that follows he lights another Sumatra, shadows rippling through his consciousness as he reviews all the things that can be discovered in one snap of the fingers. How you can step through a door to a home and find it empty, everyone gone. As all stories end.

Her eyes are upon him, and she asks, "What was your subject?"

"Literature," he says, grateful to be drawn back from the shadows. "Specifically, verisimilitude. Want to know more?"

"I think you're going to tell me."

"No. Only if you want."

"Please."

"How writers of fiction seem to create reality. *Veris similis* in Latin. *Vrai semblance* in French. The appearance of reality. The way a writer creates a credible illusion to get the reader to suspend disbelief long enough to listen and experience what the writer wants to transmit. Beneath the illusion, if the writer is serious, lies the stuff of truth, of a deeper reality, that probably has little to do with the trappings of everyday life that were used to build the illusion—unless those actual trappings are what he's writing about. But the reality beneath that illusion can help us understand something about human existence. The illusion of literature, at its best, relies on a deeper wisdom. Fiction, even the most realistic-seeming fiction, is not existence, but *about* existence. For example, Kafka uses sensory images to make us believe, or at least accept, the preposterous notion that Gregor Samsa has turned into a cockroach, and because we believe that for a little while, we experience some deep mystery of existence. But sometimes writing something defines the essence of the author and changes him. So in that sense fiction, all writing, can be truer than raw life." He thinks of Hamsun then—the building he saw this morning, where over a hundred years ago Hamsun wrote *Hunger.* "You know Knut Hamsun? The Norwegian writer? *Hunger?* In that, he abandoned many realistic devices of fiction—plot, narrative arc, story even—to portray the consciousness of a man starving to express itself . . ." Abruptly, he becomes aware of himself lecturing her, trails off.

"What is the word again?" she asks.

"Verisimilitude. It took me half a year just to learn to pronounce it right."

Her cigar has gone out, and she relights it with a Bic, trims it on the edge of the ashtray. "And now you are writing a book about bars."

"Please," he corrects. "Serving houses. So much more elegant in Danish. And what could be more existentially essential? Reason is an unreasonable faculty. It will strangle us if we take it too seriously. It needs damping, and that is why we come to these places, *n'est-ce pas?*"

She smiles wanly and they sit in silence for a time, listening to music from a CD player behind the bar. Bob Dylan is singing "When I Paint My Masterpiece." Then he sings, "I Threw It All Away," and Kerrigan finds himself thinking of his life. Looking back upon himself, he sees a man who was young and brash and full of himself and threw all his greatest potential out the window. Or maybe he had no choice. Maybe in his own way he was programmed to do precisely what he did—avoiding love, then falling hard for a woman who was hardly more than a child.

How he wishes he could go back and adjust himself somehow, do it over, do it better, but in what way, adjust to what? He has spent nearly three years trying to adjust to the deprivation of a life he had been fleeing for decades—then couldn't embrace it fast enough. Was it just because he feared age? They married when he was forty-nine. And she was twenty-nine. Maybe she feared turning thirty also. His beautiful wife. His beautiful little girl. As every story ends. In the recognition of illusion.

He tips his stout bottle over the edge of his empty glass, but not a drop slips out. He wills himself from the gloom, glances at his Associate's handsome face lost in its own distance, its own music. Such a lovely green-eyed face, he thinks, and realizes suddenly that she recognizes that she herself must also bear some blame for the fact that she did not get the education she wished for, and his awareness of her awareness of this touches in him a sense of kinship with her.

We have both been foolish. We both have regrets, and here we sit in our fifties in an old café over empty glasses, empty bottles.

He can feel the drink in his legs as they walk down **Vingårdstræde**—Vineyard Street, where years before someone had attempted, in vain, to cultivate grapes for wine. Not suited to the Danish climate. Somewhere he seems to remember reading of a Roman expedition to Scandinavia—was it in Tacitus?—in which the leader explained his withdrawal by saying: *The land is uninhabitable. There are no olive trees.*

They come out behind **Kongens Nytorv**, the King's New Square, and she points. "That's the National Bank there."

"Nine hundred and ninetynine million pound sterling in the blue-black bowels of the bank of Ulster."

"Sorry?"

"Joyce," he explains, and pats his leather satchel. *"Finnegan."* When she does not respond, he continues, "You know, Joyce visited Copenhagen. In September 1936. He was convinced he had Viking blood in him. Dublin and Cork owe their origins to Danish Vikings—but he also once told his brother Georgio that he wanted to go to Denmark because the Danes massacred so many of his ancestors. He had taught himself Danish, or Dano-Norwegian, in order to read Ibsen—Norway had been under Denmark previously. Joyce's first publication, written at the age of seventeen, was a long article about Ibsen's last play, *When We Dead Awaken* from 1899, exactly a hundred years ago. The review was published on April Fool's Day, 1900. Joyce professed to believe that Ibsen was the greatest dramatist of all time, even greater than Shakespeare."

Then he remembers one particular play Joyce had praised by Ibsen—about the necessity of an artist's renouncing love and marriage—and thinks of his own decades of such renunciation, or avoidance, only to be trapped at forty-nine by the blonde treachery. He takes refuge in thoughts of H. C. Andersen's unhappy experiences of love, taking succor in the many women he himself has known—for a night, a couple of weeks, a season . . . Kierkegaard also had a fiasco of a love life. By comparison, Kerrigan comforts himself, his is rich in experience—even if it is equally laden with regret.

"But Joyce also admired Andersen," he continues. "When he was here he even bought a toy as a reminder of Andersen for his five-year-old grandson. He called Andersen Denmark's greatest writer. He was also full of praise for Carlsberg beer, and his wife was full of praise for the Danish light, its continuous changes, which is one of the things that caused me to fall in love with Denmark, too. Joyce also had a high opinion of Brandes. Also, Tom Kristensen met Joyce when he was here. Ole Jastrau in *Havoc* is reading *Ulysses*."

She listens attentively to what Kerrigan is telling her, then stops walking and says, "Tell me something. You know so much about Copenhagen already. Are you toying with me? Why do you need my help? Do you have something else in mind?"

Kerrigan hopes the darkness hides his blush. "I only know a little," he says. "And very little about the bars or the Danish Golden Age. You know much more than I do."

"But," she says, "you . . . you are like some kind of university professor. You have read so much."

"Have read little. Understood less." He looks into her eyes and doesn't tell her that he is quoting Joyce's Stephen Dedalus.

* * *

33

He feels heavy as they enter the labyrinthine, cavelike dimness of **Hviid's Vinstue** (Hviid's Wine Room), established in 1723, the same year as the Duke pub in Dublin, older by fifty-three years than the U.S. itself, although there is the White Horse Tavern on Marlborough Street in Newport, Rhode Island, which is older, established in 1673. Hviid's survived the great fires of 1728, 1794, and 1795 and the British attacks on Copenhagen of 1801 and 1807, just as his father escaped the British occupation of Ireland and his mother the German occupation of Denmark.

They move past the bar to one of the cubbyhole tables to the side. There are many pictures on the walls, photographs, cutout articles, caricatures. She has her Moleskine book out again, and he has to concentrate on her words.

"Upstairs here," she tells him, "used to be the Blue Note and the Grand Café, and these three together were the outer rim of the Minefield that started around Nikolai Church that I told you about before. In the 1950s and '60s."

The waiter comes to take their orders, and Kerrigan asks for a pint of Carlsberg. "I can't drink any more beer," she says, and Kerrigan suggests a Campari. As the waiter crosses back to the bar, Kerrigan says, "He looks like a pug."

"That's Jørgen 'Gamle' Hansen," she tells him. "Old Hansen, they call him, because he fought until he was forty. He used to be welterweight boxing champion of Europe about twenty years ago. He also was an actor on TV—played a small part in a crime series in the eighties."

Kerrigan recognizes him then, and as he returns with their drinks, Kerrigan stands. "May I shake your hand, Mr. Hansen? You look like you're in just as good shape as when you were champ."

Hansen smiles wryly with his broad jaw and hooked, broken nose, and his hand in Kerrigan's feels like a block of wood. "Appearances deceive," the old pugilist says.

Kerrigan watches him list off. He can still remember Hansen's right that felled Dave Green in the seventies and won him the title. Suddenly, then, he notices her glass and says, "Campari red as breathless kisses." Her eyes meet his. He can't read them, but he goes on nonetheless. "Jens August Schade again. The poem is called 'In Hviid's Wine Room.' From 1963."

"Can you say it for me?"

"Night has a thousand ears, remember. Might get sued for reciting it in public. I can tell you this much—it has to do with frog-green absinthe and Campari-red kisses." He slurs a bit. Her eyes friendly, she asks, "How drunk are you?"

"Just a wee twisted," he says. "But not on beer alone."

"Meaning?"

He is picturing her in red panties and nothing else and drinking Campari and kissing him with her tongue, but he says, "Did anyone ever tell you your eyes are green as the woods?"

"Frequently," she says, but the subtext he thinks he hears is, *Never, I like it, but say it again when you're sober.* Then she writes something in her Moleskine and says, "I really must read Schade. I've heard of him but never actually read him." She closes the book and he glimpses the starfish stickers on it as she slips it into her black leather bag, and he recites:

> The starfish crawl upon the wall
> upon the floor and through the door
> the starfish with their many legs
> and not so many eyes
> the starfish that can hug and crush
> never seeing why.

She sips her red Campari. "You must spend a great deal of time memorizing verses."

"Hey, that was my own! I just wrote it right now this minute." In his own ears, his voice is hoarse from beer and cigars.

"*Sludder,*" she says, which means *nonsense* in Danish, but somehow more effectively, with the double soft *d* sound of garbage, slush.

"Not *sludder*. Sometimes when I get to a certain point, words start leaking out. Like Tom Kristensen said, intoxication is just a poem that hasn't got a form."

"Did you really just make up that rhyme? I'm impressed."

"I hoped you would be, even if it's not very good."

"Why? Did you hope?"

"Because your eyes. Like green lamps." He tries to think up a rhyme, pauses, knows he's lost it, has entered the stage that comes after the facile rhymes: "Dark is life, dark dark is death," he says. "I'm stuck. That's John Hawkes. I always start quoting stuff when I'm stuck. Like the test patterns on a TV. Remember they used to have those? To let you know it's still in function, even if there's no show."

"Recite that Schade for me again. The one with the Campari."

And Kerrigan thinks how happy he would be if she were wearing red ones. And let him see. "Here, come closer," he says. "I'll whisper it." And feels his lips moving against her warm delicate ear.

He realizes too late, crossing the King's New Square toward **Nyhavn**, New Harbor, that it was a mistake to suggest one more stop. Had they simply ordered a taxi from Hviid's to his place—or hers . . . Of course, she only asked for the poem, but he did not fail to see the glint in her eyes over the line about the red panties, which did not fail to set him to puerile speculation over what color hers were: How foolish he feels at his age to wonder breathlessly whether she is wearing red panties. Foolishly happy. Happily foolish. And at what age might that be? Late youth. Advanced late youth.

He tries to save the moment by reciting another, composed on the spot, that he feels is true in his lungs:

> Has anyone seen that friend of mine
> Who said with a smile, "This is wine.
> Have a glass. See what you think.
> Sit down. Relax. Drink."

But his anticipated pleasure of its hedonistic resonance sours. He feels suddenly like nothing so much as a drunk, thick-tongued with slurred vision, and he wonders, not for the first time, if he has become hopelessly alcoholic.

Now they walk along the Nyhavn canal, where boats sit lashed between impassable low bridges (and he thinks of Rimbaud's "Drunken Boat")—canal-narrow drawbridges actually—toward the harbor and the Malmø boats, hovercraft that take you across to the once-Danish now-Swedish city in half an hour or so, a city that will soon be reachable by the bridge scheduled for completion later this year at which time the hovercraft to Malmø will disappear. All things eventually vanish. *Ubi sunt?* He asks her to point out the different places where Hans Christian Andersen lived here. It cheers him to compare himself to loveless bungling Andersen—by contrast, Kerrigan has at least tasted love. *But what was the price?*

She shows him **Nyhavn 20**, the narrow tall house where Andersen stayed in 1835 when he started writing fairy tales, and **Nyhavn 18**, his last home before he moved in with a friend to be nursed as he died of liver cancer in 1875. And she gestures down **Lille Strandstræde**, saying, "He lived there in number 67 from 1847 to 1865."

"**Jeppe's Bade Hotel** is farther down that street, too. Jeppe's Bath Hotel. It's neither a hotel nor a bath, but good jazz CDs."

"Interesting," she says, and Kerrigan hears the chill of professionalism has returned to her tone. He regrets having suggested they stop into **Café Malmø** to see the world's largest collection of beer openers, as reported in *The Guinness Book of Records*.

They turn down **Havnegade** (Harbor Street) and step down into the semibasement pub, Café Malmø, and the first he sees across the bar section are two men passed out at a little table as Paul McCartney sings from a sound system, "I'm so sorry, Uncle Albert" which makes him think of Licia's note in the empty house: *I'm so sorry, I don't love you . . .* One of the passed-out men is wearing a Napoleon hat fashioned from a sheet of newspaper. On the wall above their slumped heads a sign offers beer and tequila shooters at a cut rate.

As they sit and wait to order, she reads to him from her Moleskine book that the café was opened in 1870 and has its name from Copenhagen's twin city, Malmö, just across the sound in southern Sweden. It is an old sailors' bar, but many international guests come to see the beer-opener collection.

The beer openers are everywhere, framed on the walls, hanging in thick clusters like stalactites from the ceiling. Kerrigan tries to imagine tourists streaming in from all around the world to study these thousands of openers, people lined up around the harbor to come in and see. He wonders if there are doubles.

Then the barmaid is there—young and punk haired—admiring the green jade cross that Kerrigan has not even noticed all day at his Associate's throat, although he does see now that it is the same green as her eyes, and he says, "It really is, really is *beauful*," and his own ear catches the loss of the syllable. "Beau-*ti*-ful," he enunciates to demonstrate that he is at least not that far gone, but he says the word too loudly, and the man with the newspaper hat lifts his head. He is leaned against the wall where Kerrigan notices yet another sign: TABLE WHORES CLUB. His face is desolated, eyelids sagging low and a smile of unforgiven unforgiving unrepentant dissoluted idiocy on his wet mouth, then once more wraps his dreams about his heart and slips away. In the course of these movements, the elbow of the man overturns a glass the stale-looking contents of which spills into the lap of the other sleeping man, who jolts upright and croaks, "That was juice-*sizzle*-me *smart!*"

"Well, you're not so *cancer*-eat-me clever yourself, you ass banana."

"Fok," the first says, and lays his head down once again, and Kerrigan begins to realize he is watching these events through nearly closed eyes himself, nodding.

"Mr. Kerrigan!" his Associate snaps.

"Shouldn't we dance?" he says.

"You'll be doing it alone, sir," she says.

"It is a lonely dance," he says. "Upon monsieur's sword." And notices that hanging just above the cross at her throat is a steel shieldlike ornament half the size of a cigarette pack. "What's that?" he asks.

"In fact," she tells him, "it is a North African chastity belt."

He misses a beat. "You puttin' me on?"

"No," she enunciates, demonstrating for him how nullifyingly nil the word's message can be. *Why would she wear a chastity belt at her throat?* He considers a deep-throat joke but decides against it.

Disgrace multiplies as he stumbles, climbing up out of the basement pub to step into the idling cab that his Associate has telephoned for.

"Nu går det hurtigt," he says to her in Danish. "It's going fast now." A Danish saying. By which he means to disassociate himself from the involuntary acceleration of his intoxication. "Intoxication," he says, "is a poem which has not found its form. That's Ole Jastrau."

"I read the book," she says. She is chill but not so chill as to make him lose all hope.

"You have experience at this. Handling slightly intoxicated gentlemen," he mutters.

"My father and my first husband gave me some practice. Second was no better, though he didn't drink. Although I would not call any of them gentlemen."

It occurs to him that maybe they are destined to repeat their lives, proceeding from wrong to wrong, she with drunken him, he adoring and losing her. He leans closer, smells her perfume, and feels the ache of loneliness in his heart. He wants so badly to touch her, for her to touch him. He wants to recite Joyce to her: *Touch me. Soft eyes. Soft soft soft hand. I am lonely here. O, touch me soon now. I am quiet here alone. Sad too. Touch touch me.* Or even to jocularize with a word of Molly's: *Give us a touch, Poldy. I'm dying for it.* What a delightful thing for a woman to say.

But he would feel a self-pitying fool for it and wills discretion upon himself. "Listen," he says quietly. "I'm not that bad. Just didn't eat enough. Cup of coffee fix me right up in case, you might like for example to come up and join me for a cup. I promise you: no uninvited monkey business."

She smiles. "Not this time, Mr. Kerrigan," she says as the cab pulls in along the curb at his apartment on **Øster Søgade**, East Lake Street.

"What a lovely view," she says, admiring the lake across the road.

"Nicer from the apartment inside," he says.

She shakes her head, opens the door for him. He manages not to lunge at her for a kiss, gives her his hand instead, which he feels her take warmly with a gentle embrace of her fingers.

"Deep down you *are* a gentleman," she says.

"Try to. Be."

He stands swaying slightly on the street outside his building as the cab rolls off. He sees her fingers twinkle at him from behind the dark glass, then the whispered roar of the engine is moving off, the rump of the car disappearing.

We followed the rump of a misguiding woman, said Fergus.

He is standing just outside the white picket fence of the building beside his own, finds himself staring at a forsythia bush—at first blankly, then slowly perceiving that it is in bloom, an explosion of yellow buds. Dimly he remembers something she said earlier about the green of the trees at the Tivoli gate and is suddenly aware that the forsythia is in fact already beginning to fade. It bloomed probably a week ago, and he has not even noticed until this moment when it only has perhaps another week left before the dazzling tiny yellow flowers fade to the green of any other bush. Yellow as the dazzling curls that frame her face.

Though of course that yellow is surely from a bottle to conceal the gray. Don't care. I use bottled stuff, too—to make life dazzle.

His eyes fix upon the bush, fighting the blur of his intoxication, and he begins to consider his age, how many springs remain for him, how many more times he will have the pleasure of seeing the yellow forsythia or the green of the Tivoli trees.

Slowly he climbs his dusty, shadowy staircase toward the little stone angel beside the door to his apartment. And he remembers then from whence these thoughts originate. One of his father's favorite poets, A. E. Housman:

> Loveliest of trees, the cherry now
> Is hung with snow along the bough . . .
> And since to look at things in bloom
> Fifty springs is little room,

About the woodland I will go
To see the cherry hung with snow.

Fifty springs? Hardly. Not half. Or half that. Or half again.

Upstairs at his desk he peers blearily across the lake to a row of night-shadowed buildings; they remind him of the sense of mystery of his youth when he believed such buildings across such bodies of water at such a dusky hour contained wondrous secrets.

Now he has the Montblanc in his hand, thinking inevitably about the mystery of Licia—When will he be free of her?—the sweet angel who appeared in his life among the faces of the students at a guest lecture he was delivering on verisimilitude one afternoon at the University of Copenhagen. He knew he didn't have a chance—she was gorgeous, twenty-five, he forty-four. Yet after the lecture she hung around, and then somehow there were just the two of them walking across Amager to Christianshavn, having a drink at the floating bar in the canal, her eyes so light and blue in the sunshine, and she said, "Men of my age are so uninteresting."

"I'm almost twenty years older than you," he said. "A brook too broad for leaping."

"Don't be so sure of that. I'm a good leaper."

He opens the lowest drawer of his bureau, where he keeps a picture of her he took on a boat sailing the Ionian Sea to Ithaca. She is smiling the smile that so enchanted him—with her lips, her teeth, her eyes, her posture—and she is wearing a blue bikini the color of her eyes. Why did he never notice how self-consciously cute she was, how posed, the angle of her head, the way her blue eyes were looking off to the side? False angel. Blue-eyed blonde treachery.

He rises, puts on a Rautavaara CD: Einojuhani Rautavaara (1928–), Finnish composer of mysterious bombastic modern "serious" music.

In his armchair he watches the flashing red-and-green neon sign of the Jyske Bank ripple across the water, disappear, reappear, as the sound of the Helsinki Philharmonic performs *Angels and Visitations,* filling the darkness of his room; the composition is from 1978, the first of Rautavaara's Angel series: *Angel of Dusk*, 1980; *Playgrounds for Angels* and *Angels of Light*, 1994.

Rautavaara explains that his angels do not originate in fairy tales or religious kitsch, but from the belief in other realities beyond those of normal consciousness, different forms of consciousness: "From this alien reality, creatures rise up which could be called angels." He compares them to the visions of William Blake and to Rainer Maria Rilke's figures of awe and holy dread.

The composer tells how the first impetus for *Angels and Visitations* came from Rilke's observation of his fear of perishing in the powerful presence of an angel's embrace. This caused Rautavaara to recollect a childhood dream of an enormous, gray, powerful, silent creature that would approach and clasp him in his arms. He struggled until he awoke. Night after night the figure returned and he spent his days in fear of it, until he learned to surrender to its visitation.

At the climax of the symphony, when the visiting angel's embrace is finally accepted, a man's deep, surrendering scream is heard amidst the exquisitely high encompassment of the violins and harps and celesta.

But before that moment arrives this night, Kerrigan has passed through the dark, shadowed rectangle of the bedroom door, shed his clothes, and crawled beneath the covers of his bed. The scream enters the shadows of the next room, fades into silence.

Two: The Seducer

I wished on the moon for something I never knew,
A sweeter rose, a softer sky, an April day
That would not dance away.
—DOROTHY PARKER

Now his eyes are open. The white ceiling floats with shadow and light. He is heavy but not unhappy, not at all, for his now wakeful mind harbors an image of the twinkling green eyes of his Associate. He pictures her face, her full lips, delicate hands with red nails, the fullness of her breasts and shadowed line between them beneath the black neckline of her blouse, how she looks from behind, narrow dark slacks on her trimly rounded hips. A butt sculpted by Antonio Canova! Dreamy again, he remembers her pointed red nail tapping the page, her sculpted fingers he would kiss.

His breath is deep and slow. Dreamily he recalls the orgasmic, terrified cry of the man embraced by the angel in Rautavaara's symphony and remembers then the Finnish girl he met some time ago at the bar in Hotel Kämp in Helsinki, teaching him the word *Multatuli*. In Finnish it means "earth and fire" but also means, as she explained in her slow ponderous English, "I haf just hod an orgasm."

His hand slides beneath the eiderdown as he thinks of her, of his Associate, of *Multatuli*, which also means "I have suffered much" in Latin. To suffer in the gentle way perhaps.

Up like a skyrocket, down like a stick . . .

Sated, happy, he meditates on his Associate, but as he rises from his bed he feels pain invade his skull. He stands in the center of the bedroom, temples throbbing evilly. His eyes cling to a shelf of books against the wall—Poe, Dostoyevsky, London, Aristophanes, Voltaire, Kipling,

Saki, Turgenev, Augustine, Dante, Gibbons, St. Jerome, Hamsun, Conrad. *The horror! The horror!*

Or, as Stanley Elkin put it, "Ah! The horror, the horror." *Mr. Kerrigan—he dead.*

He reaches for Hemingway's *In Our Time*, begins to read "Big Two-Hearted River," burns out at the bottom of the first page, reaches for Dante and opens it to a double-page reproduction of the William Blake illustration for the sphere of the lustful, coils of naked embracing bodies swirling away. Must it be bad to lust? To desire? Even if it *is* an illusion, it is a lovely one. What is wrong with illusions anyway? Especially if, in the end, everything is one? The illusion of life ends in death. But then he remembers the illusions of love created by Licia, how he was deluded by them.

The throbbing in his head slows, and he reaches to the bureau top for the jar of pills, pops two, dry. His eyes sweep past a framed Asger Jorn print from 1966. *Dead Drunk Danes*, oil on canvas, a colorful swirl of molten faces painted seven years before Jorn died at fifty-nine. (That would leave me three to go.) Cobra School painter—Copenhagen, Brussels, Amsterdam. Brother of Jørgen Nash, the mermaid killer, father of Susanne Jorn, poet.

His mind is full of cobras and dead mermaids, but he thinks of his Associate's trimly curved buttocks as he pictured them in Campari-red panties. His senses are sufficiently deranged as to inspire doggerel for his Associate:

> My mind then sold for but a rump?
> By those hips parenthesized?
> Up from the chair two comely lumps,
> Over her shoulder, that fetch-me smile.

A spasm of his colon drives him to an act less elegantly literary than Leopold Bloom's ninety-five fictional years before, and no church bell tolls as Kerrigan sits hurriedly to void with a groan and waits, elbows on knees, for more.

What do I learn, sitting here, watching what is around me? Surely there is a lesson here, perhaps a key to all of life, of my life, but what? I must see clearly. The world around me must not be some vague blur.

What do I learn then as I sit here, awaiting a possible further spasm? I learn perhaps what a marvel is the common moment, the fact of light, the height of sky glimpsed through the unclosed WC door, out the front window, aroil with cloud, the sheer mystery of this small enclosure, the blue-gray linoleum between my feet with its vague yet irrefutable suggestion of faces in its pattern—there, eyes, a nose, a stern mouth, there a sharp profile, undeniable as if ghosts were imprinted, captured there, and in that yellow corner between the blue pipe and the standing plunger, the threads of a web on which waits a spindly-legged spider with a tiny yellow button of a carcass; hidden universe, another creature, not of my species, what does it see of me?

This roll of white paper a clue to the times in which I live, the chain I pull that drops quarts of water upon my odiferous waste. Trousers to pull up, metal teeth of a zipper, brass buckle of a belt, hands and a bar of fragrant soap beneath a chrome spout of water. Marvel of modern plumbing! Gleaming white, clean, sanitary.

And through the window I see a ponytailed man in a leather vest who pauses to place the palms of his hands on his kidneys as *he* observes something that has caught *his* attention—what? A bird it seems, a sparrow, simple as that, yet what a marvel that commonplace! Lifts with a shiver of wing into the air and flies up to a chestnut tree and there stands the tree, wiser than a man perhaps. How is it that trees exist? Do trees have some manner of consciousness, thick-skinned and eternally patient?

Kerrigan stands over the guest sofa upon which he has spread out research materials, the coffee table where there are more, the dining table that he has converted to a desk for this book. His zip satchel there surprises him—wonder he didn't lose it.

His mind is atremble, his body ashiver, but to demonstrate to himself that his will is stronger than his pain, he sits and takes up his pen, puts its nib to the white-lined pad before him, and begins to write:

Just dash any words onto it when you see a blank page staring at you like some idiot. How petrifying that is, that blank staring page saying to the writer you can't! The page stares like a fool and hypnotizes some writers and turns them into imbeciles themselves. A writer may tremble before the white empty page—however, the white empty page itself fears the fearless writer with passion who dares, who has broken out of the spell that says "you can't" forever!

The words please him, even if the essence of them is cribbed from a letter written by Vincent Van Gogh to his brother Theo from October 1884, six years before his death in 1890 at the age of thirty-seven, the same year Hamsun wrote *Hunger* at the age of twenty-nine.

The Van Gogh sentences kick-start him. The words are slow and clogged at first, but he keeps the pen in motion, and a space clears in the milchy surface of his mind. Words begin to flow, and it is as if he has found the words necessary for him to know he is alive and to start the day.

He pauses, looks up from the pad, and sees the window alongside his writing table. The day smiles to him. He opens the window to gaze upon a chestnut, at the lake behind it. A man in black cycles away on a red bike. He leans out to see the tree even more fully; in its fullness, it fills his senses with its furry-green scent, its color, the gentlest rustling of its leaves beneath the cloudless blue sky. Light sparkles on the surface of the lake and he thinks of the elfin women, thinks of his Associate whom he will not see again until Monday. Two days. He wonders what she is doing, pictures her barefoot, painting, and the wondering turns to a dryness at the back of his throat, thirst. He looks at his watch. Too early, much too early, but he has to move, remembering in John Cheever's diary where he records that his days have turned into a struggle to keep from taking the first gin before noon, a fight he more often than not lost.

Will that be the end I reach?

The bathing of the head and breast in water, brushing of teeth, scraping clean the stubble from the jowels, the anointment with stinging scented fluids and donning of clear fresh raiment—his expensive Italian jeans, a tie of plum-colored French silk, a jacket of fine handwoven Irish tweed—console and heal the spirit of torment as he heeds the advice of the Divine Ale Wife to Gilgamesh: *Let thy garments be sparkling fresh, thy head be washed . . .*

Then he is jogging down the stairs, out upon the street, and stares over the lake, inhales profoundly.

A brisk walk he needs, but first he must tend to the demands of a growling belly, a hungering mouth, a brain that calls for fried fats. It is the hunter in us, he thinks, that craves fat, to sustain us over the long chase. On quick-moving legs he ducks across the streets of the Potato Rows, Kartoffelrækkerne, where he lives—workers' housing erected in the last quarter of the last century that now houses artists, writers, young professionals, politicians, architects, and self-loving curmudgeons, row after row of narrow three-story brick row houses, a dozen short streets of them, each named for a Danish "Golden Age" (1800–1850) painter or other notable.

He crosses **Webersgade** and Silver Square, **Sølvtorvet**, and visits **Preben's Pølsemester**—the Sausage Master Wagon, a tiny sausage restaurant on wheels, one of the so-called **cold foot cafés**. The first such wagons were set up on the streets of Copenhagen in the twenties by a prosperous butcher. They caught on and soon there were many hundreds throughout the city, but with the advent of international fast-food joints like McDonald's and Burger King, their numbers dwindled again to a hundred fifty or so at present.

Within the wagon, Preben sits, big-bellied, spacey-toothed, whiskered, gazing across the variety of sausages sizzling on his grill. "Got a hole to fill?" he asks.

"En ristet med brød, tak," says Kerrigan. A fried sausage with bread, thanks. And is given a piece of waxed paper with a dollop of mustard and ketchup on it, flat on the counter, a fried sausage, and a little heated bun. He asks for chopped raw onion as well, nips a sheet of napkin from the dispenser, wraps it around the end of the sausage. The sausage is hot. He likes hot sausage. He dips the sausage into the mustard and then into the ketchup, turns it in the little pile of chopped onion so that onion flakes cling in the ketchup and mustard.

The sweet smell of sausage grease touches his nostrils. He likes the smell of sausage grease. He bites the sausage and feels the hot juices burst upon his tongue. His tongue is very sensitive, and the sausage is a little too hot still. Steam rises from inside it. But he relishes the sensation, the taste. He chews the sausage and all that exists for him in this moment is taste, the fullness of his mouth, the ascent of the fats to his brain.

He dips the end of the bun into the ketchup and into the mustard and bites off an end so that the bread mixes in his mouth with the sausage. Happily he chews the two things together, smiling as he munches. He feels good. He likes this sausage wagon. It is a good sausage wagon. He likes Preben. He pops the last bit of sausage and bun into his mouth, chews, swallows, belches discreetly behind his fist, says, "*Tak*," and Preben the sausage man says, "*Selv tak.*" Thanks yourself.

"*Hej hej,*" he says, which is pronounced "Hi hi."

"*Hej, hej nu,*" says Preben the sausage man.

It tickles Kerrigan that doubling hello means good-bye, just as it tickles him to literally translate what Danes sometimes say when they receive a very beautiful present: "*Hold kæft er du ikke rigtig klog?*" Literally, "Shut up, are you not rather unclever?" *Saft susser mig*—juice-sizzle me, and "Now you're really in the *suppedasen*"—shit soup. Not to forget the Danish word for *brassiere*—*brystholder*, literally "breast holder," to contain the two happy miracles.

He enjoys Danish wisdom. *Lasternes sum er constant*, or, "The sum of the vices is constant," the truth of which he learned years ago when he quit smoking cigarettes and began to inhale his wine. Or what Danes say when they go to a dinner party where you are not urged to take more: "The food was good but the pressing was not so good." And Danish curses: *Kraft æder mig*—Cancer eat me; *Fanden bank mig*—The devil hammer me; *Fanden tag mig*—The devil take me; or simply, *For Satan!* or *For helvede!*—so innocent sounding in English, The devil! Hell!—but serious matters in Danish. And he loves the low Danish—*Øl, fisse og hornmusik* (Beer, pussy, and horn music)—and the elegant irony and understatement of the Danes, manners left from the day when Denmark was a world power for centuries, now fallen to a small power but surviving and doing it well. The year Søren Kierkegaard was born, 1813, the Danish state went bankrupt, following the British bombardments and the loss of her fleet and of Norway following the Napoleonic Wars. Fifty years later, the war over South Jutland finally reduced her to a small country. But she never lost her tongue or her culture, her eye for beauty and for harmonious surroundings—all perhaps inspired by her magnificent light and the ascendancy of her humanism leading finally to comprehensive health care for all, free education to all, and welfare to all those who need it. Three sine qua nons of a true civilization, purchased with taxation.

Turning from the sausage wagon, he realizes he has to relieve himself, considers stepping down into the **Café Under Uret,** the Café Under the Clock, an old establishment he sometimes visits on a fair afternoon when the tables are out front just at the rounded corner of Silver Square. It was established in 1883, the year Franz Kafka was born, originally as Café Roskilde, but a watchmaker moved in to the rooms above the café in 1906 and hung a large illuminated clock in the corner window above the café. When the watchmaker died, the owners of the café left the clock in place and changed the name of the café in its honor.

Instead he makes use of the green wrought-iron pissoir just across Stockholmsgade, facing toward the National Museum of Art in the square named for Georg Brandes (1842–1927), commemorated there by a bust sculpted by Max Klinger in 1902. Brandes was the influential Danish literary critic who raised the work of Søren Kierkegaard out of international obscurity some twenty years after the philosopher's death, writing about him and lecturing on his work in Germany, making it possible for the remainder of Europe to know his writings and for Frenchmen like Sartre and Camus, studying in Berlin half a century later, to fashion, of its basic tenets, braided with those of others such as Nietzsche, modern existentialism: *existence precedes essence.* And that made it possible for Camus to write *The Stranger* the year before Kerrigan was born, and for Kerrigan to read the novel twenty years later and understand from it that while each person is sentenced to death and might die at any moment, by leaping across the brook between reason and faith he could attain an hour's peace, "and that anyhow was something."

Kerrigan stands over the zinc trough, eyes closed with pleasure, his water sizzling on the residue of leaves there, pleasantly redolent of Boy Scout outings in New Jersey of years gone by, as he thinks these things. *The Stranger* saved Kerrigan's sanity, such as it is, when he read it in 1961 as a soldier stationed at Fort Benjamin Harrison in Indianapolis, undergoing a security investigation for a top secret clearance where the investigators became acutely interested in the fact that he replied honestly to the question of whether he had ever had normal sexual relations with a woman. The investigator expended many hours over many months involving polygraph machines to explore the reasons for his virginity and to determine whether he had ever had abnormal sexual relations with a woman, whatever they were, or sexual relations with another man or with a beast.

Finally they were satisfied with the obvious explanation: He was eighteen years old, had been educated by Irish Christian Brothers at all-boys schools for twelve years, and was shy. But in the meantime, Kerrigan had learned to identify intensely with the fate of M. Meursault in Algiers and with Josef K in Kafka's *The Trial*.

One scene from *The Stranger* continues to resonate in him more than thirty-five years later, straight out of Kierkegaard: Meursault sits in his prison cell considering all the things that might happen to him, one by one, all the way through to the possibility that they might come in that very day and execute him, and once he has run through the whole list of terrifying possibilities, he wins for himself an hour's peace and thinks, "And that anyhow was something." A reflection of Kierkegaard's "Leap of Faith," by which one runs through all the arguments for and against the existence of God, reaches the end point of final utter ignorance, then chooses the only way forward—the leap across the gap of that ignorance to the embrace of faith—be it a faith in God or the pleasure of sensual existence or the simple assertion that although one dies and is unhappy, one insists on living and being happy.

He shakes and zips with a nod of thanks toward Brandes Place, walks up **Stockholmsgade**—Stockholm Street—to number 20, **the Hirschsprung Collection**, named for the Danish cigar manufacturer Heinrich Hirschsprung, whose trademark was a leaping deer, the meaning of his name in German. He gazes up at the statue on the lawn of an equestrian barbarian sculpted by Carl Johan Bonnesen in 1890.

Kerrigan considers the short muscular helmeted figure, armed with knife and scimitar, mounted upon a short strong steed, two decapitated human heads dangling from one side of his saddle, a third from the other. Odd motif, thinks Kerrigan, just across the trees from the civilized Brandes, a mere bronze head in comparison to the muscular body of this armed man and powerful horse with the severed-head trophies.

Crossing back through the Potato Row houses to Østersøgade, East Lake Street, Kerrigan stands on the bridge that bisects Black Dam Lake—called the Peace Bridge, Fredensbro. Across the lake stands a tall monolithic sculpture titled *Fredens Port*, the Peace Gate, erected in 1982, by Stig Brøgger, Hein Hansen, and Møgens Møller. It rises at a tilt from the grass of tiny Peace Park: Like modern society, the monument seems locked in a constant fall that never concludes.

To his right, framed between two chestnut trees, behind the buildings on the opposite bank of the lake, the top of the state hospital looms up like a huge steamship sailing beneath a white ceiling of cloud. He stands now on the bridge and, belching into his fist, remembers the fried sausage he has just eaten. It occurs to him that the two sides of the lake are like kidneys on either side of the spine of the bridge. He realizes this is far-fetched, but it makes him chuckle nonetheless as he sees a filthy fish nip a fly from the filthy surface of the water. Big two-kidneyed lake, he thinks, remembering how vindictive Hemingway could be when ridiculed, physically attacking the author of a review of *Death in the Afternoon*, titled "Bull in the Afternoon," when he met him in Max Perkins's office one afternoon; Hemingway wound up on his butt, spectacles askew, though to his credit he came up chuckling at himself.

Those were the days, thinks Kerrigan, when an American man defended his honor with his fists, as though power and honor are synonymous or fists can do anything but silence the opposing view. He recalls Hemingway's statement about his progress as a writer, that he began by beating Turgenev and then trained arduously and beat Maupassant, fought two ties with Stendahl but had the edge in the second; however, he would not get into the ring with Tolstoy unless he got a lot better. True bull in the afternoon. As bad as the ridiculous practice of fighting duels over one's honor—which killed Alexander Pushkin and Alexander Hamilton.

Kerrigan chuckles aloud and realizes he is still slightly intoxicated from the evening before. Hemingway, he realizes, would soon have been one hundred years old had he not blown out his brains just before he was to turn sixty-two. Yet there is something else that cannot be denied: Hemingway was physically courageous; Kerrigan, he himself recognizes, is not. Amen.

He decides to remain on this side of the bridge, to take a brisk walk around the entire circumference of this lake and the next, Peblinge Lake, get his blood pumping and his lungs working. As he trudges past an old disused bomb shelter on the bank, his thoughts reach back toward the year of his birth, 1943, the year after Camus wrote *The Stranger*, the third year of the German occupation of this city, this country, and yet another century back again to 1843, the year Søren Kierkegaard published *Either/Or*, the first of his most important works, written when he was thirty. He died when he was forty-two—would have been two years before the age Kerrigan was when he met Licia and fell under her spell. He asks himself whether he is too hard on her, too easy with himself. But she did do what she did do—what else to call that but falseness and treachery? She had seemed made for him, and he for her; according to Kierkegaard, that was the moment when a couple should have the courage to break it off. But Kerrigan was in her thrall.

Somewhere in Kierkegaard's writings, he said, "Whether you marry or not you will regret it." Kerrigan both regrets it and not. Licia was such a beautiful illusion. For a time. And his beautiful baby girl, taken from him so young. She surely hardly remembers him now, or if she does at all it is as a vague fragment of a dream she dreams wherever she might be now.

He thinks about Kierkegaard and his beloved Regine Olsen—with whom he broke off the engagement, then spent the remainder of his short life contemplating and writing about it.

Subtitled *A Fragment of Life, Either/Or* is a gathering of aphorisms, essays, a sermon, and, lodged within it all, a novel in the form of a diary, *The Seducer's Diary*—all written under different pseudonyms.

The concept of "either/or" was Kierkegaard's response to the Hegelian concept of mediation—the negotiation of contradictory ideas—"thesis" and "antithesis"—into "synthesis," which is meant to include and reconcile them both. Either/or was Kierkegaard's refutation of this "both/and" approach to thought. But this aspect of it has no interest to Kerrigan. He picks and chooses from the book in accord with Kierkegaard's own prescription in that book, "The Rotation Method," whereby one picks a part of a book or a play or a poem and makes of it perhaps quite another experience than the author thought he was preparing for the reader.

The Seducer's Diary, the novel within the book, captures Kerrigan, for in it the first-person narrator, Johannes, walks the banks of this lake Kerrigan now walks, more than 150 years later, beneath the six windows of Kerrigan's apartment, dreaming of the object of his desire, Cordelia.

On the banks of these lakes where Kerrigan now pauses to watch a swan glide along the stippled glittering water, Hans Christian Andersen also stood weeping real salt tears over his mistreatment by the world while Kierkegaard's fictional Johannes the Seducer stalked his beautiful young Cordelia in the pages of the fictional diary set like a substantial dark gem in a book of philosophy and meditation. Kerrigan himself now strolls this path by the water regretting and not his marriage of four years—the length of a college education—preceded by four years as lovers, another college education. But what did he learn from it? The equivalent of a B.S. in being the victim of treachery. That while he was lecturing her about the creation of illusion in literature, she was busy creating an illusion for him with her bright, light smiling eyes. *Is this melodramatic?* he asks himself. *Is this bitterness? Am I growing to like the taste of my wounds as I lick them?*

To Kerrigan's mind, the fictional Johannes is as real, more real perhaps, than the figures of history who walked here. More real to him in any event. For though he knows that Andersen and Kierkegaard were men of flesh and blood, equally wounded in love as Kerrigan, the very intimate record available of them is still mostly indirect, while in Johannes we have a mind and a soul laid open for study in detail throughout the course of an extreme action. Even if Johannes is the cynical one in that action, Licia the cynical one in Kerrigan's life.

Then he thinks of Goethe's *The Sorrows of Young Werther*, which sorrows were self-inflicted, and he tries to see himself in young Werther. Had Goethe not died in 1832 but lived another dozen years, he might have seen in Kierkegaard's Johannes the Seducer some ironic reflection of the Young Werther whose sorrows made Goethe so suddenly famous in 1774, two years before the American War of Independence, sixty-nine years before Kierkegaard's Johannes walked the banks of this lake (225 years before Kerrigan walks it regretting Licia's falseness). Johannes is the romantic—bumbling Werther's cynical, contriving counterpart—articulating visions of a femininity that could only have been meant to reveal the true sadistic nature of the machinations of seduction. Johannes explained that in creating Eve, God struck Adam with a deep sleep because woman is the dream of man and does not awake until she is touched by love. Before that she is a dream, but there are two distinct states in her dream: first, love dreams of her; second, she dreams of love. And he remembers Johannes the Seducer's speculation that woman will forever provide an endless supply of material for his contemplation.

Kerrigan asks himself what he dreamed of in Licia and what was in Licia's mind—was it consciously false, treacherous? Or did her love just cool and turn to a malicious desire to cut free from him, with no consideration for his attachment to Gabrielle? Or to the baby she was carry-ing. If she really was carrying a baby. If the baby was even his.

Standing now on the bank of the lake, he watches the swans and the ducks, watches the continuous infinitesimal changes of the Danish light, feeling this long history of a culture around him, this speculation about women and love. He thinks of his Associate's absinthe-green eyes, and he thinks of his mother who was born here, from whence she was taken by his Irish father via Brooklyn to Dublin, to Copenhagen and back to Brooklyn, then giving birth to him and registering him as a Dane, giving him dual citizenship, allowing him to try to make a new life here after his first life was foundering there, and in his forty-fourth year to meet the beautiful Licia who would make love possible for him and then deprive him of that love.

The thought strikes him with a force that is physical. He literally staggers as he steps down through the tunnel between the two segments of Black Dam Lake, its walls festooned with ornate graffiti scrawled over with obscenities, SUPERFUCKED and FUCK SPAGHETTIS answered by FUK RACISM and BLOOD AND HONOUR and FUK YOU NIGGA and again FUK RACISM. And he looks ahead to the light at the far end and tells himself that when he comes out into the daylight again he will dismiss these thoughts of Licia and Gabrielle.

As he climbs the inclined path back up into the day, he sees the **Kaffesalonen,** the Coffee Salon, off to his right, and further on down the long narrow street the spire of the church in which he, himself, was married, **Skt. Johannes Kirke,** the Church of St. John, and he keeps walking, blanking out his mind with the movement of his legs, his feet striking the dusty path, the swinging of his arms, the breath in his lungs, the sweat in his armpits and on his back, as he fills his eyes with saving details, past the fairy-tale-like white structure of the **Søpavillon,** the Lake Pavilion, and around the foot of Peblinge Lake. He sees a green bronze sculpture of a lion and lioness fighting for the corpse of a wild boar, sculpted by an artist named Cain in 1878.

And that name reminds him of Milton's Adam and Eve in 1674

leaving Eden with wandering steps and slow, hand in hand—the work with which Milton set out to justify God's ways with man, and Housman two and a half centuries later telling Kerrigan's namesake, Terrence, first read to Kerrigan by his father and still later by Kerrigan himself at a time when he was desperate for justification,

> Terrence, this is stupid stuff . . .
> Malt does more than Milton can
> To justify God's ways with man . . .
> Ale, man, ale's the stuff to drink
> For fellows whom it hurts to think.

How fitting it seems then that just across Gyldenløves Street near the bank of Skt. Jørgens Sø, St. George's Lake, stands Andreas Kolberg's sculpture *A Drunken Faun* (1857)—a smiling boyish satyr drinking wine from a horn held high over his head so the wine runs down his face. He has feet rather than hooves and drags a half-empty wine sack along the ground behind him. His stick is discarded at his feet and his lion skin has slipped back, exposing his sex. Carl Jacobsen, the Carlsberg brewer, gave this faun to Copenhagen—a laughing, happily drunken lad, and, this being Copenhagen, there is no moral intent beyond the moral pleasure of joy.

Yet as Kerrigan crosses the little park on the bank, he stops to consider a sculpture cut from the stump of a dying elm tree, infected by the epidemic that hit Copenhagen's elms in the 1990s. This sculpture is by Ole Barslund Nielsen—a naked woman rises from the center of the broken double-trunked stump, a child to one side, and below, a seated figure in a hollowed arch in the trunk itself. It is entitled *In the Beginning Was the Word*. And in the end this tree sculpture will be worn away by the elements, like everything and every story.

He loops across Gyldenløves Street to **Ørstedsparken**, can see from the street the statue of the great man himself: H. C. Ørsted (1777–1851), discoverer in 1821 of electromagnetism as well as of aluminum, comforter of Hans Christian Andersen. Kerrigan enters the park and his feet carry him further along its paths, past rows of antique bronze sculptures as his present moment melts continuously into his past and the present adds one increment of the future to itself, beneath the willows and beeches. He comes upon *The Dying Gaul*, a bronze made from a two-thousand-year-old Roman cast, itself made from an even older Greek one. The Gaul is wounded, naked, dying, balanced on hip and hand, head lowered, mouth in pain, eyes meeting death, his sword discarded on the bronze earth alongside his bronze hand, the warrior's gold braid about his neck. What, Kerrigan wonders, is meant by the quiet agony of that face? And the response is from Chaucer, the dying White Knight's song:

> What is this life
> What asketh man to have
> Now with his love
> Now in his cold grave.

He turns back toward the lake.

Kerrigan is exhausted. His wet shirt sticks to his back as he reaches **Peblinge Sø**, the lake bank where Hans Christian Andersen wept. He sits on a bench, closes his eyes, and remembers the lake two winters before, skaters and strollers on the frozen water before the Lake Pavilion on a freezing sunny winter Sunday.

In the darkness behind his eyelids, his thoughts turn back to Kierkegaard and Johannes the Seducer and Goethe's *Young Werther*. They are both dead, Goethe and Kierkegaard, two men from two centuries, sharing a part of the nineteenth, writing about the same thing from different angles. A Dane and a German. And an Irish-Danish American contemplates another aspect of the same thing that has very nearly undone him.

The Sorrows of Young Werther inaugurated a life of fame for Goethe at the age of twenty-five. It is the story of a young upper-middle-class man of foolish sentiments, quick and self-centered, who falls in love with another man's woman and commits suicide. W. H. Auden has said that the book made Goethe the first writer or artist to become a public celebrity. Auden opined that it was not a story of tragic love at all, but a portrait of a totally egotistical young man who is not capable of loving anyone but himself. There are other views of young Werther, however—speculations that Lotte strung him along, bewitching him with touches and glances to his destruction. *La belle Lotte sans merci.*

If Werther killed himself in frustration over being unable to have Lotte, Kierkegaard's Johannes sets about with incisive determination to have Cordelia, and he *does* have her via the fact, at the source of his strength, that he always has the idea on his side, a secret, like Samson's hair, that no Delilah can pry from his mind.

It seems clear that this is *not* the philosophy of Kierkegaard—who spoke of the greater sins of reason than passion—but the casual reader of the *Diary* might take it literally and *believe* Johannes's delusion that a man's relationship to a woman is a question, her choice of life only a response to that question.

Johannes stands on Bleacher's Green (now **Blegdamsvej**) and readies his attack, his soul like a bent bow, his thought an arrowhead about to enter her flesh, her veins. And when his labors are done, when he has had her in one fizzling gulp, like a glass of champagne, he leaves swiftly, done, with no sweet parting sorrow because he views with disgust a woman's tears, which change everything but are meaningless. He has had her now and she no longer can fascinate his erotic imagination.

Kerrigan entertains an idea that Kierkegaard's *Diary* is inter alia a response to Goethe's *Sorrows*. In 1841, Kierkegaard broke his engagement to the woman he loved, Regine Olsen, and traveled to Berlin where he lived at the Hotel Saxen on Jägerstrasse 57 and wrote, first, *Either/Or* and then *Fear and Trembling*, both published in 1843, when he returned from Berlin. He had broken with Regine for reasons that he himself did not quite understand and spent years speculating about. However, he concluded that he could be happier in his unhappiness without her than with her, would be required to hide so much from her, to base the entire relationship on something that was untrue.

Whether you marry or not, you will regret it.

He sent back the ring, fabricated the appearance that it was she who broke off the engagement, but she refused to go along with that lie, explaining that if she could bear the rejection she could bear the disgrace as well. Kierkegaard was miserable but he hid his misery from the world, behaved as usual. His brother, who heard him weeping all night, wanted to go to Regine's family and tell them, to prove he was not dastardly, but Kierkegaard threatened to put a bullet in his brother's head if he did.

In his journal, on August 24, 1849—eight years later—he wrote that he traveled to Berlin and suffered with his thoughts of her every day. In Berlin he worked on *Either/Or*, completing it in about eleven months. There he would write that his grief was his castle. And that pleasure was not in the thing that you enjoy but in the consciousness of it. And finally that his yearning for his first love was only a yearning for that yearning.

Kerrigan, too, yearns for his first yearning for Licia, but what did Licia yearn for; he had thought their yearnings were for each other, and he remembers only one thing that seemed to indicate something else might have been going on behind the facade of her sweet blue gaze, her mild light manner. One summer night in the garden of their new house in fashionable Hellerup, where she had always dreamed of living, just north of Copenhagen, the baby asleep, he opened a second bottle of wine, and as evening darkened to night, the sky still yellow, she seemed to be staring at him without seeing, and she said, "You are so blind."

He could have sworn she said that. "I beg your pardon?" he asked.

"Blind," she repeated with drunken deliberateness. *"Blind!"* And stomped off into the house. He sat smoking a cigar, trying to understand what had just happened. Throwing the cigar into the still glowing coals of the grill, he rose and followed, but she lay fully clothed atop the covers, dissecting the width of their bed, and he could not rouse her.

Next morning over breakfast, he asked, "How do you feel?"

"Not good."

"What did you mean?" he asked. "By what you said just before you went to bed?"

"What I said? Did I say something?" He interpreted the fear evident in her voice as embarrassment.

He looked into her blue eyes. He loved her eyes so, her blonde hair. He loved the silken skin of her back, inside her thighs, her mild gentle manner, loved the way she made love. He adored her. Her face was still aimed at him, her own question hanging in the air, but he would not subject her to his question again, would not repeat what she had said.

Were there other things as well? Things he ignored? Things he did not see? Things he was indeed blind to?

There was that time when she seemed not displeased that he lost a contract for the translation of several significant books. He thought he saw a glint in her eye, heard a mocking taunt in her voice, but did not believe it, still does not know whether it really was there.

What else?

Of course: her gentle persistent insistence that they merge their bank accounts. And what argument did he have against it? What argument would he even think to pose against it? Not even the fact that his account contained the liquidated assets of his inheritance from his parents while hers contained only the few thousand kroner she had saved from her earnings. Not even when she suggested she take over the finances— she was, after all, better at it. And she was his wife, the mother of his newborn daughter. He loved her forever. Their lives and fortunes were joined, one.

Contemplating these ironies and conflicts on his bench on the bank of Peblinge Lake where Andersen once wept and Johannes stalked Cordelia, Kerrigan watches a swan drift past like a beautiful white question. He feels the presence of all this history, all this hurt and hurting, this love and rejection, weeping, sickness, pride, haughtiness, death, and he cannot stop feeling his own pain of absence of Licia, puzzling miserably over it still, after three years, wondering how he could have been so wrong about a person, have failed to understand her as he continues to fail to fathom what might have been in her mind.

Yet he is not specifically unhappy in his general unhappiness. He has no reason to be. Happiness would be too much to wish for, but at least there might be spells of not being unhappy in unhappiness, fits of pleasure in the senses, in the dimensions of the mind. Licia's treachery extinguished much, but not everything. Yet he was not happier in his unhappiness without her. He would take her back in a second. Perhaps. Even if he still didn't know whether she was lying? Perhaps.

In the buildings behind where he now sits on **Nørre Søgade**, North Lake Street, on the right side of the third floor is the building where Ben Webster lived from 1965 until his death. There he would sit, as Bent Kauling tells it, with the superintendent of the building, drinking beer and staring out the window over the lake. The superintendent, Olsen, could not speak English—he called Webster "Wesper"—and Webster spoke virtually no Danish, so they sat in silence, saying no more than *Skål*, and drank their beer, enjoying what Webster called "the world's luckiest conversation."

Two silent men drinking beer, watching the lake.

And a friend of Kerrigan's, Dale Smith, the African-American bluesman from St. Louis who has lived in Copenhagen for decades, tells of Webster getting fed up one night in the club Montmartre with the tootling of some very postbop saxophonists and barking, "Practice at home, motherfuckers!"

Kerrigan has a CD recorded in Los Angeles in 1959: Ben Webster on tenor sax, Gerry Mulligan on baritone, playing Billy Strayhorn's "Chelsea Bridge," seven minutes and twenty seconds of a black man and a white man fingerfucking heaven. Kerrigan knows of no cut as beautiful and moving unless perhaps it is Stan Getz blowing his tenor in alto range on Strayhorn's "Blood Count," recorded at the Montmartre in Copenhagen on July 6, 1987, when Getz had begun dying of cancer. Strayhorn himself wrote the number just twenty years before when he was in the hospital riding his own cancer to its end. Getz said that he thought about Strayhorn when he played that song. "You can hear him dying . . . you can hear the man talking to God."

Strayhorn wrote it for Duke Ellington to play in Carnegie Hall in 1967. It was the last piece Strayhorn ever wrote. He was Duke Ellington's right hand and Ben Webster had been lead solo in Ellington's orchestra at its best, Billie Holiday's favorite soloist, who accompanied her on *The Silver Collection*. He came to Copenhagen to live, the only city in the world where he felt he could go out without his knife, and he died on tour in Amsterdam in 1973. Webster, about whom, on the day of Kerrigan's birth, September 18, 1943, Jack Kerouac, at twenty-one, had written: "Caught Ben Webster at the Three Deuces on 52nd. No one can beat his tone; he breathes out his notes."

Webster, Getz, Strayhorn, Holiday, Ellington, Mulligan, Kerouac, all gone now. And Chet Baker, too, who fell or was pushed to his death out the window of the Hotel Prince Hendrick on Prince Hendrickstraat in Amsterdam on May 18, 1988. All gone. And that's how every story ends, says the "Knight of Infinite Resignation," Søren Kierkegaard, in harmony with H. C. Andersen.

But still Kerrigan can hear in his mind, clear as if he were hearing a CD, Webster's horn blowing "Chelsea Bridge," cut into wax with Mulligan's baritone eight thousand miles from here, forty years ago, finger-fucking heaven. So they live in his mind, at least until his mind is reduced to a small quantity of gray dust inside his skull.

A wind is rising on the water, and laughing in his heart he quotes foolish Werther without moving his lips: *And may I say it? She would have been happier with me than with him.* It occurs to him that his green-eyed Associate might have another man and wonders why he should be worrying about that, whether he truly cares.

He rises from the bench, feels the now swiftly moving air across his face, sees it chopping on the silver surface of the lake, alive in the ever-changing light of Copenhagen, and he has successfully banished the memory of Licia who successfully terminally savaged for him the trust and hope he had foolishly allowed her to create for him.

Silver speckles glitter on the lake, and the beggar swans float in like questions, one, another, two more. A purple-necked duck waddles up onto the bank to see if Kerrigan has bread for him. The dirty lake water rolls in harmless beads like oil down its back, and Kerrigan experiences the optimism of hunger and thirst. "Adieu," Kerrigan whispers, savoring irony. "I see no end to this misery except in the grave."

The duck sees he has no bread and waddles away, laughing.

Kerrigan laughs, too, and sets off at a brisk pace toward the opposite end of the lake, entertaining himself with the thought that in the dead of one November night in 1970, the East German authorities, in great secrecy, removed the remains of Goethe from the ducal crypt in Weimar where they had lain alongside those of the poet Friedrich Schiller since 1832, 138 years before. The flesh remaining on his bones was macerated and the bones themselves strengthened. The laurel crown affixed to his skull was removed, cleaned, and reaffixed, and then he was— still secretly—returned to his crypt, though they forgot to return his shroud and did not dare or bother to reopen the crypt to do so. No doubt some official hung it on his social-realist bureaucratic wall.

All this was discovered from records released in March 1999. The records also showed that among other things, the interior of the poet's skull had been examined, and it was recorded that found inside was "a small quantity of gray dust." Kerrigan pictures the official pilfering the dust, preserving it in a little drawstring pouch, carrying it about in his pocket for luck.

Dust particles carry on the wind that rolls across the lake, whirlpooling on the dirt walkway, smacking Kerrigan's face as he walks forward at a slant through it. At the far end of the lake, he takes a table outside **Det Franske Café**, the French Café, across the boulevard from where Kierkegaard's 1850 residence might still have been standing had it not been torn down to let **Willemoesgade**, Willemoes Street, run past between the twin towers erected there in 1892.

His table is behind the concrete planters, where he hunches against the wind to get a small Sumatra lit, then waits, smoking, with the sunlight in his face, for the tall young white-aproned waitress to bring his food—a platter of herring, crab salad, a wedge of Brie that he plans to pepper liberally. When he opened his mouth to say, "And a club soda," it said instead, "And a large draft Tuborg." Startled by these unanticipated words, he paused, and then his mouth called after her, "And a double Red Ålborg snaps if you have it!"

She smiled over her shoulder at him, one eye squinted shut against the sun, her white-swathed rump nothing short of magnificent, her breasts in a white T-shirt truly mighty, and she said, "We have it."

And there it is again: Kerrigan, a fool for love. You would be duped all over again by Licia. She was right: You *are* blind. So he just smiles politely to the cute-faced waitress's polite smile as she places the fish and drink before him. And as he eats, he watches swans and ducks, joggers, and then a single heron walking slow and precise as a tai chi chuan master along the bank of the lake, while the wind stipples the water into glittering spires of silver and black, and Kerrigan feels the beer chasing the snaps through his blood; the snaps makes a clean dash for the shelter of the brain where it does its optimistic work, and the beer plows right on after it.

He likes it here so very much, relishing with his eyes the whipping branches of the chestnuts, the potted yellow lilies framing the path line, the multi-spiring water, and the imperturbable heron. He takes out his little pad and his Montblanc, swallows more beer, and thinks of Stan Getz's three years in Copenhagen at the end of the fifties, when he came here to find serenity, freedom from drugs and drink, and played his beautiful tenor four days a week on Store Regnegade in the old Montmartre, owned by Anders Dyrup, the jazz-loving son of a wealthy paint manufacturer whose name is everywhere on Danish paint shops.

Getz played with bassist Oscar Pettiford, one of the great early beboppers—half Choctaw, part Cherokee, part black, married to a white woman—who came to Denmark to find a more tolerant social climate for his children. And he jammed at Montmartre with the musicians who came through—Art Blakey, Lee Konitz, Kenny Clarke, Gerry Mulligan. Picture Stan on baritone and Mulligan on tenor, switch-hitting, with Jim Hall on guitar playing for four or five hours in the dark morning hours on Great Rain Street.

But within two years, Pettiford was dead, at thirty-seven, of a fluke disease, and one night after dinner Getz went outside the beautiful house where he lived with his wife and children and threw a brick through every window. Then he came back in and with a poker from the fireplace smashed every plate in a collection of priceless Royal Copenhagen porcelain that the landlord owned.

The doctor put him on Antabus—an anti-alcoholic medication that causes violent illness if combined with drink—but Getz didn't take it because, he reasoned, he was not an alcoholic. On another occasion he kicked his dog unmercifully, then beat his daughter, cursing her for trying to stop him. He even put a loaded gun to his wife's head.

Too tortured to live with peace of mind, he returned to the states after not quite three years—Kerrigan heard him, saw him in Carnegie Hall in '64 and in the Rainbow Room in '70 and twice here in Copenhagen; he came back frequently to Denmark. *Standinavia* was the title of one of his albums. Kerrigan heard him play at Montmartre once in 1977, the new Montmartre which had moved to **Nørregade**, North Street. He thinks now what it must have been like to be able to go hear Getz play four nights a week.

Kerrigan contemplates the fact that a man who could play such profoundly beautiful music, lines that search into the bottom of your soul and lift it up through an agony of pleading to an angelic plain, could be so helpless against the demons that had him terrorize his own family.

He thinks again of Kristensen's Ole Jastrau, nicknamed "Jazz" in the novel *Havoc*, written thirty years before Getz's stay in Copenhagen. Jastrau lashes out to destroy a life that is destroying him as an artist, as a poet. He drives away his wife and child, smashes up their bourgeois apartment, exposes himself to syphilis, performs a wild awkward dance to the jazz of a wind-up gramophone, all the while accompanied by a younger man, Stefan Steffensen, a poet who shamelessly, scornfully uses him, abuses his hospitality, a young man fleeing from wealthy parents who are both infected with syphilis, as he is, as is the girl he has with him—a servant from his house whom he himself has infected.

Abruptly Kerrigan feels that he understands the difference between

Kristensen the creator and Jastrau his creation. For just as Stefan Steffensen is Jastrau's alter ego, so is Jastrau Kristensen's. What kept Kristensen from the dogs perhaps was his pen. He wrote it. Jastrau only lived it and even then not in the world but in the word, while Kristensen was his god, his creator; through Jastrau he both lived *and* uttered it. Getz had only the music, and beautiful as it was, as it is, it did not give him the power he needed over his demons. He only played it, interpreted it; he did not create it. But no, no, of course Getz created it, his breath shaped the notes, his being improvised the turns, the leaps.

So Kerrigan takes up his Montblanc pen, pleasingly weighted in his hand, and casts into words the spirit of the water suddenly subjected to the wind, flinging sand in the faces of the people at the café tables around him. One by one, they gather up their cakes and coffees and liqueurs and hurry indoors, hair dancing in the wind, blinking against the dust, smiling self-consciously, self-deprecatingly at their soon-solved predicament, but Kerrigan stays where he is, eyes squinted into the wind that cannot blow the ink from his page.

Grinning, he lifts his glass and drinks beer, swallowing the dust the wind has flung into it, letting the grit of it against his teeth be pleasure, and practices one of his favorite hobbies, the memorization and juxtaposition of dates:

In 1987 when Stan Getz was doing his penultimate appearance in Copenhagen's Montmartre club, dying, playing "Blood Count," which Billy Strayhorn wrote in 1967 when he was dying, the great horn man Dexter Gordon, who lived in Copenhagen from 1962 to 1976, was, incredibly, competing against Paul Newman for an Academy Award for best actor for his performance in the film 'Round Midnight, a composite portrayal of American jazzmen in Europe. Newman won. And Long Tall Dexter Gordon, the soft-spoken six-and-a-half-footer who was described by the critic Alexander Walker as moving with a child's gentleness but having an unsettling tension—that the big barrel of his body might contain gunpowder while his deep quiet voice seemed to emanate from a silence in which he lived, listening to sounds no one else could hear. Dex returned to America in 1976, twelve years before Kerrigan would meet Licia, twenty years before she would disappear with their baby, another maybe in her womb. Maybe of Kerrigan's, maybe not.

In 1943, Kerrigan was born to an Irish father and Danish mother, exactly a hundred years after the birth of Henry James and the publication of Edgar Allan Poe's "The Black Cat" and forty-five years before his meeting with the dazzling blonde Licia.

In 1831 Darwin sailed on the *Beagle*, 168 years before five states in the U.S. would eradicate his discoveries from the teaching curricula of their schools (along with the Big Bang Theory) and 133 years before Peter Higgs at the University of Edinburgh discovered, and lost, the so-called Higgs boson (the "God particle")—an elusive particle that is believed to be capable of explaining why things in the universe have mass and, thus, why life exists. In 1821 John Keats died at the age of twenty-four, the same year Dostoyevsky and Flaubert were born, two years after the birth of Melville and Whitman in 1819, which was six years after the birth of Kierkegaard in 1813, the year the Danish State went bankrupt, six years after the Duke of Wellington bombarded Copenhagen, killing nearly 2 percent of its civilian population, thirty years before Kierkegaard would write *The Seducer's Diary* in 1843 while Darwin was writing *The Origin of the Species*, one hundred years before Kerrigan was born, 145 years before Licia seduced Kerrigan in 1988, before his forty-fifth birthday—selected, seduced, bore fruit with, and abandoned him eight years later (while he was in Edinburgh, thirty-two years after Higgs made his initial discovery there), cleaned out his heart and half of his life's savings, bombarded him with tender attention until the top of his head was blown off as surely as Wellington blew the roof off the **White Lamb,** and scientists have not yet found again the Higgs boson, the God particle.

Darwin's study would later be translated into Danish by J. P. Jacobsen, whom James Joyce in 1901 would call "a great innovator" in the techniques of fiction, and in 1843 Kierkegaard's fictional Johannes was stalking the innocent young fictional Cordelia along the banks of this lake where Kerrigan sits in 1999, painfully aware that he was Licia's bitch, forcing himself to savor the taste of dust, glimpsing the beautiful willowy apron-wrapped hips of the waitress who brings him yet another large draft and another lovely, elfin smile, and just like that, he is dazzled and yearns to dance in the woods with her.

He wonders what would happen if he kissed her. Just like that—jumped up and stole a kiss from those lips, too quick for her to get away. Instead he chances to speak to her as she gathers his soiled dishes and uneaten crusts, to quote the conclusion of the Danish Steen Steensen Blicher's *Diary of a Parish Clerk*, written in 1824, when Keats was three years dead, a fictional depiction of the famous tragic love affair between a beautiful young Jutland aristocratic woman, Marie Grubbe (1643–1718), and her game warden, which ends in squalor and poverty in Copenhagen and is, still later, depicted by J. P. Jacobsen in a full-length novel:

"As for man," quoth Kerrigan from Blicher, himself quoting scripture, to the waitress, "his days are as grass . . . For the wind passeth over it and it is gone; and the place thereof shall know it no more. But the mercy of the Lord is from everlasting to everlasting."

The girl's smile is wise as Buddha's: "Can I get you something else, sir?" she asks.

Moved by another hunger now, less specific than the hunger for food or drink, he strolls up **Østerbrogade**, East Bridge Street, crosses **Trianglen**, the triangular joining of three avenues, pausing to look at the goddamn 7-Eleven shop where once stood a guest house and restaurant in which two hundred years before, Peter the Great, Czar of Russia, slept.

He passes **Det Røde Lygte**, on the west of the three angles, the Red Light Café, whose red door lamps are innocent of prurience—a soccer bar that opened in 1886, the year after the birth of Ezra Pound in the U.S. and François Mauriac in France, seven years before the birth of Tom Kristensen, who was born a year before Dorothy Parker in 1894, fifteen years before the birth, in 1909, of Kerrigan's father, who would migrate back from Brooklyn to Ireland and on a visit to Copenhagen in 1936, the same year that Joyce and Nora visited Denmark, would meet his Danish wife to be, Elene Mørk, who after the birth of Kerrigan never slept with her husband again, according to a confidence imparted by his father in his cups one night to twenty-year-old Kerrigan.

Kerrigan continues up East Bridge Street, past **Café Oluf** at the mouth of Olufsvej, and **the Park Café**, **Theodor's**, **Le Saint Jacques**, **Thygge's Inn** on Viborg Street, down Århus Street past **Århuskroen, the Århus Inn**, the **Café X-presen**, offering three unspecified finger sandwiches for a song, past **Café Åstedet**, the **Stream Place Café**, and feels like Andrew Flaws in another story, this one by the Orkney writer George Mackay Brown, "The Whaler's Return," in which Flaws returns to the Orkneys from months at sea to be married, and between the port and the house of his betrothed in the next town are fifty alehouses waiting to take from him his wages from the long whaling journey.

He stops here and there, buys rounds, ends in the field spying on a tinker wedding, is discovered, thrashed, and loses more money there. Finally, in the morning, muddy and tired, he finds his way up the lane of his betrothed's house and tells her he has just enough left of his money for the first six months' rent, while they see to the seeding and the harvest. She tells him they are also in debt for a shrouding fee and for the digging of the grave of her father who was killed by a horse while Andrew was away. But he says he already saw to that on his way in, and his betrothed replies, "There are thirty-four alehouses in the town of Hamnavoe and sixteen alehouses on the road between Hamnavoe and Borsay. Some men from the ships are a long time getting home . . . That was a good thing you did, Andrew Flaws."

Kerrigan was once in contact with George Mackay Brown. After reading the man's stories, he had wanted to visit the Orkneys to interview him, and they made plans for it by post, but Kerrigan never got there, and his last letters to Brown in 1995 went unanswered.

Then one afternoon, visiting Edinburgh in early 1996, at a bookshop on Princes Street, he picked up a new anthology of Scottish verse that included a lovely poem by George Mackay Brown, an account of an outing, of Folster's lipstick wounds, of Greve's sweet fog on a stick, of

Crusack's three rounds with a Negro, of Johnston's mouth full of dying fires, and, in the bio notes, he learned that George had died that year—that was the same trip from which Kerrigan returned to find his bride and daughter gone, his life's savings drained by half. *You are so blind.*

But he knew nothing of that yet. Kerrigan had gone on to Milne's on Rose Street, where 40 percent larger spirits are served, and the Abbortsford, for pints of black Orkney where George had drunk with Hugh MacDiarmid and Dylan Thomas and W. H. Auden. He thought about the fact that the Orkney Islands had been Danish until 1468. He thought of the wild Danish-Scottish islands he had never seen, although he might have, the fine writer he had never met, although he might have done that, too.

Kerrigan thinks now about the gaudy monument to Walter Scott on Princes Street and the modest plaque to Robert Louis Stevenson in Princes Street Gardens—just his initials and years in a plaque in the grass—and of riding a mountain bike up and down the hilly roads of Lasswade, where, at the entry to the motorway, there stands a sign: PEDESTRIANS, CYCLISTS, HORSE-DRAWN VEHICLES AND ANIMALS PROHIBITED, and he looked about in vain for bespectacled four-legged creatures who might be capable of receiving that instruction. And he thinks about Licia secretly enacting her escape from him while he was in Edinburgh. But she must have been planning it long before. Licia to whom if anyone had asked him, he would have said and truly believed he was happily wed. He'd thought they were happy together.

He doubles back and, across the street from the gateway to the stadium, pauses to gaze through the arched port at the four-meter-tall silhouetted bronze sculpture of the archer by Ernst Moritz Geyger (1861–1941) bow drawn, arrow targeted south—a giant Johannes the Seducer aiming to pierce the heart of Cordelia.

Above the archway, Alfred Boucher's three runners at the goal, frozen in green bronze, strive to be first over the line, each reaching for individual victory.

It makes him feel a little more complete to know who these two statues were sculpted by and when and that they were donated by the brewer Carl Jacobsen to the city in which Kerrigan lives. Makes him feel that the world surrounding him is no mere blur, that he knows it and the objects that furnish it, even if he did not and does not know what was occurring in the secret interior of the skull of the woman he thought was his soul mate.

On the other side of Østerbrogade, East Bridge Avenue, from Sankt Jakobs Kirke, his leather-shod feet lead him to **Le Saint Jacques Café**. This was once Sankt Jacob's Bodega, a bucket-of-blood bar, but now in the hands of a French owner, Daniel Letz, it serves excellent cuisine and boasts a magnificent icon collection—a whole beautiful wall of them behind glass, sad-eyed Madonnas with child, saints with fingers raised in benediction over the diners. He orders a draft at the bar, a little bag of peanuts, then takes a wicker seat in the ebbing sunlight. He munches the peanuts from the tiny cellophane bag on which is printed PLEASE REMEMBER THAT SMALL CHILDREN CAN CHOKE ON NUTS. Here, kids, have some nuts. He dusts salt from his palms and fires up a Christian long cigarillo. Dry tobacco. Agreeably bitter in the mouth, smoke floating blue then gray up into the late-afternoon sun that glints white on the surface of the green-lacquered tabletop and glows like yellow amber in the beer.

Music lilts from inside the café and he recognizes Billie Holiday's voice, Ben Webster's tenor. He also recognizes the song, a lyric by Dorothy Parker in which Dorothy, via Billie, wishes on the moon for an April day that will not dance away.

Billie's voice so sweet and wistful, lilting and strong; when she says "April day," Kerrigan's heart is filled with the accepted sadness of its retreating dance, and Webster's tenor softens it all with a reedy mellow cool nod. Kerrigan happens to know this was recorded in Los Angeles in June 1957 when he was still thirteen years old. The Chevy was a work of art that year. But two and a half years later, Lady Day would be dead. He thinks of Frank O'Hara's poem "The Day Lady Died."

He loves the voice, the tenor, the lyric, the poem, by four dead people, but what bothers him is that the day Lady Day died, two days after Bastille Day in 1959, he didn't even know about it because he didn't even know about her—he was pushing sixteen then, and even if he was living in the city she died in, the city O'Hara describes in his poem, where he buys the *New York Post* and sees her fateful picture which Kerrigan knew nothing about from the other side of the East River where he lived with his forty-four-year-old mother, same age as the Lady when she died and when he still didn't even know anything about her or about Frank O'Hara either who died in 1966 at the age of forty in a Fire Island car accident that Kerrigan vaguely recalls hearing about when he was twenty-three and lived on East Third Street between avenues A and B, Alphabet City, just as he vaguely recalls hearing when he was twenty-four of the death of Dorothy Parker in 1967: *An April day that will not dance away . . .*

He sips his amber beer and wonders who might be dying today that he had never even or only vaguely heard of. For a fleeting instant he pictures Licia dying, dead, relishes it, but instantly withdraws the thought, not to wish his little girl motherless, wherever she might be. Anyway, Licia will surely outlive him. And then he thinks of Licia as an April day that danced away while his back was turned.

The sun has slid away from the Le Saint Jacques tables, slants across the other side of the little square. Kerrigan drains his beer, crosses Skt. Jakobs Place to the sunny side and **Theodor's**. The tables are all taken, but anyway he sees what the pattern of his day will be: He already has to pee again. Good day to sit closer to the loo than to the bar. And he composes a bit of doggerel on his way to the gents':

A Mystery

If I sit closer to the loo
Than to the bar, I think
That's 'cause I piss more than I drink.
How that can be so, I do not know.
I only know it's true.

Inside the black-and-chrome interior he finds the gents', repeats the fate of the exasperated spirit, proceeding from urinal to urinal. Room made for more beer, he strolls across the barroom toward the outside tables, but notices a note on the glass door: WE LIKE BABIES, BUT BREAST-FEEDING IS NOT PERMITTED ON THESE PREMISES, thinks how curiously un-Danish to be opposed to breast-feeding, the breast being (in the words of Knut Hamsun in *Hunger*) a "sweet miracle" as well as the one human organ that can only nurture and cannot be used to strike, gouge, fire a projectile, or cause any manner of pain other than the sweet agony of longing.

He finds an empty chair, sits, orders, lights a Christian. He holds the match before his eyes. The air is now so still that the flame seems not to move at all, seems perfectly still yet vibrant, eating the wood of the matchstick, violent yet stable—structured in a perfect symmetrical spire, at one and the same moment beautiful, fearsome, mysterious. He wants to ask the waiter why the breast-feeding prohibition, but is in no mood for controversy. Remembers Licia allowing him to taste her milk—such a miracle.

Then he notes a newspaper section on the chair beside him, takes it up. It is the Copenhagen section of the *Jutland Post, Jyllandsposten*, folded open to an article about a hundred-year-old telephone kiosk that is about to be auctioned off on Kongens Nytorv—the King's New Square. The starting bid is $60,000. It is the first of a number of telephone kiosks designed by Fritz Koch in 1886, roomy and richly appointed with wood and copper and glass, large enough for an office with a panorama of windows. There are only a handful of them left. That they survive out on the streets without being vandalized is a tribute to Danish civilization. It occurs to Kerrigan to buy it, use it for an office. Sit there in his oversize telephone box on the King's New Square surrounded by a wide circle of elegant buildings, the Royal Theater with its great seated sculptures of Ludvig Holberg, considered the Danish Molière, and Adam Oehlenschläger, the early-nineteenth-century romantic poet whose little sister Sophie married H. C. Ørsted's older brother and was loved by many poets, including of course Hans Christian Andersen.

To sit in his elegant telephone box and write and watch the world of the elegant core of Copenhagen through 360 degrees of window all for a mere $60,000. An idiotic idea. Where would he get the money? Nowhere. He could take out a new mortgage on his apartment.

Which apartment he was able to purchase only by selling the house he and Licia had purchased on loaned money. Not a week after her disappearance, he received a letter from her lawyer with divorce papers enclosed. *I'm so sorry, I don't love you. I have to find a life for myself and the baby* was all the note she had left him in the empty house when he returned from a week in Edinburgh. Not even addressed or signed, printed in block letters. Gone with two-year-old Gabrielle and the seed that was or was not Kerrigan's and was or was not in her womb for a month. Gabrielle used to sit on his lap and have him name things for her in Danish and English: *Lamp—lampe. Table—bord. Head—hoved. Eyes—øjne. Mouth—mund. Nose—næse. Hug—kram.* And then she would give him a hug. *Kys—kiss,* then a kiss.

I'm so sorry, I don't love you. Jeg er så ked af det, jeg elsker dig ikke.

On the phone, the lawyer was taciturn. Licia was in another country. Where is she? Who is she with?

I'm not at liberty to divulge that, she said, her voice hard as business.

You're not at liberty to divulge that. She stole my kid, and you are not at liberty to divulge where she is?

The country where she is living recognizes the right of the mother to sole custody. Especially when there are allegations of, let's say, unseemly behavior with the girl.

Fury kindled in him, which he suppressed. Quietly, he said, That's a lie.

Allegation against allegation. Possession is nine points of the law. No charges have been filed about any allegations. To date. And she is not planning on asking for half the value of the house and its contents.

Oh, how kind of her. She did, however, take half of my life's savings.

Well, after all, the two of you were on a shared economy.

She told me she was pregnant again.

I'm sorry—it wasn't yours.

He hears one thing first, another second. The statement. The past tense.

She is not asking support for the child, the lawyer said. She is asking for nothing more. Only your signature on the divorce paper.

And if I don't sign?

Let go, Mr. Kerrigan. She is with another. She is happy. You won't get her back. The child is so young—she has already forgotten you. Don't get embroiled in the courts over the house and your possible other assets. And other allegations.

A pinprick of molten fury burnt off inside him, leaving him bewildered. Let me ask something? Why didn't she just tell me.

With your temper?

I don't have a bad temper.

Allegation against allegation.

Blonde treachery.

He has no money to buy kiosks. Still, he cannot put it out of his mind.

On the King's New Square, he sees it. The shutters are raised and a small truck is parked outside from which a waiter carries a tray into the door of the little pavilion, beneath its green copper spire. Inside is just room enough for a white-clothed table at which a young blond couple sit, a feast spread before them, candles burning in crystal sticks, polished silver on white linen.

The waiter pours wine into a sparkling goblet and waits while the young man tastes it, contemplates, rolling it on his tongue, nods. The waiter withdraws to the truck.

"I thought this was up for auction," says Kerrigan.

"Was," the waiter tells him, readying the next course from the back of the truck. "Went to the hammer last week. Seven hundred thousand crowns"—$115,000. "Bought by a Dane living in New York. Banker."

Kerrigan looks again at the newspaper he has carried beneath his arm. It is dated two weeks back. So much for synchronicity. He pitches it into a trash receptacle, trudges off across the square that is in fact a circle, yet finds himself stopping to look back at the kiosk. The candles are tiny yellow spires in the windows and the faces of the young couple gaze upon one another silently and the wine sparkles red in their crystal goblets as they raise them to their lips, and he thinks of his own plan to sit in there by himself writing, watching the world move about outside.

He looks across to the 275-year-old **Hviid's Wine Room** beneath where the Blue Note and Grand Café used to be and where Jens August Schade wrote about the Finnish girl who pulled up her blouse to show him her breasts. Kerrigan savors the vicarious pleasure of such a moment. And it occurs to him once again that he would never know, if she was lying to him, what she was lying about. About being pregnant. About anything. *It wasn't yours.* And he thinks the unaskable: *Was Gabrielle?*

Inside the cavelike room, he goes straight for the pay phone with beer in hand and sifts through his wallet for the number of his green-eyed Associate. He longs for her little Moleskine book with its starfish stickers on the covers. Even as he dials the number, he wonders if she will be home at all on a late Saturday afternoon, if she has a man, if she will find him out of order, foolish, and the telephone line sends its little burring sound into his ear as he waits breathlessly, convinced she is already out somewhere with someone else and not walking barefoot around her apartment painting pictures from a palette of oils or acrylics.

Then her voice is in his ear, and he is thrilled that she recognizes his at once, from the single syllable of his greeting.

"And how did you spend the day on your own without your 'Associate?'" she asks.

"Miserably," he says. "I'm no good without you and your little Moleskine. I wandered around the lakes and thought morbid thoughts."

She says nothing, and Kerrigan falls silent. He peers into the foam of his lager and lines up coins on the shelf beneath the phone and looks at a small cardboard sign propped on a table—a drawing of this place where three men in old-fashioned suits stand at the bar with a naked woman. He wonders if the woman is supposed to be a hallucination. He thinks of the Finnish girl Schade wrote about in 1962.

"And what is Mr. Kerrigan calling for at this blue hour?"

He knows she knows what he is calling for, but he tells it in another way. "I'm on my way up to the White Lamb. To hear some happy jazz."

"Happy jazz?"

"Right. That's what they call it. Dixieland, I guess. I thought you might care to join me."

Her chuckle is complex. "Oh, you did, did you? Well, you know it's time and a half after six. Come to think of it, double time on weekends."

"Oh, well, I meant, you know, like, personally."

"You mean you meant you want me to do what I do for free?"

"I thought perhaps you might care to join me for dinner."

"I think Mr. Kerrigan is the Prince of Cups this evening."

He realizes then that is the reason for the note of sarcasm in her voice, her resistance. She can hear that he's been drinking. "I'm sorry, I didn't mean to . . ."

"Besides, I've already eaten," she says. "I had a lovely pineapple sandwich."

Mr. Kerrigan, he thinks, is going to be sick. "Are you painting?" he asks. "Are you barefoot?" How he wished she would invite him over for a coffee.

"So many questions. Oh! there's the doorbell, got to run . . ."

So who needs her, thinks Kerrigan, and takes a seat at the little table near the door where he can survey the bar and the entries to the first two cavelike rooms. He drinks a pint of lager with a double Finlandia vodka in a snaps glass in honor of Finnish girls who raise their blouses. A double in Denmark is a single in the U.S. is two thirds of a single in Sweden and half a single in Eastern Europe.

He raises his vodka and says, "*Multatuli*," snaps it down, chases it with cold beer, says, "Earth, fire, I have suffered greatly, I haf just hod an orgasm." The bartender in white shirt and black vest glances over—it is not Old Hansen. Kerrigan has committed a Danish sin: *at gøre sig bemærkede*—to call attention to oneself. He raises his vodka again, but the glass is empty.

"Once more, please," he says, and when the bartender brings the bottle to refill his glass, he nods formally. This time he keeps his toast to himself, thinks, *Earth, fire, suffering, come,* and snaps down the vodka. He yearns back in memory for the Swedish girl who once fed him *svartsuppa,* black soup—goose-blood soup, and her teeth gleamed in the candlelight, her face so pale and eyes so very very blue.

Something about the Swedish girl makes him think of Santa Lucia and the Scandinavian celebration each mid-December where the young virgins dress in white, wearing crowns of candles in their hair, and march in a procession singing in angelic voices about Santa Lucia, whose eyes were put out in her defense of her purity. And he will never see Gabrielle dressed in white, walking in that procession of candles.

Everywhere he turned—a lawyer, the police, even a private detective agency—he was met by the same skepticism and doubt. If he took it to court, he was advised, the judge would likely suspect that a woman who was willing to go so far to be free of him must have her reasons. She certainly had found the means. He didn't even reveal the "allegations" that Licia's attorney had hinted at. That was a swamp he didn't want to dip even a toe in. He was left trying to guess at what was in Licia's head and trying to identify what of his behavior might have provoked judgments in her that she kept secret from him. *With your temper?* Did she perceive him as frightening? Bullshit. He thinks of his Associate—*I think Mr. Kerrigan is the Prince of Cups this evening.* Was it because he drank too much? But Licia drank plenty herself. Still, the words of his Associate bother him. Is it time to taper off?

Bullshit!

Finally he went to a psychologist, told him about what Licia had hinted at.

"*Did* you do anything unseemly?"

"No! Not that I'm aware of."

"If you had done something, you would be aware of it. Then that is just a very cheap trick that she is using." But in the end the psychologist more or less agreed with lawyer, police, and detective, advising him to drop it, get on with his life.

* * *

He perambulates. Up **Gothersgade,** Gothers Street, past **Kongens Have,** the King's Garden, hooks left at **Nørrevoldgade,** North Rampart Street, down **Fiolstræde,** Violin Street, pauses at the mouth of a slanted dash of a street, **Rosengården,** the Rosen Court, that runs quickly across to **Kultorvet,** the Coal Square.

He enters the door of a place so unremarkable it seems designed to be ignored, **Rosengårdens Bodega,** the Rosen Court Bodega. Smoke-darkened paintings with cracked oils hang on the dark brown and yellow walls, an old-fashioned claustrophobic telephone booth with a tiny O of a window in the door and an old water pump mounted above it. A single customer nurses a beer at one of maybe eight tables.

Kerrigan takes a stool at the bar, orders a large draft lager, running a rough tally of how many he has had so far today. Half a dozen perhaps. And three vodkas. A mere drop in the national bucket considering that on average every Dane drinks 104.6 liters of beer per annum. And that includes the ones who do not drink at all. And how many snaps and vodkas and other spirits? He is aware of trying to excuse his consumption, obfuscate it.

He can feel the beer, but not badly, and he's been walking a lot, too. His legs are tired and that is good. It helps keep him from thinking about whether he feels more foolish or forlorn, keeps him from remembering the impotence he felt when he dated and signed that lawyer's papers and returned them in the self-addressed stamped envelope.

The bartender is a woman, voluptuous, and she smiles at him. He orders a draft in English, forgetting himself, and she answers in English, but it sounds Jamaican. Which seems odd because she is blonde and blue-eyed. He asks.

"Just spend a lot of time in Tri-ni-dad," she says.

She has a stool behind the taps. Kerrigan offers a drink and asks what she can tell him about this place.

"Building's been here since 1850," the woman says. "There's a funny story." She puts down her beer stein. "Or maybe not so funny." She removes a stack of books from a low shelf on the wall behind the bar and points to a hole in the wall. "That's from a bullet," she says. "The bullet is still in there. From a liquidation during the war. There was a gestapo informer, a Dane, they called him the Horse Thief, *Hestetyven*. He came in here one day, and the resistance was after him. It was on Hitler's fifty-fifth birthday, on April 20, 1944. The Germans had occupied the country since 1940. Two resistance guys came on bicycles and saw another kid in the movement and asked him to watch the bikes weren't pinched—during the war, things were scarce—and two of them came in and one of them shot the Horse Thief. Seven bullets. Say he squealed like a pig, big as he was, but everyone sitting here just looked the other way. No one saw a thing. Say when the two come running out again and jumped on their bikes, they were so jittery they crashed into each other, knocked themselves to the street. But they got away. That was a birthday present for the führer."

The barmaid falls silent then, and Kerrigan isn't much in the mood to talk. He sits, looking at the bullet hole, and thinking about the German occupation, the use of force, one people subjugating another, the very idea of weapons, pistols, projectiles designed to penetrate and kill the body.

A hundred meters toward the Coal Square (**Kultorvet**), on the corner, Kierkegaard, in 1838, had an apartment in number 11 where **Café Klaptræet** (the Clapboard) is now. Kerrigan looks up at the corner building where Kierkegaard lived 160 years before, pictures him there, his slanted body hunched over a book. This would have been five years prior to the publication of his first great work, *Either/Or*, when he roamed the streets—he loved to walk in the city.

From Kierkegaard's window here, he would have been able to see **Det Hvid Lam**, the White Lamb serving house at **Kultorvet 5**, established in 1807, the year of the three-day English bombardment that destroyed much of Copenhagen and killed almost 2 percent of the civilian population, about sixteen hundred people, plus a few hundred military men. The White Lamb was hit, too—the top of the building was blown off, but the newly opened serving house in the semibasement survived intact, and beer is still tapped here today to a jazz background on the sound system, with live jazz most nights. The Duke of Wellington blew the roof off in 1807, but he is now dust in his grave, and the only duke who blows the roof off now is Duke Ellington. The building is from 1754 so it survived not only the British bombardment but also the great fires of 1794 and 1795.

Kerrigan steps back to look up at the building above the White Lamb in the semibasement, hand-lettered luncheon signs offering sardines on coarse rye or "unspecified sandwiches"—three open sandwiches on slabs of dark grainy bread. Take what you get. Caveat emptor. But they're all good with a beer and a snaps.

He looks up the red facade of the building toward the red-tiled roof and tries to imagine the cannon from Wellington's fleet in the harbor— twenty-five ships of the line, forty smaller warships, thirty thousand men—shelling that roof, smashing tiles, rubble raining down on the square, people stunned then screaming, sprinting in mad confusion, horse wagons smashed beneath falling walls, civilians—men, women, children—pitched by shells, bodies blown out of windows, falling with chunks of brick, weeping blood, bones snapping through flesh. Broken-backed horses trying to tug free of harnesses hitched to wagons buried in broken bricks and pulverized stone. He imagines men and woman amid dust clouds and smoke, flames crackling in wood buildings, running first one way then the other in a chaotic knot around the square, mowed down by yet another shell, inhaling the heat of flames, smoke, dust—three hundred buildings totally destroyed, sixteen hundred badly damaged.

England and Denmark were at peace. The two countries were friends. When General Wellesley (the Duke of Wellington) sailed his fleet into the harbor on Wednesday, September 1, 1807, passing the fortification, the fleet and fortress exchanged cordial salutes. By that evening the British artillery was in position, and England demanded the surrender of the Danish fleet, received a response that did not satisfy, and began to bombard the city for three days. The hundred thousand inhabitants, their dwellings crowded into the city, seeking to flee, bottlenecked in the winding, ancient streets. From Wednesday evening until Saturday afternoon, the bombs fell and all those men, women, children were killed.

In comparison, Kerrigan considers that at Pearl Harbor under the Japanese sneak attack 134 years later, twenty-four hundred Americans were killed.

Ultimately Denmark aligned with Napoleon in retaliation, which wound up costing them Norway—a penalty awarded to Sweden.

Anyway, he thinks, after the bombardment, when they rebuilt, they incorporated the idea of chamfered—angled or rounded—street corners, which really improves the atmosphere of inner Copenhagen and turns every intersection into a small square.

Kerrigan hears music from **Det Hvid Lam**, the White Lamb. He climbs down to the half-submerged green door. Inside, Asger Rosenberg is spanking his bass, a picture of a screaming mouth mounted on the wall just above his head. He croons George Shearing's "Lullaby of Birdland," and Kerrigan thinks this moment of Asger crooning the Shearing melody has entered his heart until it turns to dust. Asger speaks into the mike with his mellifluous voice. "We will now take a short but intense break following which we will be replaced by . . ."

Kerrigan misses the name of the replacement group but realizes he is buzzed, watching the white face of the clock that says 8:45 on the wall between two windows that look out on the still-light square while the sweet young barmaid, whose rounded form Kerrigan appreciates, puts on some pause music: Gerry Mulligan and Chet Baker blowing "Bernie's Tune," which he happens to know was recorded on August 16, 1952, in Los Angeles, with Bobby Whitlock on bass and Chico Hamilton on drums, same day they recorded "Lullaby of the Leaves," which comes on next. Just over three and a half decades later, on May 13, 1988, Chet Baker would take his fatal fall out an Amsterdam hotel window to die on the pavement. Who knows what lies ahead—tomorrow, next year, in five minutes?

Mulligan's baritone on "Lullaby of the Leaves" reaches into Kerrigan's heart while Baker's scales lift it into an agreeable melancholy. A very old woman in a large hat sits at the covered pool table with a glass of beer and a bitter dram in a little stem glass that she lifts in Kerrigan's direction, tendering a smile. He raises his near empty pint to her, and a fellow at his side says with admiration bordering on awe in his voice, "That's Lotte. She used to be an *executive secretary*. She's eighty-six years old."

Chet Baker is singing now, another fifties L.A. number: *Let's get lost . . . lost in each other's arms . . .* , his voice weird in its whiteness. Asger's bass stands face-in to a corner like Man Ray's seventy-five-year-old *Violin of Ingres*, painted on the back of a naked woman by Ray, who was born in 1890, one year before Henry Miller and eight after James Joyce.

Kerrigan decides it would be wise to take a walk and climbs up out of the White Lamb to the Coal Square, makes a right away from Kierkegaard's apartment, and another right down **Købmagergade**, Butcher Street, thinking about the fact that James Joyce was born in 1882, the year before Nietzsche proclaimed the death of God, and Heineken beer received the Diplôme d'Honneur Amsterdam, seven years before the birth of Adolf Hitler, when Queen Victoria was sixty-three and Sigmund Freud twenty-six. In the last decade of the nineteenth century, one of Henry Miller's earliest literary heroes was Hans Christian Andersen; if Lotte was eighty-six, that means she was born in 1913, when Joyce and Miller were young rogues, both in Paris or headed there.

He stops outside of **Rundetårn**, the Round Tower, the oldest observatory still standing in Europe, a five-year construction project started in 1637, completed in 1642, built by King Christian IV (1588–1648). The British bombed it in 1807 but failed to damage it seriously. In 1716, Peter the Great of Russia rode his horse up the inner spiraling ramp, thirty-five meters to the top, and his wife, Catherine, did the same in her carriage, while in 1902, an automobile drove up the ramp to the top and back down again, and recently there was a skateboard race from top to bottom. And the great astronomer Tycho Brahe, for whom it was built, never saw it, for the king, miffed at something he did, exiled him before it was completed. Still, a bust of Tycho Brahe stands on a pedestal alongside the tower.

On the moon is a crater named for Tycho, who discovered it. The Tycho crater is also mentioned in Stanley Kubrick and Arthur C. Clarke's *2001: A Space Odyssey* (1968) as the place in which the mystical monolith is found buried in moondust.

Kerrigan sits on a stone slab in the tiny square beside the tower, contemplating Tycho's crater, Kubrick's monolith, and what the actual year 2001, but twenty months away, will *really* bring, but his thoughts all float on a background of Chet Baker's eerie white voice singing—*Let's get lost*—and he remembers Keir Dullea in the Kubrick film, ancient, dying in bed, raising a trembling aged finger to point at the monolith. Kerrigan starts wondering how he himself will die. Alone? In bed? Alone?

There is bird shit on Tycho's bust, and over to his left, Kerrigan regards a monument with large medallion portraits depicting the eighteenth-century poets Johannes Ewald and Johan Herman Wessel, sculpted by Otto Evens in 1879. The monument is topped with the sculptures of two protective cherubs whom someone has crowned with a broken-down blue bicycle, which is what drew his attention in the first place.

Kerrigan lights a cigarillo, thinking of Lotte the eighty-six-year-old executive secretary, wondering if she has ever read Ewald or Wessel, both of whom were born in the 1740s and died in the 1780s, who lived in the time of Struensee, middle-aged lover of the teenage Queen Caroline Mathilde, and who were Sturm und Drang contemporaries of Goethe, whose skull was found to contain a small quantity of gray dust by East German bureaucrats one dark November night in 1970.

He considers the overview of history he labors to gather in his own skull and its fate. Gray dust that no one will even bother to peek through his eye sockets at. But just to see history *once*, almost clearly, before then. A complete history and juxtaposition of nothing less than everything—or even just a history of the place where he is living—to clothe himself in it would be very fine raiment indeed.

He looks at the medallion of Ewald (1743–1781) on the monument. Ewald is said to be one of Denmark's greatest poets, but Kerrigan knows only a few lines of his forgotten "Ode to the Soul":

Confess, you fallen, weak, wretched
Brother of angels!
Say why you spread unfeathered wings?

Confess *what*, precisely? he thinks, knowing only that the question is addressed to the fallen soul of mankind—confess why you spread unfeathered wings? *Ah!* he thinks then. *Must be to Lucifer!*

The companion medallion is of Wessel (1742–1785), who was born in Norway, moved to Copenhagen as a teenager, and produced a small body of comic-parodic anti-illusionist drama: "I sing of—well, no, not really, I'm not singing, I'm actually *telling* about it, quite directly . . ."

Kerrigan finds himself wondering whether or what Licia will directly tell Gabrielle about him. Will she tell her lies, that he abandoned them? Or maybe that is Licia's truth. More likely she will tell her nothing, deny his existence, claim that the man she ran off with is her natural father.

He drops the stub of his cigar and grinds it out beneath his shoe and realizes that he is a tad drunk, yet at the eye of his drunkenness is a sphere of startling clarity. He rises, concentrates on walking evenly along the ancient pavement back to the White Lamb, climbs down the three steps, and discovers Olie Olsen blowing his eyes out on a tenor sax, one of a five-piece jazz band: Eddie Pless on trombone, Mogens Petersen on piano, Mogens Jensen on bass, and Tue Bjerborg on guitar. No entry, no cover, beneath a white lamp, the notes of a raunchy honking sax filling the smoky air.

He orders a pint of lager and carries it to the tables in the rear, takes one all to himself, and lights a cigar, and the difficulty of doing so informs him once again that he is drunk and moreover drunk in public, exposed, and has to deal with a sudden flash of terror of this exposure.

This is it, then? Hopeless alcoholic? Where the fuck is she? Why wouldn't she come when I called her? Prince of cups, indeed!

He looks up to see the blurry sax man blowing a blurred red tenor, which evolves into "Autumn Leaves." But it is still spring, and Licia is gone with the baby, and his Associate is not here. His cigar is cold in the ashtray alongside a slender white vase of carnations, which in Denmark do not have the pungent fragrance he remembers from carnations of his childhood, pinned to his lapel for first communion, confirmation, dyed green for St. Patrick's Day, pink carnation for the prom, but he does not want to remember that anyway, so it is just as well they do not have that pungent fragrance.

His beer is empty, and he raises his face to a pair of lamps in pink shades mounted on the wall. Their twoness touches his oneness and blurs into the "Autumn Leaves" trombone solo, about an abandoned lover, or dead lover, Jazz Jastrau's Jesus moving to him like a gentle hand to a whore where he sits without his Associate; without new information to wind round himself like a cloak, without the hope of a kiss, he sits.

He stands to fetch another beer. Blurrily he sees a woman with a coarse nose sitting by herself nursing a small glass of beer at the next table from his own.

"Hello," says Kerrigan.

"Hello, then," she says in British. "I like your Italian jeans. Can see the label. Not that I was looking at your bottom or anything." Her accent makes him think of Basil Fawlty's wife in *Fawlty Towers*: *I kno-ow, I kno-ow*.

Kerrigan asks her, "Why are women so beautiful?" and she says, "Aren't you the sweet talker?"

Then his gaze skitters upward to a detail: One of the lamps on the wall above his table is dead. He sits with a thump and watches: One lamp lit, one lamp dead. And his head lolls forward, his glasses hit the hard wood surface and skitter across it. He knows more than hears the sound of a lens cracking, and without shame or care recognizes a new depth in his day, in his life perhaps, as his arms form a cushion on the table for his lowering face, and he farts loudly, twice, to his chagrin, as he gives himself to this void he has spent the day purchasing.

The nudging hand that shoves him back to consciousness is about to evoke his anger, but he looks up to see two blurred jade-green eyes. The musicians have packed up, and only a few people remain scattered throughout the bar.

"Mr. Kerrigan," she says. "Thirty dollars an hour is hardly enough to babysit a baby of your proportions."

"I can't quite see you," he says.

"No wonder. You broke your glasses. I put them in your shirt pocket. Only one lens left."

"It was I who placed them there on the table for him," says the British woman with the coarse nose, still seated over her small glass of beer.

"Good for you," says his Associate in charming English. And to Kerrigan adds, "So. *Pjanking*, too?"

"Sorry?"

"*At pjanke*. To flirt."

"Are you jealous?"

"Are you his Mrs., then?" asks the British woman.

"I think I'm his keeper," she says, without looking from Kerrigan.

"Jesus," he says. "I love you. You're jealous!"

"Please. Spare me your shit. Sit up and buy me a drink. Better yet, just give me some money, and I'll buy the drink myself."

"Me, too. Vodka."

"You can have a Danish water."

"How the hell'd you find me?" he asks, and she takes a fifty-crown note bearing the portrait of Karen Blixen from the little pile of money on the table, glancing sharply over at the British woman, who huffs and picks up her glass, retires to a table farther toward the front. Kerrigan is sorry to see her go, thinking how nice it might have been to share a bed with both his Associate and the coarse-nosed Brit.

"How *did* you find me?" he asks.

"Easy," she tells him. "You told me when you called where you would be."

"Well I might have changed my plans. After your harsh rejection of me. You said you weren't gonna come."

"I got bored."

"Ha! You were thinking about me. You missed me," he says, but she has already stepped over to the bar. He rallies a bit when she sets a small beer before him, and he lights a Petit cigar, wondering what time it is—he cannot see the clock and is embarrassed to ask. He says, "*Skål*" and "*Nostrovja*" and "*Slanté*" and "*Terviseks*" and "*Multatuli*," and "Earth, fire, suffering, and ejaculation."

The effort wears him out. "Now," he says, "We will take a short but very intense pause," and lowers his face once again to the cradle of his arms, too blitzed for shame. "Occupational blizzard," he mutters and is gone, though he hears in the distance sniffing sounds and her voice asking, "What is it that stinks of piss here?"

Three: Jax!

. . . the best way to compare
and quickest was by taking off our clothes.
O, we loved long and happily, God knows!
—LOUIS SIMPSON

The very high white ceiling to which he opens his eyes is not familiar. Two blurred, myopic flies move lazily in circles around its faintly crackled surface, the distance to which he tries, blearily and in vain, to determine.

He is in bed. A radio is playing in the next room. Gauzy curtains drift at a tall open window. Beneath an eiderdown, he is naked. And the history of his recent past is obscure. Vague clots of memory tease him from behind a dark curtain.

A door at the corner of the room is ajar and now swings in toward him so he sees his blurred Associate standing there in black jeans and a black tank top.

"He lives," she says.

He listens, uneasy, with interest, to the words that form on his breath. "I had a very unpleasant dream."

"It was no dream."

He fancies that in the blur of her mouth he can see a mixed expression of amusement, chagrin, incredulity, and sadism. He says, "No, I mean, I dreamt I . . . peed my . . ."

"It was no dream."

"You mean I really broke my glasses."

"Among other things."

"You *didn't* . . . ?"

She nods.

"Jesus." His face is hot. "How much do I owe you?"

"If I start taking money for something like that, I shall have to begin to vonder vhat my profession really is." Her v'ed w's make him aware she is speaking English. Perhaps this situation feels foreign to her. Kerrigan's face is so hot he feels sweat on his brow.

"At least," she says, "you have the decency to blush."

She leaves him to his shame, and he buries his mortified head beneath the pillow. The thought of it. Her *seeing* him like that. Removing his wet pants. *Cleaning* him like a baby, or a doddering old man.

He recalls once at a family gathering years ago an aunt had an epileptic fit after dinner—she fell to the floor and began to vomit her entire dinner, it spread like a sea across the hardwood floor. The quantity was awesome. The men present held back in uncertainty and disgust while the women went to work instantly to clean her and the mess. Women could do that. *Would* do that.

And what Licia did.

In washed and ironed drawers, clean shirt, jeans washed and tumble-dried and ironed, hung in the tall open window to air, reborn from a long steaming shower, he brushes his teeth at great length with a throwaway toothbrush, spits in the sink, and studies his pearly whites, which are less than pearly thanks to his increasing cigar appetite. The OTC codeine painkillers his Associate has given him have killed not only his pain but a good bit of his shame as well, and he fairly dances into her enormous plank-floor living room with its three-meter ceiling. Some jazz music on the stereo has him feeling spry-footed, thirties raggy stuff, and he recognizes the voice of Leo Mathisen advising himself to take it easy, smoke a cigar, and let the others do the hard work.

In the sunlight from the window, he can see her age, but she is a trim dancing fay of a girl nonetheless. He wonders if he could get her into bed with him. Always randy with a hangover. Hangover horns. He turns her once across the floor, delighted that she dances along, light as a feather on her feet, in his arms.

"Where are we, by the way?" he asks, endeavoring to slip the question in nonchalantly in hopes it will not be noticed sufficiently to spotlight the fact he was too drunk yesterday to remember being transported here.

"East side," she says. "The near east. Holsteinsgade. And I'm not surprised you don't remember."

"Know it well," he says briskly. "Home of Holsteins Bodega, where I once went to hear jazz that turned out to be rhythm and blues. Good rhythm and blues. American black guy, great big guy named Dale Smith. Sang 'Shake, Rattle and Roll,' with the original sexy words that Jesse Stone wrote for Big Joe Turner, not the cleaned-up white-guy cover lyrics." Kerrigan is feeling hot for her bod, clad in tight black. Hangover horns driving him toward her. And he can see she sees right through him. Her smile is sweetly teasing, and Leo is singing "To Be or Not to Be," turning Hamlet's question of suicide into a love song.

"I'm hungry," says Kerrigan.

"You must have *some* constitution, Mr. Kerrigan. I know a good place for lunch." She gives him a look. "You will keep your powder dry, though, won't you?"

"You," he says, blushing, "are not a gentleman."

She blinks. "My ambitions have never been that low." And, "How sweetly you blush. You know the old Danish proverb, 'A blush is the color of virtue.'"

Because she wants to show him another place for lunch, they sit in the sun over a very light brunch of morning bread and cheese, coffee and *gammel dansk*, bitter snaps, while a man and woman in dark clothes dance a tango on the concrete square outside the **Bopa Café.**

With her left hand, his Associate holds the Moleskine open on the table while eating a buttered *rundstykke* roll—a "round piece"—with her right. He notices she occasionally chews with her mouth open so he can see the bread and butter tumbling round on her pink tongue.

He says, "Don't chew with your mouth open, honey," and she pats her mouth with a paper napkin. "*Tak for sidst*, ey?" she says. Danish for "Thanks for the last time we met," but also a euphemism for revenge.

"Right. You can have it from the same dresser drawer," he says, another Danish euphemism for tit-for-tat evening up.

"This was the headquarters of one of the main resistance parties during the Second World War," she tells him. "BOPA is an acronym for the Danish Borgenes Parti, the Citizens' Party." She daubs again at her pretty lips with the napkin, chews, swallows, sips coffee, sips bitter snaps, says, "Ummm," and continues. "Leo Mathisen, in fact, played various places during the war. He was Danish but he wrote and sang in English. English was forbidden by the German occupation forces, so he just sang gibberish versions of the words. Dr. Werner Best was the German commandant under the occupation," she continues. "He picked the best house in Copenhagen, a mansion just up the coast, actually right outside the city. Your ambassador has it as his residence now."

"Do you remember the war?" he asks.

As she butters a slice of Graham's bread, she is silent. Then she looks up at his face, as though about to speak, but seems to think better of it and reaches for her Moleskine. She gives him a rundown on the occupation of Denmark, and he watches with infatuation her lips, which he longs unbearably to kiss.

On April 9, 1940, the Germans marched in over the southern border of Jutland. There was a little bit of fighting and an air assault as well, but the Danes decided not to commit heroic suicide. Unlike Norway, where the resistance had the mountains to hide in and fight from, Denmark is completely flat. There were no natural barriers. Also, unlike the Norwegian king, the Danish king, Christian X, stayed in his capital and rode on horseback through Copenhagen every day, as was his custom, all by himself, no guards, no escort.

The Danish ambassador in Washington, D.C., was astute enough to place Greenland, Iceland, and the Faroe Islands under the protection of the allied forces, so the Germans were unable to make strategic use of them, which could have been a catastrophe.

Germany plundered the Danish agriculture to feed its troops under the pretense that they would pay back. Some Danes, of course, *did* make money. There was also clandestine ferrying of Jews and communists across the sound most nights to Malmö, to the safety of Swedish neutrality, particularly during October 1943 when the gestapo attempted to round up the Jews in Denmark. The Swedes were very helpful. They also made a lot of money. Being neutral, they could help everyone. And the boatmen made money, too. But they took chances for it as well.

She lays a slice of medium-old cheese on her buttered sour bread, bites, chews with closed lips, sips coffee, and he imagines how interesting her kiss would be, tasting of old cheese and the nice bittersweet aroma of coffee with cream and the harsh taste of bitter snaps.

Yet he cannot forget that expression on her face earlier, as she looked at him and seemed to be about to tell something.

She continues: In 1943, things started getting hotter. By August, there was a general strike, shooting in the streets. Hostages were taken. The Danes scuttled their own navy in the harbor, and in September, the Freedom Council was set up. In January 1944, the gestapo, accompanied by Danish police, liquidated the outspoken poet-priest Kaj Munk (1898–1944), dragged him from his home and put a bullet in the back of his neck and left him in a ditch.

Throughout that year, there was sabotage and countersabotage. It was nowhere near what happened elsewhere in Europe, but it was bad enough. Nocturnal arrests, liquidations, random terror by the occupying forces and liquidations by the underground, too—perhaps not all of them justified. The lawful police were replaced by a makeshift police department set up by the Germans—the *hilfspolizei*—called *Hipo* for short or, more often, *Hipo svin*, Hipo swine, made up mainly of ex-convicts and criminals.

Meanwhile, in Denmark, hundreds of thousands of German refugees were streaming north from Germany, two hundred thousand in all, starved, filthy, lice-infested. It was clear Germany was losing the war; the question for the Danes was whether Denmark would be the last battlefield. But on May 4, 1945, the Germans capitulated, and Belgium, the Netherlands, Denmark, and Norway were liberated the next day.

Copenhagen was filled with fleeing German officers and Nazis speeding for the border in their jeeps. There was shooting in the streets, and candles burned in all the windows of the towns and cities—all the candles that Danes always kept in ready because the Germans frequently would cut off the power supply. It was a spontaneous display. The streets of Copenhagen glowed with thousands of candles in the windows. To this day, more than half a century later, there are still people who put lighted candles in the window on May 4 in remembrance of the end of the five-year occupation by the German "cousins."

"You know," Kerrigan says, "people say a lot about the European Union. But at least it stopped most of the fighting that's torn Europe apart over the years. Germany against France. France against England. France against the rest of Europe. Germany and Italy against Europe. England occupying Ireland for centuries. All now finally annulled by a treaty tying their fates all together. The United States of Europe."

Her green eyes sparkle, and instead of singing her praises, he sings the praise of her land.

"Shakespeare picked the right country, the right climate, the right amount of darkness for his melancholy Dane, although I admit I've grown to love the extremes of Danish seasons and light—the dark winters suit me. And the white nights of summer suit me even better. There is nothing like those white nights. The long late sunsets, the yellow skies—hell, *every* color! And the birds singing at three in the morning. You know the Belgian painter Magritte? His painting *Empire of Light*? It purports to show a paradox, as many of Magritte's paintings do—a dark city street beneath a bright sky. But to me that is a realistic portrait of a Danish summer night. You know, you're at a party that runs to half past two and step out in the garden for air and the sky is growing light, the birds are singing—even if the world around you is still dark, it's sunrise. Deep winter, too. In some ways, deep winter is even better. I remember standing on Langebro once—Long Bridge—you know, the one that connects Copenhagen with the island of Amager, in midwinter, and there was snow on the ground, and the sky was white as the snow, and everything else, the water, the bridge, the ships in the water, the smoke rising from their stacks, was shades of white and gray and black. It was a pure black-and-white world. But as I stood there watching, suddenly my eye began to pick out little blots of color—the red of a bird's plumage, a woman's long wool coat, the green of your eyes . . ."

"You should have been a painter."

"If I was, I would like to paint you." *In red panties*, he thinks. "You're quite good-looking, you know."

"In the words of the High One, 'He who flatters gets.'"

Kerrigan's eyes lower to give him time to think, and he shoves his empty plate aside. To his surprise, not only does he feel wonderful, he has also got over his embarrassment about what his Associate did for him the night before when he was unconscious. Born again. He sips the last of his bitter and lights a cigar, looks into her green eyes, and asks, "Did you know that just down the street here, on Randersgade, there's a cellar club where people go to couple openly and watch others couple? Where couples couple with other couples, and men amuse themselves watching their mates couple with strangers and women are enjoyed simultaneously by two and more men?"

Her eyes watch his mouth. "And you have been there?"

"No."

"Is this too much even for *you*, then?" Her smile is wry.

"It's not that. It's just, you can't get a drink there. What's love without wine?" He trims his cigar, smiles, can see she is titillated, and he loves it.

Then she looks teasingly at him. "Do not forget that I have seen you naked." Her eyes are bold in their greenness. "You looked interesting that way," she says, and his blush is now spiced with pleasure.

But there is an undeniable fact to be dealt with first: the emptiness of his belly. "I'm still hungry," he says.

On **Østerbrogade**, East Bridge Street, they cross **Trianglen**, pass the eastern edge of Black Dam Lake, cross **Lille Triangle**, Little Triangle, and walk along **Dag Hammerskjolds Allé**, named for the Swedish UN secretary general killed in an air crash in 1961 on his way to negotiate over the Congo Crisis—for which he was posthumously awarded the

Nobel Peace Prize that year. Past Olaf Palme's Street—named for the Swedish Social Democratic prime minister assassinated in the 1980s as he and his wife walked home from the movies, never solved—past the elegant old villas that have been purchased for embassies by the British and Russians and the ugly concrete box built by the Americans for theirs. The Americans seem always to have the ugliest embassies—Copenhagen, Oslo, Amsterdam . . .

They are headed for **Cykelstalden,** the Cycle Stall Café, where there is normally jazz only on Wednesdays from five to seven, but this season the owner, Mogens, has decided to add a single weekend. Inside the station they can see the bar, but she takes his arm and leads him to the escalator down. "We have to fill your stomach," she says. "It's just one stop on the S-Tog"—the City Train—"and then we will have a feast."

She leads him onto the train, and soon the tracks go underground and stop at an underground platform and the two of them climb up and cross Nørreport to Fiølstræde, and on **Krystalgade**—Crystal Street—they make a left, pass the synagogue, the main library, to a semibasement café—**Café Halvvejen.** Café Halfway. It is a dark, old-looking place with a curving bar that seats about eight people and five or six tables.

"This looks old," Kerrigan says.

"It is not so old," she says. "Only perhaps thirty years or so. But it is good if you are hungry."

A smiling young woman—the daughter of the owner—comes for their orders and Kerrigan's Associate asks, "May I order for us both? We'll have *biksemad*," she says. "And Krone snaps. And large Royal drafts."

The place is filling up with people ordering "unspecified sandwiches"—a kind of a potluck where you get three open sandwiches of varying fish, meat, vegetable, or egg with varying condiments and garnishes for a very modest price. That's what Kerrigan would have ordered, but then the *biksemad* arrives and he realizes he was right to follow his Associate's conviction.

The waitress places before each of them a plate deep with diced pork and diced potatoes and onions, each topped with two fried eggs and sided by a little pot of pickled beets with a basket of rye and French bread and small packets of butter and swine fat.

How optimistic, thinks Kerrigan, to be hungry and to have food, carefully lifting his brimming glass of Krone snaps to his lips. "Meniscus," he says. "Or is it menisci?"

"One meniscus," she says, her green eyes sparkling. "And one womeniscus."

"You said before that a womeniscus is called a pussy," he says.

"Can you drink a pussy?" she asks.

Eyes ablaze, he says, *"Yes!"*

Belly full of hash, Kerrigan grows meditative on the train back to Østerport station. He knows the bar they are headed for from many years ago. He was working for a private firm, before he had begun to be a full-time writer and translator, long before he met and was bewitched by Licia—or whatever she had done to him. He ate lunch at **Cykelstalden** one day and looked up to see the poet Dan Turèll sitting at a nearby table over a bitter snaps. Kerrigan was perhaps in his mid-thirties at the time, and he knew Turèll's writing, knew him as a great fan of the American beats. Kerrigan was wearing a suit and tie because he was on his way to the embassy for an interview.

Turèll saw that Kerrigan recognized him and nodded, and Kerrigan wished to show him he was more than a suit and tie, wanted to open his mouth and howl out Ginsberg's *Howl*, wanted to stand up and chant *Howl's* Whitman epigraph: *Unscrew the locks from the doors! / Unscrew the doors themselves from their jambs!*

He was eating a bowl of vegetable soup with bread and butter and a glass of water, trying to get ready for his interview, and he wanted to send a beer and a bitter over to Turèll—Uncle Danny they called him, or he called himself.

He wanted this man to know that even if he had not yet published anything, even if he had forsaken his poetry and made his living as a glorified clerk, he was more than a suit and tie and bowl of alphabet soup. But he said nothing. He sat there spooning soup and noodles into his mouth and eating bread and butter, and Dan Turèll finished his bitter and paid, nodded once more at Kerrigan, and left, a tall, slender, bearded man in dark clothes with fingernails polished black, and Kerrigan's path never crossed his again, although he did see him once more, in 1983, in the Saltlageret, where the planetarium stands now, when Uncle Danny introduced a reading by William Burroughs.

Turèll published a hundred books in his forty-seven years, and when he was dying in 1993, in his forties, he made a CD of a dozen poems with background music by a composer named Halfdan E. The next-to-last poem on the album is entitled "Last Walk Through the City," a reminiscence of a lifetime in a city, a last visit to a last bar for a last bitter, a last rummaging through the boxes outside a secondhand bookshop, a last look at the mothers leaning over the sills of their kitchen windows shouting for their children to come up for dinner, stopping here and there to watch or to shake the city from his coat as a dog shakes water from his fur, all of it so swift, so swiftly passing, and finally he takes a last stroll down the pedestrian street in the company of all his friends that only he can see. And without being sentimental, they say good-bye to it all in silent conversation, and then down by the King's New Square they disappear, and then Uncle Danny does, too, and there is one less shadow in the street.

Turèll was dead shortly after that recording, but he had written the poem nearly twenty years before, a young man imagining his own death, but never imagining it would come so early.

Perhaps it is the remnant of his hangover that causes the sound in Kerrigan's throat, but his Associate glances at him and asks, "Are you all right?"

He nods, not trusting himself to speak, thinking, The lesson here is when you see someone in a café you want to say hello to, whether you know them or not, don't hesitate, say hello.

The train glides into **Østerport Station**, and they ride the escalator up to street level and enter the bar inside the station through a glass door depicting a single, huge-wheeled bike with a minuscule rear wheel. The jazzmen are already setting up inside Cykelstalden, the Cycle Stall, a long narrow smoky serving house in the back of the station, and his Associate has been conferring with her Moleskine book. She tells him that the station has been in operation since 1897 and Cykelstalden had been a railway authority restaurant, previously much bigger than it is now, with tables out on the street in the warmer months, but now the railway authority has sold or rented most of the old serving house to Nordea Bank, and Cykelstalden has been shoved into the back. For about twenty-five years, weekly jazz concerts were held here. There was an open view from the outdoor tables all the way to the copper dome of **Marmorkirken**, the Marble Church, which rises above the low ocher, red-roofed, and red-shuttered buildings of the old naval housing, the **Nyboder** domiciles.

The manager, Mogens, in his thirties, is behind the bar, tending the taps. A strikingly pretty blonde waitress named Trine expertly carries a tray with half a dozen golden pints through the corridor of tables. The cold beer down Kerrigan's throat is a liquid field of wheat, and a curly-haired man comes over and kisses his Associate on her lips.

"*Hej*, Lars!" she says cheerily and touches his face, and a shadow drifts across Kerrigan's mind. They chat while Kerrigan, unintroduced, studies the poster announcing the Stolle and Svare Jazz Quartet featuring Jørgen Svare on sax, Ole Stolle on trumpet, Mikkel Finn on drums, Søren Kristiansen on piano, and Ole "Skipper" Moesgård on bass. Lars and Kerrigan's Associate are still chatting and Kerrigan's beer is already more than half empty, and the musicians are milling about, not yet playing. He wishes that Lars would go away, and perhaps communicates that wish, for suddenly the handsome, curly-haired man kisses her again on the mouth, nods to Kerrigan, and withdraws, saying, "I have a family to go home to."

"Who's he?" Kerrigan asks, feeling foolish.

"Lars."

"I gathered. Is he your lover?" Kerrigan can't help himself and doesn't want to—he wants to broadcast his desire.

"Vouldn't you like to know?"

The piano player starts in then, and Ole Stolle begins to sing "Blueberry Hill," and Kerrigan gazes off at what, to his uncorrected eyes, is the impressionistic barroom. Through a back window he can see the blurry harbor, and he thinks of Admiral Nelson and the 1801 Battle of Copenhagen.

Nelson, with one detachment of ships, was firing upon the city. The inferior Danish forces were responding so valiantly that the senior British admiral, Parker, signaled Nelson to cease firing. Nelson kept firing, and his first officer called the cease-fire signal to his attention. The one-eyed Nelson took out his telescope but put it to his blind eye. "I see no signal," he said, and kept the cannons going. Then he sent word to the city that he would set fire to the Danish floating batteries he had captured, with the crews still in them, if the Danes did not surrender. Olfert Fischer, the Danish admiral, carried out the crown prince's order to cease fire, a surrender. That is the origin of the Danish expression that Kerrigan has always heard translated into English as "putting the monocle to the blind eye."

Kerrigan pictures Nelson atop the fifty-six-meter-tall pillar at the center of Trafalgar Square in London, a monument to his victory over the French-Spanish fleet in 1805, and ponders with bitter satisfaction the fact that in 1966 the IRA blew up the Nelson Pillar in Dublin. He is annoyed at the thought of Nelson, although he realizes that his annoyance stems from the fact that the curly-haired Lars kissed his Associate, twice, on her pretty lips, while he himself has not done so even once, and is further annoyed that he should be annoyed at that, even as the blonde Trine so young and lovely to gaze upon walks past and smiles right into his eyes so his heart jumps. No reason for annoyance. And little sense to hate Nelson for something he did nearly two hundred years ago, but what good was history if one insisted upon putting the monocle to the blind eye? Which, of course, he realizes is precisely what he does constantly. *You are so blind.*

If he cranes his neck, he can just glimpse the green copper dome of the Marble Church through the window, just around the corner from

Adelsgade—Nobility Street—known in the nineteenth century as "the headquarters of thieves and handlers," according to High Court Justice Engelhart writing in 1815 in the daily newspaper *Berlingske*. Engelhart referred to "Jews and other people" who dealt in stolen goods in those days when after eleven at night the streets were full of thieves and burglars, and the populace was protected by watchmen armed with mace-headed spears who would look the other way for a coin.

The death penalty for theft was abolished in 1771, but in 1815 there was a cry to reinstate it for burglary. The "new" law of 1789 was described by a leading lawyer in 1809 as a "beautiful specimen of humanity and wisdom." It provided for two months to two years in the House of Chastisement for a first theft conviction; three to five years for a second offense; and life for a third offense—a nearly two-hundred-year-old legal provision that resembles a new three-strikes law in parts of America.

In 1815 the prisoners rioted against the food; cooked in a copper kettle, it was served coated with a green, poisonous film. The response was sympathetic but a third riot, in 1817, evoked a decision to execute every tenth prisoner by lottery until a forceful protest by public attorney A. S. Ørsted (brother of the discoverer of electromagnetism) resulted in a revocation of the decision. Ørsted was a strong force for the enactment of a more just penal system, but only in 1837 was interrogation by whip abolished.

Kerrigan's beer is empty and he attempts, unsuccessfully, to signal the waitress for a fresh one, which embarrasses and annoys him further.

"Are you sulking?" his Associate asks.

"Yes."

"Why?"

"Wouldn't you like to know?"

"See there," she says quietly. "The fellow with the beard three tables down. That's our minister of defense."

This stretches a grin on Kerrigan's puss.

"Oh, now you're in a good mood again."

"It just reminded me of Mogens Glistrup. Remember when he ran for office and said he would abolish the Danish defense system and replace it with a recorded announcement in English, German, and Russian that kept repeating, *We surrender, we surrender, we surrender . . .*"

She grins now, too, but says, "His party has led to an even more nationalistic and xenophobic one that has gained many seats in the parliament, you know. Some would call it almost fascist." She glances at Mogens the manager, smiling, who nods and brings a new round.

"*Is* he?" Kerrigan asks.

"Is who what?"

"Lars your lover?"

"Sometimes you remind me of Hans Christian Andersen with all those feelings you have," she says, and pokes him in the chest with her fingertip. He almost responds to the quick pinprick of indignation this evokes in him, but before opening his mouth realizes that she is teasing and says instead, "Well, you are the perfect Sophie Ørsted, aren't you? Collecting poets."

She only smiles, and Stolle and Svare are now going very cool on "Moonlight in Vermont," and Kerrigan is not afraid of anything with another fresh golden pint on the table before him. He lights a cigar and wants very much to make love to her or at least to kiss her neck or even just the palm of her delicate hand or the arch of her sweet little trotter. He remembers his Swedish friend Morten Gideon in the Casino in Divonne Les Baines once, years ago, sitting with a beautiful blonde Turkish woman he was trying unsuccessfully to seduce; suddenly, in an unexpected moment of silence in the casino, Gideon's voice was heard to rise clearly out across the entire casino, "I vant to kess your feet!"

Kerrigan is focused on his Associate's hands and her slender bare arms, thinking how good is the life of the senses.

After a pause, the quintet opens again with a Dixie version of "Toot Toot Tootsie, Good-bye," and Kerrigan says, "God, when I was a kid that song terrified me."

She looks curiously at him.

He says, "It was the lyrics, you know that line about, *Wait for the mail / I'll never fail / If you don't get a letter / Then you'll know I'm in jail . . .*"

"Why did that terrify you?"

"I don't know. Somehow it made me think of, or fear, someone I loved going to jail. I think it had something to do with a Dan Dailey film I saw once where this guy has to go to jail, and he didn't really do anything very bad, nothing violent or anything. It was like some minor fraud or something, grifter-type thing. And when he sang that song, it really scared me, like gave me an idea how unrelenting the law could be. Like fuck up even just a little bit and you're fucked. There are few things in the world that scare me as much as the thought of going to jail. Or in debt for life, being litigated endlessly, fined—"

"Are you guilty of something?"

"I was raised Catholic. Catholics are always guilty." He thinks of Licia's lawyer on the phone, quietly relentless, a light but fearsome reference to Kerrigan's house and "other assets and allegations," which Licia had provided information on to pressure him into signing the divorce and custody papers. He might have been under litigation for years, buried in debt for life, his reputation smeared—where there's smoke . . . Kerrigan feels an intensity of hatred for Licia that is alien to his nature, yet he feels it as well as despair at the thought of his daughter, growing from him year by year. How can he still love a woman who would do something like that? Yet he does love her still, which makes him wonder about himself and about what love is—delusion? How can he be so blind as still to have feelings for an illusion, a delusion?

His Associate is still watching him. Then she turns away to light a Prince with an elegant silver lighter. "My father," she says, "went to jail once. For 'borrowing' some petty cash from his office and not returning it in time so that it was discovered. It was a small amount. He had run out of money before payday, and in those days they didn't have these automatic credit provisions. He got three months. No probation. No one told me about it. I was ten, and they sent me to my aunt's for a weekend when he had to be taken away. My father brought me to her place in the country, and he had a little present for me—a coloring book. He was so loving and gentle—I didn't understand, but it was so sweet. Then on Sunday afternoon he didn't pick me up, my mother did, and when I asked where he was, she just said he had to go away for a while. No one would tell me where he was until one day in school—we were in a fine middle-class school, we lived well—one of the other girls asked me if it was true my father was in jail. I just laughed at her. And after school that day I told my mother, expecting her to say how ridiculous, but as soon as I saw her face I knew. That's how I found out."

Kerrigan put his hand on hers. "Jesus."

"Everyone has a sad story," she says. "Tell me yours."

"Let's leave my story out of this."

"Why?"

He shakes his head, takes his hand from hers.

The musicians are finishing their last set with "Love Me or Leave Me," and the sky outside has clouded over with a white-gray ceiling.

"Damn," says Kerrigan. "I want some more jazz."

"I know a place," she tells him. "It's small and dark and the jazz is on CD but it's good. Just over on Classensgade—Classens Street. We can walk there through my favorite cemetery."

Outside the train station, he glimpses the ugly concrete box of the American embassy and thinks he could hate Custer as much as Nelson, although putting everything into perspective one could as well sing the praises of any leader who, as Lincoln put it, at least sometimes "listens to the angels of his better nature." What right does a man have to complain and carp about a system that he only passively enjoys, without contributing a fart himself? Taxes. He contributes taxes. With taxes you build civilization.

They nip in through an iron gate, and Kerrigan sees they are in a graveyard.

"This is **Garnison's Cemetery**," she tells him. "We can take a shortcut back toward Classensgade. Here," she says, pointing to a broad, tall, fenced-in mansion, "is the Russian embassy. On the other side of the cemetery is the American. And across the street, during the Cold War, there used to be a Chinese restaurant called Beijing. There was great speculation about the tangle of electronics in the basement of that restaurant."

The cemetery itself is a peaceful place of well-tended graves. Near the gate on a large stone encircled by small trees, an engraving reports that beneath it lie the remains of 226 warriors who died under the Danish flag in 1864, on whose grave grows honor, for they gave all for the fatherland.

Kerrigan pictures their 226 bodies all tangled together in the earth, bare-boned now, skulls grinning at skulls, warriors who died in the last battle—so far—Denmark ever fought, the war they lost to Germany, following which the country was never again a world power, a kingdom that is about the size of an American state, same population as Missouri.

He notes that the various gravestones are cut not only with the name and dates of birth and death of the extinguished lives beneath them, but also with the positions they held in this mortal span, trades, titles, rank—as though they are all doomed to continue playing in eternity the roles they played within their lifetimes.

There lies Colonel Vilhelm de Fine Licht, 1821–1885, and housewife Anna; Baroness Ellen Schaffalitzky and Lieutenant Colonel Ludvig Bernhard Maximilian, aka Baron Schaffalitzky de Muckadell. Kerrigan tries the name on, pictures himself at a conference, offering his hand to his Associate for a shake: "Hi there, Muckadell here. Denmark. Good to see ya. Call me Schaffalitzky if you like."

"It is a very fine Danish name," she tells him solemnly as they pass the remains of Staff Sergeant N. F. Petersen and many others—a generaless (apparently the wife of a general), a mason, Customs Inspector Simonsen, a pharmacist, editor in chief; a civil engineer, journalist, priest, actor, grocer, taxicab owner, wine merchant, pilot. There is one Ludvig Fock, profession unidentified, and one Brigadier Percy Hansen.

"We've got a whole society here," he says. "Seal off the gates and you've got a complete city of ghosts. See them all on dusty planks performing their functions. But it really is a lovely place. It would be good to lie here." And he thinks of Dylan Thomas's grandfather traveling about Wales furiously in a little pony trap looking for a good place to be buried, complaining that one grave he views would not have room enough for him to twitch his toes without putting them in the sea. The townspeople point out that he's not dead yet and try to tempt him home for strong beer and cake, but the old man only looks off at the sea without speaking, undoubting, a prophet.

Kerrigan turns to his Associate. "If your last dance is not already taken, would you consider lying here beside me?"

"It would be too late for much fun then," she says with a glint in her green eyes that fires his pulse and inspires his memory with a Marvelous rhyme: "The grave's a fine and private place but none, I think, do there embrace."

Her grin is perfunctory but not lacking affection.

They pass through the opposite gate of the cemetery, step across one side of Little Triangle and into **Classensgade**. Like most of the best Danish bars, the place she leads him to is utterly unremarkable to look at, narrow fronted, tucked in between a narrow North Vietnamese restaurant named Hanoi and the blue barn-door entry of an apartment building courtyard. The door is under the numeral 5 beneath a lintel sign that says VINSTUE BAR, Wine Room Bar, the two words punctuated by the face of a die showing five, and a white-curtained plate window on which is lettered the word *Femmeren*, the Fiver.

Inside, a handful of regulars at the bar fall silent at the entry of Kerrigan and his Associate. It is a small dark room with vintage posters and advertisements on the walls—one of a strutting old-fashioned sailor advertising Tuborg, another advertising *Stjerne Øl*, Star Beer, a billboard reproduction of a Brecht-Weil play in German. Behind the bar, a substantial-looking woman in her early sixties perhaps.

They sit at a round table in the corner, and the woman steps from the bar to serve them.

"That's Ruth, the owner. She opened this place in 1967."

It occurs to Kerrigan he is sitting just around the corner from Søren Kierkegaard's 1850 residence as well as that the music playing on the sound system is Cannonball Adderley's *Somethin' Else*, which he happens to know was recorded in Hackensack, New Jersey, on March 9, 1958. The number playing is "Autumn Leaves," perhaps the best variations he has ever heard of it, with Adderley on alto sax, Miles Davis on trumpet, Hank Jones on piano, Sam Jones on bass, and Art Blakey on the skins.

He looks up at the backs of the heads of the regulars sitting around the half-square bar. They have now resumed their talk.

A gray-haired, blue-eyed, bearded man at the bar nods at Kerrigan's Associate. She returns the greeting, tells Kerrigan, "That is Ib Schierbeck, who has owned and managed many bookstores in Copenhagen." Schierbeck nods at Kerrigan, and Kerrigan recognizes a picture of Wilbert Harrison on the wall. "'Kansas City'!" he yelps to his Associate, and a very tall man rises from his table to approach theirs. She whispers to Kerrigan, "That is Niels Jørgen Steen, the conductor of the Tivoli Big Band."

"You are American," the tall man says in English. "You know Kansas City?"

Kerrigan has been to Kansas City many times, and the man asks, "Then you know Kansas City brought jazz from big band to bebop, right? The birthplace was New Orleans, but jazz was raised in K.C."

"Ah," Kerrigan says. "I never thought about that."

"You know Charlie Parker was born in K.C., right?"

"I do now."

"And Ben Webster? And Big Joe Turner? And that Jay McShann lived and died there?"

"Actually I didn't know any of that," Kerrigan admits, noting from the corner of his eye that his Associate is taking it all down.

The man stares at him for several moments, then says mildly, "You don't know shit, do you?" and moves back to his own table in the far corner and orders another triple Jack Daniel's, salutes Kerrigan with his glass. Kerrigan, feeling chastened but enlightened, raises his Tuborg.

Jazz Masters 25 is playing now, Verve label, Getz and Gillespie blowing "Dark Eyes" from '56. The mere thought of the year fills Kerrigan with wonder. Nineteen fifty-six. He can remember the Chevies that year clear as day—the way the tail fins had begun to lift a little from the angular line of the '55, softly curving up, but not yet the sharp fins of the '57. In '56 the classic rock was just emerging: Chuck Berry, Bo Diddley,

Jerry Lee Lewis, Wilbert Harrison, Buddy Holly, who would die three years later in a plane crash on February 3, 1959, when Kerrigan was still only fifteen. In 1956, Elvis Presley was still good, even if he sang cleaned-up lyrics, and Kerrigan turned thirteen, just stepping into puberty. School dances at St. Joan's and the impossible loveliness of Mary Ella Delahanty and Patsie O'Sullivan. He remembers Mary Ella's smile and Patsie's blue eyes and still can feel the sweet, pure yearning.

Another figure approaches their table, a smiling-faced man with spaces between his teeth and a wispy mustache. He says very quietly, "Want to hear some good jazz?" and goes behind the bar—apparently half the people in the place are bartenders—to put on a Danish Radio Big Band tribute to Duke Ellington, recorded in honor of what would have been the Duke's hundredth birthday that year. It begins with "Take the A Train."

"Billy Strayhorn," says Kerrigan.

"Niels Jørgen Steen," says the man with the wispy mustache, nodding back at the corner table where the big man sits drinking triple whiskeys.

It occurs to Kerrigan as he replenishes their drinks that this place is a true Bohemian bar. Nothing trendy. Just a good old low-down neighborhood joint where people who like jazz and reasonably priced drinks and friendly company can come and listen to Adderley and Davis and try to decipher the German on a Brecht poster, raffle for drinks, swap stories, play guessing games, and a man like Niels Jørgen can come and not feel that everyone is staring at his fame.

Gazing at the Brecht poster, Kerrigan yearns to hear poor dead Bobby Darin sing "Mack the Knife." He asks Ruth if she has that among her CDs, and she shakes her head with a pleasant smile, but his Associate says, "I have it. On an LP."

"You *do*?" She nods, and Kerrigan asks in Danish, "Will you invite me for a nightcap then?"

She blows a thin stream of gray cigarette smoke through pursed smiling lips and assents with a nod.

* * *

They walk back along Classensgade, and his Associate is saying, "Ruth always reminds me of a girlfriend I knew when I was about twelve." Then she begins to chuckle. "We were in the country for a weekend, at a farm. And there was a horse in the pasture. A stallion." She holds her palms out, facing each other, a foot and a half apart. "He was enormous, and we couldn't quite figure out what it was so we tried to ask the farmer, and he said, 'The horse? That's Jax.' We got hysterical laughing, and then all day, for weeks after that, all we had to do to break up laughing was one of us would say 'Jax!'"

They are laughing together now as they walk through what, to Kerrigan's weak eyes, is the impressionistic night.

In her apartment again as Darin sings about Lotte Lenya, Mack the Knife, and old Lucy Brown, she lights candles, puts out ice and glasses, a bottle of Chivas, and his breath goes shallow as they undress one another on the sofa.

"You are radiant," he whispers, his eyes full of her lovely shoulders and breasts that look much bigger uncovered, tipped with nipples the size and color and texture of berries.

"He who flatters, gets," she whispers.

Then he whispers, "*Jax!*" and she laughs, but the laughter quickly turns to something else that draws them from self-consciousness and absorbs them at once in their senses and emotions.

The night is full of amazements. Kerrigan had heard the term "multiple orgasms" before but never witnessed it. He listens in awe as she cries out again and again, lulls, begins anew, until finally he reaches his own single height and drops into exhaustion on the rumpled sheets.

Then she is weeping in his arms, and he strokes her hair. "There, there," he whispers, watching a silver triangle of moonlight on the tall white wall. "What is it?"

"So hopeless," she says. Her face is unattractive weeping, and his immediate thoughts are of escape, but he says, "*What's* so hopeless?"

"Me. All of it." She reaches to the bed stand for a Kleenex and blows her nose. "I'm fifty-seven years old—no, I lied, I'm fifty-eight—and still mourning over lost chances and stupid choices. I've wasted my life."

"Hey, it's not too late. It's never too late."

"I'll never be able to make up for all this lost time," she says. "I have never learned." She draws back to look into his eyes. "I have something in me," she says. "I *do*. But I have never been able to express it."

He pulls her close and says, "You will. You will if you don't give up," and his thoughts are torn between escape and desire. All this emotion unnerves him. The fullness of her breasts against his chest, the fear of this, his uneasiness at getting involved.

Out in the kitchen, he discovers a chilled bottle of cava and brings it back to the bedroom with two glasses, and they sit up on the mattress with fizzling flutes. She is smiling tenderly now, and her skin is dappled in moonlight through the open-curtained window. He places his lips against the silken skin of her neck, her shoulder, the passage between her breasts. They click their glasses. She sips but he drinks deeply, finds himself peering into the green shadows of her gaze.

"Tell me," she whispers.

"Tell you what?"

"What you're not telling me. What is so heavy inside you. Share it with me." She puts her flute on the nightstand and wraps her arms around him, draws his face to the comfort of her chest. At first he stiffens his shoulders, but then the sting of water burns his eyes as it brims from them, and he relaxes.

In the quiet darkness, he begins to speak.

Four: The Green Peril

We drank absinthe—light green
as the woods and as frogs,
Campari red as breathless
kisses and red panties.
—JENS AUGUST SCHADE

There are two kinds of hangover. The word for the first in Danish, *tømmermænd*, covers the physical sort, "carpenters"—hammering and sawing in your head. But the other kind is more agonizing, the moral sort.

His first conscious thought when he opens his eyes and smells coffee is enthusiastic: to continue his tavernological studies, the exhilaration of sexual meeting . . . But then he remembers her tears in the dark, then that he succumbed to the security of her flesh—Brando in *Last Tango* speaking about building a fortress of a woman's tits and cunt, and the memory of the image of that silver triangle of moonlight on the tall shadowy white wall oozes into a moral hangover, seems to speak ineffable things about the gloomy future.

He rises, steps under a steaming shower, and the hot stream of water soothes his head. He finds a brand-new blue toothbrush in the medicine chest, tears off the cellophane wondering if it was purchased specifically for him—or for whomever.

As he returns to the bedroom, toweling himself, she is there, wearing red jeans and T-shirt. Her eyes take in his naked body, and the sight of her doing that raises him behind the towel. "Coffee's soon ready," she says. "I have taken the day off. I didn't make breakfast because it's a little late for breakfast, and I know a restaurant I'd like to invite you to for lunch. It should be in your book. My treat this time."

"You don't have to."

"I know. But I want to. I insist."

As she moves back to the kitchen, she sings one of *Svante's Ballads* by Benny Andersen, almost untranslatable, about life being not the worst thing to have and soon the coffee is ready, and about a woman coming naked from the bath while her man eats a cheese sandwich.

Kerrigan wanders about the living room as he waits, runs his fingers along the spines of books on a shelf: Several volumes about Copenhagen and Denmark, its kings, fortifications, humble establishments, cemeteries, authors, artists, statuary, history . . . On another shelf are Khalil Gibran in Danish, *Dreams, Women Who Run with Wolves, The Ninth Prophecy*, a leather-bound works of Jack London in four volumes in Danish, Ovid's *Art of Love*. He tips out the latter, leafs through to two places marked with tiny red feathers, advising that the light in a bedroom should not be too bright as there are many things about a woman best seen under a dim lamp, especially with older women, although the years bring the erotic wisdom of experience.

Among her CDs he finds Coltrane's *My Favorite Things,* puts it on, and stands by the tall window listening, staring out to the vast, weed-sprung empty lot across the avenue, hearing the familiar melody devolve, spiraling away from the harmonies, becoming stronger then, when the sax seems to reach a place of pure formless sound, working slowly back down and into the melody again. He looks at the back of the CD and reads liner notes by the composer La Monte Young, saying that if the universe is composed of vibrations, the music of Coltrane can lead to an understanding of universal structure.

The hair lifts on Kerrigan's arms as he hears the soprano move back again out of the harmonies, breaking free of one structure to find a purer one, music without harmony, the supreme structure of the unstructured, pure sound, world without word . . . Or is it, in fact, destruction, self-destruction, the obliteration of structure—or perhaps what is obliterated is recognizable structure—sameness.

Kerrigan reads on the album that the number was recorded in October 1960, released in March 1961, that it was Coltrane's first recording on a soprano sax, that it was bought for him by Miles Davis earlier in

1960 when they were on tour in Europe. Coltrane would have been just thirty-four, six more years to live.

And it occurs to him that all of these improvisations are etched into his own brain already just as they are pressed into vinyl and, therefore, are no longer really improvisations. They were only improvisations when Coltrane created them and, to Kerrigan, when he himself heard them for the first time. Then they became something else, that he hears in his head, both fascinated and colonized by the notes, drawn into the rapid flow of them, but no longer surprised, abandoned to it, but in some way captive to it as well, like being buckled into a car on a familiar roller coaster, its dips and jerks and climbs and falls predictable, still exciting, but you are a prisoner of the sound now—because it keeps going inside your brain and no way to turn it off until you forget about it.

The thought is so heady he has to turn from the window, and his eye falls on a strip of pale orange wall between white-lacquered woodwork. Down the strip of wall are mounted half a dozen oil paintings, unframed, pinned to the plaster. Miniatures, each the size of a large postcard.

He has to stand close to see without his glasses. The first is identifiable, a red starfish on an abstract green-and-orange background. The next is a purple-on-purple oval. At first he thinks it is an antique portrait, but on closer inspection he sees it is an abstraction. There is a title, *Girl in a Swing*, and he can almost but not quite identify the subject of the title. Those that follow are by turn more and more abstract, figures from a dream, blue, red, white, black, but the last one leaps out at him— a red frog. He feels he's seen that picture before, that she has seen into his mind and brought forth an image from inside it. All are painted on a heavy backing that feels coarse to the tip of his finger, more like stiff cotton fabric than canvas.

He lights a cigar just as she comes in with coffee pot and cups on an oval tray.

"These are amazing," he says. "Did you do them? That red frog—"

"That one I did for you. You kept talking about absinthe green as a frog and Campari red as kisses so I thought of combining them for you. Do you like it?"

"I love it. I love them all. They're fucking good."

"No need to humor me," she says.

"I'm not. They're fucking good."

She smirks, and anger boils up in him. He snaps into her startled face, "I *said* they're fucking good!"

She is looking up at him now with a curious, naked expression he would never have expected to see on her face, and he remembers suddenly how her face looked beneath his as they made love, eyes wide, brilliant with pleasure, the surprise and surrender of her smile as she came again and again . . .

But he has told her about Licia, about his daughter, about the conception that may or may not have been . . . Somehow letting it out, letting another see it made it realer. Especially when she said that her daughters had been taken, too—by marriage—in Canada and the U.S.A. "Once a child lets go of your hand, they never take it again," she whispered in the dark.

He wishes he hadn't told her, wishes he could take it back.

Now she is still looking at her paintings. "Do you really mean it?"

"Yes."

She looks up at them as though she has never seen them before. "How could they be good? I painted them all in one weekend. Two days ago. The day I came for you at the White Lamb. I was desperate. It all seemed so hopeless, working as a secretary and playing at being an artist on the weekends."

"You *are* an artist."

"What makes you so sure?"

"I have a good eye. I can see it. It's right there." He gestures up the strip of wall. "Trust me. These pictures are fucking good."

"*Fucking* good," she teases. "Maybe it's just because you fucked me. Maybe you're just cunt struck."

"You're pissing me off," he says, and glowers at her. "Better watch it."

Her eyes brighten. "I like you that way," she says. "Do you 'ave a leetle Franshman inside you?"

"Jax!" he says, shoving his face toward hers, and their laughter combines, hers musical, his throaty, and he thinks maybe it was okay he told her.

"Now we have to choose," she says, blushing. "Is it breakfast or something else?"

"Why either-or? Why not both-and? First the one. Then the other." But he does not want to make love just now. He wants to get out of here, away from the possibility of intimacy, to consider what he has done. He has never told anybody before.

They take a long walk along **Strandboulevarden** in the late morning sun to build hunger's anticipation and optimism. She points up at the wall of number 27, at a plaque that notes Georg Brandes lived there. They pass the **Østerport Station**, then stroll along **Grønningen** with its beautiful erotic sculpture of *The Reclining Girl* by Gerhard Henning, originally a miniature from 1914, finally a full-size bronze in 1945.

They pause to gaze on her from the sidewalk where she lies on her pedestal in a grass clearing before a pond, beautiful and rounded, one arm folded over her head as if casually to draw attention to the fullness of her breasts, one foot under one calf, one knee raised, her luscious inner thigh. Kerrigan is stirred to the point that he regrets having wanted to escape from his Associate's apartment.

Their pace slows, and they move closer together after viewing the sculpture. He drapes an arm around her shoulder and she smiles up at him, and he feels himself leaning toward her. Down Grønningen to Esplanaden, across to Bredgade, past the Catholic cathedral, St. Ansgar's— with the skull of Lucius I inside his bust—and on to **Dronningens Tvær Street**, to number 12, a semibasement restaurant that used to, she informs him via her Moleskine, be named *Jomfruen*—the Virgin—and is now **Kælder 12**—Basement 12, owned by a couple from Bornholm. Eight steps down into the restaurant. His Associate links her arm into Kerrigan's, and he clasps her hand in his. The restaurant is pleasantly empty, only one table taken.

"Have you a table for two for lunch?" he asks the owner, a tall, black-and-gray-bearded fellow named Alan. "I think we can manage that," he says with the slightest of ironic garnishes at which Danes are so adept. "Are you a Dane who moved to America?" he asks. "They have accents, too."

"No, I'm an American who moved to Denmark. Everyone has some kind of accent," Kerrigan says, recalling the girl he spoke to in the New Orleans airport once who asked him where his accent was from. He told her New York via Copenhagen and asked where hers was from. "Where ah come from," she said, "we don't hayev accents."

His Associate recommends a dish on the menu called *bakskuld*—a fish in Danish called *ising*, a type of flounder, a flat fish. Kerrigan asks the waiter how the fish is prepared.

"Now that fish is definitely served dead," he says. "First it is air-cured for twenty-four hours, then it is salted for another twenty-four, then smoked for yet another twenty-four. And then I fry it."

Kerrigan scrapes the succulent, salty, smoked flesh from the flounder's skeleton and lifts it with knife and fork onto the coarse rye bread, squeezes the lime quarters over it, and closes his eyes with pleasure when the delicate, salty meat hits his tongue. He lifts his stem glass and peers into her delightful green eyes. "This fish must swim down our gullets." They are drinking doubles of O. P. Anderson snaps, and Kerrigan is at ease again. His Associate consults her Moleskine, reads, "Olof Peter Anderson, Swedish, 1797 to 1876. But the snaps was launched by his son, Carl August Anderson, in 1891. One hundred and eight years ago."

They salute with their glasses, sip, present them again, their eyes meet, they nod. "I feel so good," he says, "that I might even eat a sweet afterwards." He lifts his eyebrows, gazing at her.

She smiles—thinking, he hopes, of those exquisite moments in the dark the night before, and not of what he has told her about his life, about Licia.

"Did you know," he asks, "apropos sweets, that what you Danes call Vienna bread, *wienerbrød*, the Americans call Danish pastry?"

"Yes, and we call it Vienna bread because there was a bakers' strike in

Copenhagen in the nineteenth century, and some imported Viennese bakers taught us to like the very delicate, layered pastry we call Vienna bread. American Danish is so heavy and sticky."

"You're not a fan of sweets?" he asks in English, eager to get her speaking it, too, to hear her charming accent.

"Most are either to spice or sweets, not both. I am to spice."

"Well, I would dearly like to spice you right now. And sweet you, too. I'm to both," he adds, imitating her characteristic Danish preposition misuse, which charms him.

Her smile is dizzying with its open loveliness, and it is a blessed late April day, even if the *Politiken* he leafed through earlier predicted snow and what the Danes call *Aprilsvejr*, April weather, which runs the full spectrum of the four seasons in constant flux, practically from second to second.

The snaps and beer make him remember the pleasures of their bodies, and he smiles dreamily at her.

"You really liked them?" she asks. "The paintings?"

"No. I lied. They're terrible. And you're lousy in bed, too."

"Couldn't be worse than you. You know," she says, "instead of dessert, I vas thinking of a freshly smoked eel with warm scrambled egg on dark, coarse, home-baked rye with fresh chopped chives and new ground pepper."

"And another double O. P. Anderson?"

"Of course. Eel must swim, too, *skat*," she says in Danish, and that word of endearment, *skat*, treasure, can be either ironic or sincere, and he can hear that it is sincere passing from her lovely mouth. He leans across to touch her lips with his, tasting aquavit and lime on her tongue, then peers into her green smiling eyes.

The eel and pepper and meniscus of O. P. shoot to his brain, and Kerrigan whispers to his Associate, "Thank you."

"For what?"

"For thinking of the eel, of course!"

He notices an *Ekstra Bladet*—the raunchier of the two leading Danish tabloids—on a chair, and they titillate themselves by scanning the massage ads in the back: *Pussyclub kinky hot superbitch Susi, supersexed blonde with big tits and piquant butt carries out your special wishes. Everything in rubber, leather and plastic. Hot nude stripshow, gentle tingling bondage, urine cocktails, slave rearing, nurse sex, baby treatment, analblockage, long-term bondage, public humiliation, weight clips, thumbtacks pins and hands-macking with a ruler!*

"Here's one," she says. "*Suzette offers devil-bizarre sheep herding.*"

"*Sheep* herding?"

"That's what it says. And *Sissi, genuine red cunt hair and double D cups.*"

"Yeah," he says, "but do the curtains match the rug?"

"How's this? *Kiss my foot while your wife watches!*"

"That's original."

"I'm getting excited," she says.

"Why? Would you like to kiss my foot while your wife watches?"

Her eyes blaze at him. "*Yes!*"

"Maybe we should just nip up to my place on the lakes," he suggests. She nods toward the back. "I just have to . . ."

As he waits he refuses to worry about whether or not there is some responsibility issue involved here, whether he is getting involved, implicitly making promises. They are both adults. You don't have to fall in love. There is no rule about that.

Through the semibasement window, Kerrigan notices a few round wet patches up on the pavement as the day removes the warmth of its caressing hand. The light darkens and he hears the low music of the restaurant's sound system. Synchronistically, Diana Krall is doing "Let's Fall in Love," and he is thinking that was recorded this year but was written by Harold Arlen and Ted Koehler in 1933, ten years before he was born. Despite her wish to treat, he beats her to it and is standing, looking out the glass door, as she comes up from behind and embraces him. Something in him wants to tense but he receives her embrace, melts into it, into the moment, into the joy of a woman wanting to embrace him like this, rejects worry until later. That time, that sorrow.

* * *

"God, I *love* it here," she says afterward, standing naked at the front windows of his apartment over Black Dam Lake, gazing out onto the rippling silver water beneath the young green of the chestnut trees. He watches her from behind, where he still lies naked on the double-foam mattress they threw down there to give themselves plenty of room to roll and rock. Relieved to have located his spare eyeglasses, he can see clearly again and studies her objectively, wonders if the flaws actually matter—at their age. *What would she see if I were at the window with my naked backside to her?* He remembers Ovid's advice: let the light in the bedroom be dim, especially with older women. But old Ovid was right about the wisdom of her experience. He removes his glasses to see her impressionistically again.

He is thinking about those strange advertisements they read in the tabloid to titillate themselves, and the present in which he exists seems suddenly like some weird science fiction movie of the future in which the world is organized in a strange manner with certain people as an underbreed in which they are manipulated by economics to sell their bodies to others who live in another sphere where the repression of their carnality is required as an imagined requisite for social order. This carnal suppression, however, calls forth strange desires that they must use the money their asexual occupations accrue for them to buy satisfaction amid the underbreed. He has a vision of some rich fat-cat executive who pays a large sum of cash to a street woman to piss on him. The thought is too weird for him to pursue just now.

He stretches luxuriously to free his mind of it. "What shall we drink now?"

"There's jazz at Krut's," she says, and looks at her watch—the only thing she is wearing. "Starts in about an hour."

"Tick tick tick," he says, and his eyes fall on his *Finnegan* satchel. He hasn't been reading it, despite his promises to himself that this time he really will. "Just think," he says. "If a person's not careful, he could die without ever having finished *Finnegans Wake*. What can you tell me about Krut's?"

"It is a delightful little place. They have one of the biggest selections of whiskeys in Copenhagen, and the whiskey menu has a map so you can see exactly where what you're drinking is from."

Since he can see again, he leads the way back across the Potato Rows to the café beneath the sign in blue neon script, **Krut's Karport**. On one wall hangs a framed green-and-yellow painting of an absinthe label— Krut's Karport's own brand of the 68 percent spirit, 136 proof. The label shows a man in a dented blue top hat, chin in hand at a table, a glass of the green spirit before him, while a red-haired woman standing behind the table studies the bottle against a green-yellow impressionist wall.

Kerrigan asks the pretty smiling waitress named, she tells them, Cirkeline, "Isn't absinthe illegal?"

"This is the only place you can get it in Copenhagen," she says. "We have a special permit."

"What does your Moleskine have to say about absinthe?" he asks his Associate.

"Say my name, and I shall tell you," she says, her pouting lower lip provoking him gently.

"Your name? Seems I did hear. Think I have it somewhere on the papers from the temp service."

"You bastard."

He smiles. "Annelise," he says, and delights in the naked pleasure of the smile with which she rewards him. "Wery good," she says, opening her Moleskine book. "Now I shall tell you about absinthe."

Originally absinthe was 72 percent alcohol, more of a demon than a spirit, she tells him. It resulted in considerable social misery in the nineteenth century in France. Edgar Degas's famous painting *L'Absinthe* from 1876—a woman seated at a rough wood table at the Parisian Café Nouvelle Athènes in Place Pigalle with a glass of the drink in front of her, her eyes empty—is a kind of portrait of late-nineteenth-century French alcoholism.

Absinthe is believed to have been concocted by a Swiss woman, Madame Henriod, in the late eighteenth century. It was distilled on a base of wormwood (*Artemisia absinthium*) and anise (*Pimpinella anisum*)—

spices that date back to ancient Egypt, Greece, and Arabia. In the Middle Ages, these spices were used to cure flatulence and also as an aphrodisiac.

"Liquor is still quicker," says Kerrigan.

Madame Henriod's formula was sold to an itinerant doctor who dispensed it as a cure for bad stomachs. From him, the formula was sold to a Swiss military man, Major Dubied, who set up the first absinthe distillery with the assistance of his son-in-law, Henri-Louis Pernod. In 1805 they began production in France. Originally it was drunk by French foreign legionnaires in North Africa, both as a water purifier and as a cure for weak intestines and, of course, for recreational use. Then they brought the habit home with them, and it caught on.

During the so-called belle epoque of fin de siècle France, it was drunk by pouring it over sugar cubes in a perforated spoon balanced on the mouth of the glass. It occurs to Kerrigan that they are also at a fin de siècle, but hardly a belle epoque. Or will it be seen as such one day?

It was referred to as *la fée verte*, the green fairy, by the French poet Paul Verlaine (1844–1896)—who is also known for having shot Arthur Rimbaud, the antiauthoritarian young poet (1854–1891), in the wrist in a lover's quarrel in 1873, the year Rimbaud wrote *A Season in Hell*—when he was only nineteen.

Kerrigan says, "He was also only seventeen when he wrote 'The Drunken Boat' and came up with the idea of the *déréglement de tous les sens*—the disordering of all the senses."

Zola, Baudelaire, and Van Gogh drank absinthe as well. Van Gogh is said to have been under its spell when he sliced off his ear, although recently it was suggested that in fact Gauguin cut off the ear with a fencing foil.

"A pair of character foils, ey?" Kerrigan says. "Ear done off by the green fairy."

The French working classes also used absinthe to "disarray their senses," but more to escape the harsh conditions of their lives than to court the muse. Soon the green fairy acquired a new nickname: *le péril vert*, the green peril. By 1915 it was banned, but in 1922 a new law allowed the production of anise liquors of no more than 40 percent without wormwood; in 1938, this was raised to 45 percent, ninety proof. Here the current French national drink, pastis, entered the scene, not green but yellow in color, and when diluted with water (five to one) it turns a milky hue. "*Un petit jaune, s'il vous plaît.*" A little yellow one, please.

Jake Barnes in Hemingway's *The Sun Also Rises* drinks absinthe straight, unsweetened, toward the end of that novel and describes the taste as "pleasantly bitter," but the "correct" way to drink it is as they did in the belle époque. The original absinthe has been known to cause hallucinations, but the wormwood used now is not *Artemisia absinthium*, which is illegal, but *Artemisia vulgaris*, and the level of *thujune*—a hallucinogenic chemical—is very low. The alcohol content is still high, however.

"How in the name of God do you get all that into that little notebook, Annelise?"

"My script is very fine," she says and gazes sweetly at him. "Terrence," she adds. "To speak a person's name is like a caress," she says and touches his cheek. "Terrence."

"Shall we have a touch of the green peril, Annelise?"

"I should prefer the green fairy."

"I would prefer green panties," he suggests, fluttering his eyebrows.

She says, "I think you are quoting Schade again," making a face that somehow seems to encourage by discouraging.

The absinthe comes in tiny measures, two centiliters. They taste it straight but it is too bitter, so they dilute it with sugar and water. She consults the Moleskine once more. "Oscar Wilde said the first makes you see things as you wish they were, the second as they are not, and the third as they really are, which is the most horrible thing in the world."

Chuckling, he peers at her, one eye cocked.

"You have the leer of the sensualist about you, Mr. Kerrigan," she says.

"Thank you. And let it be remembered that my subject is Celtic and my season spring. One other thing about absinthe," says Kerrigan. "They drank it in Tom Kristensen's *Havoc* in a variation known as the Blom cocktail, a kind of martini with four parts absinthe to one part gin." He shudders. "I understand people were drinking absinthe here in Copenhagen right up to the nineteen fifties when it was banned."

The jazz group is setting up now, featuring their old friend Asger Rosenberg with the mellifluous pipes. Kerrigan orders another, though Annelise goes over to white wine. He leans back in his chair and gazes through the window behind Bjørn Holstein, the yellow-shirted drummer, at the long pale street. A child runs in the direction of the lake at the other end of the street beneath a few flurries of April snow. The snow turns to a slushy rain that ends almost as soon as it starts, and sunlight colors the gray buildings across the way.

With his glasses on, he feels pleasure in seeing every brick in the gray-brown wall, and as Asger on bass behind Mogens Petersen on piano sings Benny Carter's "When Lights Are Low," Kerrigan finds himself contemplating the bricks, thinking of the hands that laid brick on brick to construct the wall, the building, the entire city. Thinking of the hands that made the bricks themselves, the hands that drew the plans, the people who envisaged it all, who led the work. Men driven by ambition, greed, passion, the desire to be part of the force that raised a block of dwellings, a street, a city, a civilization. And the German soldiers who marched in under orders of an evil madman and seized it, tried taking it away.

Asger is now singing Frank Loesser's "I Wish I Didn't Love You So."

Kerrigan is into his third absinthe and his thoughts ride the music into their own flight of ideas, back to Germany, to Alsace, where one of his father's ancestors fled, driven from Ireland in the eighteenth century by the Penal Laws, which denied Catholics the rights of citizens. Kerrigan's ancestor ended in Baden-Baden, where *his* son's son, Fred, in 1869, under pressure of conscription in the Franco-Prussian War, returned to Ireland and ended in Brooklyn in 1880, the year Maupassant (1850–1893) published his first story, "Boule de suif" ("Butterball"), shortly before his mentor, Gustave Flaubert, died.

In a French humor, Kerrigan contemplates the story that made Maupassant famous and was about the Franco-Prussian War, a French prostitute, a hypocritical group of well-off French citizens, and a wasp-waisted

German commander. The German marches his troops into Tôtes, making the pavement resound under their hard rhythmic step, driving the inhabitants into their rooms, experiencing the fatal sensation engendered every time the established order is overturned by force, when life is no longer secure, and the people in a society find themselves at the mercy of unreasoning brutality. The detachments rap at doors and enter the houses and occupy the town.

A small group of people use their influence to obtain permission to leave in a large stagecoach to flee to Dieppe, where they can find safety. In the coach are a variety of people representing a cross section of French society, from a count down to the simple woman mentioned in the title, the eponymous *boule de suif*, a butterball, a chubby woman with a sensual mouth; the implication is that she is little more than a prostitute.

At first the others in the carriage shun her. But their journey through the snowy fields proves much more difficult than expected. They go more than half a day without food and no prospect of getting any. Then they discover that she is the only one who has thought to bring provisions, a well-filled food hamper beneath her seat. Distracted by hunger, one by one they condescend to accept her humbly offered hospitality. They gorge themselves on the delicacies she has packed—chickens, pâté, glacé fruit, sweetmeats, wine, savories. In a few hours they eat food that could have lasted for days.

They come finally to Tôtes, where they are to spend the night, but find that it is occupied by Prussians. The commandant, the tall, slim waspwaisted man, examines their credentials before they go to their rooms, and he calls aside the *boule de suif.* Elizabeth Rousset. He wants to sleep with her, but she refuses vehemently. In the morning, they find that the stagecoach does not have permission to travel on. When they inquire why, the commandant replies simply, "Because I wish for it not to."

Each day, he sends a servant to ask Mademoiselle Rousset if she has changed her mind, and each day she assures him she will *never* do so.

Her traveling companions are initially outraged, but soon think it over and tacitly agree to try to convince her to give the man that which she has so freely given so many others. They conspire to convince her it is her patriotic duty to do so. When with extreme reluctance she does give in, they gather in the dining room and drink champagne to celebrate their impending deliverance—all but one of them, Cornudet, a beer-swilling democrat. The others grow intoxicated and bawdy, tittering over what is being perpetrated in the rooms above. Only Cornudet reprimands them for their disgraceful behavior, but after he has stomped off to bed, another of them, who has lurked in the corridors, spying, tells them that two nights before, Cornudet unsuccessfully propositioned the *boule de suif,* and the others resume their merriment, content that Cornudet's outrage has nothing to do with honor or disgrace but with mere jealousy.

When the couples retire to their chambers, they are charged with passion stimulated by the act of prostitution that will soon free them.

In the morning, however, when the *boule de suif* appears at the carriage that the commandant has now released, they turn their backs on her. And as the carriage continues toward Dieppe, this time it seems that she is the only one who has not thought—or had time—to bring along provisions. The others dine on theirs and ignore her, letting her go hungry while they stuff themselves.

Finally this injustice brims up in her and tears slide down her cheeks, and one of the goodwives mutters that the woman weeps with shame. Cornudet plops his feet on the seat across from him and, with an expression of disdain for the company, whistles "The Marseillaise," and his tune and the sobs of the *boule de suif* echo between the two rows of people in the shadows.

Asger leans over his bass squinting at the sheet music, singing how in his woman's eyes he sees strange things that her kiss seems to deny, and the image brings Kerrigan back from Alsace as Licia invades his mind again, her eyes that never revealed her lack of love, so he saw no strange things in them that her kiss had to deny.

How still he feels. Perhaps it is the frog-green absinthe. The room seems frozen as he views its small movements from within the deep stillness of loss in which he is engulfed while Asger croons.

Her fingernails are long and polished a deep green, he notices now, as they lift slowly to caress the back of his neck. His eyes turn toward the green shadows of her gaze.

"Hey, Terrence," she whispers. "You're not alone."

Five: As Sane As I Am

It is forbidden
to throw foreign particles
in the VC bowl
—NOTICE ON THE OSLO BOAT

A long walk on a chilly May morning chases demons. For a time. Unshaven but bathed, he hikes briskly, fleeing a fragment of memory about his Associate that unnerves him. Away from the lakes toward Strøget, the Walking Street, a mile-long pedestrian walk curving through the heart of Copenhagen.

At **Gammel Torv**, the Old Square, he pauses to consider **Caritas Springvanden**, the Charity Fountain, Copenhagen's oldest surviving public monument, erected nearly four hundred years ago, between 1607 and 1609. A large, round, late-renaissance-style fountain, a pillar rising from the center on which stands Charity as the *Virgo Lactans* (in Danish *den diegivende jomfru*, literally "the tit-giving virgin"). Charity is holding a little child with a larger one beside, each holding a flaming heart, symbol of the love of God. At their feet three dolphins play, and the fountain's water flows from the virgin Charity's nipples.

Kerrigan gazes upward at the overflowing nipples and remembers tasting Licia's sweet milk when his daughter was an infant. The memory whets the desire of his tongue for a drink of the Lethe waters known as beer. He gazes across **Gammel Torv** to **Ny Torv**—Old Square to New Square—toward the tall columns of the City Court (**Byretten**), built between 1803 and 1816 by the architect C. F. Hansen. The building is tall and light; chiseled above the pillars in Danish are the words ON LAW A LAND IS BUILT from the Danish Law of 1241. In the middle of the square is where beheadings used to be conducted, and off beyond the courthouse is **Slutterigade** (Prison Street), beneath the Bridge of Sighs, across which prisoners are led from jail to judgment.

He hikes down toward **Pilestræde**, Willow Lane, to **Charlie's**, but stands peering in through a locked front gate, not open till four. Some twenty years before, this was a bookshop owned by an Englishman named Charlie who was losing money on books, so he turned it into a wine room that is still thriving, even after Charlie's death, though its focus now has turned to beer. Kerrigan perfunctorily rattles the metal gate, turns away, up past the **Bobi Bar** at **Klareboderne 14,** where inter alia journalists and literati drink, but he really doesn't have time. He has made a Tivoli Gardens luncheon appointment in a short while with a Norwegian psychiatrist named Thea Ylajali who has promised him much-needed advice about his Associate and about himself.

He crosses past Nørreport toward the **King's Garden** and enters the gate at **Brandes Plads** with a nod to the bust of Georg Brandes, brother of Edvard, who in 1888, having read the first thirty-page fragment of Knut Hamsun's *Hunger*, correctly predicted for him a great literary future, encouraging him to expand it into a novel, though he could not know Hamsun would end in shame due to a combination of senility and 1930s National Socialist sentiments.

The blood pounds in his pumping legs as he passes Aksel Hansen's sculpture *Echo* from 1888—a realistic representation of the doomed nymph unable to express her love, able only to call out a repetition of the last word spoken to her. Her form is alert and distressed amid the beech trees, and Kerrigan thinks of her vainly pursuing Narcissus, himself doomed to love only his own reflection. He considers the fact that this ancient Greek myth is embodied here in this sculpture in a Danish public garden. Why? As a warning? Against being lost in oneself? He wonders if he will ever again open his heart to love. If he ever really has in the first place.

Kerrigan marvels that in his fifties he is still seriously asking what love is. Beyond passion, custom, tradition, social commitment? He thinks of Licia, asks himself if his love for her had been genuine or mere delusion, and the thought touches off emotion so terrifying he feels he could be cast in stone by fear, trapped in it like Echo, like Narcissus, like a child hiding under a bed in terror of the unknown gods who drive the wind and rain, hurl spears of lightning, rouse the booming of thunder.

His legs begin to tire, but he will not slow while the demons are after him. He leaves the park at a fast clip, cuts toward **H. C. Andersens Boulevard**, loops around **Dantesplads**, Dante's Place, named for the Italian poet Dante Alighieri (1265–1321) on the occasion of the six hundredth anniversary of his death "so that the Danish people might strengthen their soul with Dante's spirit."

From the center of the traffic island in the middle of the boulevard rises **Dantesøjlen**, the Dante Pillar, sculpted by Einar Utzon-Frank. Atop the pillar stands not Dante Alighieri but his beloved Beatrice, who, in the paradise of *The Divine Comedy*, guides him to the supreme bliss of contemplating God. Inscribed on the base of the pedestal are the words *Incipit Vita Nova*; Here begins the new life.

Kerrigan crosses to the opposite side of H. C. Andersens Boulevard, wondering if he is lost in a dark wood of his life, far from the right road, if his life will ever find a place for the true bliss of theological contemplation, if he even desires or believes in that. Where is he now in truth? Back amid the song of Augustine's cauldron of unholy loves in the Carthage of Copenhagen? Or in the proper place of mankind, the temporal joys of the carnal world, for the joy of the senses is also consolation while one lives, competing with the *donna gentile* of philosophy. How could he still be so lost in his fifties?

Perhaps, in truth, the mere desire for love, the yearning for God, is all we can achieve on earth, the highest place. The question then is how to celebrate that desire, that yearning. Through rituals of blood and death and strife? Or through the enactment of ecstasy?

But in his ecstasy with his Associate in the dark of her bedroom that last night they spent together, he heard, or thought he heard, or maybe only thought or heard an echo in his mind of a phrase that terrifies him and sets the demons of his Licia hell at his heels again. And whether he heard it or thought he heard, or maybe only thought it, he needs advice from Dr. Ylajali.

As he approaches the tall front gates of the **Tivoli Gardens**, he digs into his pocket to pay, pushes through the turnstile, and feels his heart straining to be released to the innocent worldly pleasures of this place— its gardens and amusements, its concerts and fine restaurants and snack bars and bars and shooting galleries and lake and rides—all places he never had the pleasure of taking Gabrielle.

Kerrigan flees to the Ditch, **Grøften**, and the company of his favorite headshrinker, Thea Ylajali of Oslo, whom he met in Vigeland Park some years ago, strolling through the long sculpted esplanade of naked bronzes by Gustav Vigeland.

Now she sits across the table from him reading aloud the poetry of Constantine Cavafy (1863–1933)—specifically, a poem written 105 years before, "The City," about places and seas that will never be found, for the city will follow you . . .

Kerrigan responds with a quote of his own that has been singing in his mind since he saw the Charity Fountain earlier: "Blessed are the paps which you have sucked."

"Vhat is this?" she asks. "Henry Miller?"

"It's Luke the apostle. Chapter nine, verse twenty-seven. 'Blessed is the womb that bore you and the paps which you have sucked.'"

"Really? It says this in the Bible? Well, here is another," she says, turning back to her Cavafy to read a poem about erotic visions that must be kept alive, be it night or brilliant noon.

It is brilliant noon, and Thea is six feet two inches tall, and she is in Copenhagen for only a few hours. He wishes to know whether she thinks he is mentally ill. He also wishes to know her carnally, to explore the heights and depths of her. She has the longest legs and shortest miniskirts he has ever witnessed, but there is no time for that now. She will board the boat back to Oslo in four hours and just as well.

He remembers an earlier adventure with her on the Oslo boat, sailing across a storm-tossed Skagerrak back toward Copenhagen. They danced in the discotheque, gliding in a knot of people across the dance floor like some number choreographed by the pitching sea. It was to have been their night of carnal introduction—implicit in the fact of their agreeing to share a cabin on the crossing. They danced slow, close, and a young drunken Norwegian kept tapping him on the shoulder to cut in, saying grandly, "I vant to dance vith thee voman," finally grabbed two heaping handfuls of Thea's butt, whereupon Kerrigan sent him away with a sharp word, but the lad only came back a few minutes later to apologize for his brother's bad behavior, so they retired to their sea-view cabin. The pitching, however, soon had them taking turns talking to God on the big white telephone on the wall above which was printed:

IT IS FORBIDDEN
TO THROW FOREIGN PARTICLES
IN THE VC BOWL

as Kerrigan heaved into it everything he had inside him.

Somehow the crossing annulled all progress toward carnality in their friendship. Now he only wants to talk to her, yet what he hears himself say when he opens his mouth is, "Thea, have you ever considered the advantages of love with an older, shorter man?"

She blinks and smiles, unspeaking, over the edge of her modern Greek poetry and plate of smoked eel.

"Not a chance, I guess," he says.

"Do not give up so qvickly," she tells him. "Hass anyone ever told you that you are a sexy?" And the mouthful of smoked peppered eel he chews goes straight to his brain with a jolt of optimisms. He lifts his glass, says, "*Multatuli*, Ylajali."

"There is nothing wrong with you," she tells him. "You are . . . how shall I say it . . . groovy. Do they still say that? I could not bear a man who iss not groovy."

He has been telling her about his life, his project, his Associate, how last time they were together, following a hefty bout of love, clamped between her smooth sinewy legs, beneath her burning eyes and glinting teeth, he heard her whisper in the dark—or did he dream it?—the same words that Licia had drunkenly uttered to him that summer night: *You are so blind.*

Or did she say, "I am so blind"? Or did he just think it. Or maybe she said, "You are so kind." But why would she say that? He had not been particularly kind to her. And he could not remember, when he had told her about Licia that night, whether he included the detail of what she had said to him that summer night in the garden.

Whatever she might have said, whether he told her or not, or if he only thought it, it unnerved him—even if it *was* at the height of passion, even if she had reached to the stand beside her bed into a little round straw-colored basket where she kept a supply of condoms and removed a tiny flask encased in glossy yellow paper with a label that identified it as Room Incense. She unscrewed the cap and held the mouth of the flask to his nostril, and he breathed it in and ascended immediately to a peak of sensory ecstasy. Then she sniffed it herself and leaned back her head and hissed an open-mouthed, slow, serpentlike breath as he went down on her. Then, just as he was touching earth again, the flask was at his nostril once more, then at hers, and they were delirious with ecstasy. And then she said it, her lips whispered at his ear, and one of the words was blind or kind, but why would she say kind at just that moment? No, she said, "You're so blind," and why would she say that? Or he thought it, but why would he think it in *her* voice?

Whether or whatever she said or he thought, Kerrigan found himself not phoning again, or phoning with excuses (visitors, projects, business), fleeing in fear for his heart but retreating to a perimeter from which he looked back, fearing the more he wants of the same.

You're so blind, she said as they were blind with the ecstasy of a popper. Although he is not unaware of the possibility that it might have emanated from the shadowy regions of his own mind.

"There are two pos-si-bi-li-ties," Thea tells him. "Either she has said this. Or not. If the latter case, then perhaps you were hearing echoes from your memory stirred up by your passion. If the former case, perhaps it iss an ecstatic *conicedence* of thought stirred up by the *coniceding* of your climaxes. You had climax together?"

"Yes, we did."

"In that case, I would not vorry. Give it chance. And Dr. Kerrigan, you are as sane as I am," Thea tells him, then adds bemusedly, "I wonder if we shall become lovers today," a forkful of eel hovering at her lips before she bites.

The sun shines through the branches of the overhanging trees across her lippy face, and he both desires and fears her, there where they sit beneath an open-air display of miniature aviation balloons.

"This restaurant is groovy," she tells him, and flips a page in her Cavafy.

"It was opened in 1874," he tells her. "The balloon decor is in commemoration of its second manager, Lauritz Johansen, a famous balloon pilot."

"Fascinating," she says, and he wonders if it is meant ironically.

Kerrigan finishes the last heavenly morsel of his eel, convinced that it is nourishing mythological Celtic sectors of his soul as well as his body, and goes for the aged cheese he has ordered, embellished with chopped onion, jelled meat drippings, radishes bathed in a shot of Hansen's rum, a favorite among sailors. Cheese so old and strong it makes his gums ache.

"This requires a snaps," he says, and signals the waitress.

They toast with iced Norwegian Linje snaps. *Linje* is Scandinavian for "equator", every drop of it is, by tradition, shipped across the equator in oak sherry kegs before bottling. It gives the aquavit a tawny tint and flavor at once spicy and mellow.

"*Skål*," says Kerrigan, and Thea reads a Cavafy poem about a young man dazed, mesmerized by the forbidden pleasure that he has just experienced, his blood fresh and hot.

Kerrigan finds himself wondering whether she really listened when he told her what Licia did to him and what she said to him—sufficiently so to make judgment on his mental state. Easy enough for her to pronounce him sane if she didn't really listen. She pronounced him sane so quickly. And, anyway, perhaps she herself is mad.

"Tell me your fantasies," she says.

"I don't have any."

She laughs at his fear, producing in him an involuntary fantasy of himself naked and at her mercy as she prepares figuratively to tear open his heart to release myriad small red perversions to go running about the room.

"I find it hard to relax," he says.

"Relaxation is a wery much overrated state," she tells him, and looks at her watch. "By the way, a rhetorical question: How long does it take to get to your apartment from here?" she asks, smiling, blinking like a cat.

Afterward he drifts in sweat-cooled sleep, her long naked body close beside him on his narrow electric bed, her voice hushed as she seeks to arouse him for yet another bout by telling him some of the fantasies reported to her by her patients.

"Isn't that unethical?" he asks.

"Not if I do not tell you the patient's name. Anon-ee-mous da-ta."

Kerrigan tries not to listen as she speaks, watching a red spider hanging in an invisible web on the other side of the windowpane, twitching in the flow of air, limned in sunlight. He wonders whether this could be considered a breach of faith to his Associate and remains silent when Thea asks again about his own fantasies. He is thinking how it felt to have her sitting on him, her pillowy lips on his, his face between her long white thighs. What better fantasy than that? Smother me in the gentle way. But he is also thinking about his Associate. How good it was to go down on her, all poppered up. But then she said it. Perhaps, after all, he can live with the memory of her saying that. If she said it at all. If he didn't just think it. And if he thought it so vividly, what does that say about his mental state?

Her own favored fantasy, Thea tells him now, is of sitting at her work table naked. It is very hot and she spreads her legs wide to air herself while unbeknownst to her a naked man creeps in the door on all fours, crawling silently across the room, beneath her desk . . .

Kerrigan's blood begins to stir. He goes to the refrigerator for a bottle of champagne, returns to her to drown his worry in it and in her, thinking of Karen Blixen's advice always to have a little bubbly with one's predicament.

At the gangway to the Oslo boat, he kisses her. She has to lean down to his mouth. He says, "My fantasy is to crawl up out of the water and climb the long blonde legs of a giant beautiful blonde Nordic goddess . . ."

She laughs. "You are as sane as I," she tells him, and is off up the sloping ramp, canvas overnighter on her shoulder, to return to her husband, a violin maker who keeps two pet wolves.

"Aren't wolves dangerous?" he asks her.

"So too are wiolins," she says.

At the top of the ramp she turns, waves, blows a kiss from her pillowy lips. *You are as sane as I*, he thinks. And *You're so blind*. And IT IS FORBIDDEN TO THROW FOREIGN PARTICLES IN THE VC BOWL. And *I vant to dance vith thee voman!* And *You are a sexy*.

Kerrigan stands in the center of the King's New Square, Kongens Nytorv, which is in fact a circle within a square, and wonders if he is pleased with himself. He thinks of Thea, tall and golden as the monolith of naked bodies at the heart of Vigeland Park in Oslo, *The Wheel of Life*, Gustav Vigeland's monument to existence. But his thoughts drift toward Gustav's brother, Emanuel Vigeland, and his monument to death, **Tomba Emmanuelle**, at **Grimelundsveien 8** in the **Slemdal** area of Oslo. Emanuel spent twenty years constructing his own mausoleum there, a vaulted churchlike structure, bricked-in windows, dark and echoing, black, dimly illuminated walls painted with figures of copulating skeletons, women giving birth, skeletons giving birth, copulating sculptures barely visible in the dim corners.

He shivers.

Yet above the entry way is printed the Latin inscription: *Quicquid Deus creavit purum est*. "All that God has created is pure." God who brings flowers and death. Sex and destruction.

At such a moment, despite his apostasy, he might visit **St. Ansgar's**

Church on **Bredgade,** the Catholic cathedral in Copenhagen—a small and, Kerrigan once thought, holy place. But St. Ansgar's, like most churches, is rarely open when he visits, and when a man needs to visit a church he does not need to find a door that he cannot pull open. Neither can Kerrigan forget that a part of the actual right arm of St. Ansgar, Apostle of the North, is embedded in a golden shrine in the church's sacristy or that mounted on the wall to the left of the left front subaltar, dedicated to Our Lady, is a gold-coated bust of Pope Lucius I, beheaded in Rome in A.D. 254. Within the bust is Lucius's actual skull, sent to the then still papist Denmark from Rome in the 1100s. Whenever Kerrigan is in the church he does his best to not meet the gaze of the skullish bust, although he feels the thing regarding him through empty sockets from beneath its jeweled crown.

He wanders underneath a drift of clouds toward **Kongens Nytorv.** He thinks, *Green shadows on a damp afternoon in spring,* and about the green shadows of his Associate's eyes and about the fact that he has not washed away the remnants of the first two acts of love shared with Thea Ylajali. Coitus. Copulation. You are as sane as I, he thinks, wondering precisely how sane that might be, or how blind he might be, as he turns up **Ny Adelsgade** and enters the **Palæ Bar** beneath the sign of the mermaid sipping a cocktail through a straw.

Years before, this was a dive greasy-spoon coffee shop called Selandia, named for the island on which Copenhagen is situated. Since 1984, however, it has been a noble establishment, worthy of the name of the street on which it stands, New Nobility Street, host to jazz and poetry readings. It also awards, on the first day of the Copenhagen Jazz Festival in July, an annual prize of not inconsiderable prestige to a jazz artist who has distinguished him- or herself by virtue of a contribution to the genre.

The bar is already well populated when Kerrigan enters. He orders a beer and finds an empty chair at a table facing the massive painting of a long, reclining nude—Goya-inspired—that reminds him of Thea, whose secreta has dried on him. It occurs to him that people carry many manners of secret around with them. And depression descends upon him as the voice of John Lennon warns him over the sound system that instant karma is going to do a job on him if he doesn't do a job on himself.

This strikes him suddenly as funny, and his smile wanders toward the corner, where a woman with a street-worn look sits over a basket of fresh roses. Instantly she rises, picks an amber rose from the bunch, and crosses to his table. He fumbles for some change, but she gently pushes his money hand away.

"It's because of your lovely smile," she tells him, and tears spring to his eyes as he thanks her, breaks the stem from the rose, and fits the bud into the lapel of his tweed jacket. The sweet scent fills his nostrils, and he thinks of rot nourishing the rose.

Now I am terrified of the earth, he thinks. *It grows such sweet things out of such corruptions.*

He thinks of Thea on the boat, thinks of laughing in the face of love, thinks of how incredibly sexy she looked naked and how incredibly sad he feels now that he fucked her, wondering whether he is indeed insane. He wonders why the memory of her is more satisfying than the actual experience was, or whether it is the other way around.

Atop everything else, he is on his second pint and the bubbly buzz that had been settling begins to rise again into his stale mouth and takes the form of anger. Digging into his pocket for a coin, he heads for the phone booth beside the door of the women's room, dials his Associate, whose name, incredibly, he is unable to recall at this moment, even though her phone number is clear in his brain, a lapse that almost drives him to hang up in terror, but her voice is already in his ear, and he is already saying, "When we took the poppers the other night, did you or did you not tell me that I'm so blind?"

"I am not certain I recall saying such a thing," she says. "That experience was . . . wery intense." Which is no answer at all, but he plunges on. "Well, you must know what you said, and I think I have a right to know!"

"Easy boy," she says, and he leans into the wall, knees buckling.

"Did you tell me that or not? It is important that I know."

"Why? Can you not take a joke?"

"No." Then he adds, "So you *did* say it? You have to understand. It is not the content that concerns me, only the fact of whether or not those words were spoken by you to me."

"Come over and we shall talk about it."

"I can't. I have to go. But I need to know."

"Where are you going?"

He wants to goad her. "Where? Why, to the Velvet Room."

"Vhat is that?"

"A kind of strip joint right up around the corner of New Nobility Street."

"Mmmm. Take me wis you."

"Why? So you can see if I'm blind or not?"

She laughs, and he does not know whether to be enraged or amused. "Come on," he pleads. "Did you say it or not?"

"I can't remember. One says so many things. Have you ever been in the Welvet Room?"

"No," he lies, remembering the time he went there all by himself, and an impossibly beautiful woman danced just for him, slowly undressing as she danced, holding his eyes fast with hers so he hardly even saw her naked body at all, only her eyes, her powerful, hypnotic gaze, which anyway are the most exciting part of a woman's body. She might have been wearing a burka, the focus of her eyes was so intense. Well, almost. Other features had their own specific power as well. Which almost cost him a thousand crowns for a bottle of champagne; the champagne only buys you the right to negotiate for what comes next at whatever further price is decided upon.

Kerrigan never paid for it in his life. Except that once, when he couldn't even get it up. So he paid for it without even getting it. Which meant he could still brag that he never paid for it in his life.

A woman pushes past him to the toilet, and he sees a handful of familiar faces enter the bar, expatriates: an impecunious American who is an amateur mathematician writing a book about the number 1, a Scottish painter whose specialty is abstract representations of burning forests, a mustached Wroxton man who was once mistakenly arrested and incarcerated as the ringleader of a cocaine-smuggling band, held in isolation for half a year until they discovered their mistake but who, because he had been in possession of two joints, could not take action. There are others as well, and Kerrigan can hear from the sound system that John Lennon is now singing "Imagine"—a song that pisses him off: a billionaire doubting the general public's ability to imagine a world in which there is no money.

"Fucking fraud," he says aloud, and his Associate asks into the phone, "*What!*"

"I wasn't talking to you," he says.

"Who were you talking to?"

"John Lennon."

"Are you drunk, Mr. Kerrigan?"

"Sorry," he says, "I have to go."

"Vhen will I see you again?" she asks quietly, and instead of an answer, he says, "I have to catch a plane."

"To where?"

"I don't remember." Carefully he lays the receiver back into its cradle on the wall. *You're as sane as I*, he thinks, and tries to remember whether his Associate admitted to telling him he is so blind.

Gerry Mulligan on the sound system blows "Lullaby of the Leaves" on his baritone, and Kerrigan considers the fact that Mulligan is blowing a horn invented by the Belgian Antoine Sax, born 1814 (one year after the Danish state went bankrupt and Kierkegaard was born). Sax died in 1894, 102 years before the death of Mulligan, now blowing "Lullaby of the Leaves," before his sixty-ninth birthday.

He glances at the first table to the left of the door and remembers once coming in here and seeing two women sitting there, one of whom wore a close-fitting pink suede jacket and had extremely full lips, mythically proportioned, coated with glistening gloss. Kerrigan was with his Swedish millionaire friend Morten Gideon, who glanced at her and said succinctly, "Fat lips." But Kerrigan could not take his eyes from her mouth; so intense was his stare that she looked up at him, and he said, "Please. I am so sorry. But I need to kiss your lips. Please. I truly need to." And with an expression on her face of its being her duty to provide her lips to him, incapable of denying him this humble demand, she rose, and their lips joined, then their bodies welded, and he kissed her long and rotatingly and with a delightfully satisfying sensation and perfumed taste of lip gloss.

"Thank you," he said then, and he and Gideon sat at another table while she repaired her lip gloss, but no sooner was it repaired than his gaze once again fixed upon her lips and, mesmerized, he crossed once again to her table and said, "Forgive me. I have to again."

"But," she said. "I just repaired my lip gloss."

"That is perhaps why I have to again. Please. I'm sorry. I really have to."

With a tiny sigh of resignation, then, she rose, and they kissed again, long and luxuriously, and where was she now? That woman of such kindness as to be unable to deny him his humbly expressed need. Nothing ever came of it. Nothing needed to come of it. It was a kiss, two kisses, most memorable, most excellent kisses, to be remembered as long as he continues drawing breath. She left. He left. Gideon left with him. No names or numbers were exchanged.

And on the street Gideon, clearly envious, said, "So what the fuck did that prove? Big deal. A kiss."

"Two kisses," said Kerrigan.

"So two kisses. Big deal."

"I'll tell you what it proves," said Kerrigan. "It proves what Renée Ashley once said."

"So who the fuck is Renée Ashley."

"A poet."

"And what the fuck did she say?"

"She said, 'Every dark is not a shadow the dead cavort in.'"

"Big deal," said Gideon as though he didn't see, but Kerrigan could see he saw, could see that he lamented that he had not himself procured at least one of those two kisses on those mythically proportioned lips.

Remembering that, Kerrigan remembers the impulsion that surmounted any possible obstacle to those kisses, and a plan is taking form as he positions himself by the side bar glancing from the Hans Henrik

Lerfeldt Chet Baker with horn on the wall above a large early black-and-white portrait photo of Dexter Gordon with horn, diagonally across from Sonny Rollins in red, bent forward blowing his sax. Beside the front window is a five-foot wood sculpture of a sensuous woman bearing a bunch of wooden bananas and above her, from the ceiling, hangs an antique sousaphone. High on the wall opposite him is a green-and-black-and-gray-and-white abstract Lerfeldt nude, and to the right a Billie Holiday and old tin signs announcing in Danish, HERE ARE SERVED ALL MANNER OF BEER AND SPECIALTIES, ROLLED SAUSAGE AND MEATS MINCED AND SALTED. A very large orange kite in the form of a ray dangles from the ceiling, flanked by a tuba, and the plan is hatched.

He lunges for the door.

Six: A Foray into the Black Pool

It must always be remembered that his locale was Celtic
and his season spring.

—THE HON. JOHN M. WOOLSEY,

UNITED STATES V. ULYSSES

It was the woman with the roses who created a distinct picture in his mind of Molly Malone, the "Tart with the Cart," in her bronze infinity at the delta of Suffolk and Nassau and Grafton streets in Dublin, and the recollection of the impulsion that won him those kisses from the fat-lipped woman as well as the Paddy's Irish Whiskey that Cathy of Chicago served him gratis in Copenhagen's Irish Rover those days ago that made him know the time was right for the Fort of the Danes and the Garrison of the Saxons.

He was even familiar with the flight schedule and saw by his watch there was just time, and as he stepped out of the Palæ, a taxi was just rolling toward him, and Kerrigan raised one finger and stopped it dead.

"Where to?" the corpulent driver asked, attempting to turn in his seat.

"Kastrup, please. I've only fifty-five minutes to catch the last flight to Dublin. Can you make it?"

"Let's give it a try," said the driver as he threw the meter and geared out into traffic. That everything meshed so perfectly was proof to him that this was meant to be—the taxi, the last flight, the fact that he had a five-thousand-dollar credit line on his Diner's Club card, that huffing and puffing like a walrus, *kookookachoo!* he made it to the gate where a smiling, green-clad Aer Lingus flight attendant—who had been alerted from the ticket office that there was one more full-fare, one-way passenger, and her bewinged identity shield proclaimed her name to be Sheila Nageeg—awaited him holding open the portal with both hands like a protective goddess above a church door, and said, "You look like a man who needs a glass of champagne, Mr. Kerrigan."

Oh, wonders of the business class!

The fact that he could get from the Danish capital to the Irish capital so quickly—a feat that must have taken the Vikings weeks—that a room was available at Trinity College was further proof, indeed, the very room he requested in Building 38, where J. P. Donleavy had had his rooms while studying science and conceiving *The Ginger Man* in the 1940s, then known under the title of *S. D.*, the initials of Sebastian Danger-field, the eponymous *Ginger Man*, the fact that it was a balmy May evening, that **McDaid's**—established in 1779—was not only open but that the outdoor tables were set up, and he sat there on **Harry Street** with a pint of the blackest black stuff contemplating the fact that in the story "Grace" in *Dubliners*, Joyce has the main character, Tom Kernan, fall down the stairs of a bar (which, Colm Toíbín notwithstanding, Kerrigan calculates to be *this* bar) going down to the gents', as a symbol of the fall from grace and a parody perhaps of Dante, although today the gents' is *up* a tricky couple of flights (especially tricky for a man in his cups)—*but!* in the fall, biting *off* a piece of his tongue so that he speaks indistinctly, thus falling not *into* but *out of* language, in contrast to Joyce's theory of the fall from grace being the development of language—all of this convinced him that God's plan, small *g* or large, was for him to be in Dublin at just this moment, and he felt certain the reason for this might reveal itself now or later or through some affiliation with an event of the past.

Considering the fact that he had read somewhere that Joyce's own father is said to have fallen down the stairs of this bar and bitten his tongue in the process, Kerrigan feels the sweat on his forehead, smells himself, and wonders what in the name of fuck he is doing here suddenly in a bar in a city on an island in the Atlantic when he is supposed to be on quite another island in quite another capital city, Copenhagen, writing a book about *that* city's bars.

Yet he is by no means sorry to be in McDaid's at this very moment. Years ago, it is said, this bar was the city morgue, later converted to a chapel for the Moravian Brethren who were said to bury their dead standing up. The ceilings are high, he can see in through the door, the wood dark, the windows tall and gothic, and Kerrigan considering that Joyce's own father, John Stanislaus Joyce (1849–1931), was the person who in fact fell down the stairs here, contemplates how coincidental are the sources of our art, albeit touchingly so, and considers how Joyce the son credits his father with an enormous amount of his material and ideas—the spit and image of *Ulysses*.

In the 1940s and '50s, this bar was a favorite haunt of Gainor Stephen Crist, American GI Bill expatriate from Ohio studying law at Trinity, to be driven to glory as the model of Sebastian Dangerfield in *The Ginger Man*, Donleavy's classic comic novel, although said Crist, broken by drink, would later wind up bad-mouthing the same Donleavy.

Brendan Behan, after his release from Borstal, drank and sang and roared here, as did Patrick Kavanagh, a segment of whose diary was featured in each issue of the 1950s Dublin literary journal *Envoy*, edited over the tables of McDaid's.

Could any of this explain his presence here? Yet there had already been other signs that he felt might decipher the reason. First of all, a postcard handed to him for no ostensible reason by a young woman with a stud on either side of her nose and black-painted lips. Printed on the back of the card was:

Fierce talk
Loose liquor
Hard girls
The Pre-HAM Social Transgressive Cabaret
GRISTLE
Entry £5

On the obverse, however, the card said HOMO ACTION MOVIES FOR BUTCH QUEERS, filling him in, so to speak, on the meaning of the acronym HAM, so he discarded, so to speak, the card.

Perhaps the meaning then is that the world takes you, in fact, for a homosexual butch queer transgressive in disguise, he thought, but rather took comfort in his memory of the statement in some book by Norman Mailer, *The Prisoner of Sex* perhaps, that any man who proceeds to the fullness of adulthood with nary a homosexual interlude has earned the right without hesitation to describe himself as heterosexual.

"Bollocks!" shouts a lad speeding past along Harry Street on a tough-looking, stripped-down, high-riser handlebarred bicycle.

There were signs at Trinity College as well—one outside the main entrance said, CYCLISTS DISMOUNT. And one in the shower, which Kerrigan had refrained from using, said, AFTER SHOWERING KINDLY REMOVE HAIRS FROM THE PLUMBING OUTLETS. And somewhere on Grafton Street, he has seen another sign: BEWARE OF THE MOVING BOLLARDS.

In the name of God's sacred teeth, Kerrigan thinks, did she or did she not utter those words, and if so, how could two women have said the same thing to him? He had figured out, in retrospect, what Licia meant by it, but it was important for him to know whether his Associate said it, too, and if so, what she meant by it.

Another sign in Trinity on the lead-netted window of the at-that-hour-inaccessible doors of the Buttery breakfast room: NOTICE: VIDEO MONITORING IS IN OPERATION IN THIS AREA. PILFERERS WILL BE SEVERELY DEALT WITH.

A smiling waitress steps out of the doorway of McDaid's and asks if he would be wishing another pint of the black stuff or any such other thing.

"Do you think I ought?" he asks.

"Sure, a bird never flew on one wing," she tells him.

"Another then," he says, and thinks, And yet another as a propeller on my tail, as he examines the ten-pound note with which he will pay. On its front is a green-toned portrait of James Joyce (1882–1941), jovial as C. G. Jung (1875–1961), whom in theory Kerrigan might have met until he was eighteen years old, who published a psychological analysis of *Ulysses*, by whom Joyce's wealthy American patroness Edith Rockefeller McCormick tried unsuccessfully to pay Joyce to be psychoanalyzed, and who unsuccessfully attempted to psychoanalyze Joyce's mentally ill daughter, Lucia (1907–1982)—whose name, he notes not for the first time, bears an unfortunate similarity to the wife who abandoned Kerrigan, though Lucia means "light," while Licia sounds, in retrospect, sinister, with two letters of the word *blind* as well as three letters of the words *malicious* and *malice*, though it also contains four letters of the word *delicious*.

Alongside Joyce's green portrait is a mountainous peninsula that, turned sideways, bears a striking resemblance to an erect phallus and powerful scrotum ("What did Molly have on her mind?" an Irish friend once asked, pointing this out to Kerrigan). On the obverse of the bill is a map of Dublin showing the Liffy and the face of Anna Livia and the first sentence of Joyce's *Finnegans Wake*: "riverrun, past Eve and Adam's, from swerve of shore to bend of bay, brings us by a commodius vicus of recirculation back to Howth Castle and Environs." *Copyright Central Bank of Ireland 1993.*

Kerrigan wonders if the Central Bank of Ireland has claimed copyright on Joyce even while he admires the irony of the fact that Irish money depicts this great writer who was so hated here for so many years and did not set foot in Ireland for nearly the last four decades of his life.

As he sits musing over the Joyce money, Kerrigan is saddened to think that in just over two years' time, in accordance with international treaties, it will have become a collector's item, replaced along with the national currency of at least twelve other Member States of the European Union by the nondescript euro, whose notes would bear no writerly portraits.

The waitress brings Kerrigan's stout and takes away his portrait of Joyce with its quote from *Finnegans Wake* which once again he realizes he is not succeeding in reading and no doubt never will, not least perhaps because there are so many made-up words and obscure puns right from the first word, "riverrun," which play on the French *reverons* (let us dream) and *riverain* (one who lives by a river), as well as their surface meaning, facts he would likely never have discovered without a gloss.

Consider this, Kerrigan: You will no doubt die never having read *Finnegans Wake*. But at least you have, after carrying the two volumes around with you from residence to residence for over thirty-five years, read the first volume of *War and Peace*, which of course was brilliant and thrilling and entertaining. But what about volume two?

He sips his stout, thinks of all the things he will never be able to fit inside his head before it begins its process of decay and desication, a skullful of dust. Skull-alone in a dark place.

Kerrigan's slow feet walk him down Harry Street to Grafton, where yellow and white and red flowers fill the passage and a woman sits on a case awaiting customers. He steps over crunching matter on the pavement—the rubble of history? Of *his* history?—left past Bewley's Oriental Café, whose continued existence is under threat, to **Duke**, right to the familiar wood-and-glass facade at number 21. Always changing color, it is currently painted gold, a licensed premise for two hundred years, under its present name since 1889, **Davy Byrne's Bar & Restaurant**.

Here, for the first time in the 1940s, J. P. (Mike) Donleavy met Brendan Behan, and because the American did not like what Behan called him, a narrowback (i.e., one who has not worked with his body, living easy in the new world, although Kerrigan has also heard it defined as a reference to how narrow immigrants had to be if they were to be crammed into the ships that carried them across the ocean), Donleavy offered either to thrash him in the bar or to do so outside on Duke Street. Duking it out on Duke Street, so to speak.

But outside, Behan—perhaps shrewdly recognizing that Donleavy was a skilled pugilist who had trained with a professional boxing coach—offered his hand in friendship instead: "Ah, now why should the intelligent likes of us belt each other and fight just to please the bunch of them eegits back inside the pub who wouldn't have the guts to do it themselves."

Kerrigan spent a few hours with Donleavy once, at his house in Mullingar, outside Dublin, a mansion that features in Joyce's *Stephen Hero*.

Donleavy was a gracious host, served a tray of bread and scones and cheeses and tea while feeding great hunks of peat into the pungent fire. The walls of the mansion were filled with Donleavy's art, the shelves of his library were filled with various editions of his books, the music rack of the grand piano displayed the sheet music for one of his own compositions. And Donleavy himself drove Kerrigan in a vintage automobile to the station to catch the last train back to Dublin and stood there to wave him off as the train pulled away.

Kerrigan does not like to think of the sadness that descended upon him in the train, for Donleavy was the great American literary hero of his early twenties, after he had come through Joyce and Camus and Dostoyevsky, and seeing Donleavy in the last year before his seventh decade, Kerrigan himself in the last year of his fifth—the year he married Licia—he felt that one of the great moments he had always dreamed about had been fulfilled, but none of the promise that had always seemed imminent in his life ever would be, and in fact the great shock of his adult life would happen in but four years—a college education later.

As unlike as he was to this legendary writer, he felt an intense kinship to him. But it did sadden him that Donleavy took such evident relish in singing tales of fisticuffs and broken jaws, jolly barroom brawls, never mentioning the cracking of skull bones that occasionally results in partial, sometimes permanent, even total paralysis, partial edentulousness, reduced vision or hearing. Kerrigan tended to blame this attitude on John Wayne. Ironic, it has always seemed to him, that the homosexual serial killer of many young American men in the state of Illinois was named John Wayne Gacy, while another man, castrated by his wife for allegedly raping and abusing her, was John Wayne Bobbitt, who after his penis was located and reattached, founded a band called the Severed Parts and appeared in two adult films, *John Wayne Bobbitt Uncut* and *Frankenpenis*, in an attempt to pay his medical bills.

Donleavy did, however, express sorrow at the inadvertent punching out of the teeth of a woman in a brawl on the Isle of Man, an event later translated into an anecdote in *A Fairy Tale of New York* in which the main character, Cornelius Christian, accidentally punches an eyeball out of the head of a woman in an East Side New York barroom brawl.

Kerrigan's own father, a man of song and lyric, admired those who were "good with their dukes," but Kerrigan has never understood why men should wish to punch each other's faces. He had tried it a time or two himself, was moderately good at it as a lad, did enjoy the power that befell a boy unafraid to throw his clenched fist into the face of another boy, but when he was fourteen, after a particularly vicious fight one day with another boy named Theodore in which the two of them rolled over desks, tore each other's hair, punched each other's lips and teeth and jaws and skulls and eyes, Kerrigan no longer wished to. He did not lose the fight, but he knew enough later to understand that no one wins a fight like that and, further, *Theodore* means "the love of God," and even if the will of God had embodied tooth and claw and the need for every living creature to ingest the tissue of other living creatures, animal or plant, he thought it was a bum rap, and he did not wish to cooperate unnecessarily with this system.

He wonders, for not the first time in his life, despite poetic wisdom and advice that he should "to this due degree of blindness, submit," how this system of life feeding off life could have been devised. Whose imagination could have devised it? William Blake asked as much, and so did T. S. Eliot: "Who then devised the torment . . . ?" Providing teeth to tear open the throats of others in order to procure fresh, unresisting meat upon which to sup? The only exception is the sweet miracle of the breast, which can only nourish, not be used as weapons.

Then he recalls the pie-size, sculpted medallion he saw of Sheela-na-gig in the window of a shop on South Great George's Street earlier. It depicted the mysterious Celtic exhibitionist goddess whose image is found hidden away in nooks and corners of certain Christian churches in Ireland and England. The stylized image of a woman holding apart her labia, her eyes and mouth bemused, almost moronic.

> Within your stony nook you lurk
> In acrobatic pose.
> You leer, you stare, and open jerk

The petals of your rose.
Come in, you breathe, come into me.
My cunt is what you crave.
The little death is yours for free,
As is the cold, cold grave.

At the bar he orders a pint of the black stuff to keep his consciousness from pinching. On a shelf behind the bar stands a bottle of Irish vodka—Boru—named for the first king of a United Ireland, Brian Boru, who routed the Vikings in the eleventh century, whose son was Kennedy, and who was stabbed in the back by a Dane while praying on Holy Thursday, a sanctified death to which Hamlet refused to deliver his uncle, slayer of his father.

Beside him now at the bar a leather-jacketed man with a flowered neck-tie, squat-nosed, sits scowling over a pint of lager. A white-haired man at the drum table by the wall, ruddy-faced, burgundy sweatered, lifts an empty pint glass silently above his head and jerks it toward the bar. *More!* Ignored. *More!*

Three middle-aged women in flowered dresses, seated on an uphol-stered bench at a table, eat plates of ham and mustard. Kerrigan orders half a dozen rock oysters, and the barman says, "Ah, I wouldn't eat the rock oysters."

"They're usually brilliant," says Kerrigan.

"They are that, yes, usually."

"The salmon then."

"Now I'm your honest barman. You wouldn't want the salmon at this hour."

"The cheese platter?"

"The cheese platter would be agreeable," he says, and when he has served it, "Enjoy it now, there's a good Stilton," and, "Thank you very much indeed."

Kerrigan thinks it good that he eat cheese, which is provided from the sweet miracle of mammary glands. Further, he wonders if this red-haired barman would ever seek to punch his face should he be angered by him for some reason. He himself would never dream of punching that honest barman's freckled puss.

On the ceiling are art deco lamps shaped like tulip bulbs. A stained-glass door bears the same colors as the painted flowers in the ceiling recesses. The white-haired man, cane between his knees, jerks his empty glass aloft again. *More!*

Across the street, through the front window, Kerrigan can see the Baily at numbers 2 and 3, from which Mr. Leopold Bloom on June 16, 1904, in the Dublin of James Joyce's *Ulysses*, retreated in disgust from the gobbling pub-grubbing faces to dine on burgundy and blue cheese, which Kerrigan eats now, ninety-five years later:

> He entered Davy Byrne's. Moral pub. He doesn't chat. Stands a drink now and then. Cashed a cheque for me once. Davy Byrne came forward from the hindbar in tuck-stitched shirt-sleeves, cleaning his lips with two wipes of his napkin . . . Mr Bloom ate his strips of sandwich, fresh clean bread, with relish of disgust, pungent mustard, the feety savour of green cheese. Sips of his wine soothed his palate . . . Nice quiet bar. Nice piece of wood in that counter. Nicely planed. Like the way it curves there.

On the walls, painted murals of smiling people in a dark wood over a bright beach behind a light mountain—painted, Kerrigan knows, by the father-in-law of Brendan Behan.

Joyce drank here, too. And across the street in **The Duke**, where he and James Stephens had their first meeting. The Duke was then called Kennedy's, and Stephens invited Joyce in for a tailor of malt whereupon, according to Stephens, Joyce confided that he had read the two books Stephens at that time had published, pronouncing that Stephens did not know the difference between a semicolon and a colon, that his knowledge of Irish life was non-Catholic and so nonexistent that he should give up writing and find another job he was good at, like shoe-shining, as a more promising profession.

Stephens claimed to have responded that he had never read a word of Joyce's and that, if his protective wits were preserved by heaven, he never would read a word of his unless asked to review it destructively. Yet years later, in 1927, when Joyce was near despair over the negative critique of the bits of *Finnegans Wake* he had so far published under the title *Work in Progress*, he is said to have entertained the idea of inviting Stephens to complete the book for him.

Stephens was born in 1882, the same year as Joyce and Franklin Delano Roosevelt, seven years before Adolf Hitler, the year Charles Darwin died. Joyce died in 1941, FDR and Hitler in 1945, and Stephens in 1950, at the respective ages of fifty-nine, sixty-three, fifty-six, and sixty-eight, Hitler's life the shortest of the four. Stephens had been one of Kerrigan's father's favorite poets, especially the poem he had read aloud to young Terrence on frequent occasions about a rabbit caught in a snare whom the narrator of the poem can hear crying out in pain, but cannot find even though he is searching everywhere. Rumi, the thirteenth-century Persian poet, his real name Jalâl al-Dîn (1207–1273), born in north Afghanistan, wrote a similar poem about the helpers of the world who run toward those screaming in pain simply because they can hear them.

Kerrigan smokes a cigar thinking of this, and of the fact that he doesn't do much for anyone in a helpless situation. The old man jerks his pint up once again. *More!*

This time the response is immediate. A fresh pint of Guinness before him, cane between his knees, glowering, he surveys the room like an Irish king. Kerrigan nods with respect and moves out into the May night.

Through the gates of **Trinity** (CYCLISTS DISMOUNT), he treads across the cobblestones to **Building 38** where, watching himself in the mirror brush his brownish pearly whites, he fears sleep, recognizing that he will die someday, that he may die in bed feeling sweaty and alone beneath an overwarm blanket, knowing he is going far away and not a friend in sight to understand this journey, the awareness of which we all block out as long as we can, are almost incapable of thinking about, an ending which, though known, comes always as a surprise we secretly believe we might be exempt from simply because of the very special nature of being one's own unconditionally self-beloved self, self-contempt notwithstanding.

If there was a phone in this room, he would call his Associate and berate her, make her pay for his unhappiness for no reason other than that he suspects she would allow him to do so because of her apparently great heart.

For a moment he thinks he loves her and will propose marriage, but quickly dismisses the thought, knowing that it would involve other people, too, her daughters, witnesses, officials. In any event, marriage will do nothing to alleviate this pinpoint of death fear. It is all illusion, delusion, and the job of human beings is to maintain that delusion in order to enjoy themselves and accomplish their work upon this earth: to live and be happy and love the heady liquor of the drink known as air, and that, anyway, is something. The word *delusion* is immediately accompanied in Kerrigan's mind by an image of Licia in her bikini blue as the false blue of her eyes.

Because he cannot face the task of removing his hairs from the plumbing fixtures, he plops still unwashed onto the bed in his skivvies, considering how Thea's fragrance will still be there somewhere yet, probably stale now, and even as he reaches for himself, he is off in a distant land, and his father waves from an even more distant shore, smaller now, but glad of face as Kerrigan calls out, "Dad! Dad! Come over for a pint!"

And he is in the house where people sit in darkness; dust is their drink and clay their meat. They are clothed like dark birds with wings for covering, they see no light, they sit in darkness . . . the house of dust.

Ireland has a standing army of five thousand poets, Patrick Kavanagh once said, though the Irish do not, he asserted, give a fart in their corduroys for culture.

And near as many pubs or more, Kerrigan cannot but think. He considers volunteering to do a volume on Dublin's pubs for the series, as he sets off to visit some of Kavanagh's old haunts, having dreamt inter alia of his own father waving from across the river—his father who had read him Kavanagh's "The Great Hunger" years before Kerrigan was capable of appreciating more than the music of its language, of the narrator's being suspicious as a rat near strange bread when a woman laughed.

But first he visits **St. Andrew's Church** to light two candles for the dead and one again for the still living but stolen from him, kneels in a pew to which is affixed a plaque that says, PRAY FOR THE SOULS OF JOHN AND ELIZA D'ARCY.

Instead of praying for the D'Arcys, Kerrigan retreats from the church and stops at the **Chemist Shop Sweny's** at 1 Lincoln Plaza, where he sniffs a bar of lemon soap, thinking of Bloom buying one of these, even as he knew Molly was preparing to cheat on him with Blazes Boylan. He buys a soap oval wrapped in tissue paper and stores it in his hip pocket in honor of Poldy, poor peaceful cuckold onanist Jew—just like me, though I'm not Jewish—planning to give it to his Associate if he ever sees her again. Soap successfully delivered. For her, not for me.

"Is it for herself?" asks the sweet elderly lady with a twinkle behind the ancient wooden desk, and Kerrigan smiles, nods, steps out to note that what used to be called **Kennedy's** public house across the street, mentioned by name in Beckett and Joyce, is now called **Fitzsimmons**. He strolls north a block toward **Merrion Square**, past the birthplace of Oscar Wilde at number 1, who died in 1900, same year Nietzsche died and Thomas Wolfe was born, Joseph Conrad's *Lord Jim* appeared, and Joyce's first piece of writing, "Ibsen's New Drama," was published, a review of Ibsen's last play, *When We Dead Awaken* (1899):

> We only see what we have lost
> When we dead awaken.
> And then what do we see?
> We see that we never have lived.

You are so blind.

Remembering another of Ibsen's plays, *An Enemy of the People*, published the same year Joyce was born, the quintessential modern play about the willful poisoning of the environment for profit, and *The Wild Duck*, equally about blindness as was Sophocles' *Oedipus Rex*, he pauses to look at the door of number 82 Merrion Square, where Yeats spent six years—remembers that Yeats had been one of the first to experiment with mescaline, imported by Havelock Ellis from Mexico in 1894 when Joyce was twelve years old. Kerrigan recalls his own experiments with LSD in California in the sixties, can recall standing on a cliff over the Pacific in Ocean Beach, San Diego, thirty-three years before, watching the sea crash on the sandstone in a wild splash of electric color, droplets of red and green and yellow flying up into the moonlit evening. He remembers lying on the floor of an adobe cottage with a young woman, both of them wearing jeans and nothing else, his fingers on the denim at the fork of her thighs, and she held his hand there, projecting images upon the ceiling of writhing blissful bodies in embrace that in some mysterious way they *both* claimed to have witnessed. And he can remember convincing himself that, since his body was composed of atoms in movement and the door was composed of atoms in movement, if he would only move purposefully and with true belief, there was no need to open the door, for his atoms could slip right through the spaces between the door atoms. The trick was to do it quickly, not to get welded in there, like *The Fly*. And he did that.

His painful bloodied beak brought him back to earth fast and ended his psychopharmaceutical experiments forever. And just as well. Those sixties were dismal in truth.

He moves on to 84 Merrion Square, where Æ (George William Russell, 1867–1935), lifelong friend of Yeats, wrote *Voices of the Stones*, which Kerrigan's father so loved:

> Uncover: bend the head
>   And let the feet be bare;
>   This air that thou breathest
>   Is holy air
>   Sin not against the breath . . .

And J. P. Donleavy reported receiving a letter signed Æ in 1957 in which the letter writer suggested that *The Ginger Man* made men worse than brutes, poisoned the minds of children, dragged the Savior's name in the mud. "The Holy Name of Jesus," he wrote, "belongs to a Person who will judge you soon."

Donleavy called it his first-ever fan letter. This Æ of the 1957 blue-nosed fan letter could not be the Æ his father so admired, for that Æ shuffled off twenty-two years before, in 1935, at the age of sixty-eight, having repented of his initial dismissiveness of Joyce's *Ulysses*.

"And there's no use giving you my name," the bogus Æ declared, signing only with those two letters.

Sin not against the breath.

And what else is poetry but a struggle for breath, a column of breath, the spirit jet upon which the soul conveys its desire and its wisdom in words? *Are you in possession of wisdom, Kerrigan?* he asks himself, thinking how wrong he was about Licia, how he had ignored signs, imposing on himself the belief they were happy together. The sex had been great until the last year or so. Then she didn't want as much anymore. None at all, in fact. He still loved her, decided that there were seasons to everything and congratulated himself on his wise patience, his patient wisdom in not forcing the matter, when in fact she was no doubt already getting it somewhere else. Who was her lover? The neighbor? But no, the neighbor stayed on when Licia disappeared and abducted Gabrielle. So who?

Then once when he had come home from a weeklong literary conference, suddenly she welcomed him into her bed after months of not wanting him. Once. She locked her feet at the small of his back forcing him to come deep in her. Once. And announced a week later that she was pregnant. And she was gone six weeks after that.

He foots on to Grand Canal to look at the door with the fox-head knocker at 33 Haddington Road, one of Patrick Kavanagh's many south side residences, a poor place with a tiny broken door pane, and Kerrigan asks aloud, "Who bent the coin of my destiny that it sticks in the slot?"

remembering his own father reading him Kavanagh's "The Great Hunger" in which that question is posed, apparently thinking it applied to his life of a loveless marriage, but Kerrigan thinks now it was prophetic of his own life. Did the reading by his father of that poem to Kerrigan at the tender age of thirteen, did that very act bend the coin of Kerrigan's own destiny so it stuck in the slot, had him running from involvement as from the smell of strange bread until he was ready to be duped by a beautiful young woman of false blue eyes?

He expects no answer and lets his oxblood-shod feet trot him past Parson's Bookshop, now a sundries store, and down to the **Waterloo** and **Searson's** on Upper Baggot Street. Not certain which one to visit for a pint, he visits each for a glass, finds himself mumbling Kavanagh lines into the second, which causes two persons at the bar to look with surreptitious deadpans his way. *I'm not the only one in Dublin muttering to myself,* thinks Kerrigan, who has seen several already in protracted conversation with themselves.

But takes his leave all the same and crosses to the **Grand Canal** and sits on the bench of Percy French, dead in 1920 at the age of sixty-six:

> Remember me is all I ask
>> and yet
> If the remembrance proves a task
>>> forget.

Kerrigan blushes remembering having written an epitaph for himself. Licia chided him for being morbid, and he thought he could see fear of his death in her eyes. *You are so blind*, he thinks, feeling his stupidity and vulnerability and his belief that she truly loved him, as he did her.

.

INSTRUCTIONS ON MY DEPARTURE
When I die, please cry
Big tears from your blue, blue eyes.
Moan, *No! How? Why?* Then sigh.

Take from the buffet a tasty cake,
Strong beer. Marvel that I am not here.
Return to the open box and peer
At my pale, closed face, and smile,
Remembering some foolishness of mine.
Think, That old guy was okay. He was *okay*.
And in time, then, just go your way,
As I know you must do anyway.

His face reddens with shame now at his stupidity, his blindness, thinking that her heart would break when he died long before she, and she had tried to tell him the truth in her drunkenness in the garden that night. He put the monocle over the blind eye and surrendered to Licia's treachery to an extreme that she must have felt he was her plaything. How cynical she must have been, how mindful of her manipulations, and he was ripe for it. She must have seen that and could not resist such a temptation, saw how she had him in the palm of her hand. In fact, he heard her say that once about a boss—*Jeg har ham I mine hule hand*—I have him in my hollow hand.

"*You asshole*," he mutters aloud there on the Grand Canal. "*Asshole!*"

He crosses the lock to the other side of the canal to another bench, this one made of bronze and fitted with a long-legged, rumple-suited, life-size bronze of Patrick Kavanagh, dead himself in '67 at sixty-two, arms crossed, legs crossed, staring through his bronze glasses into the real water of the canal, crumpled bronze hat on the bronze bench beside him, engraved with the wish to be commemorated where there is water, where a swan floats past with head low in apology and a fantastic light peers through the eyes of bridges.

Kerrigan sits and imitates the poet's stance, watching a gray swan float past like all the questions it didn't occur to him to ask himself, after all the blindness with which he accepted Licia's act.

Stopping at **Toner's** for a small Bunratty he is thinking again of Joyce. He has spent many hours in the company of Joyce's prose, and *A Portrait* *of the Artist as a Young Man*, decades before, saved him from the living death of Irish Roman Catholicism and Irish-American jingoism:

> I will not serve that in which I no longer believe, whether it call itself my home, my fatherland, or my church: And I will try to express myself in some mode of life or art as freely as I can and as wholly as I can, using for my defence the only arms I allow myself to use— silence, exile, and cunning.

It occurred to Kerrigan that in 1968 he turned twenty-five years old and that was the first time he succeeded in reading Joyce's *Ulysses* and saw Joseph Strick's film version of it as well as listening to Siobhan Mc-Kenna and E. G. Marshall's excellent recording of the Molly and Leopold Bloom soliloquies.

That was also the year he sheltered a deserter from the Vietnam War in his apartment in New York, his single "concrete" act of resistance against that war. He identifies that act with Joyce, with his declaration from *A Portrait* of what he would no longer give allegiance to—religion, family, country—and with the hero of Joyce's *Ulysses*, who was not a warrior like its eponymous Greek hero but the pacifist, mild, cuckolded, humanity-loving, passionate Jew, Leopold Bloom.

The power of Joyce's literary stance aided Kerrigan's escape from the jingoism that four years earlier had him, without reflection, wearing on his jacket in the chill autumn New York City streets of 1964, in the wake of the Gulf of Tonkin Resolution, a BOMB HANOI! button. Why he wore that button, other than an unhealthy childhood diet of John Wayne and Senator Joseph McCarthy, he did not know; but he takes some comfort in the fact that both Steinbeck and Kerouac were also confused about Vietnam, and he will as long as he draws breath be grateful to Joyce, who worked so hard to contribute intelligent visions of the world to the world.

Kerrigan has dedicated more than one June 16 to a meditation on the lives of Joyce and Nora as he followed the real path of the fictional Leopold Bloom strolling Dublin streets on his long day's journey back to

Molly's now famous *Yes*. In life, on June 16, 1904, Joyce took his first stroll with Nora Barnacle. "Barnacle by name and barnacle by nature," complained Joyce's father about his son's alliance with the uneducated hotel maid with whom he would spend the rest of his life. His choice of that date as the one upon which Leopold Bloom took his walk was a tribute to Joyce's love for Nora, whom Molly Bloom (and Anna Livia Plurabelle of *Finnegans Wake*) so closely resemble. Since 1924, many others have also commemorated that day and those characters, year after year, in many cities of the world, celebrating Bloomsday.

Joyce and Nora lived in Zurich briefly in 1904 and again from 1915 to 1919, when the First World War forced them from Trieste. During those four years he wrote much of *Ulysses*, supporting himself on private language lessons and gifts of money. When the war ended, he left, but returned frequently to consult ophthalmologists for his failing eyes and psychiatrists regarding his daughter Lucia's declining mental condition.

In mid-December 1940 he again fled to Zurich, this time from France, to escape the Nazi invasion, and there he died just a few weeks later, on January 13, 1941, just before his fifty-ninth birthday, and was buried there in Fluntern Cemetery. Nora remained there with their adult son Giorgio, a singer, until she died in April 1951 and was buried in Fluntern as well; fifteen years later, their separate graves were united there.

Ulysses, to Kerrigan, is a successful artistic experiment, an innovation, that led to a new way of expressing and perceiving something of human existence, a complex fictional presentation of Western culture that functions on many levels. If one takes Homer as the beginning of Western literary history, embodying classical Greek metaphors, values, and symbols upon which the culture builds, then Joyce's novel might be seen as the conclusion or counterbalance two and a half millennia later.

Joyce's *Ulysses* parallels the ten-year journey of Homer's *Ulysses* (or Odysseus, as he is known in Greek)—from the Trojan War back to Ithaca where his wife, Penelope, holding off many suitors who think Ulysses dead, and his son, Telemachus, await his return—with the story of a single day in 1904 in the life of a lower-middle-class Dublin Jew,

Leopold Bloom, also living on a group of islands, who spends the day of June 16, 1904, walking around Dublin aware that his wife is at home committing adultery with a theater agent named Blazes Boylan. Toward the end of the day, Bloom meets the Telemachus equivalent in Stephen Dedalus.

The chapters of Joyce's *Ulysses* roughly parallel the episodes of Homer's epic, and the levels of meaning of the book are myriad. One of its aims is to celebrate the human body, so each chapter is also characterized by a body organ—for example, in one chapter, Bloom defecates while a church bell rings in the background, a brilliant literary response to the church's hypocritical suppression of human bodily joy and necessity. The fact that Bloom is a pacifist everyman, a non-macho, non-nationalist humanist as an emblem of modern twentieth-century society, contrasts in a number of ways with Homer's representation of Ulysses, a heroic warrior journeying home from battle to his faithful wife, and makes a profound and prophetic observation of the possibly increasing strains of our times—feminist, pacifist, anti-jingoist, contra-dogmatist.

Among the many other things that Joyce's novel does is parody various writing genres, styles, and techniques, and also introduces and develops William James's concept of stream of consciousness via an interior monologue also employed and developed by others, most notably perhaps Virginia Woolf.

Kerrigan concedes that some of the "experiments" in the book may fairly be viewed indifferently and as largely inaccessible to most readers without critical guidance as to what Joyce is doing, but the interior monologues, most particularly those of Leopold and Molly Bloom— when he read them for the first time, then heard them orally interpreted on record—instantly changed him, brought him into a profoundly more intimate contact with his own consciousness. And there, he recognized the possibility of accessing his own deeper thought processes and the simultaneity of time as a feature of the makeup of human psychology— not academically, but practically. Society, it seemed then to him— religion, convention, conformity—severely attempted to keep each human being skull-alone with her or his own secret thoughts, fearful of expressing anything but what is sanctioned by conventional consensus thought.

Many decades after the first publication of *Ulysses* in 1922, stream of consciousness—or its simpler counterpart, stream of experience—is no longer considered avant garde or innovative; it is a standard feature of literary practice throughout the world and a direct reflection of how we are. So even if some experimental fiction is a challenge to read and some readers may not wish to accept that challenge, it is nonetheless an important feature of our literature, of our culture, of our lives as human beings (as opposed, say, to our lives as zombies).

But Kerrigan is convinced that not many readers with even a modicum of sensitivity—whether or not they are literature majors—would fail to be moved by the Bloom soliloquies, most notably Molly's gorgeous celebration and affirmation of human life and sexuality on which the last sixty pages or so (depending on your edition) of the book flows, giving a view into the mind of a woman character and concluding with her resounding *Yes*.

To Kerrigan's mind, people who insist that all fiction must be "realistic" have a problem seeing the difference between life and art. Which was a considerable part of the point of his Ph.D. dissertation about verisimilitude, at a lecture on which Licia was one of the faces in his audience drawing his eyes again and again, following which eight years of his life were derailed by the delusion that she loved him as he loved her. He *did* love her, he thinks. Or he loved who he thought she was. But she was not who he thought. He considers that the darkest piece of humor of his life—that while he was lecturing her on the illusion of the real in literature, Licia performed a practical demonstration for him of the creation of an illusion and delusion of love whose thrall lasted for eight years.

So, he thinks, *she was* la belle dame sans merci. Perhaps if he had looked into the stream of his consciousness, he might have seen signs. But he did not. And was left alone, palely loitering. And no birds sang. Yet he is compelled to ask himself again and again how conscious of this was she? How cynical? And the fact that he still is not certain convinces him that he is still as blind as he was the day he fell into his enchantment. She must have thought, As well him as someone else. He has status. Money. He's not the most exciting-looking guy—could be taller, slimmer, with broader shoulders, narrower hips, long legs, not as big an ass . . . But he looks okay. He'll do. Why not? And then she saw him growing older year by year, his flesh sagging, the wattles . . .

Kerrigan takes a long walk past the **Shelbourne**, where Kipling and Dickens once slept, past **Stephen's Green**, and circles round to the **Long Hall** on **South Great George's Street**, alongside Upper Stephen Street, whose curve is said to follow the edge of the Dubh Lin, the black pool for which Dublin is named and where the Vikings moored their longships in A.D. 838. Here it was that the Danes settled, founding this capital, older by two centuries than their own. On this street, according to his father, the double-dark Kerrigans lived: *No doubt*, he thinks, *this is all myth, family myth, a father's fictions.*

Inside the Long Hall he sits behind the sixteen taps, watching his face in a fish-eye mirror by the cash register. The taps offer Guinness, Guinness, Guinness X Cold, Guinness X Cold, Kilkenny, Smithwick's, Bulmers Vintage Cider, Carlsberg Lager, Harp, Heineken, Heineken, Budweiser, Murphy's Irish Stout, Budweiser, Miller Genuine Draft. He sits beneath crystal chandeliers by a stained-glass bar partition. On the back bar shelf a little brass mermaid on a polished marble rock advertises Carlsberg's Continental Lager, and a man-size grandfather clock with one hand bears a sign announcing CORRECT TIME.

Kerrigan swallows half a pint of half-and-half and wonders about the family tales of his father, persecuted ancestor fleeing to Alsace and turning pacifist and leaving Baden-Baden and Belfort for Bedford-Stuyvesant to avoid conscription in the Franco-Prussian War in 1869. Fictions, delusion, monocle over the blind eye.

He understands then the purpose of his flash decision to visit the Black Pool was a blundering toward a clarification of who he is by viewing where he had come from, but it is all blindness and blundering. He has tried to clothe himself in history and literature, but he is naked as Andersen's emperor, fit for nothing but the pursuit of pleasure in the present moment as his time melts into the black pool of the past.

Passing the **Hairy Lemon** on his way to **Temple Bar,** he thinks of the lemony soap in his pocket and of his Associate and of giving it to her. If he ever sees her again. He steps into the Hairy Lemon to use the facilities. Moving past the bar he notes a backpacker, tall and thin with dark-browed narrow eyes, open the satchel on his pack to pull out his wallet and, in so doing, drop a double thumb-size brown hard lump on the floor.

Kerrigan stops. "Excuse me, my friend, but I believe you dropped your lump."

The young man's narrow-eyed face pales. "Not mine," he says, eyes full of white.

"I'm sure I saw it fall from your kit," says Kerrigan, but the boy shakes his head and backs away. "Not mine I tell ya." American.

Kerrigan bounces the clump on his palm. "You're sure?"

"*Told* ya, mister. Not mine."

Kerrigan shrugs, pockets the lump, and exits the back door without visiting the gents' after all. His heart is beating. He steps into the doorway of a secondhand bookshop to see if he is followed and thinks then, *Why the hell did I do that?!* He regrets pocketing the boy's stash. *For what reason?* He should have left it on the floor. But now it is too late, so he continues across **Drury.**

Through **Dame Court,** across **Dame Street,** down **Temple Lane,** he enters the Temple Bar, where he retires to the basement, closing himself into a stall to empty his bladder and study the brown lump. He smells it, touches the tip of his tongue hesitantly to it. Then worries that it might be literal shit. But he returns it to his pocket and jogs up the stairs to breathlessly order and carry his pint out into the sunny backyard, where he takes a seat alongside a barrel.

He can't catch his breath, can't get air comfortably deep into his lungs. From jogging up a flight of stairs? Maybe need to cut down on the Petits. Maybe just one. No inhaling. He lights a cigar, observing the antique tin signs mounted on the walls advertising Powers Whiskey; Bagots, Hutton & Co. Fine Old Whiskey; Murphy's/From the Wood That's Good; Bulmer's: Nothing Added but Time; Crested Ten: John Jameson & Son; Murphy's Extra Stout: On Draught and in Bottle; Lady's Well Brewery-Cork; Cantwell's Café au Lait . . .

And he recalls Kathleen Cantwell, who never so much as poured him a kind word, in his first-grade class in Blessed Mother Catholic School in Elmhurst, whose sweet young Debbie Reynolds face caused all the boys to dream of sweet tender love. But it was the mouth of little Ellen Childe who caused his string to thrum. Maybe a clue to Licia there. Maybe Kerrigan, by virtue of his double diminutive dark name, is prone to the darker nature of women, sees the dark as light, the treachery as blonde, the false as bright blue eyes.

Finally the air breaks through to his lungs and he inhales deeply, abandoning the Petit in the ashtray. A yellow crane lifts up above the rooftops against the blue sky with its scatter of soft white clouds. A young man at the next barrel says to him, "I like your green tie" and reaches to take it between his fingers. Kerrigan nods, concealing his annoyance at this transgression of perimeters, and the young man's young woman says hoarsely, "You are a luvlie man."

Kerrigan remembers once in McDaid's then, years ago, he had come from some literary conference and inadvertently forgotten to remove his name badge, which said, DR T KERRIGAN. A woman approached him and said, "Now what would you be a doctor of?"

Kerrigan, taken aback, noticed his tag then and said, "Oh, of, uh, literature actually."

"I think you are a doctor of bullshit," she said.

He laughed, thinking she could scarcely have known how closely that description fitted his dissertation on verisimilitude, and the woman's husband appeared.

"And what are you drinking?" the husband asked.

"I was actually having a mineral water," Kerrigan said. "Fizzy."

"You'll have a large whiskey," said the man, and as things progressed, in the morning, the three of them sailed on the choppy green water through the chill misted dawn air of Dublin Bay in the couple's ten-meter sloop. They parted swearing to stay in touch but never did of course, and in honor of that memory, Kerrigan now goes to the bar to request a taste of potcheen. The bartender gives him half a tumbler for which he will accept no payment.

"Sure it's hardly a taste at all, and it is not the real stuff anyway. If you want the real stuff you'll have to go to the Garda. They confiscate it all to keep on hand for their celebrations."

"*Uiske beatha*," he says, raising the glass of clear liquor. "Whiskey. It keepeth the reason from stifling." Wise words spoken 422 years before by the Chronicler Raphael Holinshed.

While he nips the potcheen to keep his reason from nipping too tight, his lungs rebel again and he begins to cough, which leaves him gasping, seriously short of breath, frightened now.

What is happening to me?

After several moments the air begins to filter down, just as a lad of perhaps nine in a dirty T-shirt steals in the back door, peering cautiously over his shoulder to be certain the bartender has not seen him.

He approaches Kerrigan. "Would you like to buy a solid gold pen?" the lad asks, his hair red and face pale, his eyes puckish. Kerrigan waits until he is sure his lungs have settled, then asks where he got the pen, and the boy says, "Me mother was tired of it so she give it me, but I cannot write."

"How many karats is it?" Kerrigan asks.

"Oh, 'tis not a vegetarian pen atall," the boy says, and Kerrigan laughs and gives him all the coins he has in his pocket. "That's not enough for the gold pen," the boy says, and Kerrigan tells him to be off. The boy complies, but stops at the back door and shouts in "*Bollocks!*" before he takes off running.

Instantly Kerrigan regrets that he didn't buy the pen.

In Donleavy's old room at Building 38 in Trinity (CYCLISTS DISMOUNT and KINDLY REMOVE THE HAIRS FROM THE PLUMBING FIXTURES AFTER

SHOWERING and PILFERERS WILL BE SEVERELY DEALT WITH), it is not reason that stifles Kerrigan as he bathes in the tiny cake of hand soap provided, thinking gloomily that he has no faithful Penelope nor even an unfaithful lusty Molly to bring the soap to, and is not in a mood for a honeymoon of the hand. Perhaps he will bring the Bronnley's to his Associate, fulfilling the unfulfilled by Leopold. He cannot be certain that he even has a chance with her, who may or may not have whispered that he is so blind.

He sits on the edge of his bed gazing out the tall window to the green, breathing heavily, and quotes Donleavy's O'Keefe aloud: "In this sad room / In this dark gloom / We live like beasts."

Then he recalls a fact he acquired from an article in *Time* that he glanced through on the plane, that most heart attacks occur between four and six P.M. on Mondays and Fridays. It is currently, he calculates, Friday, but the hour of six P.M. is long past. His legs are tired, and he wanders to the sink, which he leans over to look at his face in the mirror, mouth shallowly gulping in air.

Is he having a heart attack? He is not unwilling to die, should this be what this event signals, but not at this specific point in time because he still has a book to complete, and he will be damned if he will allow all this expensive research to lie fallow—he has not even submitted his expense report this month—even if he does not wish to complete the book at all but merely to continue researching it without end amen.

Regretting ever more greatly that he did not purchase the golden pen, he rinses his mouth, sees his face in the mirror over the sink, pouchy eyes, not quite able to get the air where he wants it, deep in his lungs. He looks at the eyes, thinks of George Seferis, Nobel Laureate from 1963—*if the soul is ever to know itself it must gaze into the soul*—noting that the pouches are now more than incipient; they are in fact greenish of hue and definitely pouched.

And he lies sidewise naked on his bed to sleep, relishing the chill through the open window, curious to see if he will dream, fears he will die without an opportunity to observe himself doing so.

And naked in the chilly dark, curved atop his knubbly bedspread, he fancies he can hear the streets outside his window, the river beyond the Trinity walls, the voices of strangers in the courtyard speaking softly, the sound of a runner's feet moving swiftly over the barbered grass.

Taxiing out to the airport, Kerrigan stares, gloomily unseeing through the side window, breathing shallowly and thinking about death while the driver complains about his wife.

"She's moody, y'know, and like I'm out last Sunday for me birthday, and I come home, she asks me next day when did you come in? I says, How do I know when I come in? I was blind drunk. I don't know, I don't know. She's moody."

Kerrigan nods, pays lip service. "With the best of them it's hard."

"And isn't it the truth? Been here on business?"

"Escape really."

"Wife lets?"

"She's, uh, we're separated."

"Ah, I figured as much, y'know. No excape without. Like the French fella says, what's his name? *No Exit*. How you say that in Frenchie, y'know?"

"*Huis Clos*," says Kerrigan. "Hell is other people."

"That's exactly right. And no excapin' it. She's moody."

All my life, on and off, at least ever since Licia tooketh away her illusion, but even before, even as a child, I've more or less wanted to die, thinks Kerrigan. And perhaps now I will. For real. Comes to every man, also to me. Why not now?

He lights a cigar outside the door into the airport but immediately begins to cough and flings it to the ground and twists it out beneath his shoe. If I am dying, he thinks—the breath not quite deep enough into his lungs—and if there *is* an afterlife, I will perhaps have the opportunity there to meet many of the people I have admired. That is if, in the afterlife, there is not the same kind of ranking system as here upon this earth. No reason to suppose so, however. For that matter, no reason to suppose there is an afterlife at all. Or that even if there is, the egos that distinguished us while living will still be in function.

He steps into the airport just as his flight is announced, and he heads for the departure gate. A tall black-T-shirted professional man is boarding the plane just in front of him and laughing happily over something he apparently is reading on the last page of the *International Herald Tribune*, and Kerrigan feels on the edge of death that he should do something, but doesn't know what.

He should have bought the golden pen.

Seven: Pint of View

We have a huge barrel of wine . . .
Every morning we glow and in the evening we glow again.
They say there is no future for us. That's right.
Which is fine with us.

—RUMI (TRANSLATED BY COLEMAN BARKS)

The early flight from Dublin on Scandinavian in a Boeing 737 is nearly empty in business class. Handful of suits scurrying home after doing business with the Green Tiger. Early, but not too early for a chill champagne with warm scrambled eggs and a single sausage, fried cherry tomato, and a chanterelle mushroom. To which the young professional in the black T-shirt, Kerrigan notes, four rows up the aisle, is also amenable. How the stewardess smiles in this section. Smile fades when they go aft, through the curtain to the economy class, where they dole out raw fish from a wicker basket.

"You know what Churchill said about champagne," he says as the flight attendant beams and cracks the seal of the little bottle of Lanson's bubbly for him. She tilts her head obligingly, as if to say, *No, what?*

"Three prerequisites: It must be dry, it must be chill, it must be free."

Oh, you kid! She smiles and touches his arm. Maybe she genuinely likes me. *You're a luvlie man. You're so blind. Can't you take a joke? You're as sane as I. I vant to dance vith thee woman. IT IS FORBIDDEN TO THROW FOREIGN PARTICLES IN THE VC BOWL. Pilferers will be severely dealt with. Sin not against the breath.*

He uses the tiny red plastic clothespin to attach his napkin to the lapel of his shirt and digs in. The eggs are runny, the champagne lukewarm. Luxurious problems. Kerrigan sees a picture in the *International Herald Tribune* of a very young-looking American soldier and remembers himself at Fort Dix in '61. Wanted to be a true American. Fantasies of action in Cuba. Jump the wall at Guantánamo, bayonet between the teeth, BAR beneath the arm, lobbing hand grenades. Medals and decorations for service above and beyond the call. What a sap! Him and Benjamin Blicksilver, the six-four wiry-black-haired and bespectacled intellectual from Columbia who was so good at absence.

Blicksilvah! First Sergeant Robert M. Coover used to bark breathily. *Whar the hail is Blicksilvah!*

And where is Blicksilver today who had recommended Kerrigan to read the last sixty pages of *Ulysses* to find the blue parts. "That," said Blicksilver with a smile on his slightly wobbling face, "is the reward that awaits you after plowing through the first few hundred pages."

And Kerrigan quotes: ". . . how he kissed me under the Moorish wall and I thought well as well him as another and then I asked him with my eyes to ask again yes and then he asked me would I yes to say yes my mountain flower and first I put my arms around him yes and drew him down to me so he could feel my breasts all perfume yes and his heart was going like mad and yes I said yes I will Yes." *Trieste–Zurich–Paris,* 1914–1921. [THE END]

But the past is not a dimension it is wise to cavort in with all the dark of its disappearances so he is grateful for the fact that some manner of hard thing irritating his hip brings him back to the here and now. He digs into his pocket to find a kind of dusty stone there that he drags out precariously, careful not to upset the breakfast on his fold-down table. He finds himself staring at a large brown lump resembling a petrified turd. Then, just as recognition finds its way to his consciousness, he senses a figure standing over him, looks to see the shining stewardess whose smile indicates she is fully aware, beneath her respectful gaze, of the nature of the thing in his fingers.

"Would you like to buy some duty-free items, sir?" she asks, indicating the many sleek and shiny cellophaned packages in her trolley, but her smile says something quite else. And now a businessman in the seat across the aisle is also looking at the brown lump, though not smiling at all, and Kerrigan feels the blush ignite his face. He wonders what the fellow in the black T-shirt would say.

"Hairy lemon," blurts Kerrigan. "Soap."

"We do not have soap, sir. Just liquid soap in the lavatory."

"No, no. This. Hairy lemon soap. Bought it at Sweny's Chemist. Featured in *Ulysses*. Joyce. You know, Leopold Bloom bought a bar on June 16, 1904. Poldy Bloom. Give us a touch, Poldy, Molly said. I'm dying for it. And he kissed her under the Moorish wall."

Now she looks frightened, escapes with a wilted mouth as Kerrigan stuffs the lump back into his pocket. How to get rid of it? Cram it in the obsolete armrest ashtray. But they would know. Too large anyway. Already alerted perhaps. Witnessed. Their records show who sat here. Seat 7C, left two-seat aisle. Kerrigan, T. E. Too old for this. Could go to jail. Smuggling. Mule. Alert the captain to have a SWAT team waiting at Kastrup. Swat him like a fly. Journalists, too. UNKNOWN EXPATRIATE WRITER APPREHENDED AT KASTRUP. HASH COUP. Held in isolation for thirteen days.

He sips bubbly with his predicament. Could bury it in the remains of his runny scrambled eggs. Not deep enough.

The businessman across the aisle is sneering openly at him. Kerrigan says, "*Tyv tror, hver mand stjæler.*" Old Danish proverb: Thieves think everyone steals. And "Drunks fear the police, but the police are drunk, too." And "You have the leer of the sensualist about you. I am the proverbial *l'homme moyen sensuel.*"

The man removes his gaze slowly. Very un-Danish to strike an attitude over another's vices. Must be a Swede. Or Norwegian. You're as sane as I. Aren't wolves dangerous? So are violins. You are so blind. Did she say that? Sin not against the breath.

Kerrigan thinks of the sniffing dogs that patrol American airports, trained to nose out the goods, tries to remember if he has ever seen such a beast in Kastrup. See here, I hold an SAS Star Alliance Gold Card. Many, *many* air miles to my name. Entrée to the gold lounge, where they serve complimentary champagne and Christian of Denmark cigarillos.

Disposable toothbrushes in the loo and gratis newspapers in five languages. Bright row of bottles of strong spirits at your free disposal along with an ice bucket, tongs, sturdy drink glasses (no plastic cups there) and savory snacks. They even distribute free volumes of Scandinavian literature in the original Scandinavian with English translation, including Strindberg's *Alone*, Brandes's *Thoughts on the Turn of the Century*, Hamsun's *Hunger, A Fragment*, Munch's *Notes of a Genius*, and Ibsen's *When We Dead Awaken*, which James Joyce reviewed at the age of seventeen. *We only see what we have lost / When we dead awaken. / And then what do we see? / We see that we never have lived.*

I know these things. I am the man and I was there and I will be there again, puffing a Christian, tippling bubbly in the company of great Nordic writing, and I will breathe easily and deeply again, as soon as this temporary obstruction in my lungs is overcome, and I have a press card issued by the Danish Association of Magisters Joint Committee for Danish Press Organizations that entitles me to cross police lines, though subject to the provisions of the Ministry of Justice Circular No. 211 of 20 December 1995. Freedom of the press. I instruct you to let me pass. But it stipulates on the card that one is subject to obey instructions from the police at the site of the crime. Such as: *Please empty your pockets, sir, and assume the position.* Maybe one of those good-looking policewomen. Hurt me a wee bit, please, so I at least get something out of this inconvenience. Just a wee bit. Tingling of the flesh, as old Poldy said in Night Town.

Now you're fucked, Kerrigan. All these years of surfing only to wipe out over a stupid bit of greed. Robbing a frightened backpacker of his stash.

UNKNOWN AMERICAN WRITER HELD FOR QUESTIONING IN KASTRUP HASH CASE.

Hashish (Arabic), n. (1598), the concentrated resin from the flowering tops of the female hemp plant (*cannabis sativa*) that is smoked, chewed or drunk for its intoxicating effect—also called *charas*.

Female hemp.
You're so blind.

Can't you take a joke?

Sin not against the breath.

Everything will be all right. Optimism, said Voltaire, is a mania for insisting all is well when things are going badly. *Candide.* Fine novel that, published more than three hundred years ago, and Voltaire had to run for it. Police after him for every manner of sin in print, against God, the church, the priesthood, sexual propriety, king and country. Man will not be free until the last monarch has been strangled in the intestines of the last priest. Or the other way around. To protect himself he had the book published simultaneously on the same day in Paris, Amsterdam, Berlin, and London, and ran his bloody arse off to the little town of Ferney, just across the border from Geneva, where he built a chateau, convenient for a Swiss getaway, planted poplars along the entryway, and the town became known as Ferney-Voltaire and the townfolk called him Le Patron.

French cabdriver once when I insisted on being allowed to sit in the front seat bellowed at me, "*C'est moi qui est le patron, monsieur!*" Unlike the sweet waitress to whom I once said, "*Merci, madame,*" and she replied, "*C'est moi qui dit merci, monsieur,*" and slapped her ample rump as she passed me. Another missed opportunity that one remembers on the very lip of extinction. Die in prison of lung cancer. *Do you 'ave a leetle Franshman in you?*

Kerrigan clicks the telephone out from beneath the armrest, swipes in his plastic, and dials her number. He wants just to hear her voice once before they lock him up. Ironic to be able to reach her like this, so near yet so far, years about to separate them. Time goes by so slowly. Long lonely nights. And this is why I sojourn here, alone and palely loitering.

She answers on the first ring. "This is Annelise," she says in the Danish manner. He only listens, the rush of the jet in his ears, as she says, "Hello?" and he can think of nothing to say to her.

"Is it Terrence?" she asks. "Why are you breathing so heavily?" He hangs up.

Is it Terrence? You're so blind. Pilferers will be severely dealt with. Beware of the moving bollards. Why are you breathing so heavily?

Am I breathing heavily? Enough to be noticed? Will they think he's nervous.

The chief cabin steward requests the passengers to fasten their seatbelts and place their seatbacks in an upright position, so Kerrigan feeling less than upright sits strapped in and upright, looking out the window at the shadow of the plane over the green sea (not snot but jade, like his Associate's eyes), moving landward, alongside a sailboat, over the fields of Amager, over a bunch of tiny cows in a field, a herd of tiny horses, over glittering miniature scale-model cars and roads and houses, finally larger, much larger than before, over the airfield where the great wheels bang down and roll along the tarmac.

Pilferers will be severely dealt with.

He knows he must easily be subject to suspicion, a heavily breathing man without luggage, not even a cabin bag, only his *Finnegan* satchel, in rumpled clothes, who has been sighted by a cabin attendant with a double-thumb-size lump of hashish in his hand—the word *assassin* originally was *hashishin*, thugs who smoked hash and went out on a rampage of killing—yet he does not dare discard it for fear he is being watched. He recognizes that this is unreasonable yet his mind is awash with fleet fishlike thoughts of scientific methods by which they can test the fingers and pocket lining for hash residue and the fear that his fate will be harsher if he tries to escape it. At least he was honest. Owned up to his sins. So lock him up but keep the key handy.

He can think of no more horrific fate than jail. To be forced into close quarters with no escape from confronting terrible types. Supposedly the Danish penal system is much more humane than the American where, in the year of 1999, 1.8 million people are incarcerated with the total ever increasing, more than half for nonviolent offenses under the new, tough, mandatory no-parole drug sentences, but Kerrigan doubts the Danish jails are all *that* humane, set up not to correct but to punish. Even the Danish minister of justice has been quoted as saying that no one ever became a better person by doing time. You are locked in a room, subject to the whimsy of brutal types who belong to secret societies, and no escaping their rule unless you are one of the "strong" prisoners.

Kerrigan once had a tour of a maximum-security prison in Denmark and was in a group shown around by a very well-spoken prisoner with impeccable manners. The group was told about conjugal visits that could be with wives, girlfriends, boyfriends, or prostitutes—said to reduce the instances of violence in jail. They were shown cells that were only slightly worse than certain no-star hotel rooms Kerrigan had stayed in—toilet, shower, bed with bedspread, coffee table, minifridge, TV, writing desk, easy chair. The difference was that these rooms were locked, from the outside, between seven P.M. and seven A.M. You had to remain locked into about an eight-square-foot room for half of every twenty-four hours. Afterward the group was gathered in the prison conference room for a Q&A. Kerrigan asked, "I've heard that there are strong prisoners and weak prisoners. What actually transpires?"

The guide—obviously a strong prisoner—gazed at him with intelligent, unwavering blue eyes, thought a moment, and finally said, "What are you asking me? Are you asking if a fine is laid on the weak ones each time they have to use the toilet? That doesn't happen."

Answer enough for Kerrigan. Negating the suggestion a mere formality.

Kerrigan knows that he would not do well in prison. If only he had his pistol with him, he could retire to a restroom and plug his brain. Keep his reason forever from stifling, unless of course he would end in hell or purgatory for such an act or, as the Buddhists were said to believe, would be immediately recycled as an insect: Oh, no you don't, buddy! No exit for you. Go immediately to worse shit, do not pass go, and collect nothing but more misery.

His pistol! If they apprehend him, search his premises, they will find it. Last exit closed. No excape, as his Dublin cab driver said. They could pin whatever they want on him. Yet isolation would be preferable to the society of criminals. God knows if the stories are true of what they do to each other, what they do to the weak, anal rape the classic method by which victorious soldiers demonstrate their power over the vanquished, even as James Dickey indicated in the climactic scene of his novel *Deliverance* as standard practice. There are even jokes about this on TV sitcoms, and it is not funny. It would hurt. Very much. Not even masochistically pleasing, just goddamn downright ugly brutal pain, tearing of the rectum. Humiliation and pain. Miserable society that allows such practices. Some people even applaud it. Make jokes of it. Gloat.

Your honor, this man completely *forgot* he had hashish in his pocket. Therefore I call for immediate dismissal. Why is he breathing so heavily if he's innocent? Simple obstruction of the air passages. Temporary.

On the other hand, he knows a British fellow who was one of the hostages in Iran and who used his imaginative faculties to ward off ill treatment—he fed his captors "secrets" gleaned from the pages of a Tom Clancy novel. Perhaps the imagination can serve even there. Perhaps Kerrigan could start a writers' workshop, thus becoming a valued colleague of the stronger cons who would then refrain from bestial practices, come to him as a senior, request his guidance.

Kerrigan, in terror, confesses to himself that he is a physical coward.

After a long swift walk, Kerrigan presents his identity card to the uniformed man at the passport control booth. He glances at Kerrigan's card, looks at his face, regards his heaving chest, and says in Danish, "Ah, here's an American who has had to learn to master this horrible Danish language."

"I try anyway," says Kerrigan in Danish, and they both laugh.

"Welcome home," says the Dane in Danish with a smile, and Kerrigan smiles, too, saying in Danish, "Thanks shall you have," though he is wise to him: It's a test; they speak Danish to you cheerfully, but if you don't understand you reveal yourself as a possible thief of a national identity card for purposes of illegal entry into this social democratic kingdom's welfare.

No dogs on leashes are sniffing about the baggage area, and with a distinct sense of watching eyes all about him, his legs stiff and heavy, lungs laboring (*Why is this happening?*), he strategically positions himself behind a black man and walks through customs unmolested while the black man in front of him is stopped and questioned.

Saved by Nordic racism! You should be ashamed. But you're not.

The tall young professional fellow in the black T-shirt comes out behind him, and as they pass through the automatic doors to freedom, he gives a sidewise smile and a wink. "Hash and eggs, ey?" he says, and is gone.

Kerrigan leaves the train at Nørreport station, deliciously, deliriously relieved. A free man. Yet he cautions himself against optimism. *Ingen kender dagen for solen går ned*, he thinks. Danish proverb: No one knows the day before the sun has set. Like Sophocles, *Oedipus*: Count no man happy until he is laid in his grave. And remembers then what Kreon says to blind Oedipus when he objects to having his children removed from him: "Think no longer that you are in charge here. Rather think how when you were, you served your own destruction."

The sun is brilliant. Rare day of spring. Soon time to blind his consciousness. Soon time for *en hivert*. Lovely Danish word, that, for a drink: A pull. Sounds better in the Viking tongue: *Hivert*.

What'll it be, sir?

A pull of beer, please. You mean a hivert? Yes, please.

He crosses **Kultorvet**, the Coal Square, where the outdoor cafés are folded out to the late-May sunlight. Can hear Happy Jazz playing from within the White Lamb, singer and chorus: *I'm the sheik of Araby, your love / belongs to me / (He's got no pants on!)* Written by Harry B. Smith and Ted Snyder in 1921.

On **Amagertorv**, he pauses to observe the tabloid headlines mounted on placards outside a newspaper kiosk, all apparently dealing with the same heinous crime, like some medieval ballad: BABY CORPSE FOUND IN STREAM and BABY CORPSE FOUND IN PLASTIC BAG and BABY LIVED TWO HOURS IN BAG IN STREAM . . . Why do we so relish this gore?

A little girl outside a bakery window says in Danish to her mother, "I want my cake *now*, Mommy! I want it *now*!"

Kerrigan pauses and looks down at her. "So do I," he says, "And I've been waiting *much* longer than you."

The girl closes her mouth and gazes up at him with large blue eyes. The mother's mouth is mirthful. Kerrigan, the hero of the moment, smiles at Mommy, whose cleavage is lovely as this spring day. Known in Danish as a *kavalier gang*—cavalier passage. Such a beautiful thing, the passage between the breasts that bear the milk of human kindness, two tiny miracles.

A woman cycles past illegally on the Walking Street, but Kerrigan doesn't mind for she wears a miniskirt and each pumping turn of the pedals flashes the peachy cream of inner thigh, visions of eternity, the immortality of humankind. *Write an ode to women's inner thighs.* She sees him looking and smiles. And that is another reason why he loves Denmark. Write an essay: "Why I Love the Kingdom of Denmark," by Terrence E. Kerrigan. Women don't mind if you take a discreet peek. *Yes, I'm beautiful,* her smile says. *Thank you for noticing. Did you enjoy the look? And you're a noble gent yourself, despite the rumpled clothes and cheek stubble—manly that. And I can tell your jeans must've cost. Hundred dollars I bet. Ceruttis, no? You're a luvlie man. Love your green tie. Nice Italian jeans there—don't want you to think I was looking at your bottom. May I squeeze it?*

Of course, madame, yes, and you are a vision in a dream of all the lovely weightless lightness that causes the heart to soar with poetry. Light as a bird, not as a feather.

A man slouches by with two rottweilers on leashes held short. His sleeveless muscular upper arms adorned with dark-blue tattoos, bracelet-like. Viking designs perhaps. Or Celtic. It seems to Kerrigan this man must be very afraid in his heart and therefore perhaps dangerous.

A hand-lettered sign near the Amagertorv fountain proclaims that ALLAH IS THE ONLY GOD while a representative of the Association for the Advancement of Islam stands ready to field questions, and from farther down the walking street, a group of marching fools appear bearing placards that pronounce:

NO SEX NO CRY! And FAMILIES FOR PURE LOVE! And NO MORE FREE SEX! And SEX IS NEVER FREE!

The Association of Families for Pure Love descends upon him like a flood, hollering, "Yee-*ha*!"

Will you please shut up! he thinks.

The Pure Lovers recede toward the King's New Square, and Kerrigan eyes a pregnant girl who bears her belly proudly. *Must* be triplets. Touch it for luck? You are so beautiful with your swollen nose and lips so all abloom and stuffed with the life growing inside you. Oh how I would love to lie with you, touching with most gentle respectful affection your body swollen with the gift of life to the world, you beautiful humble life-giving goddess!

There a young man keeps a small beanbag of some sort constantly in the air by the deft manipulations of his feet and knees, and two women walk past, one with a sleek midriff and crumpled-up face. O city of the hundred vices! Kerrigan sees a poster plastered to a trash basket that says LA PETIT GAGA and another advertising a play by Hans Christian Andersen about a mother. The cunt giveth and the cunt taketh away.

The walk has once again winded him. *Why is this happening?* Has he sinned against the breath? He cannot get air into the bottom of his lungs. He reverses direction, heading back up Købmager Street toward the Coal Square, and looks up as he approaches the central post office to see a green bronze statue of **Mercury** leaning out from high up on a roof across the way. Always astonishes him when he accidentally glances up to see it there—long, lean body, seeming to be about to leap into the air, to fly, sculpted by Julius Schultz in 1896, another gift to the city from Carlsberg. Drinking beer and smoking cigars benefits art here!

He wants to think about his Associate and whether or not it is important whether or not she said that thing, particularly in light of the fact that he might be dying, but a plan is hatching in Kerrigan's skull for a nonlaborious exercise in point of view that will allow him plenty of sitting. He once had a professor of creative writing who complained about manuscripts that kept shifting point of view from character to character, saying, "It's like going to the theater and being forced to change your seat every five minutes."

Kerrigan's plan is to drink a pint of beer in every café on the Coal Square, moving full circle around, clockwise perhaps for the sake of symmetry, to see what variety of wonders this exercise in point of view— pint of view rather—might reveal to him, changing his seat after every pint whilst keeping his consciousness from pinching. And then, when he has done that, perhaps he will have a new perspective on his Associate, whom he longs to see.

Stepping onto Kultorvet, the Coal Square, he gazes around at the trees and cafés and bustling people. This square was established in 1728, after the first great fire which raged for sixty hours and destroyed nearly 30 percent of the city.

He stops first at **Vagn's Beef and Sausage Wagon** to fortify his stomach from among the wares offered:

Wienerpølse	Vienna sausage
Knækpølse	Elbow sausage
Medisterpølse	Medister sausage
Hot dog	Hot dog
Fransk hot dog	French hot dog
Ristet pølse	Fried sausage
Almindelig pølse	Ordinary (boiled red) sausage

Settling on a Vienna sausage on a tiny bun, the ends hanging out on both sides, center piled high with mustard, ketchup, chopped raw onion, and paper-thin slices of pickled cucumber, he bites. A treat! His cholesterol sings marvelous hymns in his blood, and he munches happily as the sexy woman in the flower stall wraps a bunch of pink carnations in white paper for a smiling, snub-nosed woman who clearly intends to brighten her rooms somewhere while a wiry blond fellow in the fruit stand alongside sings out, "Hey ten delicious plums for a tenner! Ten Danish plums for a tenner!"

Another bite, tangy mustard on the palate and onion sweetening the breath for an earthy kiss perhaps. Nibble those drooping ends with their little stubs of fried string. Yum. You are what you eat: Kerrigan pictures himself as a hot dog consumed by a lovely young maiden without mercy. There's a fantasy for his giant Norwegian headshrinker, who once called him mini-Terry, giving him an erection of irritation and humiliation. Aren't wolves dangerous? So are wiolins.

Now the flower lady is calling out, "Hey ten pretty roses for a tenner! Ten pretty roses for a tenner!"

Before starting his cycle of Coal Square cafés, he weaves through the benches at the southeast corner of the square where derelict Inuits loiter, drinking export beer with gold foil at the neck.

"Any surplus today, friend?" one of the Inuits asks, and Kerrigan tosses a five-crown coin into the man's hat.

He enters the Biblioteksboghandel—the Library Bookshop (now, alas, replaced by a candy shop), so named because the business school alongside it used to be the main branch of the Copenhagen library, now moved to Krystal Street, alongside Café Halfway.

He drifts down to the basement and rummages among cut-rate offerings—novels, poetry, history, coffee-table books about airplanes, war machines, Madonnas, art, masks . . . There are how-to's and opera books, travel guides, a wall of cheap classics that he feels as though he has read and would not admit to not having read, though in truth he has barely ever more than scanned a good many of them. Read a few, though, more than a few, yes. He takes down Lucretius, reads on the back what is said to be the only existing biography of Lucretius, by St. Jerome: "Titus Lucretius, the poet, born 94 B.C. He was rendered insane by a love philter and, after writing, during intervals of lucidity, some books, which Cicero amended, he died by his own hand in the 43rd year of his life." Then he takes down a slim paperback volume of Matthew Arnold, looks to see if "Dover Beach" is included. It is. "Dover Beach" is an essential poem for him. Written in 1867, two years after the end of the American Civil War, three years after the loss of the southernmost Danish province to Germany. *Where ignorant armies clash by night.* He remembers reading it to Licia, and her false blonde enthusiasm for it. Dover Bitch more like it. Dover Cunt. But he will not turn against Arnold's masterpiece because of Licia. No.

Kerrigan buys both books, two ten-crown bargains, buck and a half, that fit into either rear pocket of his Italian jeans (*Don't want you to think I was looking at your bottom*, said the lady from the Isle of Man) and goes back out onto the Coal Square. Still smacking his lips with the memory of his sausage, he starts his café carousel at the **Rice Market**, little tucked-in section of four or five tables with a slung-jaw Turk happy to provide him with a pint glass of amber lager.

Who can be happier than a man with a pint and a cigar (no inhaling today and I did not have sex with that woman) at a table in the early afternoon sunlight with a book of pre-Christian Latin poetry, purchased for a pittance, on the table before him?

Here in this very café he once sat with the Danish novelist Lotte Inuk, whose real name is Inuk Hoff Hansen, christened Inuk because by chance born in Greenland, and who in addition to writing also reads tarot. She read Kerrigan's cards and the last card she turned down was of a man lying on his face with seven swords buried in his bleeding back.

"This is not an unalterable future," she told him. "And please remember that the swords are metaphors for devotion to quests for something base."

What does he quest for that is base? he asks himself, but is distracted by a gal in rust-colored pants clinging just so to her big powerful butt! He gazes with devil-slit eyes upon it, imagines horns upon his own head, a love philter emptied in the beer that drenches his parched mouth. Let me die of love, then. Let me die of dedication to the beauty of the feminine species. Let me, as the Danish poet Karsten Kok Hansen once advised me, "Love love love as though your life depended on it 'cause it does." Or as the Frenchman gesturing to the fork of a woman's thighs once said, "*Rien sans lui.*"

But he is aware that he has been running from involvement all his life. Until Licia. And that was an error. He wonders if it will be an error with his Associate. Whether you marry or not you will regret it.

From where he sits he can see diagonally across the square the opening into Rosengården Street where the night men and executioner used to reside, thinks of the night men in their "chocolate wagons," collecting the shit of the city in the days before sewers, right up to the early part of this century on whose outer edge he perches, imagining himself as a curiosity being studied by some citizen a hundred years hence, the year 2099.

Kerrigan greets the eyes that read these words. Is *anyone*, in fact, reading this? Who are you? Are you free or slave? Do you have to read this in secret? Do you have beliefs, or is all belief long dead? Even the withdrawing roar finally utterly withdrawn? Do you live in fear and shackles? Do you know the passionate joy of intellectual speculation? The beauty of the human body? Do you have a lover to caress? Do you know the golden pleasures of beer? Do you know, dear children of a future time, that love, sweet love, was once a crime?

You can see me but I can't see you, and by the time you read this, *if* you ever do, please remember that my blood was Celtic and the season spring, and Georg Brandes's *Thoughts at the Turn of the Century*, published in 1899, will seem a true antiquity, two hundred years old, longer than any person can ever hope to survive unless medical science and the world economy make leaps not yet imagined possible. But where will there be room for all the surplus population of those long lives? And foodstuffs?

Kerrigan will ask no questions of his reader a hundred years hence for he is aware he is ill equipped to do so, just as Brandes was when he said in 1899 that the prime question about the future of European politics was whether the twentieth century's greatest world power would be Russia or England.

And the world Brandes described in 1899 was one in which the great powers were dividing the globe among themselves. Their aim was to do so as peacefully as possible to avoid a world war. But still, for their own economic advantage, they victimized not only the unlucky nation but all the smaller surrounding nations, subjected to sword, fire, horror, and engulfed in the interest of national unity, used for barter, or delivered to brutality so that peace could be preserved. It was in that manner, while

Christian Europe looked on with consent, that the sultan permitted the slaughter of three hundred thousand Armenians.

With but four fingers of beer remaining in his glass, Kerrigan's mood turns glum, considering the place that used to be called Yugoslavia, the bombs and missiles, slaughter, rape. He considers the fact that but eight years before, in 1991, he was the happy editor of a small anthology of Yugoslavian literature, and none of the work he gathered for it seemed to focus anywhere but on the profound, universal, existential matters that go beyond national concerns. Yet there were horrors to come, concentration camps, slaughter, massive rapes when the country fell apart after Tito's death, separated into its five republics with only a single one, Slovenia, escaping from war, a country of two million that was so well organized that it could escape that fate.

And what happens now? What is the great question of the century about to begin? Between Eastern Europe and Western Europe? In the Middle East? The Muslim world? China? Africa? What?

Go to the next café.

He drains his beer, moves three meters south to an outdoor table at **Ristorante Italiano Pompei Pizzeria**, obtains a pint of green Tuborg at the counter, and places himself at the outer perimeter, and it occurs to him that, for him, the great question of the century about to begin is perhaps far more personal. Perhaps more like, What is he going to do with whatever years remain to him? He might have as much as a quarter century remaining, even more, although not, perhaps, at the rate that he is attempting to keepeth his reason from pinching. Perhaps he has a future with his Associate. Or perhaps that is a blind alley. Which way to regret it?

To his right, a commemoration of the past: a 1990 bronze sculpture by Hanne Varming of a bench with an elderly man and woman seated on it, a representation of the couple from Hans Christian Andersen's "The Elder Tree Mother," first published in 1845 by P. L. Møller, a womanizer, who eventually would, according to Henrik Stangerup's fictionalized account of Møller in *The Seducer: It Is Hard to Die in Dieppe*, die in syphilitic madness in Normandy. The old couple fit right in on the square, watching the world through century-and-a-half-old eyes.

A ladybug lands on the back of Kerrigan's hand, alongside a pale age spot. He blows her off his hand into the air with a fanning out of spotted wings. She lights up in the sun, and what could be more beautiful and full of hope than the new full pint of golden beer he hoists into the air to toast the unknown faces watching from the future?

Who are you, my friends? Singular, really. For you can only read this on your own, one person and a book, I can only address one of you at a time; only one of you at a time can let me in. Unless you are being read aloud to by a third person. Maybe you found me in some carton in a basement or an attic, and out of curiosity you turned back the cover and began to read. Perhaps you are leafing through, reading a page or a paragraph here and there. Kierkegaard's "rotation method."

Or maybe books are obsolete in your world. Maybe you are reading me on some manner of screen, all books having been abolished in this paperless world. Or maybe these pages have been fed into some manner of machine that converts them to a voice, perhaps speaking into earphones. No matter.

If you have come this far, you could only be a friend. Let me tell you where I have buried my fortune, and if you hurry you can find it before anyone else gets there. It requires the ability to decode black scratches that are symbols of the sounds we make with our mouths and allow any human being to transmit the secrets of his or her mind to the skull cages of others. Lucretius, Arnold, Andersen, Joyce, Kierkegaard, Kristensen, Cavafy, et alia.

The Coal Square most likely still will be here, but housing what? Owned by whom? Dedicated to what pursuits? What changes might occur here—even in a decade? A dozen years? This square might be torn up completely and reshaped, trees torn out and others replanted. Sculptures changed, facades, a fountain dug—nothing is permanent. He looks across at the White Lamb café from 1807. Even the Duke of Wellington's entire fleet of gunships did not succeed in undoing the

Lamb, barely nicked its roof. Nelson and the Duke of Wellington are dead, and in 1966 the IRA blew away the pillar in Dublin commemorating Admiral Nelson, who put the monocle over the blind eye, but the White Lamb's golden beer flows on nearly two hundred years after Nelson and Wellington's attacks on this city, and perhaps will still serve its useful function one hundred years from now, at which time virtually all currently treading or crawling the earth will have dust for brains. After all, Hviid's Vinstue is still around, and it is ninety years older than the White Lamb.

What else? That corner building that houses **Klaptræet**, the Clapboard Café, where Kierkegaard lived in 1838—surely, yes. And these trees? How many of them? He sits up, rotating in his chair, and counts. Ten of them, spaced irregularly around the square. Larch trees and beech. How old are they? Some are large and old, some slight and green and new, witnesses to all this life and bustle of shoppers, mothers and fathers pushing baby carriages, Vagn selling sausages, a bookshop that for a mere ten crowns a volume, a dollar and a half, gives me this slim back-pocket volume written two millennia past by a Latin poet driven so mad by a love potion that he took his own life at forty-three, a fact Kerrigan considers at the age of fifty-six with his suddenly impaired lungs. Yet managed to make use of his lucid moments to record words still read now, more than two thousand years later. And another volume with "Dover Beach," written in 1867 by the then-forty-five-year-old Arnold who then had twenty-one years left and who summarized in one poem of thirty-seven lines the then-contemporary society's loss of faith in God, likening it to a receding wave on the beach, in "its melancholy, long, withdrawing roar"—still withdrawing for nearly a century and a half.

And these two books he has for a mere three dollars.

In truth, how vast is the culture of this brave new world!

He shifts his chair and tips back his head to gaze upward—and is surprised to discover his lungs fill better in that position—at the spreading branches of the beech tree above him, the little fig-shaped leaves, branches overlapping to form a protective mosaic whose shadow drifts on the ground beneath—shelter from sun, from rain. Who would cut down these trees?

Then, incongruously, he remembers the love philter which his Associate produced on the occasion of their last meeting when she whispered, or he imagined her doing so, that he was blind, or possibly kind, or maybe he only thought it—in his Associate's voice?! That tiny phial concealed in her hand. Poppers. Amyl nitrate. She shook it and sniffed, held it to his nostrils, and the sensations of his palms against her skin were charged, electric. For but a few seconds, their copulation was truly golden, then, and he should have purchased that golden pen with which to write about it all.

Kerrigan sits with his head tipped back to better access air with his lungs, and from a distance he hears tramping, and the Pure Love Brigade comes marching across the square again chanting, "No sex! No cry!" and "Yee-*ha!*"

American bluenoses out on a spree, damned from here to eternity, Lord have no mercy on such as ye. He promises himself that if they come again, he will, by God, moon the bluenosed fools with his hairy fat pimpled pink butt.

Yee-ha!

He can see a window open on Peder Hvitfeldts Street with bed covers hanging over the sill to air out all the sex and fuck germs. Just think of all the prick, cunt, asshole, armpit, feet germs clinging to them. Then the breezes carry them away in the air, floating right over the heads of the marching prudes—Yee-*ha!* Take a shower of sex germs!

Free as the air. Over Kerrigan's head, too. They land on his scalp, remnants of love illicit and sacred, perversion, inversion, missionary couplings, and the partakings of oral joys and solitary pleasurings. Love whippings, cock suckings, cunt lappings, and humpings galore! Golden showers, secretory overflows. The germs dust down over his face and shoulders and his rod goes stiff. He breathes through his mouth ingesting sex pollen, washes it down with the remainder of his pint of golden beer, and moves to the next café, **Phønix**, slightly hunched to conceal his secret, thinking, *God's sacred teeth, I'm half pissed already and my lungs are not filling right, and I am so fucking horny still even at my advanced age sweetening all lamentation!*

I'm pissed and I'm proud! he chants privately, crossing the few meters to Phønix, noting that it says *UFF* on the storefront behind the café in yellow and black letters with black outline. UFF. And QUALITY USED CLOTHING. Ironically he detumesces in the Phønix, where he should rise from his own ashes as a fiery bird.

He settles with a beer delivered by the plump-wristed hand of a daughter of God whose taps are in a kiosk like the one on the King's New Square that he wanted to bid on in auction. Her smile as she hands over the frothy glass would change the mind of Gilgamesh from going off to seek eternal life.

Oh you gorgeous bitch!

The beautiful women are multiplying. Their men must neglect them or they would not be out parading their loveliness this way. Or perhaps they parade their loveliness because their men have made them mindful and proud of their magnificent forms.

Or maybe they are the goddesses of the new paradigm calling forth the most beautiful of desires, to gaze with joy and wonder upon the body, to create new life. Even if those new lives were stolen by the Dover Bitch.

But there is no denying these women are all gorgeous bitches. People of a future time, if you still have the concept sexist, please know that I am *not* one, I just adore women. So, okay, maybe I am a sexist. But I don't know any better, okay? I am an exception.

The sunlight through his beer gleams on the table before him, a glass of golden fire, cool and wonderful in his mouth as he swallows deeply, and deeply again.

On the back of his hand he tallies the pints with the strokes of his Montblanc, just to know, because one loses count so easily, and sees there are already four strokes as he takes his table at the **Clapboard Café** and surveys the square from this pint of view, taking inventory:

There are seven outdoor cafés, one sausage bar, four restaurants, a business college, a bookstore, one employment agency, a fucking 7-Eleven, one used clothing store (UFF), one unused clothing store, ten trees, a flower stall, a fruit stand, a travel agency named Albatross ("Upon my word I slayed the bird / That made the breeze to blow . . ."). The apartment that Søren Kierkegaard called home in 1838 and the White Lamb serving house that the Duke of Wellington's cannon failed to destroy in 1807, though it did dent the roof. The duke was then known as Arthur Wellesley (1769–1852), born in Dublin and commemorated there in Phoenix Park by a 205-foot granite obelisk (1817) located just inside the park's main gate, on the eastern side and but a stone's throw from the feet of Finn MacCool, who sleeps beneath Dublin, dreaming the history of the Irish race.

Yellow leaves blow across his table. The sky above Kerrigan's head, as he tips it back to increase his air intake, is blue and tarnished silver, and he watches a woman with a rump he would give an award to if he were chairing a committee charged to do so. She sits. Happy the chair beneath her, said Leopold Bloom.

There goes a woman eating a big green apple with her white teeth, how her lips compress over the tight green skin, and see, that infant there can hardly walk, tottering after the copulating pigeons who move on, hopping with a scurry of wings, foiled in the act by a tot: *Yee-ha!*

Now comes a party of Rollerbladers swooping through like marauders, at the speed of frustration, as Lance Olsen put it in *Burnt*, and there up above the Niels Brock International Business College, Kerrigan remembers, on the fourth or fifth floor, are or were the offices of *Det Danske Selskab*, the Danish Cultural Institute, whose publications department once was run by a woman named Kate Hegelund whom everybody loved for her gentleness and who one day for unexplained reasons at a most untimely age was dead.

Her smiling face, her braided golden hair, her gentle ways never to see the new millennium.

Now he runs a line across the four strokes on the back of his hand and buys a little bag of crisps to munch along with the green Tuborg draft purchased from the **Nico Café** alewife, trying to remember the books that Kate Hegelund gave him, and there must have been one by Sophus Claussen (1865–1931) because Kerrigan recalls a poem by Clausen in which he asks who does not think that the forest's thousand silent branches witness, though we think we are alone. And another in which the poet Thorkild Bjørnvig explores the many facets of Karen Blixen's identity—as an idea of nature, a marionette, a wild animal, a teller of tales, and a creature free of identity, relieved of and escaped from identity, in a state of "permanent adventure and pleasure."

Kerrigan thinks now of that escape from identity to a state of permanent pleasure and wonders whether that is possible. He has been attempting something similar, although he is also trying to construct an identity out of a mosaic of facts, dates, names, statistics, history. But now he can barely get sufficient breath to fill his lungs and will lie in his bed this night, his only partner the dread of extinction.

The glass is empty, and Kerrigan's intoxication has ebbed with five strokes of his Montblanc on the back of his hand as he glances from tree to tree around the square, their leaves trembling with the life of the air that touches them, wondering if their silent branches sense his presence, immediately dismissing the thought as worthy only of his own ego cage, for it is the question of an ego, the least important part of his being, albeit the only conscious part.

The outdoor tables administered by **Det Hvid Lam,** the White Lamb serving house, are few, a double row of two, and he strokes the back of his hand with the nib of his Montblanc, beginning the second set of five pints, his mood heavier than he would have expected it to be.

It occurs to him as he swallows the first of his sixth pint and gazes up at the green leaves above his head that he has never even asked himself who he is. He has tried to construct an identity but what *is* he underneath the construct? *Perhaps I am nothing but a drunkard. Perhaps, because I do not even ask, I doom myself to being no one, nothing.* "I'm nobody, who are you?"

Dickinson's words lift in his blood with the beer, and he thinks perhaps it is all right not to have asked that question. It is difficult enough work just to be, without having to know quite who it is you are being:

> How dreary - to be - Somebody!
> How public - like a Frog -
> To tell one's name - the junelong day -
> To an admiring Bog!

The red frog his green-eyed Associate painted for him.

Halfway down the beer, his eyes fall again on the front of the building where Kate Hegelund worked. He lifts his glass to her, wishes her well in her eternal rest or eternal joy, and feels water in his eyes.

This day is not proceeding as the celebration of his deliverance and the carefree carousel he anticipated. His lungs are still not functioning optimally, and still he has not solved the enigma of whether he was accused of being blind. Then he remembers the Lucretius in his back pocket and slips it out, swallows the rest of the Tuborg, and leaves the White Lamb behind, crossing the center of the square with Lucretius.

The bar of the last of the Coal Square's seven cafés—**Kultorvets Restaurant,** the Coal Square Restaurant—is housed in a shack where Kerrigan marks the seventh stroke on the back of his hand as the bartender taps his beer. The bartender is Japanese, so Kerrigan says the only word he can remember in the language of the country he visited but once, decades ago: *"Arigato."* Thanks. The waiter exhibits polite surprise, bows graciously, his smile friendly and Western, slightly mischievous.

Kerrigan sits in the sun with Lucretius in his hands, but he is thinking of the possibility that he might be dying. It seems somehow a fitting end for a writer, a failed poet, to die of a lack of breath. Sin not against the breath. The wound of the mouth.

He closes his eyes. The day is hot now and humid, but with an occasional saving breeze. He is dying, it seems, near an end he has no doubt hastened with his imprudent but most enjoyable behavior. And with his eyes closed or with his eyes opened, it is the same, for he is alone and that startles and unsettles him. At such a moment there ought to be a witness. A woman who loves him. A man who admires his work—a man whose own work he himself admires. A woman whose work makes him see. An artist perhaps, who saw into his soul and painted a picture for him of a red frog perhaps.

How public like a frog.

An image appears in his mind of the table beside his bed. It is as though he is lying in bed on a humid night, motionless, the hand of death closing ever so slowly, almost imperceptibly, around him, smothering him, and on the bedside table is an 8½ × 11-inch white pad with pale blue lines the color of water too beautiful to be real—the color of Licia's bikini. How lovely the pad is. If he could only reach it, he would caress it like a lover's back, a woman he knew whose back beneath his palm was joy, splendor.

Who *was* it? Her again. The Associate. Will he never be free of thoughts of her?

You have not lived right, Terry boy. I've lived the only way I could. You could have done better, been more prudent, careful, you would have lasted longer.

Who wants it?

You do. You *do*.

Opening his eyes, he realizes he is almost asleep there for a moment. He sees on the surface of the round metal table before him a half-full pint of beer and a book. Lucretius. He opens the book at random, as the Romans used to do to find a sign, and he reads a passage about the dread of death, that men so wish to escape that dread that they are greedy for wealth far beyond their need and shed the blood of others in pursuit of riches, allow others to live in poverty to attain it, and from the same dread envy the power of others, the wealth of others, the fame, the dignity, feel that they themselves live in darkness and filth. To such extremes the dread of death drives the man that he begins to hate life and commits self-murder, completely forgetting that this is the very thing that has driven him with dread from life and toward every sin . . . It is the dread itself that is to be dreaded. He closes the book, looks into his glass, focuses on the age spot on his hand as the tramping of feet approaches up Butcher Street:

"*Yee! Ha!*"

The Pure Love Militants again. Kerrigan remembers the promise he made to himself to moon them if they came back, but does not move. A life is built on promises unkept.

It seems such an indifferent number of pen strokes to stop on. Seven. Seven pints of view.

Perhaps another circuit, maybe this one counterclockwise, starting here with this fine place, with this fine Japanese, Danish-speaking bartender. He thinks of his father's oft-quoted lines from Housman:

> For I have been to Ludlow Fair
> And left my necktie God knows where
> And carried halfway home or near
> Pints and quarts of Ludlow beer . . .
> And down in lovely muck I've lain
> Happy till I woke again.
> And then I saw the morning sky
> Heigh-ho the tale was all a lie.
> The world it was the old world yet.
> I was I, my things were wet,
> And nothing then remained to do
> But begin the game anew . . .

However, he remains seated before an empty pint glass, thinking: *She positively could not have said you're so blind. What are the chances? How many people say that? Who would say it? Licia and Licia alone. A onetime occurrence.*

And she reached into your heart and drew out the image of a red frog. And you are fabricating excuses not to be with her because you are afraid. You opened your heart to her, so wide that she could reach in, and now you are trying to close it again.

Eight: The Smoke Eaters

Sin not against the breath.

—Æ

Instead of recycling the Coal Square, he follows his seventh pint with a walk back down Butcher Street, east over Højbro Place, past the equestrian statue of **Bishop Absalon**, founder of Copenhagen, wielding the ax of battle and domesticity. Past the **Parliament** and the old **Stock Exchange**, Kerrigan's lungs labor again so he stops on the pavement and flags a cab to take him over Knippels Bridge, spanning the slit of harbor between Zealand and Amager islands, to **Strandgade**, left to **Christianshavns Kanal** and the masts of small pleasure craft tipping with the breeze on the lightly billowing water, mast fittings clanging agreeably. He pays and stands on the wooden bridge for a moment, Wilders Bridge, watching the surface of the water change with the minuscule constant changes of the Danish afternoon light.

And he calculates: Because all of the seven "pints" he drank were really only four tenths of a liter, he has only had the equivalent of a little over five pints. That he is able to make this calculation so deftly refuels his confidence and renews his thirst.

Past a stucco wall of ocher yellow, he enters through the door of the **Færge Caféen**, Ferry Café, with its porthole window. His mouth cannot room more beer just now, or his belly house it, so he orders a *gammel dansk*. The woman behind the bar, red-gray haired, a face that has lived, her nose broken, its tip twisted, serves him his bitter dram (dram being a measure for snaps originating from the Greek word *drakhem*—a weight unit equaling 4.25 grams, same root as the Greek currency unit, *drachma*, soon to be replaced by the European currency unit, foiling all future plans by Greek taxi drivers to pull the old 5,000-to-50,000 drachma-note switcheroo, which trick was once pulled on Kerrigan). She answers his question that the café dates back to 1850. The walls are paneled with ship planks, and a ship's-wheel lamp hangs from the ceiling. Beside the bar, a brass ship's bell stands ready to be rung should some generous customer buy a round for the house, and a pool table shrouded with a sheet of green plastic.

He takes his drink on the canal side of the establishment, gazing across to Wilders Place and the tipping masts while a couple of bureaucrats from the Culture Ministry across the street finish their lunches of liver and bacon and onions and mushrooms. He orders a plate of it for himself and a beer and another bitter snaps, and the nourishment fills the empty pouch of his optimism and enthusiasm.

The black bitter liquid, he imagines, opening the cells in his lungs to admit more air. You have to go to the doctor, he knows he will be advised if he reveals this to anyone. But like Bartleby the Scrivener, he would prefer not to.

Kerrigan has developed his own plan of treatment in case of serious disease. In a **Vesterbro** bar he knew, he visited a fellow he had once met researching an article about the drug culture in Copenhagen. From this fellow, for an exorbitant price, he purchased a Browning No. 1 pistol from the land of Antoine-Joseph Sax (1814–1894) which he loaded with seven cartridges and placed in a cigar box, wrapped around with two stout rubber bands, at the back of the highest shelf in his bedroom closet.

His plan, should that day come before his health was so badly deteriorated that he could not, is one sunny day to rent a pedal boat and pedal out into the middle of Black Dam Lake. There he will unpack the picnic lunch he will have brought with him in a wicker basket. He will dine on smoked eel and dark rye bread spread thick with fat. And because fish must swim, he will drink cold bottles of beer. Many of them. And iced snaps in his favorite Holmgaard aquavit glass, many of them. While he dines he will watch the swans float past like beautiful white questions that are about to be answered. And to encourage the seagulls— for they are an important part of his plan—he will fling bits of bread and eel up into the air to get them hovering overhead in an excited, crying cluster.

And then, when he is sufficiently satisfied, sufficiently besotted, but not yet incapacitated, he will take the pistol from his belt, place the snout in his mouth, pointed upward toward his cranial cavity, and pull the trigger to administer one large lead pill to the rippled brain. It will tear a broad path through his skull, spraying bits and clumps of gray matter upward, which the seagulls will catch in their beaks and gobble down, wheeling over the lake, their gullets full of morsels of his thought and personality so that he will sweep across the lake like a great pointillist consciousness on his way to forever.

He wonders whether he will be able to carry out that plan if he cannot breathe.

Two bitters and his lungs seem reasonably well functioning again, and head tipped back, Kerrigan wanders off down the cobblestoned street of **Wildersgade**, named for an eighteenth-century shipbuilder named Wilder, to the **Eiffel Bar**, over the door of which a red rectangular sign hangs bearing a likeness of the Eiffel Tower. A list of beers and liquors in the window of the gleaming facade announces prices that transport him back a dozen inflationary years.

The bartender, dressed like a French waiter in a snug black vest advertising Tuborg Classic beer on the back, greets Kerrigan when he enters.

"Good day," he says. "So pleased you could come." A Band-Aid is stuck to his freckled front bald spot. Kerrigan orders a cognac to put a knee on the content of his stomach. He knows that, at this price, it is not cognac but brandy—two-, one-, or no-star brandy no doubt, but welcomes the coarseness of texture. He chats with an elderly man who, he learns, has been the owner since 1960 when he emigrated from the Netherlands. The building is from 1736 and the bar dates back to the 1930s, originally called Café Wilder, then Café Jakob, finally the Eiffel Bar since 1960. At the end of the barroom is an ornate spiral staircase that seems to lead nowhere—at the top of which, he has heard, ladies of the night once held court, though he cannot ascertain if this is mere legend. Kerrigan peers up the spiral staircase anyway, thinking that prostitution in Denmark has in fact been legal since March 17, 1999—a St. Patrick's Day event, though Irish birth control would surely have ruled over eros that day: Pour it down till you can't get it up.

Outside again on **Wildersgade**, his feet, for which he is thankful, follow the cobbles back to the canal, turn him right to **Overgaden Neden Vandet**—High Street at the Water—and stroll him slowly past more tipping masts. Over the doorway at number 51B a plaque on the brick wall announces that the resistance group **Holger Danske** was founded and housed there during the German occupation, 1940–1945.

Holger Danske is a legendary Viking hero who is said to have been sleeping for hundreds of years and who, it is told, awakens in time of Denmark's need to come to its aid. Beneath *Helsingør Slot*—Elsinore Castle, where Shakespeare set Hamlet, based extremely loosely on Saxo's account of the seventh-century Jutland King Amlet—is a large concrete sculpture of the sleeping giant, seated, sword across his knee, head tipped in slumber, in the shadowy catacombs. And his was the name taken by this Danish resistance group—the sleeping giant who woke to aid his country in need. This legend is similar to that of the warrior giant who sleeps in the earth beneath Dublin, Joyce's Finn MacCool, dreaming Ireland's history.

His feet lead him farther to **Christianshavns Boat Rental & Café**. Here, on this 101-year-old platform mounted low to the water upon the canal, Kerrigan sits with a glass of beer, gazing upon the view beneath the bridge where covered boats bob on rippling water. A poster beside him celebrates Ernest Hemingway's hundredth birthday, an event Hemingway himself of course never got to see, having consigned his brains to a shower of shotgun pellets thirty-eight years before when Kerrigan was but eighteen, reminding him of the beginning of a story written the same year by Robert Coover, "Beginnings," which begins something like, "In order to get started he shot himself, and his blood, unable to resist a final joke, spattered the cabin wall in a pattern that formed the words: It is important to begin when everything is already over."

The Hemingway poster includes portraits of two leopards that Papa no doubt would gladly have blown away. Kerrigan once stayed in the Swiss chateau of Hemingway's German publisher, Heinrich Maria Ledig-Rowohlt, who introduced paperback books to Germany. He was the German publisher not only of Hemingway but also of Faulkner, Nabokov, Updike, Camus, Sartre, Henry Miller, Thomas Wolfe, and Harold Pinter. During his stay, Kerrigan was given the chateau library to write in for a fortnight, and among the books and papers there he came across a letter from Hemingway to Ledig-Rowohlt from the 1930s in which Hemingway reported being in hospital with an arm broken on a hunting trip. He noted, however, that before he injured the arm he had shot a big-horn mountain sheep ram, two bears, and a bull elk and written 285 pages of his new novel. He mentioned that Dos Passos had been with him when the accident occurred but was not hurt himself and did not succeed in shooting anything. He went on to complain about the German translation of the title of *A Farewell to Arms*, and with a threat to take his new novel to "a big Jewish publisher" if he is not treated better in future, he closed the letter with warmest regards from himself and Mary, and then no doubt went out to pick a fight with Antoine de Saint-Exupéry.

Kerrigan enjoys the beer in his throat and the sunlight on his face, thinks of the time he was here with his friend Thomas McCarthy, an Anglo-Irish story writer and novelist who was supporting himself as an executive for an automobile tire company. How many years ago? McCarthy used to edit the literary journal *Passport*, which, like many another literary journal, had gone under after a dozen or so semiannual issues. McCarthy himself has published a good many fine short stories and a couple of novels over many years.

How many people are working like that, Kerrigan wonders, writing and publishing their stories and poems in obscurity for little or no pay, for the sheer pleasure of doing so, of putting into language some deep inner thoughts and visions in order that the envelope of their solitude might be breached, that their inner landscape might be viewed by another, in celebration of human communion.

He thinks of Calvino's observation in his essay on "Quickness," quoting Galileo that the greatest of all inventions was the alphabet, which allowed a person to communicate his deepest thoughts to any other person regardless of how distant in place and time, all via the arrangement of twenty-something characters on a page (in the case of Danish, twenty-nine characters).

And in that way, thinks Kerrigan, the writings of any other of the thousands, millions of little-known authors might be stumbled upon in the years to come, beyond our lifetimes, a hundred years from now when Ernest Hemingway would have been two hundred years old and long beyond shooting any animals or having imaginary or real punch-ups with other writers. Some curious reader might find a yellowed copy of a book or literary journal in a bin outside a used-book shop, if such still exist then, or on the back shelf of some library, written by an unknown or forgotten author, and leaf through it, reading at random the most private thoughts of men and women now long gone from the earth, bringing them back to life for a time in the reader's mind.

Then he notices the sunlight moving on the water and remembers—how could he have forgotten?—that first day with Licia. How they had walked here from the university. How she said, Men my age are so uninteresting. (And you are so blind.) How she looked naked back at the west side flat he owned then. He has been thinking about her for years and still she is not finished with him.

Kerrigan sips his beer, takes out a cigar, feels in his pockets for matches, and finds the lump of lemon soap in one, the hashish in the other, and thinks about hashishinating his consciousness if his lungs will permit. He climbs from the floating bar to the street.

The hashish is solid and large in his pocket, and he remembers those days decades past when he smoked himself into a languageless trance, sublimely self-hashishinated. He thinks of the Freetown of Christiania, and fingering his stolen pocket hash stash, considers the old Danish proverb, *"Hvo der vil have kernen må knække nødden"*: "If you want the meat, you have to crack the nut."

Across the canal to **Skt. Annæ Gade**, past **Vor Frelsers Kirke** (Our Savior Church), and left on **Prinsessegade** to **Christiania**—so-called **Fristaden**—Freetown. A former military fort, it was taken over by squatters in 1971. An area of about 750 acres with 150 buildings, woods and ramparts and moats and a thousand inhabitants. One of the exits is through a gateway over which hangs a sign: YOU ARE NOW ENTERING THE EUROPEAN UNION. Kerrigan contemplates the sign from within the Freetown, smoking a little cigar in the sunlight.

The Danish population is split fifty-fifty over Denmark's membership in the, at this writing, fifteen-country union, with ten others waiting to enter and three in special relationship with the union. The Danish opposition fears that Danish life will become standardized, that the Danish language will be lost to the international English that is rapidly becoming the lingua franca of a political entity whose twelve languages are increasingly difficult to manage in administrative meetings. They also fear the common European currency, the euro, against which Denmark, Sweden, and the UK have taken a stand.

However, the value of the European Union for European civilization is clear—the importance of binding these nations together legally for the future of a continent torn by centuries of internal war.

The population is also no doubt equally split over whether the Freetown of Christiania should be allowed to continue to exist. In the beginning, the squatters who took it over paid neither taxes nor water nor electric bills. In 1973, the government decided to allow the squatters to run a Freetown there for three years as a social experiment, but five years later, a decision to level the area was supported by the Supreme Court. Some violent episodes, clashes between police and Christianiters, were followed by a continued political tug-of-war, but Christiania is still standing, twenty-eight years after the squatters took it. It is the second-largest tourist attraction—after the Little Mermaid—in

Denmark, but that weighs against the fact that it also includes 750 acres of most attractive urban real estate on which developers could turn an enormous profit.

There was a drug problem for some time involving motorcycle gangs and hard narcotics, but the thousand inhabitants managed to rid the place of the violent elements and hard drugs. Attempts to purchase or sell hard stuff there today are dealt with harshly, but soft drugs are allowed, sold openly (when the police are not around) on a broad dirt pathway called **Pusher Street**, where varieties of hash, skunk, and pot are sold by weight.

Various other enterprises also flourish here, most notably the restaurant Spiseloppen—the Eating Flea—and the concert hall where, inter alia, Bob Dylan has sung. There are also a good jazz club, art galleries, and other enterprises. Many artists live here as well—painters, goldsmiths and silversmiths, sculptors, musicians, writers—and the living quarters and social establishments, kindergartens, nurseries, a "womansmith" blacksmithery, a small bicycle factory, even an enclosed skateboarding hall, are originally and strikingly appointed. It is also now possible to have a guided tour of the area by someone living there. But the only way for a new inhabitant to come in is by becoming the lover of someone who already lives there.

Kerrigan owns paintings by two Christiania artists, Wiliam Skotte Olsen and Finn Thorstein, and one of his friends, Per Smidl, lived here in a construction wagon while he taught himself to write and went on to publish numerous books, one about his life here, *Wagon 537, Christiania*.

He follows the rutted dirt roadway toward Pusher Street. There are no motor vehicles here, only bicycles, and many unleashed dogs wander about or lie in the dusty sunlight. At one of the stalls in the shopping bazaar area, he buys a chillum from a man with one eye and proceeds down Pusher Street. The **Christiania Jazz Klub**, in the Opera Building, is locked up tight until this evening. Kerrigan has spent many nights in the company of friendly guests and management, stepping outside to share a joint with new friends, where entrance is as cheap as the bottled beer or shooters of Havana Club. At closing, the bartender often brings out an alto or tenor or soprano sax from under the bar and continues jamming until dawn or beyond.

Continuing past the Klub and past **Nemoland**, another bar with open concert stage, he comes to the **Woodstock Café**. From the bar at the end of the long room inside, he orders a black bottle of gold-label beer that he carries to an outdoor table and sits in the sunlight among Inuits and their grumbling, restless dogs. Using his notepad as a workplace and the blade of his tiny Swiss army knife, he cuts a sliver of hash from the lump he has carried in his pocket all day, then segments the sliver and fills the bowl of the chillum.

Lowering his eyelids in honor of the poor backpacker from whom he filched this hash, he lights it with a Tordenskjold stick match and tentatively, slowly draws the smoke into his lungs. So far, so good. Holds it, not too deep. Then exhales again. He draws three times on the pipe, then lets it go out, tucks it into his shirt pocket, and soothes his palate with strong beer.

Soon he is joined by three young Asian-looking men, perhaps Inuits. One of them rolls a fat joint and lights it, tokes, and passes to Kerrigan, who thanks him no. The young Asian man glowers at him. Kerrigan smiles. The young man begins to tell the story of his life. He's thirty years old, born in Taiwan, moved to Denmark as a child, was sent to New York as a teenager to play football in some high school league. Despite his small stature, he was an outstanding kicker from years of playing soccer. He still looks wiry and muscular, good-looking in a sullen way. "I was good," he says. "I should have stayed. Now I'm bad boy. I'm all the time on hash, on coke." His older brother, a bank adviser, is the biological son of his Danish mother. Apparently he himself was adopted. Kerrigan doesn't ask. Instead he suggests that the young man's multicultural background could be an advantage—all the languages he speaks.

He glowers at Kerrigan. "Are you fucking blind?"

Kerrigan freezes in startled silence, hearing echoes of Licia's words.

Then the young man continues. "You live in Denmark—don't you see what racists they are! I get nothing but welfare. Twelve thousand kroner a month. After rent and cigarettes and drugs, what do I have left for myself? A hundred?"

One of the other boys—he looks very young—laughingly speaks to the Chinese fellow in a language Kerrigan doesn't understand. He glowers and flings his half-smoked joint in the boy's face. It bounces back to the table with a scatter of sparks. "You laughing at me! You think I'm a fucked-up Inuit?"

The boy's throat bobs as he tries to swallow his fear. The Chinese boy glowers at him, at Kerrigan. He seems to be deciding something—maybe who to punch. Finally he says, "I'm in a bad mood." He stands, extends his hand. "It was good to talk to you," he says, and is off and soon the boys follow. Kerrigan thinks, *Those anger-management classes paid off.*

Across from where Kerrigan sits, at a broad outdoor café, a woman on a bench piles her long hair upon her head, elbows raised. The sun sparkles in her yellow locks. He smiles. How do they know that makes us long for them?

He watches a Christiania bike—a three-wheeled bike with a large wooden transport case in front of the handlebars—rumble past, three giggling children in the transport case. An extremely large man in his mid-thirties, wearing shorts and a white T-shirt, stops in front of Kerrigan's table and asks, in English, "You know about the twelve families that run the world?" Kerrigan says that he'd heard something or other about them. He sits across from Kerrigan at the table. "My name is Viggo, and I'm drunk," he says, "but this is a fact." He says that America was an experiment which these twelve families, all royalty, decided to allow, to see what would happen. But now the twelve families are displeased, and America is going down. Somehow then, seamlessly, Viggo is on another subject, telling about his wife, Dorthe, who is twenty-eight and has found a forty-one-year-old plumber who makes her happy. That's okay with him. He loves his wife for the love that she gives to his two-year-old boy, and he wants her to have love from the plumber. That's completely okay, but he does not want this plumber to try to be a male role figure for his boy. He plans to advise the man about this. So he will have a warning. But if he doesn't take the advice, a car will pick him up and take him out into the woods where his bones will be broken with bats by the French mafia.

"No one knows about the French mafia," Viggo says. "It's been around for twelve centuries, and I know the son of the leader."

Kerrigan appeals to Viggo not to do that, not to have the plumber's bones broken. He will risk losing the right to see his son at all, ever again.

He shakes his head. "There will be no proof, no link to me."

Another man appears, not quite as large as Viggo, and says that he has called for a taxi, and the two of them salute good-bye with stiff arms and set off along the dirt street.

Kerrigan finds himself staring at the earth, which is very interesting to look at. The texture of the dirt is fascinating and several tiny ants wander about, tiny reddish-brown marvels gliding over the brown dusty earth. Specks of magnificent design—living! His mouth is agreeably dry and the chill glass of the beer bottle against his fingertips wonderfully pleasant, and the air of the spring day seems to be sliding unimpeded again into his sipping nostrils.

It occurs to him that one strategy might be to throw his wallet into the moat on the other side of the flowering ramparts, and then to die here where no one knows who he is. He might never be identified. This seems an interesting strategy.

Then he thinks of his Associate again, how she would look with her elbows in the air piling her hair up upon her head, and the thought of his Associate reminds him that if he obliterates himself here in Christiania, he will never complete his book about Copenhagen, even though he does not want to complete it but only to continue researching it forever, which would give him some measure of immortality. So to break it off before then, at this particular critical juncture, would seem a sloppy way to die.

The sun on the skin of his face and hands and the tips of his ears is marvelous as he floats down Pusher Street past the stalls and scales and roaming dusty dogs, the bearded tattooed men and nose-jeweled women. He stops at a barrel manned by a fellow in beard and leather vest who smiles. "Yes, sir. Can I help you?" Kerrigan asks how much for the little bag of skunk buds and is told that it is eighty crowns, the large a hundred. "I think the large then."

"Yes, sir. Thank you. Hope you enjoy it."

Kerrigan pockets the transparent bag, thinking, *A boy never outgrows his need for skunk.*

Out of the sun and into the shade again on the wheel-rutted earth. Kerrigan experiences himself as very far away in this strange place, re-enters the EU through the wooden archway, and floats up Prinsessegade toward Torvegade, where he waits for a taxi across from Elephant's Bastion. No taxi comes. Then he remembers a place just up the road he has passed a thousand times on his way out to the airport and has always meant to visit but never yet has.

A raveline is a triangular defense work standing in a moat between two bastions, the two outer faces of the raveline protected by ramparts. The **Summer Restaurant Ravelinen** is built upon the site where a raveline once lay outside of the defensive gate of the island of Amager, a so-called Zone of Servitude, where until 1909 building was limited in order to keep a free field of fire and deny cover to any enemy approaching the city.

The Restaurant Ravelinen stands where the old fortification used to be. The old yellow sentry building, which dates back to 1728, is now the restaurant's kitchen. The restaurant consists of two roofed-in sections built of strips of brown wood and an open gravel yard of outdoor tables that look out onto the old city moat and embankment.

This is where Kerrigan sits with a tall glass of lager staring down to the gravel that crunches beneath the soles of his shoes. He is the only guest.

> The bird of amnesia
> Nests on the head of the smoke-eater
> And steals his wits.
> Thus spake the High One.

Nonetheless, the gravel reminds him of something very sad, so sad he does not wish to think of it, for his stomach seems to be falling toward its own bottomless center as the not yet recognized memory rises to the surface of his thought. He sits there a long time staring at the gravel. Then he looks up at the wall beside the kitchen doorway across the gravel yard and the ancient yellow sentry post where he sees an advertisement for a *Pinse Frokost*, a Whitsun Lunch, celebrating Pentecost, Monday, May 25, and he remembers then what the gravel reminds him of.

He had been at another restaurant with his Associate—**M. G. Petersens Family Garden** in Frederiksberg, established in 1799, at Pileallé 16, on the west edge of Copenhagen. They sat outside with a drink, and she had gazed down at the gravel, a distant look in her eye. When he asked what she was thinking, she told how she and her first husband's family used to have a traditional Whitsun celebration each year. They would eat an enormous Danish *smørrebrød* lunch on the Saturday. *Smørrebrød* means literally "butter bread," but such a lunch consists not only of three or four different kinds of bread with butter and swine fat, but also a couple of dozen courses on the table, three or four kinds of herring—pickled, fried, curried, sherried—smoked eel with scrambled egg and chives, caviar, cod roe, smoked salmon with dill and freshly ground pepper, fried plaice fillets, smoked halibut, fresh calf liver paste, wild boar pâté, corned beef, country ham, lamb meatballs, calf meatballs, pork meatballs, half a dozen Danish cheeses . . . They would drink bottled beer and iced snaps, would *skål* and sing drinking songs in honor of the women, in honor of the company, in honor of the papa eel that would never come home to his eel family again. They would party all night and on the Sunday morning, at sunrise, they would move over to Hansen's Family Garden "to see the Whitsun sun dance" as they ate breakfast with strong coffee and morning snaps and many kinds of bread and cheese and sausage and pastry. There was music and dancing to Happy Jazz and people wore old-fashioned straw hats.

A celebration of this sort requires a certain sense of pace regarding the drink, and this pace was something that her first husband had never mastered. As in many other places, it is customary at Danish gatherings for wives and husbands not to sit together. Thus she and her husband were at separate tables. At one point she saw him down on the ground, swimming in the gravel. He swam from his table through the gravel over to her and reached up to pinch her on the inside of her thigh. *Very* hard.

"Did you enjoy dancing with Martin?" he hissed, and then swam back to his own table. Martin was the man on her left with whom she had just danced. Everybody was dancing with everybody. But even while her husband danced with another woman, he watched his wife dancing with another man, and sometimes he pinched her afterward if he didn't like the way she danced or who she danced with. Or he would tap the tabletop in front of him with his index finger until she stopped dancing and came to sit beside him. If she didn't stop dancing, she knew what was in store for her later.

On this occasion, however, one brutal pinch had been sufficient. She rose and went off by herself into the Frederiksberg gardens, through the hedge maze and the stone-path pond. She looked at her leg. There was a still-stinging, nasty red-black spot where he had pinched her. Then she decided not to return to the party. She walked all the way home to their apartment on the other side of the city, packed a bag for herself and for her daughters, who were staying with her aunt, and she left him.

Two months later she was alone with their three daughters in a two-room apartment. Her husband had cleverly registered everything they had in the name of his parents' company so she had no claim on it, wanted no claim on it. She wanted only no longer to be pinched and accused of things of which she was not guilty. She wanted her daughters not to be shouted at by a drunken father. She wanted to be free of living with a man who became someone else when he was drunk, which was nearly every evening.

Kerrigan stares at the gravel, gray and black and white pebbles that slide beneath his shoe as he shifts his feet on them. The sound saddens him. It makes a sound that somehow calls up the word *children*. He pictures his Associate's husband swimming in the pebbles, reaching up with a crazed face to pinch her leg, then swimming away again. Kerrigan is sad for the man, that he lost such a beautiful wife, the mother of his daughters, because his ego was so weak it required her subjugation to it.

The entire world is full of madmen, he thinks. *There is no such thing as civilization; it is all just a behavioral veneer. Or rather we live in an illusion of normalcy, of normal, reasonable behavior.*

Close to the surface of his consciousness are images of Licia and his girl he wishes not to see. Faces so far away. How do you survive that? You survive. On the flow of time. You get over it. One day you tell yourself, get over it, and you get over it. Even if you never do.

His mouth is dry again and he has not touched his beer. He drinks off half the glass in one long succession of swallows, working it down his throat, cold and delicious.

He wants very much to comfort her at this moment, his Associate, to make her believe in comfort, for it seems to him if he can make her believe, then it will be true. And he wants very much to go and sit alone by his front windows and watch the sun set over the lake, to watch the light—pale red, pale blue—ripple on the water while silhouettes of men and women and children and dogs and joggers move past beneath the silhouetted trees like a picture in some forgotten childhood book.

He pictures the sad green shadows of his Associate's eyes. She deserves a man who is not a drunkard, who is not drunk every day, who is not drunk most days.

Outside on the grassy ramparts beneath the shelter of trees, he watches the sun move lower in the sky and marvels at the thousand colors of light on the water, stippled like an oil painting, and he feels the ellipse of the universe on its slow elliptical course around him and, around that, the mysterious darkness.

He walks slowly along **Torvegade**, head tipped back, toward Knippels Bridge, toward the center. On the other side of the street is the small, white, old-fashioned face of **Spicy Kitchen** at number 56. He stops and looks across, thinks of their spicy lamb curry, their chicken masala, their inexpensive beer and wine. But despite the hashish, he has no appetite. Just as his lungs begin to labor again, he sees the green "free" light on the roof of a cab and raises two fingers.

Back in his apartment, he sits by the window, hunched over his work, but merely peers at the Montblanc cradled in the crook between his thumb and forefinger, raises his eyes to the lake outside, silent figures jogging past on the dusky lake bank.

He reaches to his back pocket and slides out the book of Arnold, thumbs through to "Dover Beach," and begins to read, hearing within his ears, within the silence of the apartment, the melancholy, long, withdrawing roar . . .

Nine: Land of Dreams

> . . . the world, which seems
> To lie before us like a land of dreams,
> So various, so beautiful, so new,
> Hath really neither joy, nor love, nor light,
> Nor certitude, nor peace, nor help for pain;
> And we are here as on a darkling plain . . .
> —MATTHEW ARNOLD

From a dream in which his wife is chiding him for not having properly divided the fruit in an enormous bowl and offering it around, he wakes with a jolt realizing that he is no longer married and that the wife in his dream was not Licia and that the telephone has been ringing for some time.

By the time he reaches it, the machine is recording a message. A voice with a Swedish accent speaks into the recorder. "Terrence! Kerrigan! Are you all fugged up or what? Pick up the fugging phone!"

It is the insistent, demanding voice of Morten Gideon, who visits him from time to time, always unannounced, when he is in from Stockholm to find peace to smoke cigars and drink alcohol, to converse and fulfill secret assignations with the many women with whom he dallies.

Kerrigan decides he is not up to Gideon today.

He met Gideon years ago at the Casino Divonne Les Bains, first noticed him there by the loud and clear pronunciation of his Swedish-accented English addressing a ravishing blonde Turkish baccarat table-mate in these words: "I vant to kees your feet!"

To which the Turkish beauty—a gynecologist by profession Kerrigan would later learn—replied, "Yes, yes, Dr. Gideon. Down, boy."

Spying Gideon again next morning at the breakfast buffet where he sat nursing a Fernet Branca and soft-boiled egg, Kerrigan could not resist extending his compliments and inquiring whether Gideon's proposal had brought him into contact with the lovely Turkish trotters.

"It is all a dream in the dark," said Gideon, inviting Kerrigan to join him in a Branca, the beginning of an extended friendship.

The message now is: "Meet me, Kerrigan. Let me invite you out to dinner. I want you to meet this woman and tell me what you think. Meet me in the bar at the D'Angleterre. My plane gets in in two hours. Meet me there at three. I want you to tell me what you think of this sweet kid I met. Skin like milk! Be there!"

But the subtext is: *Legitimize the fact that I am having dinner with this sweet kid and then disappear so I can shag her.*

Gideon is the chairman of half a dozen different international companies. With kinky blond hair and thick lips, big dark-framed eyeglasses and black Armani suits and big glossy black shoes, he rules whatever he puts his hand to. To Gideon every woman is a challenge, but he is not content to look. He wants the comfort of their bodies, of their acquiescence.

"Hey," he says, "I'm a passionate guy. I need love."

He has just married his fourth wife, who is thirty years younger than he. He has seven children by various women. He is an intellectual businessman and has excellent taste in cigars with a budget to keep it busy.

Kerrigan splashes several palmsful of cold water into his face, leans on the sink for a while, assessing how he feels. His lungs are heavy but seem to be functioning. So far.

Moving barefoot to his dining table, he sees a fat stack of freshly written yellow pages, inspired by his reading of Arnold and Lucretius and the hashishination of his frontal lobe. He does not dare read them. He peeks. First sentence looks good. Second, third, fourth, too. Cheered, he decides not to read further just now.

His head is light so he switches on the radio to the classical channel, hears Johann Strauss II (1825–1899), "Little Woman of the Danube," and the swaying rhythms of the waltz soothe his mind. His gaze rests on the smooth lake, paddling ducks, bobbing joggers. A couple strolls beneath the green chestnuts and a woman passes pushing a stroller as memories carry on the strings of the Vienna Philharmonic—the New Year's Day brunch Licia always prepared for the two of them to dine on as they watched the Vienna Concert on television, "Tales of the Vienna Woods," "The Blue Danube," "On the Beautiful Blue Danube," "The Champagne Gallop," Von Suppé's "Charge of the Light Cavalry" . . .

They ate scrambled eggs and drank champagne, and the year that had just begun could not have begun more elegantly. None of the petty cares of daily life mattered then, no quibbles, grievances, petty jealousies, nothing. There were only the Strausses, I and II, the century-and-a-half-old music, the bubbly, the winter sun through the living room's plate window, the food on the smoked-glass coffee table—yellow eggs on a blue china platter, smoked eel in gray-white strips on a bone-white plate ready for the chives and pepper, delicate sausage slices, black pudding, cheese—of the cow, the goat, the sheep—fresh fruit, juices, toast, jams and marmalades, a basket of assorted rolls fresh from the bakery. And on the color screen of the TV the beautiful young Austrian women in their colorful gowns, the young cavaliers in their waistcoats and colored butterflies and cummerbunds, waltzing with such fluent grace.

And Kerrigan with a good cigar, Cohiba perhaps, Esplendido or Robusto, gifts from the generous Gideon, or a Davidoff Tubo No. 2, hand-rolled in the Dominican Republic. A cigar that might have burnt for an eternity, its thick, redolent smoke coiling up into the motes of icy sunlight through the frosted window, a single candle in the Irish crystal stick he gave her for Christmas, his beautiful wife with her beautiful slender legs seeing to him, replenishing his plate and cup and flute, because this was her New Year's gift to him, her husband, and if the gowns of the Austrian women were a tad gaudy, if their blue gazes were a tad vacuous, it did not matter, for these were moments of supreme success and there was no happiness like theirs then.

Beneath the decorated tree, unwrapped gifts in large, colorful department-store boxes, yet-unread books of gleaming freshness, and out the window their cherished lawn now white with snow beneath a freezing perfect blue sky, the magnolia's winter-bare black bones dusted with snow, a mere few years before it all would be taken away—the meaning of existence, of family, a net of human beings joined by blood and marriage, a tiny clan devoted to one another despite the occasional argument or jealousy, despite trouble, always stronger in the long run than the puny threats to it, stronger than all but one—blonde treachery.

He has been through it all. Taking the kindest possible tack. That she no longer loved him, that she had to get away. An adult human has that right. But it didn't hold. Because she planned it over a long while. She took half his money—okay, she had the legal right, but it was his inheritance, and she took Gabrielle, too, and she planned it and had it all ready to do when he was away in Scotland doing research. And she had to have had a man on the side who offered her a life in another country—maybe the United States, and he only hoped that the poor bastard fared better than he had. No matter what, Kerrigan felt, he did not deserve that.

He showers, dresses, thinks, remembers the wise words of Karen Blixen: *It is always advisable to take a little bubbly with your predicament.* And your brunch.

And there happens to be tucked away in his billfold two free drink chits from a new café that has opened a while back on the west side, on **Istedgade,** which happens to be the real street on which the fictional Ole "Jazz" Jastrau lived in Tom Kristensen's *Havoc,* and the real street Dan Turèll wrote about in *Big City Trilogy* with "Life on Isted Street," a long blues reflection on the life of this street in the 1960s and '70s with its hookers, addicts, pushers, serving houses, the residents and the "tourists." What better choice of a place for scrambled eggs and crisp bacon, cheese and bread, juice and the bubbly?

So when he climbs down to East Lake Street, he can only conclude that the appearance of a taxicab at just that moment, green taxi lamp glowing in the mild early afternoon, means that the universe and all the laws of synchronicity salute and support his decision.

"I love this street," the freeloading fictional poet Stefan Steffensen says to Ole Jazz in *Havoc,* looking down Istedgade from the block where it starts.

"Why?" Jazz asks, and Steffensen tells him, "Because it's long."

Words Kerrigan ponders while listening to the jolly Pakistani cabdriver tell him about a friend, Akhtar, in Bangladesh who owns two things only: a shed and a coconut tree. From the sale of his coconuts, Akhtar earns enough to support himself in his shed for the entire year, and even has a surplus so that he can give something to the poor.

The cabdriver laughs merrily. "Akhtar does not know, you see, that he himself is poor! And so he is wealthy!"

The story seeps into Kerrigan's consciousness, and he says softly to the driver, "That's a beautiful story."

"It *is* a beautiful story!" the driver shouts. "I never forget this story!"

"And I'll never forget it either," says Kerrigan as they cruise past **Jernbanescafeen**, turn right onto **Istedgade**.

"I hear from your accent you are from a country other than this," the driver says. "I am guessing you are from America, and I am guessing that I am right in my guess."

"You *are* right," says Kerrigan, thinking of the parable of the coconut tree and the poor man wishing to give something to those poorer.

Kerrigan watches porn shops zip past to left and right, drug addicts and hookers leaning in doorways, clustered on the street amid the shawarma grills and the gentrifying cafés and shop fronts.

"I think," says the driver, and looks at Kerrigan via the rearview mirror, "that you once loved a tree. Very much. You loved that tree."

Kerrigan tries to think of a way to calm the man, but picking through his mind, he remembers the peach tree. "How did you know?" he asks.

"I know. What tree was it?"

"A peach tree. It was the only tree that grew in our yard in New York and every summer we picked the peaches, and they were so delicious. We had peaches for breakfast and for dessert and for afternoon snacks. We had peach pie and peaches with cream and sugar. They were so delicious. I loved that tree. I did. Then there was a hurricane and it blew down. Our poor tree. I missed it so much."

"I think," says the driver, "that everyone in the whole world should be required on their birthday to plant one tree. The tree is the cousin to the man, to the voman. I think you come from America and you have lost your tree, you must plant one tree in this country!"

He pulls up alongside number 128, the long front of **Café Strassen**, which used to be **Café Zach**. Kerrigan pays, and the driver turns with a smile and solemn demeanor. "Remember," he says, and raises one finger. "The tree. The tree is going to help you."

Then Kerrigan notices that the café's windows are dusty and brown papered and rubble is piled outside. Across the street on this side of Istedgade at 126 is another corner establishment, this one not a café, however. Here he will not get brunch. Maybe he'll get a knuckle sandwich. It is a dark, small-windowed place, billed as Copenhagen's west side's western bar, named **McKluud's** in honor of the 1970s TV series about Marshal Sam McCloud, played by Dennis Weaver, aka Chester of the wooden leg in *Wyatt Earp*, with big James Arness and a whore named Kitty. This serving house of dark-brown wood is a low-light venue and a sign on the door says that it is open Monday to Sunday from two P.M. to two A.M., and on weekends the party continues until five A.M. at **Isola RockMusicCafé**.

On the pavement, gazing at the horseshoe-shaped doorknob, he realizes they will not have champagne so decides to order a double Stoli which he does not really want. He is barely conscious of the fact that a small brown-complected man with crooked teeth stands alongside him, smiling with all his snaggled teeth.

Kerrigan reflexively smiles back, then quickly nods dismissively as the man moves even closer, disagreeably close to Kerrigan's face, and utters some strange foreign words.

"The same to you, I'm sure, sir," says Kerrigan dryly, withholding his gaze, and the man turns away, hobbles to the corner, turns, and is gone, yet even as he withdraws, the foreign words ring clear of their heavy accent. What he had said in Danish was, "I wish everything good for you in your life. We are all in the palm of God. And now I am going again."

Kerrigan steps quickly along the street to the corner, looks down the sidewalk, but the little brown man is nowhere to be seen. He feels inordinately sorry at his rude response to the man, finds himself gulping in air that does not quite fill his lungs. He looks across the street at the **Café Blomsten**, where he once saw two very large men drinking from a bottle of vodka and arm wrestling while two beautiful women necked at the bar. Then he thinks he might go around the corner of **Enghaves Place** to **Dybbølsgade**, where **Café Snork** is—a place with a good vibe—and where he once met two French girls and spoke to them, which made him feel he was inside a Bob Dylan song—"Stuck Inside of Mobile (with the Memphis Blues Again)," to be exact—speaking with some French girls . . . but maybe what he wants now is bubbly.

He looks the whole long length of Istedgade toward the Central Station and begins walking toward it, but is quickly winded and has to lean on a mailbox to catch his breath, which doesn't want to be caught, thinking that if he had a glass of champagne he would be fine.

Champagne, he thinks, is an apt topic for the **Café Petersborg**, a mere twelve minutes by taxi, on **Bredgade**. It was here, one evening in 1845, that the light-music composer H. C. Lumbye (1810–1874), who lived nearby on **Toldbodgade**, heard a champagne cork pop and was inspired to begin to compose his famous "Champagne Gallop," although he completed it farther up Toldbodgade at the Toldbod Bodega.

Established in the mid-eighteenth century, Café Petersborg was named for the old imperial capital of Russia and in honor of the fact that the Russian Consulate was then housed in the same building; the Russian Orthodox church still stands across the street from it. Also where Hillary Clinton ate lunch when visiting Copenhagen as first lady of the U.S. a year or two before. But he decides to go down the street to the **Toldbod Bodega**, choosing a table in the second room, and orders a split of Moët. Named for the customs house where the Esplanade ends in Copenhagen harbor, near the royal landing dock, the bodega is some two hundred years old. In this building, the same H. C. Lumbye lived and composed.

Even as Lumbye began to introduce the Viennese waltz and gallops and polkas to the emergingly affluent Copenhagen middle classes, Kerrigan thinks, a man named Ole Pedersen Kollerød, awaiting his execution for having slit the throat of a coachman named Lars Petersen, was writing the story of his life as a vagrant and petty criminal in and out of jail, entitled *My story of the unhappy fate that has pursued me since my 6th year and until my 38th year, the age I have reached while I write this.* He not only wrote but illustrated the story and, clearly, had his talent been nurtured as a child, he might have found useful work. He reported the time of writing his story as "the best time of my life, because I have known no pleasure or been allowed to do nothing useful since I was stupid enough to commit the first offense for which I was punished." At the age of six. In Denmark, the death penalty was only employed for murderers at that time, unlike in England, where theft was a hanging offense.

Kollerød ended his account: ". . . my tale is at its end and what does it amount to when death approaches now? From its dark throne the night wields its heavy sceptre. The world sleeps . . . darkness . . . the grave's silence. My gaze stares. My ears listen in vain. Creation sleeps. The pulse of life will end. The wheel of the world fearsomely stands still and proclaims destruction. O, let the blade fall hard . . . Let it fall. No more can I say."

Ole Kollerød was executed by decapitation during the autumn of 1840, just over a year after the first Straussian concert, held on June 10, 1839, in the D'Angleterre Hotel on Kongens Nytorv, bringing Copenhagen at last up to date with Vienna, Paris, Berlin, and London, where the waltz and gallop craze already was well under way in replacing the staid music of the past.

Following the Napoleonic Wars and the Danish bankruptcy of 1813, the spirit of Danish society was subdued, but in the late 1830s people were getting rich again and wanted to express their new wealth in the freedom and eros of the new dances. The waltz was what they needed, considered so sensuous that only the humorless Germans were said to be able to dance it without giving in to its erotic allure.

H. C. Lumbye was a key person in the new lively music which, ironically, was seen to support the existing conservative order of absolute monarchy against the constitutionalists. People subscribed to the monthly publication of Lumbye's piano sheet music, and on August 15, 1843, the Tivoli Gardens opened, heralded by the music of Lumbye's Tivoli waltzes and polkas. (There is a statue of Lumbye in Tivoli playing violin, a group of naked, violin-playing boys at his feet.)

The antiestablishment periodical the *Corsair*—then in the process of making a laughingstock of Kierkegaard (at first they praised his work, but he scorned their praise so they attacked him personally, his appearance, his bent posture)—also complained about Tivoli's popularity at a time of censorship and other social ills. As to "The Champagne Gallop," the *Corsair* commented that it was only for the rich and that Lumbye ought to compose a "Beer & Snaps Gallop" for the people.

Kerrigan sips his champagne with "The Champagne Gallop" dancing in his head, thinking of Kollerød slitting Petersen's throat, denying his guilt, and having his own head chopped off even as Lumbye's cork popped and the bourgeoisie galloped gaily across the D'Angleterre dance floor, contemplating what tableaux might be painted of contemporary Denmark and contemporary Europe as popular sentiments swing further and further right and nationalist affinities approach pre–Second World War levels.

He thinks of Morten Gideon's wealth. He is a champagne socialist who always traveled with at least two hard leather pocket humidors, Cohibas Exquisitos, cigars that cost thirty dollars apiece and were worth it—if you could afford it. Kerrigan remembers the day he sat in Gideon's office in Gamla Stan in Stockholm smoking a corona while Gideon, with a young woman on his knee, spoke into the phone to the sixty-year-old chairman of the ethics committee of one of his organizations, reprimanding him quietly for a confessed indiscretion with one of the staff.

"Bob, listen," he said. "It is not that I give a fuck but we can't be seen to do these things. You gotta get with the times."

Bob had, according to his account, accidentally placed his open palm on the woman's breast while attempting to help her on with her coat; according to the account of the much younger woman in question, the palm in question had been inside the lapel of her blouse and midway down the cup of her bra. The girl was from New Jersey. She said, "He was coppin' a feel!"

"Bob, don't help them on with their coats," Gideon said, and puffed his cigar and kissed the secretary on her lips; she was having difficulty stifling her laughter and Gideon rested his cigar hand on her slender, stockinged thigh. "Let 'em put on their own fucking coats and no one can accuse you of things you didn't do." Under the circumstances, Gideon had to request Bob to deliver a written apology, which he did, following which he was sued, the written apology serving as the prima facie evidence, and the matter was settled out of court for six American figures—expensive feel—although Bob still had to deal with his wife after that and with his own image of who he was.

"The old pig," laughed the young woman on Gideon's knee when the phone call was completed.

"Gimme a fuckin' kiss, you're beautiful," said Gideon.

"You know he wants to play *doctor* with me," she said over her shoulder to Kerrigan, her slender arms laced around Gideon's neck.

"Hey, I *am* a fuckin' doctor," said Gideon. "I don't fuck around *playing* doctor. You got the real thing here, baby."

"I'm a doctor, too," Kerrigan said.

"Yeah, a doctor of bullshit. What was that word again?"

"Verisimilitude."

"A doctor of fucking verisimilitude."

"And you're the doctor of love, ey? Professor of desire. Set their souls on fire."

Gideon, a man of many parts, surprised Kerrigan by flinging some Carlos Fuentes at him: "Hey, love is doing nothing else. Love is forgetting spouses, parents, children, friends, enemies. Love is eliminating all calculations, all perceptions, all balancing of pros and cons. That's my fuckin' motto."

"Order! Order!" said Kerrigan.

"Order has nothing to do with love, my friend Kerrigan! Columbanus: *Amor non tenet ordinem.* Get with the program."

And Kerrigan considers Fuentes's words, his Associate, and calculations, perceptions, pros, cons.

He doesn't mind lying for Gideon. It was only for the sake of appearances—the young women always knew that, too. But there is Gideon's young wife in Uppsala, and Kerrigan remembers reading the Arnold poem again last night over the lake, alone: ". . . love, let us be true to one another!" And he thinks of his Associate and the husband who pinched her, drunk every night. And he wants her to have better than that.

Kerrigan signals for the bill.

"Something wrong with the champagne, sir?"

"Not as thirsty as I thought," Kerrigan says. "But do you have any cigars? A Cohiba perhaps? Robusto?"

It was his plan to taxi over to Holstein Street, surprise her, but it takes so much effort to flag and get into the cab that he decides what he needs is a night's sleep first.

Kerrigan wakes and cannot get his breath. He *really* cannot get his breath. He sits up in bed and wonders if he will ever get breath into his lungs again.

He wakes again a moment later, pitched diagonally across his bed. Apparently he stood up and fell down again.

Dreams about strange rooms in a strange apartment in which he is lost. His eyes open in the dark, look at his wristwatch: 11:20 P.M. He's slept for seven hours just like that. He turns on the overhead light. He doesn't feel so good. He stands up and looks back toward his bed, wondering if he can sleep or whether he ought to have a snack and a glass of wine.

The air in the room marbleizes with shadow. He takes a step.

Then he wakes to find himself flopped on his back on the carpet. He has pissed his pajama pants. He tries to inhale but cannot. He has no air. He begins to understand he is dying. It hurts to die. Life will not leave him peacefully. It requires painful tearing from his body, his throat, his chest. He is suspended in his dying, in its pain, the pain of breath that will not come.

Flat on his back, he points with a quivering finger upward at the white ceiling above his face, which seems to want to smother him. Then something opens in his chest and a tiny fistful of that most precious of commodities—air—enters. Replenished, he manages to rise to his feet. He feels drunker than he has ever been, though he can't remember having had a single dram all day. He staggers to a hard-seated chair, aware and ashamed that he has wet himself, and his lungs once again lock. They will not permit breath to enter. He gulps with impotent impatience to fill them with the black-and-white air all around him, and it scratches frantically at his throat but is granted no entry.

At last, a drop of breath slips in, another. He notices again his pee-soaked pajama pants, tugs them and his drawers down, kicks them an inch away where they lie in a soppy, stinking heap.

He begins to understand he will die here. Now. Not, as he always expected, a calm dignified guttering out. No, it comes with pain. Death takes it all and takes it hard. Nothing is easy. His eyes glimpse the phone on the table just beyond arm's reach. He half rises and his hand palms it—one finger punches three numbers—positions the receiver at his mouth. His throat ejects airless words that his tongue and teeth and palate sculpt to fit into the mouthpiece. It feels strange to request an ambulance for himself. He hears his voice straining over the message, giving his address.

The doorbell rings, and he supports himself along the wall, buzzes them in, opens the apartment door. Then he is far away, beyond pain. A narrow light indicates the crack of untroubled peace he hoped for and into which his being has slipped. But the light widens, invading this sublime nothingness—which only *becomes* sublime with the splinter of awareness that has found him. Instantly, emotion follows: profound annoyance that he is still alive. He opens his eyes. He is in his apartment again, lying on the floor beside his blue metal waste basket, which is on its side. Two strange men are moving toward him. Their mouths move, bulbous eyes observe him, hands reach to drag him from his crack of peace.

The stretcher is rolled out the vehicle's back into chill night air, good on his sweated face. Wide automatic doors swing open with a whoosh of welcome to the dismal empty space inside. And his stretcher rolls fast along a corridor, rounds a corner, slips away into a bare, dimly lit room where a nurse wearing a short-sleeved, low-cut white blouse takes his right hand.

"My name is Sara, Terrence," she says. All visible patches of skin on her arms and shoulders and chest and neck are adorned with tattoos of shooting stars and exploding rockets and color-illuminated constellations. There is a fiery red-and-yellow Big Dipper over the lush curve where her left breast disappears into her blouse.

"We are going to take a sound picture of your heart, Terrence," she says, squeezing his hand in both of hers, and he squeezes in response, in syncopation to the drops of saltwater dribbling off his lower eyelids. He wants to explain to her what happened, all of it, how he fainted, how he couldn't breathe, how he pissed himself, but realizes all he needs is her hand.

There are two or three nurses around him. One of them is feeling with both her hands down his legs to his feet. She sees him looking at her from behind his plastic oxygen mask and smiles mischievously with a dimpled cheek and cute small teeth from the foot of the gurney; touching his feet, she asks with a teasing threat, "Ticklish, Terrence?"

She doesn't realize what a randy old goat he really is, but then he thinks that she *does* know and is just trying to engage him, to keep him alert and interested and alive—that all these people around him in this big colorless empty room are here for one reason: to keep his sorry arse alive.

The nurse who tickled his feet comes closer, and he focuses on her dimple as she asks, "Does anyone know you're here?"

He shakes his head.

"Do you live alone?"

He nods.

"Isn't there a girlfriend? An ex, at least?"

He shakes his head, and her expression is so profound with deeply concealed pity that he blurts, "Well, I do get laid once in a while!"

Smiling, she asks, "Is there no one to call?"

He glimpses the large round face of a clock affixed to the wall. "It is two forty in the morning," he says, begs the question. "It's too late to call anyone at this hour." Could he call his Associate? The thought of her not being here fills him with terror, but more terrifying is the thought of her refusing to come.

Then he realizes that the fact that they want him to call somebody throws a serious light on things. It occurs to him once again that he might be not far from death. He remembers not being able to breathe earlier; he does not want to experience that again.

"Shouldn't we give you some more comfortable hospital clothes?" the nurse asks.

Something bothers him about this. Then he remembers that earlier when he passed out and pissed himself, he removed his briefs and pulled on jeans without underwear. He whispers, "I don't know how to say this, but I don't have any underpants on." Immediately he sees the absurdity of what he's said, but she plays along. "It's okay," she says. "I won't look."

They tug off his jeans and pull a pair of hospital shorts up his legs, fit his arms into the sleeves of a white top that snaps up the front. His left arm aches and his left leg and his left knee, too, and he is given a plastic baggie that contains his ID card and keys and crumpled money.

"You can just keep that under the covers for now," the dimpled nurse says. "We want to take you up to X-ray."

A very large porter rolls his bed to the elevator bank, along a hall to an X-ray room. A dark-haired woman in white asks, "Can you stand up against this?" indicating a large blank screen. His oxygen mask is removed and he is helped to stand. He's seeing stars. "Press your chest against here," she says, and steps out of the room. The stars begin to brighten and move very fast. There is an electronic grinding sound and he is fainting, but the gurney is behind him again and the mask is over his nose and mouth. He hates the feel of the clammy plastic, but he does not want to part with that thing again.

Back in the big empty colorless room, a dark-haired young woman standing on his left tells him her name is Laura. "I'm a doctor," she says, and rips open the snaps of his shirt to slather on some kind of lubricant. She produces a wand, on the tip of which she smears more lubricant.

"Turn on your left side, can you do that for me, Terrence?" He does as told, though his left arm and leg throb under the weight of his body. He glances at his left knee; it is three times normal size. Beside him on a chest-high rolling stand is a computer and screen and switches and pinpricks of green and red and yellow light. She jams the lubricated wand hard under his ribs and tacks with the fingers of her free hand at the computer keys.

He hears an odd, wet, deep-barreled tympani, irregular in its cadence, and manages breath to ask, "Is that . . . my heart?"

"Yes," says Dr. Laura, all business, while she continues to rejelly the wand and thrusts it beneath his ribs. Then he sees it. He sees his heart. It is dancing on the computer screen. It looks a little like a black-and-white version of a Class V Ectoplasmic Manifestation from *Ghostbusters*, but this Manifestation is full of emotion as it angrily tries to do its work. It is dancing; it is a serious dance his Ectoplasmic Manifestation of a heart does in black-and-white on the computer screen. He can see that one segment of the heart is not participating in the dance. It occurs to him that death is not participating in the dance; death wants to stop the dance, and stopping the dance means tearing life from his heart. The upper left quarter is flattened and arrhythmic while the rest of it, doing all the work of the dance, is angry at the nondancing part because it has to dance harder and harder.

Is the upper left quarter of the heart dead? he wonders. *Will the dead meat rot?*

Dr. Laura relubricates the wand and presses it none too gently in under his ribs as she is joined by a male colleague. "See that?" she asks him.

"Yeah," says the male colleague, who glances at him. "My name is Troels," he says. "I'm a doctor." He shakes his hand.

"Clotting in the lungs," says Dr. Laura.

"Yeah," says Dr. Troels, and then the gurney is speeding on its wheels along another corridor, an invisible man with muscular tattooed arms that frame Kerrigan's face propelling it from behind, and Dr. Troels hurrying alongside. "You're going to have a CT scan," he says.

"They won't take my oxygen mask," he says flatly, too proud to plead.

"No," Dr. Troels says. "You need your oxygen. I won't let them take it."

"Thank you."

In the CT room he is assisted by the doctor and the muscular-armed attendant in transferring onto a narrow bed, and an invisible woman says, "We're going to shoot contrast through you. You'll feel very warm in your body, and like you have to piss, but you won't." Impressed by her frankness, he feels the warmth spreading through his body, and he doesn't feel like he has to piss. But he does feel like he has to shit, and he prays to whatever forces enabled him to call the ambulance to also help him keep a tight asshole for it is one thing to die, yet quite another to have the last thing he witnesses his own ignominy.

A voice that sounds like the deep bass of James Earl Jones commands through a speaker inside the big metal doughnut into which his narrow bed now slides: "Breathe in! Release! Thank you. Breathe in! Release! Thank you."

There are indeed things to be thankful for in any situation. In this instance, he is thankful that he does not shit.

Now the gurney is racing back down to the anonymous blank room where his heart danced on the screen, and Dr. Troels, who he now notices is a dark-haired handsome man of perhaps thirty-two—is jogging beside it, saying, "You have clots in both lungs. That's why you can't breathe. Have you traveled recently?"

"Couple times."

"Did you wear support stockings? Move around in the plane to keep your blood flowing?"

"Not really."

He shakes his head ruefully. "The only thing to do now is a massive injection of blood thinner—heparin. That should dissolve the clots. Did you hit your head when you fainted?"

"Don't think so."

The doctor is running his fingers over Kerrigan's skull, pressing here and there. "Any soreness?"

"No."

"Have you urinated blood recently?"

"Not since a few years ago when I had a bunch of prostate biopsies."

"Did they find anything?"

"Not a thing."

The doctor's young eyes meet his, smiling faintly in collusion. "Does, uh, your, uh, still function at all for you?"

"It still knows what it wants, and it does okay."

He looks with interest at Kerrigan, and for a moment—Kerrigan, the old dude, and he, the young doctor, are men in a bar, ready to exchange stories of rapture, but the young doctor seems to remember himself and instantly grows serious again. "Have you ever had blood in your feces?"

"No."

"This procedure should do it for you," Dr. Troels says. "But I am required to tell you there *is* a risk."

The stretcher is back in place in the big dim anonymous empty room now, and it occurs to Kerrigan, face clammy behind the mask, that this is a fitting room in which to die, a blank empty colorless room in the bowels of a modern state hospital with a sculpture outside somewhere of a monolith that represents civilization in constant fall but never actually landing. Kerrigan closes his eyes and visualizes the sculpture.

"What is the risk?" he whispers.

Dr. Troels meets his gaze. "The massive dose of heparin we have to give you might induce bleeding in your brain. You might have a stroke."

The young doctor's eyes tell Kerrigan that there is no other way. Either risk this or let the lack of air rip life from him. And he has already had a taste of how that is and does not want another.

Two plump warm hands take his right, and he turns his face toward Sara with her shooting-star tattoos.

He looks again at Dr. Troels. His lips are sweaty behind the plastic oxygen mask as they form the word *Okay.*

A needle is stuck into the side of his stomach, and he can feel liquid rushing in as another needle slides in under the knob of bone in his left wrist, and he is surprised that he can register pain at all anymore. Sara has his right hand again. He looks up into her eyes. "You are so sweet," he whispers.

"My partner might not agree," she says with a twinkle. "Actually I'm something of a bitch."

He smiles.

Her eyes grow serious. "The heparin was injected about five minutes ago," she says. "The risk of stroke generally lasts for an hour. I'll be here with you." He follows her eyes to the large round face of the wall clock. Its hands say 3:45. He watches the second hand spastically twitch away spent instants as he waits to see what is next. Paralysis of left side? Right? Loss of speech? Loss of bowel control? Drooping drooling lips that cannot speak? A brain that cannot produce and develop words, that cannot truck them to the page?

Sara seems never to tire of squeezing his hand with her two, perhaps because he has them trapped in his chilly claw. The phrase "death grip" floats to the surface of his mind as the clock blurs before his eyes. It is not possible, he thinks, to fall asleep during this part of his own story, but he feels his eyelids sagging, his vision losing focus as his thoughts grow dreamy to the rhythm of the oxygen blowing into his lungs; its hiss as it leaves the tank hooked to the foot of the stretcher fills his ears to overflowing, and his thoughts are dreamy collages, scraps of face and talk and gesture. The dimpled nurse's pitying expression asking whether he has a girlfriend, Sara's twinkle and her tattoos, and a fleeting image of his Associate beside him on Grønningen, gazing at the sculpture of the reclining girl, his Associate—Annelise—leaning into his body. The image is a weight belt that sinks him a few feet beneath the surface of consciousness. He hears a snore burring at the back of his throat, which makes him smile; he didn't know he could snore into an oxygen mask. It is a cozy sound, and he is safe as long as Sara's warm grip anchors him.

There is nothing then. A shallow immersion.

Until his eyelids lift, and his vision focuses on the clock face: 4:50. His eyes turn to Sara. She is smiling. She seems very, very happy. Her tattoos blaze like celebratory fireworks. Her green eyes—why did he not notice before that they are green?—fix his, and her fingers move against his cold but warming hand.

* * *

The street door buzzer rings without hesitation, and he wonders as he crosses the lobby what she will look like, whether she will be as lovely as he remembers. Barefoot. Fingers and smock spattered with oils.

She is already at the door as he turns down the hall.

"Are you drunk?" she asks.

"No," he says, and she steps back to let him in.

"Long time no see," she says. "Where were you—oh, you're limping, what happened?"

"Had a fall."

"Drunk?"

"No, I wasn't drunk. I fainted. I'm not going to drink anymore," he says.

Her green eyes explore his face. "This is new."

"Not going to drink any less either."

She continues to peer silently at him, moving him to add, "Maybe a little less."

She keeps staring.

"Okay, maybe a lot less. If that's what it takes."

"If that's what it takes for what?"

"You do realize that I like you quite a lot, don't you, Annelise?"

"I like you quite a lot, too, Terrence."

"But no twelve-step city for me. I'm not on that road. Three drinks a day is what I'm told I may have."

She peers at him. "Told by whom?"

"The health authorities. They tell everybody that."

"Oh, well, did that ever stop you?"

"I'm hoping that we can have our three drinks a day together."

Once again he finds himself not wanting to tell her something; he doesn't want to tell her about his lungs and his blood, the blood thinner he has to take every day. He doesn't want to tell her that the whole left side of his body is one big purple bruise, or how close he came to dying and having a stroke. Neither does he want to tell her about the optimism, the sense of beauty that has opened in him from being so near death, from coming back.

"I'm not a fanatic," she says. "Would you like something now?"

"Any of that cava left?"

She brings the bottle on a tray with two flutes and a jar of caviar with crackers and a spoon and chopped raw onion and sliced fresh lemon.

"That looks delicious," he says, unwrapping, unwiring, and uncorking the champagne with an agreeable pop. Then he adds, "You look delicious, too."

"The same," she says with lowered eyes, pursing her lips into a faint smile.

He pours. They toast. Then she sits—not beside him on the sofa, but on the two-man sofa across from it. They don't speak for more minutes than he is comfortable with.

He says, "I brought you a tiny present from Dublin," and takes the Bronnley's lemon soap from his pocket, rises to hand it to her. "It's"—he begins, decides on not going into the whole story about Joyce and Bloom, content to have succeeded in bringing it to her—"lemon-scented."

She puts it at her nose, smells, hums with pleasure.

He gazes at her. She is as lovely as he remembered, lovelier. "Have you read Proust?" he asks.

"No," she says. "Do I have to read Proust to be your friend?"

"No, no, I've read very little Proust myself. I only pretend that I've read him. But what he said about love is really worth thinking about, I think. He wrote about the impossibility which love comes up against, that we imagine we can know someone because we can know the body that encloses him or her, but we can't know all the points of space and time he or she has occupied, and will occupy, so we don't and can't know them completely. We grope toward the person but can't find them." He wets his lips with cava. "I'm very attracted to you, Annelise. I'd like to be your friend. I'd like to be your best friend if I can. And try to help you be happy. I'd like to know you—as much as I can."

She peers into his eyes. "There is something about me that almost no one knows but me," she says, and is silent.

"Will you tell me?"

"Do you really want to hear?"

"Very much."

"On March twenty-first, 1945, I was trapped in a bombed building. Bombed by the British. It was an accident. They were aiming at the building the Germans had taken over as their gestapo headquarters and they succeeded but they also hit a school and some apartment buildings, including the one that I lived in. The girl who was watching me took me to the basement when the bombs started exploding, and we were buried in the rubble for a whole day. I kept speaking to her, asking questions— her name was Mette. After a long time, I realized she was not answering me. She could not. She was dead. I understood that she was dead. Then I decided that I had to dig myself out. I was four, nearly five. I remember it in detail. There was a lot of fire. And water from the pipes filling parts of the basement. I heard years later that several other children boiled to death. I heard the screams."

"Oh, God," he says. "I'm so sorry."

"It was an accident. The British bombers were doing their best. They liberated us. Montgomery was our hero. And all his men who risked their lives and gave their lives for Europe. English and Scots and Welsh and Irish, too. And of course the Americans. But those hours in the basement . . . talking to Mette, and her not answering . . . and then I knew . . . I still get frightened sometimes . . ." She sips from her cava, blinks, looks at him. "Why in the world are we talking about this?" she says lightly, chuckling, closing the subject.

"Look," he says. "Let's go ahead and finish the book."

"Do you really want to finish it?"

"By my calculation there are a total of 1,525 serving houses in Copenhagen. I have that figure from a report of Copenhagen County's Health Committee. They recently issued a plan to reduce alcohol consumption by five percent by closing seventy-seven serving houses. The public laughed in their communal faces, so they dropped the plan. There are still 1,525 serving houses, but we only need to pick a hundred of them for the book, only about fifty more. Then we can move on to some other project. I think we work well together. Will you?"

"What's in it for me?"

He thinks for a moment, reaches to his breast pocket, lifts out the Cohiba he bought all those days ago, unwraps the cellophane. "You like music?" he asks. She nods, and he hands her the paper ring from the Cohiba. "Here's a whole band for you."

She slips the gilt-paper band over the pointed red nail and knuckles of her slender ring finger and stretches her hand out as if to admire a diamond.

He says, "I lied before when I said that I liked you quite a lot. Actually, I adore you."

She smiles at him with her sad green eyes. "I'm just a girl, Terrence."

"You're a goddess to me," he says. *"Je t'adore."*

She says nothing, but her eyes smile. Then they lower. "Thank you," she whispers.

"Maybe we should, like, plant a tree together somewhere," he says, and can barely hear his own voice. "It could be our . . . tree."

"We could do that, Terrence."

"Who knows what sorrow might await us?" he says.

"Den tid, den sorg," she replies. "Old Danish proverb: That time, that sorrow."

He raises his bubbly to her. "Love, let us be true to one another, for the world . . . and so on and so forth."

"May I hear the so on and so forth?" she asks.

He sits forward on the edge of the sofa, watching her, about to recite, and she asks, "Why are you sitting all the way over there, Mr. Kerrigan? All by yourself."

He rises, crosses to her CD rack, hoping, finds just what he wants, and puts it on. As the first lilting notes of "The Beautiful Blue Danube" drift across her century-and-a-half-old rooms, he bows beneath the three-meter ceiling, extends his arm. She accepts it, smiling, and leading with his good leg, he believes himself transported to a higher salvation with his lady as his hand takes her slender waist and they dance, turning, across the broad plank floor, and the world spins dizzily with them.

Bibliography

Ackroyd, Peter, *Dickens*. New York: Harper Collins, 1990.

Andersen, Hans Christian, *Forty-Two Stories*, tr. M. R. James. London: Faber & Faber, 1930, 1968.

Arbaugh, George E. and George B., *Kierkegaard's Authorship*. London: George Allen & Unwin Ltd., 1968.

Arnold, Matthew, *Dover Beach and Other Poems*. New York: Dover Thrift Editions, 1994.

Berg, A. Scott, *Max Perkins: Editor of Genius*. New York: Washington Square Press, 1978.

Bertmann, Annegrett, ed., *No Man's Land: An Anthology of Modern Danish Women's Literature*. Norwich: Norvik Press, 1987.

Billeskov Jansen, F. J., and P. M. Mitchell, *Anthology of Danish Literature*, Vols. I and II, Bilingual Edition. Carbondale, Ill.: Southern Illinois University Press, 1972.

Bjørnvig, Thorkild, *The Pact: My Friendship with Isak Dinesen*, tr. Ingvar Schousboe and William Jay Smith. Baton Rouge, La.: Louisiana State University Press, 1983; Souvenir Press, 1984.

Borum, Poul, *Danish Literature: A Short Critical Survey*. Copenhagen: Det Danske Selskab, 1979.

Brandes, Georg, *Tanker ved århundredskiftet/Thoughts on the Turn of the Century*, introduction by Jens Christian Grøndahl, tr. Martin A. David. Bilingual edition. Oslo: Geelmuyden, Kiese (Scandinavian Airlines), 1998.

Bretall, Robert, *A Kierkegaard Anthology*. New York: The Modern Library, 1946.

Britt, Stann, *Dexter Gordon, A Musical Biography*. New York: Da Capo Press, 1989.

Brown, George Mackay, "The Whaler's Return," in *Winter's Tales 14*, ed. Kevin Crossley-Holland. New York: St. Martin's; London: Macmillan, 1968.

Calvino, Italo, *Six Memos for the Next Millennium*, tr. Patrick Creagh. New York: Vintage, 1996.

Carr, Ian, et al., *Jazz, The Rough Guide: The Essential Companion to Artists and Albums*. London: The Rough Guides, 1995.

Cavafy, C. P., *Collected Poems*, revised edition, tr. Edmund Keeley and Philip Sherrard, ed. George Savidis. Princeton, N.J.: Princeton University Press, 1992.

Coover, Robert, "Beginnings," in *The Literary Review: Stories & Sources*, ed. Thomas E Kennedy, vol. 42, no. 1. Madison, N. J.: Fairleigh Dickinson University, 1998.

Costello, Peter, *The Dublin Literary Pub Crawl*. Dublin: A&A Farmer, 1996.

Deane, Seamus, Introduction to James Joyce's *Finnegans Wake*. New York: Penguin, 1991.

Donleavy, J. P., *The History of the Ginger Man, An Autobiography*. New York: Penguin, 1995.

Ensig, Kirsten, *Turen Går til København*. Copenhagen: Politikens Forlag, 3.udgave, 1996.

Erichsen, John, *Et Andet København, Sociale Fotografier fra Århundredskiftet*. Copenhagen: Gyldendal, 1978.

Fargnoli, A. Nicholas, and Michael Patrick Gillespie, *James Joyce A to Z*. London: Bloomsbury, 1995.

Friar, Kimon, ed. and tr., *Modern Greek Poetry*. Athens: Efstathiadis Group, 1982.

Gilgamesh, The Epic of, introduction by N. K. Sandars. New York: Penguin, 1977.

Goethe, Johann Wolfgang von, *The Sorrows of Young Werther*, tr. Elizabeth Mayer, Louise Bogan, and W. H. Auden. New York: Vintage, 1990.

Hendriksen, F., *Kjøbenhavnske Billeder fra det Nittende Aarhundrede*. Copenhagen: Foreningen Fremtiden, 1927.

Höm, Jesper, *The Faces of Copenhagen, 1896–1996*. Copenhagen: Forlaget Per Kofod, 1996.

Housman, A. E., *A Shropshire Lad*. New York: Illustrated Editions Co., 1932.

Ibsen, Henrik, *When We Dead Awaken*, tr. James Walter McFarlane. Scandinavian Words 6. Bilingual edition. Oslo: Geelmuyden, Kiese (Scandinavian Airlines), 1998.

Igoe, Vivien, *A Literary Guide to Dublin*. London: Methuen, 1994.

Jacobsen, Jens Peter, *Mogens & Other Stories*, tr. Tiina Nunnally. Seattle: Fjord Press, 1994.

Johansen, R. Broby, *Gennem Det Gamle København*. Copenhagen: Gyldendal, 1948.

Joyce, James, *Finnegans Wake*, introduction by Seamus Deane. New York: Penguin, 1992.

————, *A Portrait of the Artist as a Young Man*, introduction by Anthony Burgess. London: Secker & Warburg, 1994.

————, *Ulysses*, introduction by Declan Kiberd. New York: Penguin, 1992.

Kennedy, Thomas E., ed., *New Danish Writing: The Literary Review* (Fairleigh Dickinson University, New Jersey), vol. 51, no. 3, Spring 2008.

Kiberd, Declan, *Inventing Ireland*. London: Jonathan Cape, 1995.

Kierkegaard, Søren, *Enten-Eller* (*Either/Or*), Bind 1 & 2. Copenhagen: Gyldendal, 1843, 1996.

Kinsella, Thomas, tr., *The Tain (from the Irish Epic Táin Bó Cuailnge)*. Oxford: Oxford University Press, 1969.

Kirkenin, Heikki, and Hannes Sihvo, *The Kalevala: An Epic of Finland*, tr. M. Lauanne and A. Bell. Helsinki: Finnish-American Cultural Institute, 1984.

Kollerød, Ole Pedersen, *Min Historie*. Copenhagen: Foreningen Danmarks Folkeminder, 1978.

Kristensen, Tom, *Hærværk* (*Havoc*). Gyldendals Tranebøger, 1930 (reprint).

Lauring, Palle, *A History of Denmark*, tr. David Hohnen. Copenhagen: Høst & Son, 1973, 4th edition.

Ljungkvist, Carsten, and Herbert Meinke, *Jazzanekdotter*. Århus: Forlaget Ildhuset, 1997.

Lucretius, *On the Nature of Things*, tr. H. A. J. Munro, in *Great Books of the Western World*, Vol. 12, Encyclopædia Britannica, Inc., 1952.

Lundgreen-Nielsen, Flemming, ed., *København læst og påskrevet: Hovedstaden som litterær kulturby*. University of Copenhagen: Museum Tusculanums, 1997.

Madsen, Hans Helge, *Østerbros Herligheder—en bydels identitet*. Copenhagen: Nationalmuseet, 1986.

Maggin, Donald L., *Stan Getz, A Life in Jazz*. New York: Quill/William Morrow, 1996.

Nørregård-Nielsen, Hans Edvard, *Kongens København, En guldaldermosaik*. Copenhagen: Gyldendal, 1994.

Nygaard, Georg, *H. C. Andersen & København*. Copenhagen: "Fremtiden," 1938.

Poetic Edda, The, tr. Carolyne Larrington. Oxford: Oxford University Press, 1996.

Raabyemagle, Hanne, and Claus M. Smidt, eds., *Classicism in Denmark*. Copenhagen: Gyldendal, 1998.

Rasmussen, Peter Bak, and Jens Peter Munk, *Skulpturer i København*. Copenhagen: Børgen, 1999.

Rumi, *The Essential Rumi*, tr. Coleman Barks with John Moyne. San Francisco: Harper, 1995.

Scavenius, Bente, *The Golden Age Revisited, Art & Culture in Denmark, 1800–50*, tr. B. Haveland and J. Windskar-Nielsen. Copenhagen: Gyldendal, 1996.

Schade, Jens August, *Schades Digte*. Copenhagen: Gyldendal, 1999.

Scherfig, Hans, *Stolen Spring*, tr. Frank Hugus. Seattle: Fjord Press, 1986.

Seibles, Tim, "Bonobo," in *Poems & Sources: The Literary Review* (Fairleigh Dickinson University, New Jersey), vol. 44, no. 1, Fall 2000, pp. 71–72.

Smidt, Claus M., and Mette Winge, *Strolls in the Golden Age City of Copenhagen*, tr. W. Glyn Jones. Copenhagen: Gyldendal, 1996.

Spink, Reginald, *Hans Christian Andersen and His World*. London: Thames & Hudson, 1972.

Stangerup, Henrik, *The Seducer: It Is Hard to Die in Dieppe*, tr. Sean Martin. London: Marion Boyars Publishers, Ltd., 1996.

Stephens, James, *Songs from the Clay*. New York: Macmillan, 1925.

Strømstad, Kirsten, and Poul Strømstad, *Rundt om søerne*. Copenhagen: Christian Ejlers Forlag, 1996.

Strømstad, Poul, *Residentsstaden Kjøbenhavn, Gader, Torve og Pladser Indenfor Voldene.* Copenhagen: Skandbergs Forlag, 1991.

Theisen, Torben, *Billeder fra det nu forsvundne Østerbro.* Lyngby, Denmark: Dansk Historisk Håndbogsforlag, 1984.

Thomas, Dylan, "One Warm Saturday," in *Portrait of the Artist as a Young Dog.* New York: New Directions, 1955.

———, "A Visit to Grandpa's," in *Quite Early One Morning.* New York: New Directions, 1955.

Thomsen, Allan Mylius, *De Ydmyge Steder (The Humble Establishments).* Copenhagen: Dansk Hotel-Portier Forening with *Copenhagen This Week,* 1997.

Turèll, Dan, "Behind Every Single Window," tr. Thomas E. Kennedy, in *New Letters*, vol. 75, nos. 2–3 (2009), pp. 137–39.

———. "It Isn't Easy," tr. Thomas E. Kennedy, in *Poet Lore*, vol. 107, no. 1/2 (2012), p. 102.

———. "Last Walk Through the City" and "Life on Isted Street," tr. Thomas E. Kennedy, in *Absinthe: New European Writing* no. 12 (2009), pp. 40–46.

Turèll, Dan, and Halfdan E, *"Gennem Byen Sidste Gang,"* in *Pas På Pengene!* Copenhagen: Mega Records (MRCD 3220) (undated).

Valore, Peter Braams, *Sophie Ørsted og Digterne.* Copenhagen: Bakkehusmuseet, 1991.

Van Gogh, Vincent, *The Letters of Vincent Van Gogh*, selected and edited by Ronald de Leeuw, tr. Arnold Pomerans. London: Penguin, 1996.

Vinding, Ole, "James Joyce in Copenhagen," tr. Helge Irgens-Moller. Unpublished.

Wamburg, Bodil, ed., *Out of Denmark*. Copenhagen: Danish Cultural Institute, 1985.

A NOTE ON THE AUTHOR

Born and raised in New York, Thomas E. Kennedy has lived and worked in Copenhagen for three decades. His books include novels, story and essay collections, literary criticism, translation, and anthologies. *Kerrigan in Copenhagen* is the third novel in his acclaimed Copenhagen Quartet to be published in the United States, following *In the Company of Angels* (2010) and *Falling Sideways* (2011). The fourth, *Beneath the Neon Egg*, will follow in the near future. His websites are www.CopenhaganQuartet .com and www.thomasekennedy.com.

KEEP READING . . .

Discover the other novels in Thomas E. Kennedy's

COPENHAGEN QUARTET

"Kennedy's ambitious, inspired project to do for the Danish capital what James Joyce did for Dublin in *Ulysses* is an exercise in seduction by stealth." —*The Guardian*

In the Company of Angels

"Simply an unforgettable novel." —*Los Angeles Times*

Available now in paperback and as an e-book
ISBN: 978-1-60819-467-4
eISBN: 978-1-60819-152-9

Falling Sideways

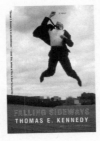

"Touches on the contemporary moment with a deft precision."
—*Financial Times*

Available now in paperback and as an e-book
ISBN: 978-1-60819-442-1
eISBN: 978-1-60819-443-8

Beneath the Neon Egg

Available August 2014 in hardcover and as an e-book
ISBN: 978-1-62040-141-5
eISBN: 978-1-62040-142-2